THE FIRST PAIR OF
THE ZEPHYR SERIES

Kismet

HER STORY

J. JAMES WHEELING

FEATHER
WATCH
PRESS

Feather Watch Press, LLC
www.jjameswheeling.com

Hardcover ISBN: 978-1-968526-00-9
Paperback ISBN: 978-1-968526-01-6
eBook ISBN: 978-1-968526-02-3

Cover and book design by Jess LaGreca, Mayfly book design
Map illustrations and design by Map Hero

Library of Congress Catalog Number: 2025913431
First Printing: 2025
Printed in Canada

Dedication

I dedicate this story to those whose unique gifts
are underestimated and the glorious feeling that comes
when those talents are understood and appreciated.

A Note to the Readers

The book you are holding (or listening to) has taken fourteen years to complete mostly because I had to learn to write correctly and I strive for historical accuracy. When this story's inspiration first came to me and I accepted the challenge to steward it into being, I began by alternating chapters between the man's story and the woman's story which are happening, more or less, simultaneously. As the story matured, it became clear that it had become too vast for one book. I was advised to divide it into two books and created *The Gantlet* and *Kismet*. It makes no difference which one you start with but, if you want to know the whole story, my advice is to enjoy both books.

This first pair signals the beginning of the Zephyr series. The stories begin in Boston with the California gold rush in 1849 and will run through the Silver Panic of 1893 in the Red Mountain Mining District in the San Juan Mountains. All will be released as pairs and I anticipate there will be multiple pairs to get this magnificent story to its end.

Buckle up, it's going to be a fun ride!

Contents

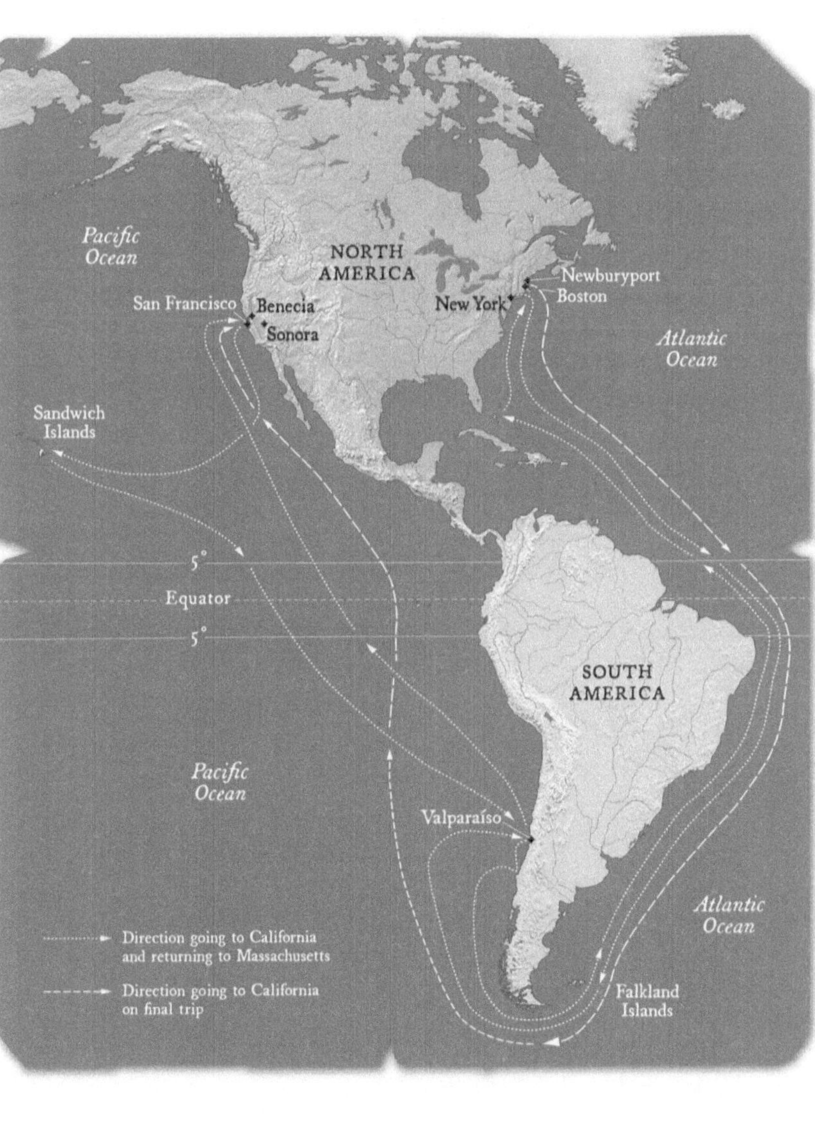

Pacific
Ocean
NORTH
AMERICA
San Francisco
Benecia
Sonora
New York
Newburyport
Boston
Atlantic
Ocean
Sandwich
Islands
5°
Equator
5°
Pacific
Ocean
SOUTH
AMERICA
Valparaíso
Atlantic
Ocean
Direction going to California
and returning to Massachusetts
Direction going to California
on final trip
Falkland
Islands

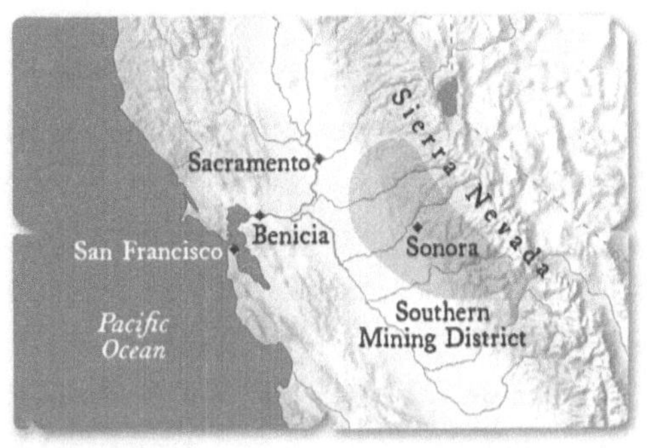

Prologue

MAY, 1851

SOMEWHERE IN THE HILLS AROUND

SONORA, CALIFORNIA

The summer breeze whispers through the branches of the broad oak tree, rattling the leaves overhead. One branch, its diameter the size of a child's waist, stretches wide from the tree's colossal trunk before making a graceful arc toward the sky. From it hang three empty nooses swaying over a buckboard wagon's empty bed.

In the tree's shade, a parody of a trial is underway.

"At least I'm not a scqundrel passing myself off as a credible law officer. Your time is coming. You see just three of us, but there are many more aware of your misdeeds. It's only a matter of time before you are brought to justice."

"I've heard enough out of you, woman."

Lillia watches with despair as the buckboard is backed up under one of the oak tree's sweeping branches. Three ropes with crudely fashioned nooses hanging from one end are flung over the branch's girth. A zephyr breeze whispers through the dark green leaves ironically contrasting with the ominous sway of the three dangling nooses.

With a remarkable calm settling into her mind, Lillia fondly remembers the other occasions when a zephyr had visited her.

"Boys, string 'em up," says the tax collector, with a jerk of his head.

Her calm switches to dull disbelief as she, Rupert, and Donatello are roughly herded toward their makeshift gallows. Muted by her horrific reality, Lillia prays to herself:

It's going to happen. I'm going to die by hanging. Our son is going to be an orphan. Oh, my dear God, help us.

After some formidable resistance, the bound trio are roughly hauled into the wagon bed and the nooses jammed over their heads. The noose's coarse rope scrapes open the clotted brush wounds on Lillia's face and ears as it slides down to her neck. She detects the low murmur of Rupert and Donatello mumbling to each other, but the deafening throb in her ears keeps her from understanding their exchange.

Time slows to a crawl. Wisps of her dark hair brush against her cheek and she fidgets against the binding rope. Sweat streams down her temples, and when she looks over at Rupert, then at Donatello, she sees sweat beading and running off the scruff of their unshaven faces.

"Lillia, you've made me so happy," Rupert whispers softly.

Tears well in her eyes such that when she turns to look at him, he is a blur.

"Oh, Rupert, our love can't end this way. We have so much more to live for."

A shrill whistle interrupts her, and she squeezes her eyes tight before bracing for the wagon bed to move out from under them.

Suddenly, two rifle shots crack the air. When the anticipated movement of the wagon does not happen, Lillia's eyes spring wide open. The horses make a deflated sound, their whinnies of pain issued only with an agonizing sigh. When she twists her neck around to look in the horse's direction she sees instead, the canyon walls swarming with multitudes of men racing toward them. Moments later, she hears Giorgio's familiar voice replace the pounding in her ears.

"Lillia, I'm going to cut you down."

The upward pressure on her neck releases, and she gasps for air as her feet find the floor of the wagon's solid bed. Looking around, she sees Giorgio release Rupert and Donatello from their nooses.

Once their hands and feet bindings are severed, they loosen and rip the nooses from their necks before jumping from the wagon. Rupert embraces Lillia, the strength of his grip resuscitating her from her shock.

"Dear God, that was close," he softly says into her ear.

Content to bury her face in his chest, she hears Giorgio and Donatello join the hunt for the men that, only minutes before, had been their captors. Her breathing returning to normal, Lillia's attention is drawn to the canyon wall and she sees Luca in conversation with a bearded stranger.

In the same line of sight, she sees the horses lying in their death pose, blood pulsing from the holes in their respective chests. When Luca and the stranger turn away, their movement catches her attention again, and she watches them disappear beyond the rim of the canyon wall.

The area churns with Mexican miners bent on revenge as they single out the tax collector and his cronies. There is the occasional pistol pop and taunting shouts as the men are forced to beg for mercy. Her fingertips absentmindedly exploring the noose's raw mark under her jawbone, Lillia, still in Rupert's protective arms, turns away from the violence. That is when she sees Luca striding through the crowd toward his oldest brother, a broad grin spread across his dirt-smudged face.

"Bet you never thought you'd come that close to hanging, did you, Perty?"

Rupert grabs his younger brother by the shoulder and pulls him in for a hug saying, "You've got a lot of explaining to do, but I've never been happier knowing how good of a marksman you've become."

"I can't take all the credit."

Turning to Donatello, Luca says, "Giorgio and I found him, just like Rafael said. Clear over in San Fran. Found him doing road work. Sheer, unadulterated luck, I'd say. We rode as fast as we could and not a moment too late!"

"Found who?"

Luca turns to Lillia to address her question directly.

"Rafael said if we couldn't find the judge, we were supposed to hunt down a sharpshooter by the name of Dash Truepenny. He's the one who took the other shot so's we killed both of them horses simultaneously."

Lillia's mouth falls open in shock. Her mind explodes with only one detail from Luca's statement.

My Dash Truepenny?

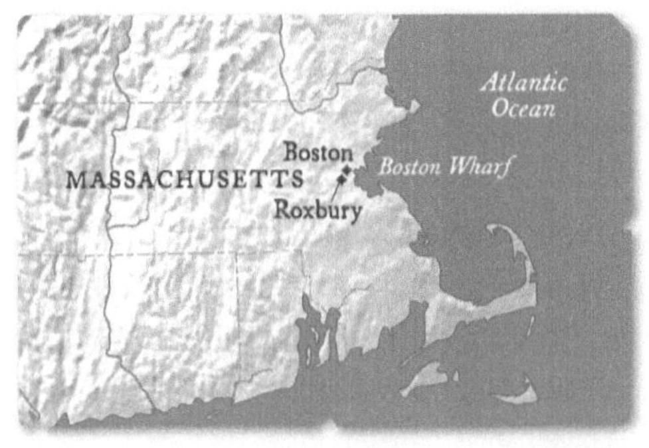

Chapter 1

APRIL, 1849

ROXBURY, MASSACHUSETTS

*L*illia Soilleux startles and drops her needlework at the sound of a sharp rap at her door. Two days have passed since she received Donovan's Morse coded note. Now, the time has come.

A knock comes again, the distinct sound of a brass-tipped walking stick against the solid wood of the Soilleux family's front door. She has been anticipating the slippery smooth style of Donovan's father, the way he slides his words together to form innocent-sounding inquiries. In actuality, he is sleuthing for the information he desires from his unsuspecting victims. But she had also been exposed to his dark side when she had witnessed his verbal lashings on Donovan.

She steels her composure, rises, and unlatches the door. It is whom she expected, the handsome and stylishly well-coiffed William O'Creigh, his face slightly drawn, but his sticky sweet smile staring down at her.

"Good afternoon, Miss Soilleux. Would it be possible to have a conversation inside with you and your parents?"

Bowing her head slightly, Lillia answers his question by opening the door wider. When he passes her, she smells his body odor and some concoction designed to cover it . . . mint or, perhaps, horehound. As she closes the door, her father, Henri, enters the hallway, stepping briskly toward them.

"Hello, William. What brings you to our home this afternoon?"

"I've a . . . well, I've a delicate matter I need your and your daughter's help with, Henri."

"I've just added wood to the parlor fire, and it will be comfortable for conversation. Lillia, will you join us after helping your mother with the tea tray?"

"Yes, of course, Father."

Lillia watches the men leave, her belly churning with butterflies of dread and anticipation. She hears her mother, Phoebe, bustling in the kitchen and decides to wait until she hears the kettle's whistle before lending a hand. In the meantime, she rushes to the adjoining hallway and takes a position in proximity to hear the men's dialogue.

Henri sanguinely asks, "So, what is this delicate matter you'd like to discuss?"

"My son has gone missing. I have searched everywhere. Given his marriage to your daughter next week, I'm here to inquire if she knows of his whereabouts."

His confirmation of Donovan's flight makes Lillia grip her apron tightly. When his note had arrived by messenger two afternoons ago, she had anticipated it to be a love note. Her heart had fluttered when she opened it, his pet name for her, Dot, gracing the outside. She had squeezed her eyes tightly, conjuring Donovan's image—patched eye, crooked grin, and the way he cocked his head to one side while he waited for her to decipher his words. But then she had decoded the note only to find each word becoming more horrifying than the last.

Dearest Dot . . . Learned illicit family business . . .
Must flee Boston . . . For your family's safety say nothing
to my father . . . Meet me in San Francisco . . . Please . . .
Love Dash

She remembers having barely been able to look her parents in the eye over their supper that night, the gravity of the note's words reverberating in her mind. If she had doubted its legitimacy then, William's presence now only confirms the note's truth, and its warning.

"Where did you see him last?"

Henri's question to William refocuses her mind to the present.

"I sent him on an errand requiring no more than a day's worth of travel. Three days have passed. Something has gone wrong. Since he carried a considerable sum of money, I'm starting to fear the worst."

An insistent nudge of a tray's edge interrupts Lillia's eavesdropping. She turns and sees Phoebe pressing it against her ribs. Taking the full tray, Lillia enters the parlor with Phoebe following close behind. As Lillia sets the tea tray on the low table between them, she feels the air become close and stifling.

"Lillia, it seems Donovan has disappeared while on a family errand. Have you any word from him?"

Donovan's words, *say nothing to my father*, flash in Lillia's mind, and resolve fills her soul. Reaching for the teapot, she puts on her best neutral expression and focuses on her practiced words, their truth giving her strength.

"We spoke several days ago. He told me he had many tasks to do before our wedding. When I answered the door just now, I was sure it would be him."

"Who else have you questioned? How else have you searched?"

Lillia can tell Henri's probing questions have pricked into William's paternal consciousness when he growls, "I hope you are not doubting my diligence to find my youngest son. Normally, his older brothers would be assigned to the task I gave him, but they were occupied elsewhere. I had hoped Donovan, given his infirmity . . . it is clear now that I've sheltered him too long. I regret to say this, but his only future value is working as a clerk, if he has a future."

Curiously, William's tone drops away to a pitiful whimper, something quite unfamiliar to Lillia. Immediate doubt of his sincerity fills her heart.

"By the time I was notified Donovan had not arrived with his delivery, almost two days had passed. I'm plagued with worry about an assault on my dear boy."

Lillia feels her composure waiver. As the only one familiar with Donovan's note, affectionate words like "dear boy" and "plagued with worry" ring hollow coming from William's mouth. She fights the temptation to reveal her secret but discretion wins.

"William, I can offer you my personal word to employ our efforts and connections within our areas of influence to assist in your search," Henri offers.

Lillia realizes, almost too late, that she should probably display some worried emotion. Filling her eyes with fake tears, she looks up at William.

"Please, Monsier O'Creigh, please find him! We've our whole lives ahead of us."

Phoebe draws near and hugs her around the shoulders, allowing Lillia to bury her face there, grateful not to have to engage with the sly demon before her. When she hears boot heels clicking against the wooden floorboards toward the door, Lillia gently pulls away from Phoebe and rests her face in her hands. She hopes Phoebe will interpret the act as sadness, but knows it is really one of pure relief.

While helping to prepare their evening meal, Lillia's mind whirls with memories of Donovan—of their bourgeoning romance when all had been exciting and new just a year ago. Each moment flashes before her, until her mind settles on one particular day, when she shared her pet name for him.

"Dash Truepenny, you are Dash, because I am your 'Dot.' We met in our study of Morse code together, so it's perfect, right? And Truepenny, well, I've always been blessed with ample literature from my Uncle Sebastian. His favorites are Chaucer and Shakespeare. When I was perusing a volume the other day, I came across Shakespeare's use of 'Truepenny' to describe someone who is true to himself, trustworthy, and an honest fellow. I can't think of a better way to describe you."

Donovan's sweet expression fills her memory, his left eye's patch crinkling slightly when he grinned at her. The memory of their stolen moments together, brief and fleeting due to his father's demanding nature and disapproval of her as Donovan's choice in a wife, swell in her heart now. Secretly, they had been working together to learn the latest technique in communication, Morse code. They were both afraid if William learned of their plans to leave the family business, he would find a way to ruin them. And then she got Donovan's note.

A whiff of sadness seeps into her memory. But, where she had been distraught at his exodus, she now feels less shock and more resolve. She understands, after today's exchange with William, why Donovan had to leave. Whatever he did was justified. Her current emotion centers more around his leaving her behind without even being asked to go with him. She has been left to remain in the suffocating society where she is misunderstood by most and condemned to keep his secret from all, including his enraged father.

Lillia shares few words with her parents at the supper table. Henri comes to her side, putting both hands on her shoulders, whispering, "There will be another, ma chéri."

She nods and fights back tears. From outside, the crunch of gravel under approaching boot treads brings her tears to a sudden halt. A pounding knock rattles the kitchen door. When the familiar voice calls out, their startled expressions are replaced with joy.

"*Bon nuit, mon frere et famillie!* Let a traveler into the warmth of your hearth?"

Uncle Sebastian!

Lillia rushes to open the door as brothers and business partners greet each other heartily. While the men return to the hired carriage for Sebastian's luggage, Phoebe prepares a fresh plate of supper.

Lillia clears the dishes and confides, "Oh, Mother, what am I to tell Uncle Sebastian after he sailed from the Mediterranean to be at my wedding."

"We don't know the whole truth about Donovan yet. Hold onto your faith. Let your uncle wash away the day's pain with his laughter and stories."

No, Mother, I know the whole truth.

Once settled in the house, Sebastian pulls Lillia into a bear hug, engulfing her tall, slim figure before bussing both of her cheeks and whispering close to her ear, "Ah, Lillia, your father told me of your unfortunate circumstance."

Lillia musters only a slight resignation to his words before Phoebe asks, "What of the other woman in this house?"

"Now Phoebe. You know I've plenty of love for all the women in my life . . ." Sebastian replies and winks at Lillia over Phoebe's shoulder, ". . . and for those I barely know, as well."

Phoebe affectionately swats him with her dish towel, saying, "Sit, sit. Eat some supper, and then we'll take tea in the parlor."

Sebastian obediently sits and places a napkin in his ample lap.

"When I am finished here, we will unload my travel trunks of their bounty."

Sebastian crows his delight at not eating ship's food before retiring with Henri to the parlor. When Lillia and Phoebe arrive with the tea tray, Lillia stares in disbelief at the six wrapped packages next to her chair.

"Go ahead, *ma chérie*, open them. There are so many because I was shopping for a betrothed woman. Who says they won't be useful to you still?"

Lillia opens one gift after another, each more exquisite.

Exasperated, Phoebe protests, "Sebastian, these are not gifts of an uncle to his niece. They're too extravagant!"

"Phoebe, your daughter is no longer a child. She deserves women's gifts. Besides, I left the Bengal tiger and Arabian stallion at the ship. Do you have space in the barn?"

Lillia and Henri break into laughter until Phoebe succumbs to small giggles. Once the others open their gifts, they settle into tea and conversation.

"Here's an interesting story: I gave a ride to a young man headed to the California goldfields this morning," her father says. "He was completely convinced he would come home rich. He's not alone. Practically every young man I see on the docks has their eyes wide with frenzy."

Lillia looks up from her teacup and asks, "Has there been any proof of the plenty in California?"

"I've seen nothing substantial, only vague claims meant to feed the fury."

"Fools," Phoebe mutters.

"They might be, Phoebe," Sebastian agrees, "but our ship from Nice was full of those willing to pay for deck passage to catch the next ship to California. I wouldn't be surprised if our sailors are joining them at this moment. We'll have to pay handsomely to keep them."

Henri snorts, "We can't afford an increase after the American tariffs."

"Then prepare to raise your prices. No sailors, no French perfume, or Belgium sweets."

Uncomfortable silence engulfs the room until Henri comments, "We need to pray gold fever passes quickly."

Lillia wonders if Donovan will make it before the gold runs out.

Henri breaks into her thoughts and asks, "Lillia, how about joining us in our trip to the wharf tomorrow?"

Lillia thoughtfully bobs her head and answers, "Yes, Father, I believe I will go with you. I'd like to witness this gold fever and see the Bengal tiger Uncle Sebastian brought me."

The men laugh, while Lillia rises to collect the cups onto the tea tray. On her way out, she hears Sebastian call after her, "I brought you the latest periodicals from Philadelphia and New York as we worked our way up the coastline. I'll set them on the stairs for you."

"Thank you, uncle," she says. "We can always count on you to keep us up on the world's events. I'll take one for reading before bed tonight."

As promised, the stack sat on the stair steps after Lillia finished with the dishes. She takes the top one from New York. Eager to review its contents, she rushes through her undressing and slips into her nightgown. After setting a freshly lit candle on her bed stand, she settles into her bed and opens the paper to the center broadsheet.

Her heart flips when she reads the full-page advertisement leading with the title of "California Association of Women." Barely able to read fast enough, she finishes and then starts again, more slowly, studying every word of every sentence. After the second read, she folds the paper and lays her head back against her pillows, her eyes tracing the lines in her bedroom ceiling while contemplating what she has just learned.

A woman, Eliza Farnham, is soliciting young, single women to sail to California in order to bring civilization to the chaos there. She has already hired a ship and is undertaking a rigorous selection process. She has been endorsed by politicians and civil leaders alike. Why would young women do this? Better yet . . . why wouldn't they?

If she thought reading would help her fall asleep, Lillia is very disappointed; her thoughts were whirling with the California Association of Women. By the time sleep takes her, she is content simply being aware of other women in New England's strict society who share her sense of suffocation and are willing to escape. That is enough.

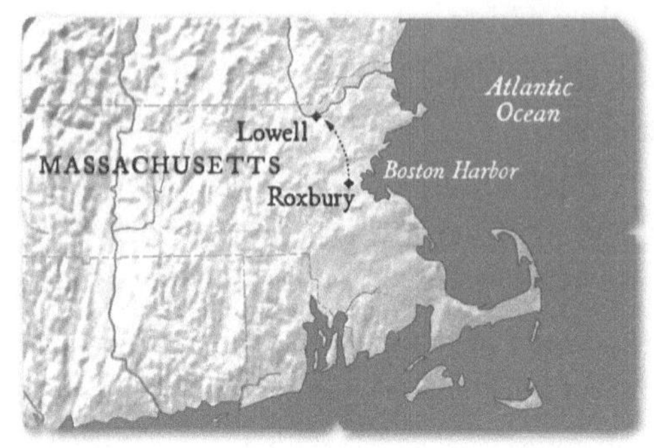

Chapter 2

APRIL, 1849

ROXBURY, MASSACHUSETTS

Uncle Sebastian has been with them for a week, when Lillia overhears him in close conversation with her father. She stands at the stair's railing and strains to hear what the men are discussing so passionately. When Sebastian details his proposal, she can hardly believe her ears.

"I just got a tip from a contact at India Wharf. If we can obtain a volume of cotton canvas from a Lowell mill and sail it post haste to California, we stand to make a killing. It's in high demand for everything from temporary housing to shipping containers to men's trousers. The opportunity for success is without reproach. I'll take Lillia away from her woes and use her quick business mind and bargaining skills to solidify negotiations. You

10

see the advantages, don't you? Think of it, Henri! My information is too good to pass up."

"How are you going to manage to keep Lillia safe? Besides, I can't imagine operating our business without her, Sebastian. She is my greatest asset for keeping track of all our imported goods, who owes us what . . . all of it."

Lillia feels her chest tighten at her father's appeal, her loyalty to him beginning to swell beyond her own needs. Sebastian drops his voice.

"Henri, have you seen your daughter? Ever since my arrival, she has been morose. The Lillia I know has a bright spark in her eye and a tease on her lips. This young woman is devastated at the disappearance of her betrothed. You must let me take her away. I promise to return her to you along with a multiplier of your investment so vast your head will spin."

"What of Phoebe? Lillia is her mother's pride and joy. Leaving Phoebe alone . . ."

Imagining Phoebe's poignant reaction to Sebastian's idea is so overwhelming to Lillia that the end of Henri's statement goes unheard.

"When do you propose leaving?" she hears Henri ask.

"Time is of the essence, Henri. The sooner we get to Lowell and understand what kind of wait there is for the fabric, the sooner we can make arrangements for a westbound ship. I'd like to leave within the next day or two, if that is possible."

"Lillia can't possibly be ready on such short notice."

"I wouldn't be surprised if she hasn't unpacked her wedding trunks, brother. We owe it to her to at least ask, don't you think?"

Once again, silence grips the parlor while Lillia maintains her perch at the second-floor railing, her damp hands gripping and releasing the smooth banister.

"I suppose we could ask her, but don't do it in front of her mother. If Lillia decides to stay, Phoebe need never know of the scheme. If she decides to go with you, I will handle the conversation with my wife in private."

"I will respect your wishes. Before we retire tonight, I'll speak with Lillia. That will give you tomorrow to tell Phoebe if Lillia chooses to sail to California."

The shock of Lillia's sudden departure has Phoebe wrapped in dull sadness with red-rimmed eyes while standing in the kitchen with her daughter. An awkward silence hovers between them. When her older brother left for the Northwest, Lillia had watched her mother grieve and helped her make the adjustment. Could Henri help her overcome the sadness of Lillia's departure?

Suddenly worried for her mother, Lillia is surprised when Phoebe takes her shoulders in a passionate grip and hugs her tightly. Lillia returns the strong embrace until Henri arrives from loading the carriage.

"Alright then, you two, time for Sebastian and Lillia to begin their journey."

Lillia follows her father to the carriage. Before handing her up to her uncle, Henri turns to his daughter and takes her hands in his and says, "Lillia, watch over your uncle, temper his enthusiasm, and have courage in your trials. Your mother and I will get along. Promise to write us. Never forget how much we love you."

"I love you, too, Father. Please watch over Mother. She took Bernard's departure so hard, I can't leave without knowing you will help her adjust to my leaving."

"I'll do my best, *ma chérie*," Henri whispers before plucking a gentle kiss on her forehead.

Sebastian's determination to get to Lowell is surprising. He has driven the road to Lowell so fast Lillia wonders if he might not also have an ulterior motive for getting to California as fast as possible. When the next pothole bounces her hard against the lightly padded seat, Lillia winces and bites her lip against the pain, shooting her uncle a sideways glance, which elicits only an empathic shrug.

"Sorry, *chérie*, impossible to miss them. Winter hasn't been kind to your New England roads."

"Any idea how much longer we have to endure this torture?"

"While unfamiliar with this route, it seems to me Lowell should be somewhere just beyond this upcoming hilltop."

Lillia takes his explanation and turns away, hoping to hide her pained expression. Since leaving her parent's house in Roxbury at dawn, she has been haunted by the echo of Henri's words—*never forget how much we love you*—and regret for not telling them the truth about Donovan's escape raises its devilish head. At that moment, the need to return to her parents almost overwhelms her.

Just as quickly, bold determination boils in her veins and her motivations clarify. Donovan knew her feelings about the limitations of Eastern society. Without a husband, she was doomed to a life of dependency on her parents and a limited opportunity for self-expression. Given her age and unusual temperament, she had accepted that she had no choice but to settle for anyone who would marry her. Donovan had his own set of societal limitations, so their match had benefitted them both. Or so she had thought.

But, deep in her soul, she feels a calm, confident voice assuring her there is more to life. This trip needs to prove her instinct is right.

She knows some people will question Sebastian's judgment of taking her along and making her a business partner. The reality is the two of them will be a force to reckon with given

Sebastian's history of good fortune and her bargaining skills. Henri had given her their money belt to wear under her skirts and its weight sits heavily on her hips, reminding her of his confidence in her shrewd financial skills. He had also assured her the money wasn't going to strain their Boston import business for liquidity, but she knew better.

Lillia takes confidence that Henri must believe in the potential of this trip. But, when he put her in charge of the belt, he told her to mind it carefully, be frugal, and to not let Sebastian's enthusiasm get the better of the operation.

They find accommodations at a comfortable inn and enjoy their evening meal. As their plates are cleared, Lillia is certain Sebastian must be as exhausted as she, but his tone picks up with renewed vigor.

"Lillia, time is of the essence. Ships are leaving every day. My source assures me we're in a very profitable race, but we must strike quickly to see our greatest return."

"Still, Uncle, I'm worried about my parents. Is it reasonable to think we'll return to Boston within the next two years?"

"That will depend on what we find in California. I'd be lying if I said gold fever hasn't had an effect on me. Mind you, I'll not be toiling in the mud. We'll gather the nuggets in exchange for goods. You, on the other hand, you are young and should grip the elephant's tail with gusto!"

"I'm grateful for your confidence."

Sebastian removes a slip of paper from his coat pocket, unfolding it with care before handing it to Lillia.

"This is our ship. After we make our fabric order, we'll visit Beverly to arrange for passage. The ship is scheduled to leave on June 15, which will put us in California in late December."

"Uncle, that is over a month away! We cannot wait that long."

"I agree, but we must allow for the fabric's creation. I agree we should search for a ship that could leave earlier, but for now, this is our only option."

Lillia scrutinizes the paper Sebastian handed her. "This says the ship has furnished staterooms including meals for two hundred fifty dollars per person. Is that what we should expect?"

"For comfortable passage, yes. What we consider exorbitant now may save our sanity in the end. It is a very long trip."

Lillia's mouth forms a tight line before she says, "And that is before knowing what they are going to charge for shipping our cloth. I think we should also consider a ship that isn't quite so expensive."

Sebastian sighs heavily at her words.

"I have a good feeling about all this. It will work out."

The following morning, Sebastian's voice coming from the inn's dining room urges Lillia to rise and dress quickly. She hears him in enthusiastic conversation as she twists her hair into a low bun. Securing the hair pins, she takes a deep breath and steps out of her room. Predictably, Sebastian sits at a table of men who all look up at her when she enters the room.

"Here, gentlemen, is my niece and business partner, Miss Lillia Soilleux. Lillia, I present to you a fine collection of travelers with whom we share many interesting similarities."

Lillia nods politely to the group as Sebastian pulls out her chair and she takes it gracefully, saying, "Gentlemen, good morning."

An older man, who doesn't conceal his raised eyebrows says, "Your uncle has shared his enthusiasm for California, but I'm surprised at his choice in business partners. How do *you* intend to find your fortune alongside the men?"

Lillia stifles her offense and says, "I assure you, the men in California's goldfields have nothing to fear from my presence.

I have no intention of competing for a creek bed or a muddy hillside."

A different gentleman asks, "What will be your contribution to the partnership?"

"With my family's merchant background and financing, I have a unique perspective. I'll determine what the wilderness is lacking and fill the void."

Lillia notices the mens' raised eyebrows. She pours herself a cup of tea, and an uncomfortable silence settles around the table like a foul odor. All but two men find excuses to leave the table. Sebastian skillfully uses that moment to set his trap with the remaining two men.

"Our initial foray into the California market will be with heavy canvas, a modest but necessary item. The key to success is its rapid acquisition, as well as finding a fast-sailing ship to speed our arrival. I'm wondering if either of you have any insights that might aid us?"

While waiting for a response, Lillia observes the older of the two gentlemen. Sporting a pure white, stylishly trimmed beard, she is puzzled as to why he doesn't make eye contact with anyone, choosing instead to stare at the tatted tablecloth. With this focus, he speaks hesitantly.

"I know of a ship and captain. Would you entertain a conversation with him? I have a meeting arranged with him this afternoon, but perhaps we could all share supper together?"

"*Très bien*! That's exactly what we had in mind."

At this, the gentleman raises his face, revealing the milky grayness of sightless eyes but showing a pleased grin as Sebastian continues.

"We'd be most pleased to share the evening meal with you and your captain friend. May I ask your name, sir?"

"Charles Forsythe. It will be my pleasure to introduce you to Captain Eagleton."

Pouring herself another cup of tea, Lillia notices the second man make a quick motion toward his coat pocket, removing a small leather booklet and a thick pencil. Dressed in the peak of fashion, she guesses he is only ten to fifteen years her senior.

"How do you propose to make payment for the goods?" he asks, his tone clipped and efficient.

"Ours will be a cash transaction," Sebastian replies.

From lowered eyes, Lillia sees the man stare at her before tearing a page from his book and offering it to her.

"You will find this useful in your dealings at Lowell Mills. I'll inform the mill agent of your venture's urgency."

Lillia takes the page without looking at it, saying, "You are very kind, Mr. . . . ?"

"Wellingham. Howard Wellingham. I've a knack for discerning the merits of business propositions. I'll admit to being doubtful of a woman's capabilities, but your uncle's experience can compensate. You'll serve as a novelty, an attractive oasis to the starved miners' eyes. Consider it an asset for which other merchants will have no counter."

Lillia dips her face away to camouflage her shock at his condescension, biting her lip against verbal retribution. Sebastian's eyes flash before he rises to shake Wellingham's hand, both men exchanging measured smiles.

Choosing to walk to the mill agent's office, Lillia takes Sebastian's arm, and they proceed in silence until Lillia can't deny her burning question.

"How do you know that Mr. Wellingham is on the up-and-up? We just met him this morning."

"If his connection at the mill is as solid as he lets on, it will be a good omen to our venture. By the way, your earlier restraint is noteworthy. His underestimation of your skills is your new advantage."

"I suppose you are correct," she says with a sigh.

A sign on a red brick building at the outside edge of the mill's complex designates it as the mill agent's office. From outside the building, Lillia flinches at the riotous clatter of the loom shuttlecocks and wonders what the sound must be like inside.

Sebastian opens the door, allowing Lillia to step into the shadowed interior, before following her. Once their eyes adjust to the dim light, Lillia makes out a desk, a bookcase, and three chairs positioned on a rug island surrounded by a sea of polished hardwood flooring. The agent looks up from his work, leaving his desk to greet them without pushing back the chair. Trying not to stare at his diminutive stature, Lillia smiles as he approaches.

"Welcome, sir, madam. I'm Oscar Plenworth. What brings you to Lowell Mills?"

"Hello, Monsieur Plenworth. I'm Sebastian Soilleux and this is my niece, Lillia Soilleux. We're in urgent need of a quantity of your canvas."

"Tell me more, Monsieur Soilleux."

Sebastian outlines their needs while Lillia watches Plenworth for any clue about his willingness. His inert expression gives her no satisfaction. When Sebastian finishes, Plenworth thumbs through papers on his table finally saying, "I'm afraid your order falls into a difficult category."

At that, Sebastian removes Wellingham's note from his coat pocket and offers it to Plenworth, along with a slight bow, before saying, "Perhaps you would consider this credential on our behalf?"

Lillia studies Plenworth as he unfolds the note, reads it, and bursts into laughter.

"Ha! Oh, my, my, my! So this is you! Wellingham arrived earlier informing me to take no other business until your order is satisfied."

Energized, Plenworth quickly returns to his desk and spins a large ledger toward him for examination and says, "Here's what I can do: we have half your required amount of fabric in our warehouse. The other half will be available in a week's time."

Sebastian gapes as he looks at Lillia. Equally baffled, she looks from one man to the other. Suspicion clouds her mind as she wonders how all this could be so easy.

Grinning widely, Sebastian says, "Prepare the paperwork, my good man."

Without looking up, Plenworth scratches wildly into his ledger.

"How fortunate for you Mr. Wellingham is willing to take his percentage when the goods are sold in California."

Lillia feels all the air escape from her lungs. "His percentage?"

"Why, yes. He expects a ten percent partnership. That's why he had your order bumped ahead of the others. He can be very persuasive."

Lillia shoots Sebastian a look.

"What if we don't agree to this partnership?"

Plenworth slowly puts down his quill and meets her gaze.

"That would be unfortunate. As he stated to me, no Wellingham, no deal."

He reaches for a stack of papers, licks his fingers, and counts through the pile.

"There are twenty-odd orders ahead of you, ready sometime in June, maybe July. Considering you'll be traveling together, I'd strongly suggest you reconsider any notion of reneging on this partnership."

Lillia's scowl deepens at the news of Wellingham's travel plans. Sebastian gently pulls her to the side and whispers, "We both know waiting until June will doom this venture. Wellingham sounds better as a partner than an adversary. For now, I believe this is our best, and only, way forward."

Upon their arrival at the inn, Lillia rolls her eyes when she notices five settings at the table.

"Welcome, Soilleuxs! A glass of sherry while we wait?"

"How did you know?" Sebastian starts.

"My blindness has made my other senses quite attuned to things like scent and sounds. In your case, I detected a simultaneous woman's step to a man's step. It had to be you two!"

Chuckling, Sebastian fulfills Charles's request, Lillia feels her ire rise when Wellingham and a tall man enter the room trading comfortable camaraderie. Sebastian raises the sherry decanter in their direction and offers, "Just in time! Sherry?"

Accepting, the men stand by as Charles boldly makes the introductions, "Captain Rupert Eagleton, may I present Monsieur and Miss Soilleux of Boston, my newest friends and potential business partners and yours, if we're lucky."

The captain politely bobs his head in Lillia's direction before shaking Sebastian's hand.

Charles continues, "Theirs is a grand adventure. I'm wondering if we might all benefit from each other's needs."

Wellingham seats himself next to Lillia. He leans toward her and says, "Miss Soilleux, I understand all went well at Lowell Mills this morning."

"Yes, your assistance was quite astonishing."

Sebastian seats himself on her other side, leaning around her to address Wellingham.

"We learned you're planning to sail on the same ship to California. Had you planned a trip earlier or did we provide inspiration?"

"I'm to courier a valuable item to California from New York requiring the quickest passage available. Eagleton tells me he is up to the task."

Following their meal, Captain Eagleton shifts their casual conversation to business.

"Monsieur Soilleux, what has Charles told you about my ship?"

"He mentioned it's the fastest that can be found in this bay."

"What goods are to be stowed in the ship's hold?"

"A large quantity of cotton canvas, about twenty tons."

Lillia cuts in, "Captain, how long will we be at sea?"

The question makes Captain Eagleton square his shoulders before replying, "Most ships take six to eight months. Those with bad luck, who don't fail completely, can take a year sailing to San Francisco."

Everyone looks at Captain Eagleton as he compellingly swirls his brandy.

"I have an idea, however," he says. "It requires imagination, courage, and the ability to invest."

Looking at her uncle, Lillia knows he has swallowed the captain's hook. Wellingham's cheeks flush while Charles sits quietly, gently stroking the snifter's bowl with his index finger.

Captain Eagleton chuckles softly, and then says, "Good, I have your attention. After several years in the ice trade with Boston's Frederic Tudor, I'm ready to make my education pay off. Fresh water and decent food are the Achille's heel of the Cape Horn trip.

As it happens, I've come into possession of a quantity of ice. Without the frequent stops for fresh water and replacing stale food, we'll arrive a month ahead of other ships departing simultaneously and, due to better victuals, berths will demand top dollar."

The captain's eyes glitter at his final statement. Wellingham asks the first question.

"Rupert, is your ship already prepared for the journey?"

"That's where your investment comes in. I was forced to sell my ship. But I'm debt-free and own two hundred tons of ice."

Sebastian asks, "Where is your ship now?"

"Docked in Newburyport."

"Captain, what is your financial requirement?" Lillia asks.

Warm satisfaction rolls over her when Wellingham flinches at her question.

Unfazed, Captain Eagleton replies, "Beyond the expense of improving her insulating qualities, she can be had for five thousand. My contribution is the ice and sailing skills to get us to California."

After a few moments, Sebastian makes his counter saying, "If we have to come up with the money to purchase the ship, along with improvements, I propose partners, and their cargo, travel at no cost. Additionally, any monies received from passengers and other potential freight, will be shared by the partners based on their percentage of contribution."

The proposition gets considerable contemplation until Charles suggests, "Let's sleep on Rupert's idea and reconvene at breakfast."

Agreeing, everyone pushes back from the table. Sebastian escorts Lillia to her room and comes inside to light the lamp for her. Taking a seat on the bed's edge, Lillia waits for what she knows is bottled up inside him. It doesn't take long to emerge.

With wonderment in his voice, Sebastian says, "Never in my life, when I thought this day couldn't get any better, this, this—"

"Fantasy?"

"Now, now," Sebastian coos, "I agree it's unconventional. I've heard of Tudor, the Ice King. Captain Eagleton could be right about getting ice all the way to California. Tudor sails his ice to Calcutta!"

Lillia takes a sober tone as she says, "With what we spent today at the mill and our expenses before we sail, if we partner with Captain Eagleton, success will be mandatory when we get to California."

"But with Charles's and Wellingham's participation, we'll share the costs."

Aware that this irrational behavior is what her father had warned her of, Lillia stifles her concerns and lets Sebastian take her hands while pleading, "I know this will put our finances on a knife's edge. But we've been presented with an uncommon opportunity. Perhaps Charles or Wellingham will consider investing more than a third."

"Beneath the polish, I find Wellingham to be sneaky. Possibly conniving. If he had been honest about our cloth venture from the start, perhaps I wouldn't be so worried."

Sebastian opens his arms to her, and she falls into his solid embrace.

"Do not fret, time will reveal his secrets. More importantly, I sense we're in the grips of kismet."

"Kismet?"

"Yes. Our fate. Our destiny."

"Does kismet pay the bills?"

"Not more than fate does, but to have had so many details of our venture unfold so perfectly, I have no other answer, do you?"

"No, I don't. Though 'perfectly' may be overstating it some," she sighs, resigned.

"It certainly seems like we are being put into a fortunate position, doesn't it?" Sebastian coos before adding, "Sleep peacefully, Lillia. We are truly under the influence of kismet. I promise you."

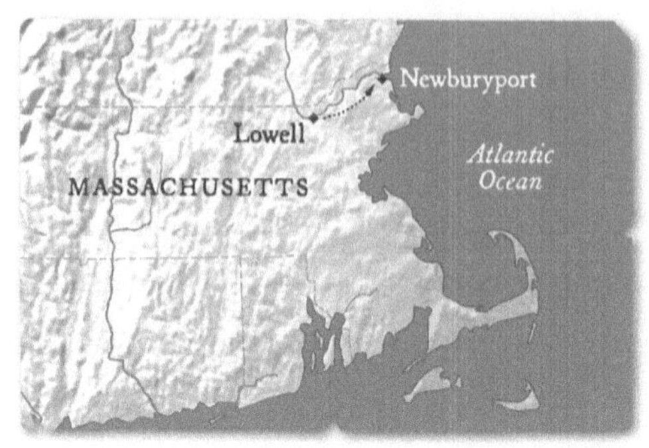

Chapter 3

MAY, 1849

LOWELL, MASSACHUSETTS

All parties reveal their investment capabilities at breakfast the next morning. With roughly similar amounts, they agree to a four-way partnership with Captain Eagleton. Due to the Soilleux's liquidity, they agree to accompany the captain to Newburyport to release the ship's debt with their portion.

Sebastian guides the carriage toward Newburyport while Captain Eagleton rides horseback next to him. Lillia holds the newly inked partnership papers firmly in her lap. When neither man attempts conversation, Lillia seizes the opportunity to further understand the captain.

"Captain Eagleton, how is it that you had to sell your ship?"

After an uncomfortable pause, the captain says, "I suppose an explanation is due. The truth is, I took a risk, came up short, and had to satisfy the creditor."

Lillia considers his vague answer for a moment before asking, "Given the California-bound craze, isn't it likely the creditor has already sold your ship?"

"Rest assured, she's waiting for me. I requested my creditor give me notice of a pending sale, and I haven't heard anything."

Dubious, Lillia shoots Sebastian a sideways glance and asks, "How can you be so sure of the creditor's integrity?"

"She's my mother."

"Your own mother forced you to sell your ship?" Sebastian bursts out.

"She's a stickler, whether it's her son or another debtor."

Incredulous, Sebastian asks, "What on earth would force your mother to be so harsh?"

"My brothers."

"My good man," Sebastian says, now laughing, "as your new partners, I believe you should elaborate."

Captain Eagleton heaves a confirming sigh.

"To begin, I'm the oldest of six brothers and four sisters. My father was a shipping merchant. When his ship was lost at sea, I was sixteen and my youngest brother was still nursing. My mother raised us with her wits, the proceeds of shrewd investments, and the skills of Father's accountant. As it turns out, our father had created an investment fund for his children to use, as long as the original amount borrowed was repaid."

Sebastian nods with approval saying, "Your father had admirable foresight."

"Agreed. As the sea is in my blood, I started as a packet ship's boy, going back and forth across the Atlantic. After several trips, I hired on to one of Tudor's ice ships as first mate. We made runs to the Caribbean with New England ice."

Sebastian approvingly nods his head toward Lillia as the captain continues.

"When my brothers matured, they joined me on the Tudor ships. With my last run, I made back my portion of the family loan money."

"Well done!"

Sebastian's enthusiasm is dampened as the captain continues.

"Yes, well, rather than pay it back, my brothers convinced me to pool our respective monies and buy one of our father's schooners to begin our own freighting business. In doing so, we exhausted Father's investment fund. Mother wasn't pleased."

Curiosity getting the better of her, Lillia asks, "How much was loaned?"

"Forty-five thousand between us."

Lillia covers her gasp with her gloved hand.

"The next time we made port, we learned one of our sisters was to be wed and justly due her share. Mother threatened to seize the ship if we didn't repay. In a desperate attempt, we put in a bid to haul war provisions from Charlestown Naval Yard to Mexico's Pacific Coast. Surprisingly, we won the contract. That was eighteen months ago."

Sebastian lets the time frame sink in before saying, "Surely the proceeds from that venture paid off what you owed."

"After delivering the supplies, the officer handed me a voucher and told me to redeem it at the Charlestown Naval Yard, which meant returning around Cape Horn."

As the carriage crests the hill overlooking Newburyport Lillia asks, "Why are you alone in this effort, when your brothers have their debt to pay as well?"

"They know how serious Mother is about honoring our repayment, but news of gold in California was just spreading along the Pacific Coast when we were there. They convinced me to sail north to see the commotion firsthand before heading around the Horn."

Lillia makes a face at Sebastian.

"I should have known they would desert me. The stories of finding gold were too much for them. Adding to my injury, my personal bag containing the voucher got mixed up with one of theirs. By the time I figured it out, I had no choice but to gather a crew, sail back to Newburyport, and face Mother."

The horse's hooves clop rhythmically until Sebastian asks, "And your ice acquisition?"

"I've lived off the ship's proceeds until a good friend of mine found himself in a bad spot, so I swapped him for a house full of ice. That's how my idea was hatched. When it works, I will have solved most of my problems."

"Are you going to entice your brothers to return or just fetch their portions back?" Lillia asks.

"A good question, Miss Soilleux, for which I have no good answer. All I know is I must redeem that voucher."

Over supper that night, the captain outlines the next morning's activities, "We'll visit my mother in the morning, show her the partnership agreement, and your earnest money, so she will release the ship."

Still skeptical about the ship's true availability, Lillia sets her fork down and says, "Perhaps we should visit the ship to confirm it is available for repurchase?"

"Don't worry, she'll be right where I left her."

Dabbing her napkin to her mouth, Lillia smiles saying, "I find an evening walk to be refreshing."

Sebastian grins broadly and nods. "I agree. What's the name of our ship, Captain?"

Captain Eagleton scrutinizes them before offering a slight wince with his nod, "I suppose you're about to learn the name. Mind you, it was my brothers' idea. I was outvoted. Ships should bear respectable names; names that illicit confidence in their speed or strength. Mine? She's christened the *Ornery Agnes*."

"Your mother's name . . ." Lillia begins.

"Is Agnes."

Lillia and Sebastian suppress laughter while he continues, "She's as seaworthy as they come. Given the right winds, she can keep pace with some clippers, even though she's designed for hauling. She's not fancy, but then, neither is Mother."

Sebastian offers a toast, his composure restored.

"'Tis all one can ask of a ship. Here's to *Ornery Agnes*."

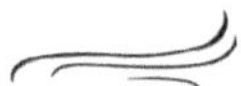

Newburyport's sea air chills as dusk settles on their walk to the docks. Lillia imagines the small but busy seaport in the daylight, her only reference being the tumultuous Boston Harbor. For now, she enjoys the peace and warmth of Sebastian's arm as they stroll toward the waterfront.

When they reach the ship, Sebastian illumines the hull with his torch's flame. The dim light catches the image of a carved eagle gracing her bow along with her iconic name.

"We may have to dress her up to lure paying passengers," Sebastian observes.

"On the contrary," Lillia points out. "If, as you say, fresh food and water is valuable, the discerning will appreciate those benefits more than the ship's façade."

Captain Eagleton looks at Lillia approvingly, saying, "I agree. It sounds like a compelling argument."

Lillia and Sebastian return to the docks the next morning to find Captain Eagleton perched on the ship's railing above a group of men. When they step closer, he looks up and hails them, "Ah, there you are! I'll be with you shortly."

Lillia turns to Sebastian and asks, "Why is he engaging workers before we know if his mother is going to release the ship?"

"His diligence tells me he's confident and a good captain. You'll see soon enough. Let's take a look around while we wait."

He gestures toward the boarding plank and Lillia climbs it hesitantly, this being her first time on a ship. Heading toward the bow, they find the passenger deck locked. Sebastian uses his elbow to wipe the salt spray from the exterior windows allowing her to peer inside. Several berth doors, some ajar, line the passenger's common area.

From over her shoulder, Sebastian says, "It looks well kept . . . better than some I've seen. The galley should be at midship as well as berths for the cook, carpenter, sailing master, and boatswain."

"Where are the crew and captain housed?"

"The crew will be in the forecastle, one deck below us. The captain and his mates will reside below the helm at the stern."

Lillia looks toward the stern, and she sees Captain Eagleton gesturing them toward the boarding plank to make their exit. To join him, they maneuver past stevedores hauling bulky bolts of burlap toward the hold.

As the bolts pass him, Sebastian motions, and asks the captain, "For the ice?"

"That's right. First, three layers of burlap. Then five inches of compressed sawdust. Once the ice blocks are positioned, there'll be just a paper's width between them with no exposure to the air. When all the ice is loaded, we reverse the process."

"What about drinking and cooking water?"

"We'll leave one corner of burlap loose to chisel out chunks. A drain will catch any melting ice for personal use. Now then, Miss Soilleux, I've learned you enjoy a lively walk. Shall we take a stroll to my mother's home?"

"Absolutely. Lead the way."

The trio follow the main road past the town's busy center and a marketplace. Again, Lillia compares this pleasant little town to the chaos of the Boston marketplace and she feels completely comfortable. Continuing up a gentle grade, they stop to catch their breath and Lillia observes the change from the business center to a serene residential neighborhood. The clapboard homes are well-appointed, two- and three-story structures, each painted in tasteful hues with contrasting shutters that highlight the multi-paned windows. One in particular catches Lillia's attention. Admiring its windowed turret perched on the roof, the captain notes her gaze and leans over her shoulder from behind.

"The Home for Aged Women is mostly widows of whaling captains. It is a comfort for them to have each other but my mother insists on maintaining her independence."

They continue down the street lined with well-maintained yards, each home's exterior reflecting the bright morning light. Captain Eagleton stops them and points.

"Third one on the right."

Lillia detects a slight warble in the captain's voice as she looks in the direction where he's pointing. The house is the largest on the lane. Lillia tries not to gape at its groomed shrubbery and garden beds. A broad staircase leads to a generous wraparound porch and, even from her distance, Lillia sees the white paint has no blemish.

Upon approach, the captain clears his throat and says, "Now, then, about Mother. She's a stellar example of a self-sufficient New England merchants's widow. Direct in her observations—some say too direct, I urge you not to take offense."

Lillia and Sebastian glance at each other as they climb the home's front steps. The beveled-glass door swings open, and they see a tall, slim, older woman dressed fashionably but frugal in pure black taffeta from chin to hem, her chignon of flashing silver offering a pleasing contrast. The angularity of her face suggests a stern countenance, and Lillia isn't surprised at the woman's first words.

"Rupert, who've you snared this time?"

"Hello, Mother."

The captain strides up the steps, plants a generous kiss on her cheek, and gives her a firm hug.

"Now, now, no need to throttle."

"Mother, I'd like to introduce Monsieur Sebastian Soilleux and his niece, Miss Lillia Soilleux of Boston. Monsieur, Miss, my mother, Agnes Eagleton."

Lillia leads Sebastian up the front steps. Agnes's smile warms at Lillia's approach.

"I'm delighted to meet you, Miss Soilleux," she says.

Sebastian comes to Lillia's side and takes Agnes's hand.

"Madam, it is our pleasure."

Agnes's eyes light up at Sebastian's words, her eyebrows raise at his graciousness, and perhaps at the lilt of a French accent. She gestures them inside with elegant grace.

"Come in, please. Rupert, show your guests to the parlor while I put the pot on."

Agnes disappears down a central hallway as the captain escorts Lillia and Sebastian through a generous foyer, sweeping staircase, and finally to a tastefully designed sitting parlor. The upholstered furniture gives an immediate tone of elegant comfort. The hardwood floors gleam with polish, but it's the soft rug that makes Lillia sigh.

She says, "Your mother is a lovely woman, Captain."

"She's quite a specimen. But watch yourself, Miss Soilleux. She's full of surprises."

"Would it help to discuss our business sooner than later?" asks Sebastian.

"Good question, and the answer is I'm not sure. I've never understood what makes my mother work."

"Understood. We'll tread lightly. Will you tell us more about your father?"

"Certainly. I have fond, but few, memories of him. When I was very young, he was gone, mostly whaling in the northern Atlantic. Later, he purchased a packet ship and a few schooners to start his freighting business, one of which is waiting for us in port. She's an Isaac Webb-built ship from the twenties. She's seen some years, but we've made improvements to keep her running strong."

Agnes arrives with a tray laden with delicate cakes and a tea service. Once everyone has their tea, Agnes settles into her chair.

"Tell me, Monsieur Soilleux, how has my son entangled you and your niece?"

Sebastian shifts in his seat as he answers, "We are seeking to establish a business in California. Your son has offered to sail us there with our goods."

Agnes takes a long sip of tea, lifting her gaze toward the captain before returning to Sebastian.

"What is this business you speak of?"

"The idea is to take a simple item, cotton canvas, as our entrée into the California market to learn what is in demand or missing before establishing ourselves as importers. Our business today, other than the pleasure of meeting you, is to offer partial payment against the indebtedness of the captain's ship."

"The *Ornery Agnes*?"

Agnes raises the teacup to her lips. Lillia detects a sly smile on the woman's face at the use of the unflattering name.

"Yes, madam."

"How is it you are only offering partial payment?"

Captain Eagleton interjects, "There are two other investors whose money isn't quite as liquid as the Soilleux's. The whole amount has been legally committed besides all operational expenses in California."

The captain produces the partnership agreement from his coat's breast pocket, and hands it to his mother. She puts down her teacup and examines the document. After a moment, she lowers the papers and levels her gaze to the captain.

"Rupert, it looks like you've got a solid partnership agreement here."

With a quick side glance, Lillia catches the captain's dumbfounded expression, realizing he was not expecting her endorsement today.

Agnes turns to Sebastian and smiles warmly, saying, "Monsieur, I'm pleased a businessman of your talents has become acquainted with my son. On a selfish note, I hope he'll find the rest of my sons in those California hills."

"I appreciate your confidence, Madam."

Captain Eagleton stands to leave, but Agnes gestures swiftly with her hand.

"Not so fast, Rupert. Stay here with Monsieur Soilleux and finish your tea. I'd like a private conversation with Miss Soilleux."

Agnes stands and motions for Lillia to follow her. Tentatively, Lillia sets down her cup and rushes to catch up to Agnes's brisk stride. In the kitchen, Agnes casually begins wiping the wooden countertops with a towel before stopping to look intently into Lillia's eyes. Lillia boldly returns her gaze, studying the fine lines and contours of Agnes's visage.

"How old are you, my dear?"

"I'm in my twenty-fifth year."

Agnes's expression turns wistful.

"Rupert was ten years old when I was twenty-five. Justus, Rupert's father, was at sea and Rupert had to help me deliver my seventh child, Paulo, who wasn't willing to wait for the midwife. I believe Rupert has felt burdened with a father's role since then. The others enjoy their freedom more than Rupert has or ever will, I'm afraid."

Lillia is speechless after this admission.

Agnes continues, "What is it that motivates you to make this horrendous trip? California is full of barbarians."

"Mrs. Eagleton, while some say California is uncivilized, New England society judges a woman's worth based on marital status. I'm simply trading one incivility for another."

"Do you intend to remain a spinster?"

"I don't consider the idea to be a death sentence."

"Dear, I don't wish to offend. Simply put, I'm of like mind. A man who appreciates a woman's intelligence must be stronger than most, since your intellect will challenge his own. Most men expect to be the only one in the relationship with the ability to reason."

"I'll gladly brave life's trials alone with what grit and brains our Maker gave me before living with a condescending man."

Realizing she may have crossed a line, Lillia quickly adds, "Forgive my boldness."

"No need. Our conversation has been quite refreshing. I was required to nurture the same spark after Justus's death while rebuffing the advances of many suitors; word had spread of the wealth Justus had left me. It took determination, but I believe I've weathered the storm. From what I've been hearing, I believe California is an opportunity for strong, enterprising women. You'll be at the spear tip, so keep your wits about you, but I'm envious of your circumstances. I wish you only the best, I really do."

"Thank you, Mrs. Eagleton. Your confidence means more than you know."

When the women return to the parlor, both men quickly stand. Agnes addresses Sebastian directly.

"Sir, the Soilleux portion of the ship's value will be enough to release the ship for renovations. Please see Mr. Hensley at the Institute for Savings. Once the other investors have paid the full amount, he will release the *Ornery Agnes*."

Sebastian extends his hand to take Agnes's where he lightly passes his lips over her knuckles saying, "Very well, Madam. Thank you."

The captain smiles and says, "Thank you, Mother."

When Agnes turns to Lillia, she whispers, "I give you my strength in all your efforts. Go with God."

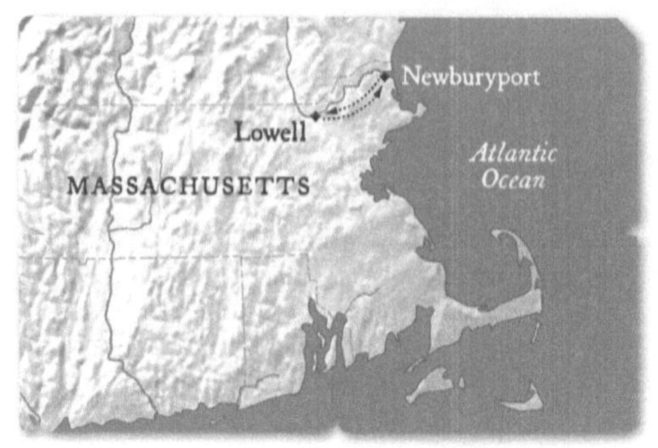

Chapter 4

MAY, 1849

LOWELL, MASSACHUSETTS

After a week spent advertising their available berths to potential travelers, Lillia learns from Captain Eagleton it could be another two weeks before the ship's renovations are complete. Eager to monitor their cloth's progress, she and Sebastian return to Lowell leaving the berth sales until the time for sailing is closer.

Sebastian notices Lillia's eyebrows are knitted into a deep crease as the carriage rolls across the countryside and asks, "Are you fretting about the fact we've only sold two berths?"

"I don't understand why so many have scoffed at our price. Don't they value the speed and uniqueness of this voyage?"

With no good answer to her petulance, Sebastian changes

the subject, saying, "Did Agnes give you any indication as to why our captain has never married?"

"Only that she attributes it to his having become the head of the household too early. Why do you ask?"

"He's commented about the difficulty an intelligent and strong-willed woman has finding a suitor."

"As if those characteristics are unsavory?"

"No. Rather, it takes a certain kind of man to appreciate a woman who challenges his authority."

"I would venture to guess his opinion is based on his mother's formidable facade created to maintain control of the monies left to her. Our captain only sees a hardened woman and doesn't appreciate why."

Sebastian pauses, clearly choosing his words carefully before saying, "Have you become hardened after young O'Creigh's disappearance?"

Lillia sits with Sebastian's question for a long moment before answering, "What have you said about that to the captain?"

"Only that you've had a recent tragic event which has shifted your focus away from love."

If Sebastian's idea was to shift Lillia's rumination from selling berths to Captain Eagleton, he is quite successful.

At the Lowell Inn's dining room, Lillia and Sebastian find Charles sitting in his familiar spot in the company of Wellingham. She sighs as they approach, relieved Wellingham is present to join them.

"Hello, my friends!" Charles says, waving a hand in greeting before adding, "Sebastian, you should have a blacksmith look at your carriage's loose hitch pin."

Marveling at Charles' keen senses, Sebastian faces Wellingham and sticks out a welcoming hand and says, "Good to see you, Howard! Were you successful in your efforts to tie up your loose ends?"

At Sebastian's side, Lillia observes what has to be an imposter. Gone is the trim, well-dressed Wellingham they had left only a week ago. In his place is a mussed and unshaven man, his face drawn with fatigue.

"In a manner of saying, I suppose," Wellingham replies, offering only a thin smile before returning his downward gaze to the sherry glass his fingers are idly spinning.

Charles gestures toward them saying, "Join us, both of you."

While he calls for more sherry, Sebastian pulls out a chair for Lillia across from Wellingham where she observes, with lowered eyes, Wellingham's behavior.

Something is very wrong.

"Did you meet Rupert's mother?"

Charles's question makes Lillia and Sebastian exchange amused looks before Sebastian responds, "We did. Have you met Agnes?"

"I proposed to her several times. When my interest was not returned, I abandoned the effort. That's not to say I've not found ways to be involved in the Eagleton family, but Agnes knows nothing of it. Rupert has been a fine captain for many of my shipping endeavors . . . until his last one."

A fresh set of expressions pass between Lillia and Sebastian.

"I should like to join you when you haul the canvas to Newburyport. It has been my tradition to see Rupert off when he sails."

"And perhaps renew an old friendship?"

Charles cracks a big grin at Sebastian's suggestion.

"Yes, perhaps. But, more importantly, Howard has had a turn of events you should know about."

"Is that so, Howard?"

Wellingham heaves a long sigh, his pompous tone completely deflated when he says, "Life's twists bring joy and cruelty. I've had more of the latter lately. After less than a year of marriage, I lost my wife by her own hand, her actions brought on by the remorse over not being able to conceive."

"Oh no, I'm so very sorry," Lillia offers.

Wellingham continues, "To help me heal, my New York banking friends offered me the opportunity to courier a wager to California. In my mental disarray, it sounded like just the right antidote. I left you a week ago to prepare my business interests for my prolonged absence. In Springfield, I discovered my business partner left weeks ago, fired all the employees and sacked everything of value. I spent days trying to piece the business back together. But short of me being present to rebuild the company, no one was interested. Given my courier commitment, I had to walk away."

"When you arrived, Howard was telling me he doesn't have the wherewithal to invest in our venture."

Heavy silence settles over the table. All attention turns to Charles, whose expression gives no hint of his thoughts. Lillia toys with the idea of reminding Wellingham of the ten percent interest in their canvas proceeds he had connived but decides to hold her tongue.

Wellingham continues, "My courier position will pay for my passage. This delay further underscores my need to travel by the fastest means available. Eagleton is the best."

Silence continues until, as if poked by a pin, Charles jerks his head upright.

"How many paying berths are left?"

"Excepting ours and Howard's, there are still seven available."

Charles falls silent at the news as the others discuss the *Ornery Agnes*'s progress, the few passengers willing to pay their price, and the anticipated date of departure.

Sebastian says, "Tomorrow, we will visit the mill to learn of the hauling logistics and when we can start for Newburyport."

Charles abruptly asks, "How many crew have been hired?"

"I believe the captain has fifteen plus the cook, carpenter, master, and boatswain."

Charles smacks the tabletop with his open hand saying, "For my plan to succeed, we must make every effort to get to the ship before Rupert sells any more berths."

Following a two-day mad scramble for wagons, drivers, and loading their cloth, Sebastian's carriage leads their procession to Newburyport. Charles had insisted on interviewing the wagon drivers and, after careful selection, had chosen to ride next to each driver rather than in the more comfortable carriage. The echo of his occasional jolly guffaw makes Lillia wonder what their new friend and business partner is scheming.

Captain Eagleton heartily hails the wagon train when it arrives at the *Ornery Agnes*'s side with some light in the sky. Once the wagons and horses are boarded and the drivers' accommodations are arranged, the partners return to the inn. After supper, Charles begins the difficult conversation.

"Rupert, our partnership arrangement has shifted, but Howard should tell of it, not me."

All attention turns to Wellingham as he recounts his story. When finished, Lillia feels the air ladened with disappointment until Captain Eagleton cuts the tension.

"So we're financially short."

Wellingham bows his head sheepishly, "Afraid so, my friend."

Charles quickly sips his drink, setting it down gently while clearing his throat. "I have an idea, but before I share it, I must have a few answers from you, Rupert."

The captain offers a welcoming gesture.

"How many crew members have you hired?"

"I've everyone save a few deckhands."

"Any other paying passengers?"

"None since Sebastian left. I'm not as smooth talking as he is."

Lillia's heart leaps when Charles abruptly claps and howls triumphantly, "Then consider the ship full and ready to sail!"

"What do you mean?" Lillia asks.

"Weren't those wagon drivers pleasant? They could be trustworthy partners."

Wellingham's face is wrapped in confusion.

"In which venture, Charles?"

"The California goldfields. While I'm physically unable to participate, I can enlist them to do the work. I will pay for their passages and thereby pay off the lien against your ship and put you, Howard, in charge of getting them established in California."

Lillia asks, "How will you ever see your returns?"

Charles grins widely.

"I've not been blind my whole life, only the last ten years. My family has always had investment money. Deprived of sight, I trust others like Rupert to sail my ships and, until recently, Wellingham to create my firearms. Without something to anticipate each morning, I would have no reason to go on living."

Captain Eagleton grins widely and announces, "Right then, Charles saves the day! Now that the cloth is here, there is nothing stopping a timely departure when then ship is ready. I would guess we will have her prepared for the ice in about a week. We will load the cloth before the ice, use the same wagons and drivers to haul and load the ice, and sail the following morning. All things considered, I believe we will be underway in ten days."

Charles nods in agreement before saying, "I must ask for Miss Soilleux's assistance at the bank and solicitor's office tomorrow morning. Would you be willing?"

Without hesitation, Lillia says, "Of course, Charles. It would be my pleasure."

A warm spring breeze swirls around Lillia and Charles as they enter the Newburyport Institute of Savings. As the first customers of the day, Agnes's account manager, Mr. Hindsley, is efficient in his work. Before any other patron enters the bank, Charles places the paid-off lien papers in his coat's breast pocket. Outside the bank's door, Lillia takes his arm and starts down the front steps, but Charles hesitates.

Cocking his head to one side, he whispers, "Oh, my."

"What is it, Charles?"

"I haven't smelled that fragrance for years. Belongs to only one woman. You're about to witness a very interesting moment, young lady."

Puzzled, Lillia snuffs the air but detects nothing foreign. Glancing over her shoulder, she sees Agnes Eagleton round the street corner, striding confidently toward them.

"Charles, it's Agnes Eagleton. Would you like me to leave you to have a conversation with her?"

"Despite my frequent business with her son, Agnes hasn't seen me in fifteen years, and she's ignorant of my condition. It's best you stay to help her understand my circumstances. Don't worry, I'll happily do the talking."

Charles turns his back to the oncoming Agnes. Waiting until she is only a few strides away, he turns and faces her.

"Agnes, it has been too long."

Agnes halts in her tracks and stares at him while Lillia glances expectantly between them.

"Charles Forsythe, is that you?"

Charles smiles charmingly and says, "Not quite the same man as then. An accident took my sight ten years ago. You were announced by your distinct perfume. I regret not seeing the light in your beautiful eyes."

"How do you know? What brings you here?"

"I'm only too glad to answer all your questions but not on

the steps of the bank. Perhaps a cup of tea at the shop around the corner? After you have finished your business, of course."

"Oh, I'm afraid I could be hours sorting out the payments on my son's ship. I wouldn't want to inconvenience you."

"Ah, well, busy as usual. Perhaps you could advise me? I must find a solicitor to draw up some papers. Do you have a recommendation?"

"Why yes, Mr. Cless is a fine solicitor. His office is down the street on the right."

"I believe it's in the tea shop's same neighborhood. If it suits you to reacquaint, Miss Soilleux and I will meet you at the tea shop. If not, I'll leave heavy hearted but grateful to have heard your voice and delighted in your fragrance."

After a quick nod, Agnes enters the bank and Charles takes Lillia's arm.

"What say we find Mr. Cless's office?"

"Why didn't you tell her you have already settled the debt on Captain Eagleton's ship?"

"Agnes is an enigma. I have never figured out why she rejected me, but that is in the past. She's going to make her decision to meet us soon enough."

After only a half hour, Lillia and Charles step from the solicitor's front door, Mr. Cless proving to be just as efficient as the banker.

"I've built up quite a thirst with all this contract business," Charles says. "A cup of tea will hit the spot."

Lillia smiles at his tenacity, now admitting she is eager to know of Agnes's choice.

"Charles, it is none of my business but, how confident are you Agnes will be waiting in the tearoom for us?"

"There's a sixty percent chance she'll be there. If there's one thing I remember about Agnes, she's more curious than is good for her."

"Perhaps, once she knows of your relationship with the captain, her opinion of you will change. It could be her earlier objection of your proposals stemmed from a distrust of suitors."

They round the block's corner and find the tearoom's door open, the breeze wafting the aroma of tea and pastries out to the street. Charles halts his step, a wide grin spreading across his bearded face.

"Well, I'll be."

Once again surprised at his ability to sense, Lillia surveys the room and sees Agnes at a table facing the door. The older woman's face lights up when she sees Lillia and waves them over. Charles takes the seat across from Agnes and Lillia pulls up an adjoining chair.

"I hope you don't mind, Charles, I ordered for us. By the way, do you have something you'd like to share with me?"

"Agnes, I've a great many things I'd like to share. Are you referring to something in particular?"

"My financial manager tells me the lien on my son's ship has been paid in full. He said a blind man and a young woman arrived first thing this morning. I assume you hold the papers on Rupert's ship?"

Lillia detects a snap of tension in the air. She quickly says, "Charles, Agnes, I think you're going to need some time together. I'm pressed with some ship responsibilities. If you'll excuse me."

"I'm to find my way back to the ship alone?" Charles asks.

"Not to worry, Charles," Agnes says, as she leans in and takes his hand, "I promise to walk you back. You've got a fair amount of explaining to do."

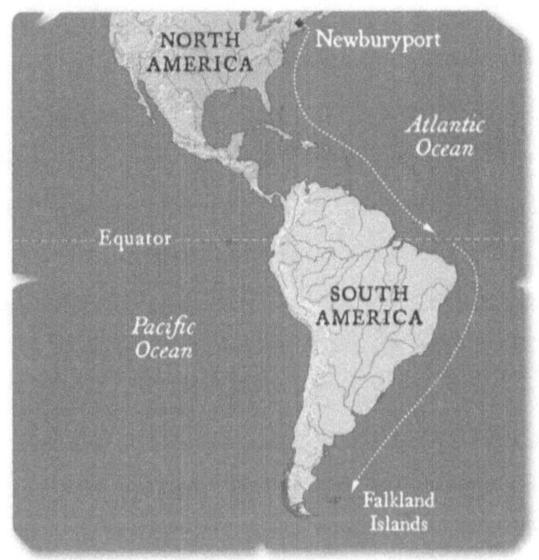

Chapter 5

MAY, 1849

NEWBURYPORT, MASSACHUSETTS

Lillia walks to her berth well before the ice loading is complete, and closes the door behind her. Having never sailed on a ship, despite her family's import business's reliance on them, she stares at the compact space. Just enough room for her trunk and the rope cot for her bed. But it is her space, away from the ship's noise and activity.

Sitting on her trunk, she wrestles off her boots and proceeds with undressing while contemplating what she has gotten herself into. Never before has she been this far from her parents and their home. With so many unknowns ahead, she feels a tingle of distress at the idea. Or is she feeling excitement?

She wonders where Donovan is in his journey westward, what kind of challenges he is facing, and what the likelihood is of ever seeing him again. Whatever misgivings she may have about making the journey, California represents the freedom she longs for. Donovan knew her feelings. His note would have never pleaded the way it had if he doubted she would not make such a voyage.

It is not long before the ship's motion lulls her to sleep. Her mind wanders from thoughts of Donovan to the recent characters she has encountered. Following Donovan to California might seem impulsive, but having Sebastian and Captain Eagleton emerge as facilitators once again speaks to Sebastian's notion of kismet. As the veil of sleep settles over her, she embraces the future with all the strength and courage she can muster. That's why Donovan had entreated her, wasn't it?

Lillia wakes to the sound of a woman retching and it jolts her upright. Blinking a few times, she rises from her berth's cot, the taunt ropes protesting against her movement. She rubs her aching shoulders, briefly considering what in her trunk might provide extra padding. A renewed bout of female discomfort spurs her into action. Forced to brace herself against the ship's exaggerated motion, she dresses quickly.

Stepping into the brisk sea air, she sucks in a quick breath while staring at the wide expanse of water surrounding the ship. The wind instantly whips tendrils of her dark hair from the hastily created low bun, leaving her to wish she had thought to cover her head with a scarf. Turning around, she sees the thin outline of the shore in the distance silhouetted against the setting sun. The notion occurs to her that she doesn't know when she will come back to this place.

She sees Dr. Gibbs holding his wife, Miriam, clinging to the railing. As they were the first to buy passage from Sebastian, she feels a personal responsibility for their welfare and asks, "Is there anything I can do to ease her distress?"

"Thank you, no. I'm afraid no one knows of their motion intolerance until they sail. For some, seasickness never abates, thereby eliminating ocean travel. I'm afraid this foretells our traveling by coach."

Lillia considers his grim forecast and replies, "I hope Mrs. Gibbs's affliction eases. It will be a long four months."

On his way to the helm, Captain Eagleton passes and asks, "Not a bit of trouble then, Miss Soilleux?

"I'll admit to a queasy stomach early on, but my body has accepted the pitch and roll."

"Good. Nothing bothers me more than a woman in travail."

Leaving the Gibbs to follow the captain, Lillia struggles to keep up, her steps awkward to his confident strides.

She says, "Speaking of travails, I understand you were asked to assist your mother in birthing once."

The captain pauses his quick step to let her catch up.

"Why did she tell you that?"

Lillia shrugs, replying, "She offered it as explanation as to why you've never married."

Furrowed brows foretell the captain's consternation before he says, "Mother is a tough woman. When I was younger, her rigid behavior was very confusing. Now I've come to believe my marital status is due to the high bar she set. I've yet to find her match. If you'll excuse me, we're going to anchor offshore for the night before beginning our tack into New York's harbor in the morning. We've made excellent time since leaving Newburyport, but I'd rather not test my new sailors after last night's loading marathon."

With that, the captain redirects his attention to his crew. Lillia notices Sebastian at the bow and joins him.

"Uncle, our stop in New York City tomorrow is for Mr. Wellingham's benefit, correct?"

"Yes, he's fetching the trunk from a bank which he is responsible for couriering to California. Shouldn't take long. How are you adapting to the ship's motion?"

"Better than Miriam Gibbs. I hope she can overcome her sickness, or at least choose not to vomit over the railing opposite my berth."

"They are an interesting couple, those two. They have chosen to put all their energy into civilizing the wilderness. California is their first foray."

Lillia recalls the California Association of Women broadsheet, Agnes's encouragement, and now the Gibbs's motivation. She believes they all lend confidence and credibility to her instinct.

"Dr. Gibbs says some never adapt to sea travel and are forever bound to land. I should hope I'm never limited in that way."

"If you haven't felt the effect by now, I should think you are immune. It's a good thing. I find ocean travel invigorating. I think we both will be doing quite a bit of it."

"Why do you say that?"

Sebastian chuckles,"*Ma chérie*, this venture of ours is just the beginning. For those who are willing to take calculated risks, the world is wide with opportunity. Remember, kismet is in force."

"Once we're done with Mr. Wellingham's business in New York City, do you really think we won't stop until we are in Chile, like Captain Eagleton proposes? Two months without touching solid ground?"

"Seems that's what the captain is determined to accomplish. I've never been aboard a ship for two months straight. Two months is optimistic. It could be longer. By the way, did you pen a letter to your parents?"

"I did. After I left Charles and Agnes at the tea shop, I wrote a long letter filling them in on all the details and developments in our venture. Then I posted the letter before settling in for the night. What did you do last night?"

"Regrettably, I stayed up to watch the ice being loaded. I was so fascinated by the process, I couldn't pull myself away, but now I'm dreadfully tired. I'm looking forward to a solid night's sleep."

Since Wellingham's stop in New York City would be brief, and in accordance with the captain's order, too brief for anyone to leave the ship, Lillia stands at the ship's railing and watches the activities of New York's busy wharf. Not unlike Boston's wharf, she finds the perspective of being on a ship looking ashore to be unique.

It is afternoon by the time she spies the carriage bearing Wellingham and several armed guards. When he and those carrying his trunk are surrounded until they board the ship, her suspicions flare. What kind of valuable cargo could such a small trunk contain?

Eager to be on their way, the captain calls out for the crew to prepare for sailing. Lillia turns her attention from the wharf and Wellingham's entourage to watching the sailors scamper up the shrouds to their respective yards and unfurl the great billows of sails from the yard arms. Never tiring of the sight, her breath is taken by the sight of the bright white cloth shining in the mid-morning sun.

The captain's call rings out as the ship leaves New York's harbor, heading into the great Atlantic expanse. As they sail, Lillia's heart fills with the anticipation of freedom and seeing Donovan again.

After a week of southbound sailing, Lillia happily finds the fresh ocean breeze to her liking as well as the gentle roll of the ship cutting through the ocean's waves. As has become her habit following the noon meal, she takes a spot on the stern deck. She casually scans the vast blue horizon and observes the captain and crew at their daily activities, usually using a book to disguise her interest. One particular activity is so fascinating she can hardly camouflage her curiosity. Only recently has she understood its importance to the voyage.

When the captain wants to measure their speed, a crew member tosses a device called a chip log overboard. Connected to the chip log is a knotted cord with precisely measured knots wound on a spool. The first mate, Nathanial, holds the spool with one hand and takes the cord between his other hand's thumb and forefinger, counting the knots as they pass once the chip log catches the water.

A different crew member holds a sandglass which runs for precisely twenty-eight seconds, and as the last grain passes to the lower globe, he calls out. Nathanial reports the number of knots which have passed through his fingers to the captain who, after a calculation, dutifully records the information in his log.

Today, she watches a broad grin crease his unshaven face.

"Good news, Captain?"

"We're well ahead of schedule. I couldn't have asked for better conditions. It's a good thing; the doldrums are approaching. A true test of a sailor's patience and skills."

"The what?"

"The doldrums, an area on either side of the equator where the wind and ocean currents go slack. Difficult to say how long it will take to get to the southern currents."

"No wind at all?"

"None. Rest assured, the crew and I will do everything we can to catch even the slightest whisper of a breeze."

"And you've calculated for this delay?"

"All captains must. It's a fact when sailing from one hemisphere to another, Miss Soilleux."

Two weeks later, Lillia lies on her cot clad only in her pantaloons and camisole. A thick cloak of humid air envelopes the ship, with no hint of the ocean's pitch and roll. Despite her efforts to fan herself, she lies hostage to it, her understanding of the doldrums complete. When her stomach grumbles, she reluctantly rises to dress for dinner.

Just as she steps into her skirt, there's a gentle knock at her door, the unexpected sound causing her to halt mid-step.

"Uncle?"

"Miss Soilleux, it's me, Howard."

"Oh, yes, Mr. Wellingham. What is it?"

"I should like a word before supper."

"Certainly, Mr. Wellingham. I'll meet you on the passenger's deck in a few moments."

"Thank you."

Continuing to dress despite her damp skin making it difficult, Wellingham's request has piqued her curiosity. She lifts and coils her sweat-moistened hair into a neat bun, securing it with her carved bone combs. When she steps from the passenger's quarters onto the quarterdeck, she is surprised to see Wellingham at the railing, his shoulders slumped. She steps to his side and sees his usual clean-shaved face covered with several days' worth of whiskers.

"Mr. Wellingham, are you ill?"

"Physically, no. But I've slipped into melancholy. After all my losses, it's too much to bear. I'm wondering what you're doing to stave off this ship's unbearable boredom?"

"We were walking the deck with Dr. and Mrs. Gibbs until the heat became overwhelming. My uncle doesn't do well in the heat."

"Would you consider allowing me to join you, once we are underway again and your walks resume?"

"Certainly. I'm sure everyone would welcome an additional companion with new perspectives."

Five days later, the breezes pick up and everyone feels the levity of progress again. Lillia, Sebastian, and the Gibbs resume their deck debates, now with Wellingham joining the group. Lillia notices Wellingham refraining from comment until he understands Dr. Gibbs's or Sebastian's view, before adopting the opposing position. She wonders if such behavior is just his nature, or if it's a tactic he has cultivated.

After observing his demeanor for several days, she decides to get to the bottom of it.

"Mr. Wellingham, do you really hold those radical beliefs you express in our debates?"

"What do you think?"

"I believe you're aggrandizing to force a more robust, thus prolonged, debate."

A smile creases his face as he says, "One must stretch the bounds of thinking for continued mental progress if we are not to be doomed by mental confinement."

"I agree. Your tactics are working on the doctor. He's not used to being challenged. When forced to parry to your jab, he acts surprised by the logical progression to a greater idea."

Wellingham wears a shocked expression and asks, "My goodness, Miss Soilleux, how are you educated?"

"Oberlin College. I was forced to leave before I finished, but I enjoyed my time around the likes of Lucy Stone. I had limited experience debating with the school's women."

"Your uncle never mentioned your schooling."

"It's unlikely he would, given we've only seen each other every other year. We share a passion for business and curiosity. Given society's limitations, he is the voice during our business dealings, while I keep track of the accounts in the background. All things considered, we make a good team."

"What of your parents? I don't mean to pry, but how is it they agreed to let you embark on such a voyage?"

"They trust my uncle to shepherd me through our venture's trials. Uncle Sebastian and I also share a wandering soul."

"Whose idea was it to buy the cloth and make the trip to California?"

"My uncle got a tip, and we decided to capitalize. But I should like to ask you some questions."

"My pleasure. Fire away."

"How is it that by producing a simple note, you advanced our cloth order with Mr. Plenworth?"

"Plenworth owed me considerable favors from past business dealings. I believe we are now square."

"Speaking of square, we were shocked to learn of our unwitting partnership. Granted, it was quite fortuitous for all but made without consultation with me and my uncle prior to our visit to the mill."

Wellingham looks away for a while before cocking his head toward her and speaking over his shoulder.

"I regret my earlier behavior. Had I not been so adrift with grief, I might have been more reasonable, but the contract's been signed."

Lillia looks away knowing that without their canvas partnership, he would arrive in California virtually empty-handed. Finally, she waves her hand in a quick flourish and says, "Thank you for your honesty. I should retire. Have a good rest tonight."

"Allow me to escort you to your berth."

"If you wish."

At her berth door, Wellingham faces her, saying, "Thank you. Your generous inclusion of me in your walks has helped pull me from my gloom."

Twenty-six days from Newburyport, Lillia watches as the captain directs the crew in the sails' adjustment. The sailors lithely climb up the cords of each mast's shrouds, bare toes and fingers gripping the rigging on their way to the royal sails. Once there, their voices raise into a chantey, the song's meter helping the men, now unrecognizable dots to her eyes, furl the sailcloth in equal armloads.

By now, she has learned all the captain's commands. She admires the respect he gives to his crew and their reciprocity is clear. When Nathanial arrives to take his shift at the rudder wheel, Lillia observes their easy camaraderie. Captain Eagleton steps away from the wheel and notices Lillia's gaze.

"Miss Soilleux," he says, smiling and doffing his cap.

"Captain."

"Wouldn't you be more comfortable in the security of your berth rather than enduring the wind and salt spray on deck?"

"On the contrary, Captain, I find it invigorating. The ship's operation is quite entertaining."

"Entertaining?"

"Indeed. Your calls to action and the crew's instant response are quite educating. I'm learning what wind conditions initiate the sails' adjustment."

Captain Eagleton pauses for a moment, his smile turning mischievous.

"Tell me, Miss Soilleux, how fast have we gone today?"

Without hesitation, Lillia states, "We've been traveling at the rate of . . ."

She falters when she realizes his trick even as he prods, "Go ahead. I know you know how to make the calculation."

Determined to maintain her dignity, she states, "As of noon today, we are traveling at a rate of eight nautical miles per hour."

"Correct. You're a good student. We are within three hundred miles of the Horn. Until the weather becomes inhospitable, I invite you to continue your education."

"My presence isn't a distraction?"

Captain Eagleton drops his voice. "A good sailor maintains his focus. Any distraction—woman or graybeard—tests the concentration."

"Graybeard?"

"The monstrous waves we will encounter at the Horn. Named for the gray froth on the wave's lip before it cascades into its deep trough. You'll become familiar enough, but the deck won't be safe at that point."

"May I ask another question, Captain?"

"Certainly."

Lillia points to the crew scuttling around on the royal yards.

"Is it frightful up there in the royal yards?"

"Frightful? I don't think so, but I've spent my adult life aloft. I find the heights freeing. One can see forever from the royals. The wind sings through the rigging. I see my life with more clarity as if I'm closer to my Maker."

Lillia pauses as she absorbs his description.

"Would it be possible for me to know that freedom?"

The captain's expression suddenly washes in disbelief, his mouth opening and closing as he gropes for unspoken words until he looks away from her earnest expression. Lillia realizes her audacity and rushes to regain credibility.

"I'm aware of my request's impracticality. I wouldn't consider it unless I was properly prepared. Perhaps I could borrow some trousers? Climb at night so no one sees me? Perhaps when the moon is full for extra light?"

Captain Eagleton stares toward the South American coastline. Lillia is sure he will dismiss her when he finally clears his throat.

"I'll keep your request in mind. Perhaps when we are in the calmer waters of the Pacific. Strength is the key. You must be strong enough to not only go up but to descend as well."

"I can build my strength."

Captain Eagleton turns to walk away. He stops abruptly and turns back.

"I've had some interesting requests, Miss Soilleux, but I believe your request tops them all."

On their previous deck walks, Miriam Gibbs and Lillia had maintained the distance of a step behind the men, doing more listening than debating. Occasionally, they had made a contribution but never had they taken the lead in an exchange. Lillia observed Miriam and judged the woman to be about fifteen years her senior and the picture of society's compliant female.

On this day's deck walk, Lillia notices Miriam intentionally slow her step. When the women are several paces behind the oblivious men, Miriam initiates the conversation.

"Tell me, Miss Soilleux, what takes you to California?"

Lillia pauses before making a calculated reply. "My uncle and I are scouting business opportunities."

"But what of your womanhood? Your role as a proper wife and mother? Have you read the latest Godey's Lady Book? There's a wonderful piece outlining the attributes of pure womanhood to which all women must aspire. I've brought it along and would be happy to loan it to you."

"Ah, thank you for your offer. If you must know, I was engaged but my fiancé disappeared before we could wed."

"Oh, my. You have my sincere condolences. Time will heal the wound. But you mustn't give up on the idea of fulfilling your natural place in a man's care. Believe me, it has its benefits."

"With all due respect, I refuse to believe a woman can only find her true expression by living in the shadow of a man's benevolence."

Lillia's statement leaves Miriam temporarily speechless until she whispers, "What of your feelings for Mr. Wellingham?"

"Feelings? What feelings might you be referring to, Mrs. Gibbs?"

"I've seen how he looks at you. I should wonder if perhaps he wouldn't make a fine husband. I'm surprised you haven't noticed."

Oh, I've noticed.

"I can assure you my relationship with Mr. Wellingham is strictly as my uncle's business partner."

"Even better, keep the business relationship in the family."

Lillia feels her cheeks heat with frustration toward the woman's singular focus. Before she can respond to Miriam's comment, the men stop walking.

"Shall we retire to the galley for dinner?" Sebastian offers.

Lillia quickly nods. "I must stop by my berth. Then I will meet you there."

She leaves and deliberately walks toward her berth, her thoughts congealing around the ironic fact that the very societal behavior she is fleeing is actually sailing with her.

When the Falkland Islands appear in the distance, Captain Eagleton curiously hauls in the ship's sails forcing the *Ornery Agnes* to come to a halt. Missing the ship's rhythm, Lillia joins Sebastian and Wellingham at the passenger's deck railing to find it awash in bright white sailcloth. The captain's commands are distant and unfamiliar to her ears.

"What is happening?" she asks.

"The captain is changing the sails. Says those we sailed with from Newburyport won't survive Cape Horn."

Wellingham adds, "I heard Charles insist on spending money on new sails before we left."

They spent the next three days watching the change while other ships sailed by. Once the sails are set, Lillia ventures to the stern deck at sunset to admire the bright white sails reflecting the sun's last light. Captain Eagleton comes up behind her.

"She's a beauty with her new sails, isn't she?"

"Captain, why weren't the other ships stopping to change their sails like we did?"

"There's only one reason I can think of; they don't have them to change."

"But what if their sails fail as they cross the Horn?"

"It is a disaster. A risk only a fool would take."

"Is there anything more to do before we begin our travails around the Cape?"

"Only to recognize it may be the hardest test most sailing on this ship have ever endured. While July in Newburyport is warm and lovely, July in the southern hemisphere is winter. Ice will coat every surface of the ship, and it will be treacherous for everyone."

"As part owner of this ship, I'd like to contribute to easing the hardship. Is there a task suitable for me to undertake?"

Captain Eagleton pauses before saying, "This part of the journey will be the most tedious, especially for the passengers. If you could devise a clever way for them to forget their misery, be it by conversation, debate, games—anything that would take their minds off our slow progress—I would greatly appreciate your efforts."

Lillia grins widely and says, "Consider it done."

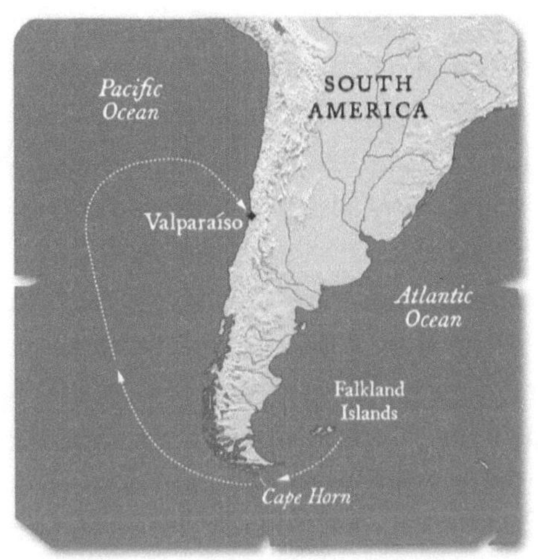

Chapter 6

JULY, 1849

CAPE HORN, SOUTHERN HEMISPHERE

Days later, Cape Horn manifests itself with a violent overnight storm that turns the seas into a roiling tempest. Sensing an unfamiliar commotion at the passenger's quarters' door, Lillia steps cautiously from her berth to investigate. Elias, one of the younger crew members, his shoulders crisscrossed with canteen and food pouch straps, shuffles awkwardly inside. He slams the door shut just as the ship tilts aggressively to port.

Staggering to keep his balance, Elias frees himself from his burden and says to Lillia, "Barnabas says this will be all you get until tomorrow morning, so ration accordingly. Says there won't be nothin' fancy 'til we get to the Pacific. Some days'll be worse than others. I will stop by at nightfall for the empty canteens and sacks. Just hang them here on these hooks."

As he motions to the referenced hooks, the other passengers arrive to take their rations. When the ship's bow dives, everyone grabs for something stable and holds on. A blast of salt spray splatters against the quarters' door as if reminding them of the fierce, watery beast lurking just beyond.

Sebastian says, "Thank you, Elias. Be careful out there."

Elias doffs his cap to the passengers and quickly opens, steps through, and closes the door behind him. Cautiously, everyone takes a canteen and food pouch and retreats to their berths.

Lillia takes her role as mental stimulator seriously. With nothing but time on her hands, she devises word games and puzzles on a slate in chalk. Passengers receive the slate and pass it to the next to solve, finally returning the finished product to her.

In the coming days, the passengers become quite discontented with the rations as well as the sea's constant abuse. This malaise translates into limited participation with Lillia's efforts, as well. Lillia discovers that discouragement is hard to fend off.

After eighteen days of fighting the rough seas, there is no talk of an end to it. Ever hopeful that this day will signal the end of the horrible weather, Lillia rises stiffly to meet Elias at the door for the morning food delivery. Stepping into the open area of the passenger's quarters, she sees Elias's shadowy figure approaching through the opaque windows. Getting closer, she determines the windows aren't covered in salt spray, but ice.

Propelled through the door by a gush of icy water, Elias slams the door behind him and says, "Ma'am, it's a frightful one today. Lucky to get here with the rations. Captain says to tell the passengers he's making progress. About halfway. Won't be long before we're in the peaceful Pacific."

Thanking him for the news, Lillia offers to help untangle the cords and straps from his shoulders. With all but one tangle resolved, the pair are so engrossed in their work they do not notice the prevailing darkness outside. Finally free of the cords, Elias turns to leave. Just as he releases the doorknob's bolt, a mighty wave cascades into the room. Both Lillia and Elias lose their footing and are swept from the room in a tangle of arms, legs, and canteen straps.

Instantly shocked by the cold and wet, Lillia's body is swept forcefully across the deck, a random canteen strap linking Elias to her. In her panic, she scans the deck for something securely bolted down to grip. The launch's secured frame comes into view just before an explosion of sea spray temporarily blinds her. Desperately, she reaches out for the frame, but her grasp finds nothing but air.

Another colossal wave crashes against the ensnared pair, picking them up and tossing them across the deck. Caught in the frigid water's blast, Lillia gulps for air only to find more water. She and Elias desperately flail their arms and legs to stop their free fall. The mizzenmast's solid form provides the required abrupt stop. She gasps as a stabbing pain shoots from her side and Elias becomes limp as a rag. She groggily watches the seawater drain away through the scuppers, unsure of what to do next.

As the ship rolls into a deep trough, she sees the foredeck's low wall. Its thick baluster should be solid enough for her to hold onto. She wraps her right arm under Elias's right armpit and begins to crawl, the additional weight of her saturated skirt tangling around her legs, making her progress slow. It seems like an eternity before she gets to the wall.

Just as she wraps her free arm through a baluster, the captain calls out, "Find your cover! 'Tis another about to hit!"

The ship rises, precipitously, and the steep angle helps her pull Elias's limp body tight against her. But when the deep green wave's water hits the railing, it arcs gracefully over her head before crashing mightily against the ship's deck.

Now in the wave's trough, Lillia tentatively releases the baluster to secure Elias by rewrapping her arm around him and cradling his head against her belly. The ship lifts again and she resecures herself. Once again, the wave arcs overhead, the powerful gush falling impotently through the scuppers opposite her.

"Elias! Wake up!"

He doesn't move. She squeezes her eyes shut and hears faint voices. Then she feels a pair of firm hands on her shoulders, saying urgently, "Miss, we've got 'im. Turn loose so's we can get to cover afore the next'un hits us."

The crew member's request cuts through her mental fog. When she feels Elias being pried from her grasp, the canteen strap keeps the pair entwined. A bright knife quickly cuts the cord and she feels the sweet release of Elias's weight. Just as the ship begins its climb, a different set of hands grip her under the armpits, and Lillia feels her body slide across the smooth deck.

By the time the next wave crashes across the deck, she is in the galley, the men around her bracing against the ship's acute angle. A blanket is wrapped around her shoulders and she sees Elias's blanketed form laying on the galley floor.

A crew member probes his neck for a pulse and announces, "Still beating."

Lillia watches listlessly as they pump on Elias's chest.

Barnabas puts a tin cup to her lips and says, "Here, Miss, drink this."

She allows Barnabas to tip the liquid into her mouth, the alcohol burning her tongue as it moves down her throat, its fire gagging her.

"Heat 'cha up, Miss, it will. Best ta swallow slow, no good ta gag."

The galley door opens with a spray of saltwater revealing Dr. Gibbs and Nathanial. Simultaneously, a cheer rises from the group working on Elias.

"Yay! There he is! Welcome back, youn'un!"

Unsure if it is the alcohol or the good news, Lillia relaxes. Her eyes droop with fatigue, but she hears Dr. Gibbs approach.

"Miss Soilleux, can you hear me?"

Lillia lazily turns her foggy gaze toward the doctor and sees him smiling at her.

"Barnabas has some dry clothes for you. You can change in his quarters. Can you walk or do you need assistance?"

Lillia lifts her face to his at the question, the movement making her head throb. She realizes her entire body is quaking uncontrollably.

She replies, "I can walk."

In Barnabas's dim quarters, she is escorted to the cot where she sits down. Dr. Gibbs arrives with a stack of clothing and sets it next to her, saying softly, "I'll leave you to change. Call out when you're done."

Lillia watches him leave, her gaze falling on the clothes stack. Unfamiliar, she touches them. Coarse wool. Men's clothes, but warm and dry. With unsteady hands, she fumbles with the buttons of her blouse. Her throbbing head makes it hard to focus.

"Miss Soilleux?

"Not yet."

Finally, Lillia stands naked and trembling. She wraps the wool shirt over her shoulders. Its cedar fragrance is familiar but she can't place it. The coarseness of the wool makes her skin tingle as she slides her arms into the sleeves. She rolls the too-long sleeves slowly, her fingers fumbling. Pulling on the large socks, she feels her feet getting warm in the thick material.

Last, the pants. She has never worn pants. Pulling them up over her bare buttocks, she buttons the fly and waist button. The ship lists again and she thumps down onto the cot, her feet trapped in the pant leg's length.

Rolling the pant legs into cuffs, she says, "Dr. Gibbs, you may come in."

Dr. Gibbs enters the cramped and dark space. Lillia had never seen him without his tall hat. Balding with a full fringe of hair, it looks like he has a fur wrap resting on his ears.

"How's Elias?" she asks.

"He has a nasty bump on his head and drank a fair dose of seawater, but he's going to be alright thanks to your heroic efforts. Let's have a look at your head."

Lillia feels the pressure of his practiced fingertips exploring her skull and yelps when a lightning bolt of pain explodes.

"Ah, found it. Only a nasty bruise, no open wound. Let me feel your side. I suspect you've got a couple broken ribs after the mizzenmast broke your fall."

The ship lurches again, slamming the doctor against the wall.

"Dear God, how much longer must we endure the sea's abuse?"

Her wince against his gentle probe confirms his suspicions.

"I must say, Miss Soilleux, you saved the young man. My recommendation is to keep to your quarters for the duration of this Cape Horn ordeal. Let those ribs heal and build your strength."

After eighteen days of confinement, Lillia greets Sebastian's knock with enthusiasm. Taking his bent arm for support, they carefully step from the dimly lit passenger's quarters into the bright sun. Still gripping his arm for support, Lillia squints against its glare while straining toward the railing.

With a gentle tug, he says, "Take it easy. No sense in overdoing your first day on deck since your accident."

"Uncle, I'm fine. Bed rest has been good, but I've got to get my strength back. There are far too many things to do yet."

"At a measured pace."

"Look there! Are those trees I see?"

Captain Eagleton answers her question when he walks up from behind them.

"No, Miss Soilleux, those are wrecks, the "trees" you see are what is left of the ships' masts. Been sailing through the wreckage all morning."

"Oh, my."

"Nathanial tells me we passed a recent wreck during his early morning watch. We avoided her misfortune by sheer luck and a watchful bow post using a lantern."

"Was there any chance to give aid?"

"Nathanial said one lifeboat was gone. I hope the crew using it survived their escape."

"Did he see the vessel's name?" Sebastian asks.

"I believe he said it was the *Night Call* out of New York City. I'll report it to the authorities when we get to Valparaíso."

Lillia detects a difference in Captain Eagleton's calls to his crew. She emerges slowly from her berth to the passenger's deck and is greeted by a dense bank of fog. Peering into it, her eyelashes lace with moisture, such that she can barely see the ship's railing. From above, she hears the sailors singing their chantey as they furl the topmast's royal and gallant sails.

She climbs to the helm and sees the captain glancing from the murk to a handheld compass and back.

"Captain, where are we?"

"We are navigating into Valparaíso. Coming in from the south at this time of year is difficult."

After a moment, Captain Eagleton removes a brass telescope from his coat pocket.

"Would you consider helping me with something? Nathanial would normally do this, but he's aloft."

"Of course."

He flicks his wrist three times, each time expanding the retracted length before handing it to Lillia.

"Use this to find the sun through this soup, please."

Lillia takes the telescope, raises it to her eye, and points it into the upper realm searching for an orb of brightness.

As she searches, the captain continues, "We should be within ten miles of the coast, coming in on a northwesterly line. Without the aid of the sun or the mountains, I'm concerned our speed could cause trouble. There's a lighthouse that sits on a peninsula guarding the city's port. Useless in this soup."

Lillia finds the sun's glow radiating rainbows through the water vapor.

"The sun is to our port side at eleven o'clock. It looks distorted, like there's something blocking its fullness."

Captain Eagleton grins broadly and says, "That's Mount Aconcagua, the highest peak in the Andes range. Quite a sight from a distance. This'll be my first time using it as a navigational tool."

"A mountain helps you navigate?"

"Before we entered the fog, we were fifty miles offshore. I was centering Aconcagua's peak between two other mountain peaks. If we can stay on that heading and take it slow, it should guide us through the fog and right into Valparaíso's harbor."

"How long have we been in the fog?"

"Roughly thirty minutes. Keep your eyes on the sun. It will help us know the fog's density as well as our direction."

The crew emerges from above the fog's gloom—a foot, a leg, and finally a torso at a time. Captain Eagleton directs them to positions along the railing as lookouts. Nathanial returns, and Lillia relinquishes the telescope. Captain Eagleton leans toward her as she turns to leave.

"Thank you for your help. If you are going to the galley, I could use a cup of tea if Barnabas has it ready."

"Certainly, Captain."

In the galley, Lillia finds three tin cups and fills a canteen with hot tea before returning to the helm. After thirty minutes more, all the passengers are on deck in anticipation of seeing land. One instant they are entombed in the fog, the next the bow pierces through the veil revealing a lush green coastline. The aforementioned white lighthouse, perched on its peninsula, passes by on their starboard side.

Lillia finds her way to the bow for a better look. Not used to seeing an entire city all at once, she admires how Valparaíso looks like an ornate, layered confection. Low, shaggy roofed buildings line the lowest level at the waterfront, while taller, sturdier shops and warehouses are positioned above and behind them.

Three rolling green knolls make up the city's second tier where her gaze rests on stylish white mansions surrounded by orchards and vineyards. An officious two-story building is chiseled into the rock-strewn hillside and serves as the city's crown. Every structure faces the seaport.

Once the ship is anchored in the bay, Lillia stands with Sebastian and the captain at the bow and watches a flotilla of small boats row toward the *Ornery Agnes*.

Eager anticipation for standing on solid ground makes her feet dance beneath her skirts and she wonders out loud, "What are those boats carrying?"

Captain Eagleton replies, "Sweets and fresh fruit mostly. They know our cravings will overwhelm our financial sensibilities. The empty ones are for hire."

Lillia's eyes shine as she imagines sweets, the idea of something other than oatmeal and crackers making her mouth water. The fresh fruit and vegetables they had enjoyed for most of their trip had run out during their crossing of Cape Horn, so it had been weeks of the same dry sustenance.

Turning to Sebastian she says, "The merchants are right to think we would pay anything to have a break from our mundane fare."

Winking, Sebastian says, "There's much to look forward to with this stop."

"Our stop will be relatively brief, if all goes according to my plan," the captain says before calling the crew and passengers together.

"Before we disembark, there are a few things you should know. We are in Valparaíso only as long as it takes to attend to the ship's business and resupply our larder. It is likely we will be here for more than one night, so find a comfortable hotel bed and enjoy the local hospitality without getting into trouble. Make all our lives easy and don't miss our departure. I will fly the ship's flag when we are a day from leaving, so watch for it. Enjoy your time in Valparaíso. Our next dry ground will be in San Francisco."

The local rowboats arrive, and rowdy calls interrupt the captain's final words. He adds, "These young men expect to be paid for your passage, so be prepared."

Lillia watches Charles's boys flip the Jacob's ladder over the railing, the rope structure musically slapping against the ship's hull as it falls. Sebastian and Wellingham join her at the railing to watch the jubilant young men climb into the rowboats. Arriving in the shallows, the young men rediscover the use of their legs while comically wobbling their way toward dry land.

Sebastian chuckles, and says, "I wish I could say I'll have an easier time of it, but I know better."

Captain Eagleton joins the group and announces, "I'm off to report to the customhouse. Nathanial's in charge. I can hardly wait to see the agent's face when he sees I have roughly one hundred and fifty tons of New Hampshire ice bound for California."

Sebastian smiles wide and says, "I think all the partners should share in that experience. After our Cape Horn ordeal, such a sight will bring levity to this old man's mind."

"Captain, what are your plans for the ice?"

After reviewing Captain Eagleton's logbook for an inordinate amount of time, the Chilean customs agent's casual question causes Lillia to shoot a knowing look at Sebastian. They had been anticipating his reaction to their unusual cargo since arriving in his office.

"It's been our freshwater supply and ballast around Cape Horn. Now that we're on the continent's tranquil side, we'll drink it as it melts," the captain replies.

"Would you entertain a business proposition?"

Captain Eagleton turns to his business partners and then looks back to the agent before asking, "What do you have in mind?"

"My brother established a merchant house in San Francisco in January. I've received several communications from him about the need for more perishable goods, but alas, no ship has had the room or the ice. If you have space, he'll pay you a premium."

Lillia subtly takes Sebastian's hand and squeezes it.

"Additionally, if you have any spare berths, we've a few unfortunates who have limited funds for passage. One, a survivor of a shipwreck a month ago, is especially in need. Spends most of his time in our jail. The sheriff would like to send him on his way."

Captain Eagleton turns to the others. In unison, all nod yes to the first proposition, and no to the second. He turns back to the agent.

"I'll calculate the amount of space available for additional cargo and return with a figure tomorrow. I doubt we will have any open berths."

The agent feebly throws up his hands and says, "I had to try. I'll await your calculations."

Chapter 7

AUGUST, 1849

VALPARAÍSO, CHILE

Between her featherbed's starched sheets, Lillia chooses to snuggle deeper into the warm blankets rather than rise. She lazily observes the stream of sunshine through the room's single window, as the bright reflection moves across the polished white walls. Outside the window, her view soars over the rooftops of the city and toward the distant mountain range where Mount Aconcagua reigns.

Like a switch, her rambling thoughts converge into focus. She leans from her covers to fetch her satchel, retrieving her calendar. Flipping through the marked pages, she determines today is August 28. It's been nearly three months aboard the ship, just as Sebastian had suspected. Donovan and his progress toward California suddenly springs into her mind. With trepidation, she realizes that since her accident during the Cape Horn crossing, he has not been the subject of her thoughts.

Perhaps it is because of her arrival at the Pacific Ocean or finding herself halfway to her goal of San Francisco, she contemplates what his progress could be. She wonders if he has encountered any trials of his own, sure that he would have despite not necessarily being the adventurous type. Physically, she knows he would have had to become stronger. But what challenges would he have faced with his useless left eye?

But hers is an analytical process, not a heartfelt longing or all-consuming worry for his well-being. Unable to keep her mind from drifting to Captain Eagleton, she realizes this is the first morning when the captain's familiar orders and the ship's routine has not been her call to rise. And she misses them both.

Lillia finds Sebastian and Wellingham seated at a table facing the bay, an empty chair welcoming her. She pulls back the chair and is greeted by them both and a lovely display of familiar baked goods, and rich, warm coffee.

"There is a surprising influence of Europe here, isn't there, Uncle Sebastian?"

"Indeed, we learned from our server that Germany, Italy, France, Spain, and Portugal all have ties to this city. I'm eager to walk the streets and learn more of the history during our short stay," Sebastian replies.

Through the open window, the mournful chatter of seagulls mixes with the full-throated calls of vendors from the streets below, forcing Wellingham to raise his voice when he asks, "How was your rest?"

"In a word, indescribable."

The hostess arrives with a fresh tray of pastries as Sebastian says, "I've just asked Howard what his plans are for California after he completes his courier assignment."

"Yes, Mr. Wellingham, can you share the details of your courier position?"

"I suppose it needn't be a secret. Some collegians staked a wager on who could get to San Francisco first—one group going by the overland route, and the other around Cape Horn. My assignment is to arrive before them, to advertise my arrival, and wait for the winning team to claim the wager. There's a chance those traveling by sea may have already arrived. They sailed on a ship named *Night Call* out of New York City on April 10."

Lillia coughs into her coffee cup. Wellingham nods slowly, exchanging a puzzled look with Sebastian, just as Captain Eagleton briskly steps into the room and says brightly, "Good morning, all."

"Captain," Lillia starts in, "the wrecked ship's name Nathanial had you record in your logbook . . . it was *Night Call*, wasn't it?"

"Indeed. Out of New York City."

Wellingham looks at his companions before dropping his chin to his chest.

"It seems my courier position may have just become more difficult, or perhaps easier. Now I only have to wait for the overland team to show up. I've agreed to advertise my arrival for two years. If no one claims it in that time, the money is mine to do with as I wish."

"There's your answer, Uncle. He'll stay in California for at least two years."

"Indeed, I have nothing and no one to go back to in New England. I suppose this endeavor holds the key to my future."

Captain Eagleton cuts through everyone's somber tone with, "Well, then. Shall we discuss my spatial findings?"

"Proceed, Captain," Sebastian says.

"The crew and I worked into the wee hours. We've determined that only twenty-five percent of our ice has melted. There's enough space for ten crates of ordinary dimension adjacent to the ice for preservation purposes. We also found space for another five crates or twenty sacks worth of trip provisions. Barnabas is coming ashore to begin his procurement."

Sebastian sits contemplatively with the captain's numbers before saying, "Our customs agent is used to having the upper hand in negotiations, so we will have to be shrewd. That said, we hold a card he will never suspect."

"Such as?" the captain asks.

Sebastian folds his hands over his paunch, grinning and staring at the men. "Lillia."

Lillia slowly lifts her eyes from her coffee cup to see all three men gazing at her.

She says, "Me? Why?"

"There's a strong likelihood he's never negotiated business with a woman. His underestimation of you will tip the scales in our favor."

The men silently digest Sebastian's suggested strategy before Wellingham asks, "Miss Soilleux, what would your strategy be with the customs agent?"

Lillia gently sets her cup down into its saucer before saying, "It's quite simple, really. By offering ten crates' worth of space, we ease the agent's problem, a significant opportunity he'd be a fool to pass up. Three spaces for paying customers will help offset our operating costs. The key will be to get the agent to pay us for the cargo before we leave, so we don't get stiffed by the brother. To get our best price for the cargo, we'll use the jailbird to our benefit in the form of a bargaining chip."

The men stare at each other until Sebastian chuckles to himself, and the captain says, "I agree with Sebastian. Miss Soilleux should be our negotiator."

Wellingham nods in agreement before asking, "Captain, did you determine if there were any additional berths created?"

"If we shift the canvas between the decks, it could create space for as many as three passengers."

"Before we use him as a bargaining tool, perhaps a personal interview of the ill-fated character is in order," Lillia suggests.

Wellingham concurs, "It would be helpful to understand his full story. Very well, Captain. Shall we do the interviewing honors?"

"I suppose. Following the interview, we should all proceed to the customs office to learn the nature of the cargo."

In agreement, the captain and Wellingham leave for the jail, while Lillia and Sebastian remain in the dining room.

"Uncle, do you really think I can do this negotiation?"

"You proved my point when you offered the idea of using the shipwreck victim as a bargaining tactic. Well played."

"So much depends on the value of the agent's cargo."

"Indeed. Use today's conversation to observe him. You should be able to understand how motivated he is—both by the sheriff and his brother. When the time is right, he won't expect the terms coming from you."

Lillia smiles knowing he has confidence in her negotiating skills.

"I should post a letter to my parents before we leave. With any luck, it will arrive in Roxbury about the same time we arrive in San Francisco."

"Good idea. When you are done, fetch me, and we'll post it on our way to meet the captain and Wellingham."

August 28, 1849

Dearest Mother and Father,

I have much to tell you but most important, I am penning this letter from Valparaiso, Chile. Our ship's captain has conducted a superb voyage. We made no stops until Valparaiso as we had fresh drinking water and plenty of provisions chilled by the ice. We are on pace to be one of the quickest passages from Newburyport to San Francisco. Uncle Sebastian and I are well, glad to be standing on solid ground for a few days before setting sail for California. Only ten weeks left before we enter our new adventure! Love to you both. Will write when we arrive.

Your Lillia

Lillia and Sebastian stroll down the cobbled, waterfront road looking at the shops and chatting with vendors on their way to the jail. After so many weeks of blue ocean, the quaint, spring blossom-lined dirt road makes Lillia walk slowly while admiring the many colors and scents. Overhead, the songs of foreign birds mixing with the din of seagulls makes her sensory overload complete.

At the jail, only a few moments pass before Captain Eagleton and Wellingham step outside, a small boy slipping past before the door shuts behind them. Lillia watches him dash down the road, but her curiosity is interrupted by Sebastian's eagerly blurted question.

"Well? Knave or fellow?"

"Not sure. One thing of importance, I determined he is not a member of the Yale team whose money I'm couriering. He's just a passenger they picked up in Buenos Aires before starting their ill-fated Cape Horn crossing. He told us a remarkable story of how he escaped when all the others onboard perished. He released the lifeboat, climbed aboard, and launched it without assistance. He washed ashore a few days later, traded the boat for a donkey, and rode along the coastline to Valparaíso. With no money, he stole food and ended up in jail for it. Captain, what was your impression?"

Captain Eagleton snorts, "That is quite a feat of survival, even for a seasoned sailor. It's hard to tell if his behavior is natural or the result of his ordeal. One thing is clear, the town officials want him out of their hair. The sheriff gave me the impression he has somehow made them quite uncomfortable. No one wants to be specific. That said, he seems quite contrite to me."

"Good, they're motivated to remove him from their city, which makes him a decent tool to drive a harder bargain with the customs agent. Once we know what the cargo is, we can decide if we need the complication. To the customs office we go!" Sebastian enthusiastically calls out.

By the time the partners get to the customs office, the sun rests just above the western horizon. They learn the cargo is citrus, lemons, and oranges, harvested two months ago, but stored in cool mountain caves. Lillia quietly observes the customs agent as the men discuss the fruit's required space while noting the need to cull out spoiled fruit is going to add one more day to their stay in Valparaíso.

"With regard to your question about additional berths, after doing the calculations, it seems we have enough space in the 'tween decks for three passengers," the captain says.

"I heard you met with the shipwrecked soul," the customs agent says casually.

The partners exchange surprised looks until Lillia notices the same small boy who had scurried away from the jail sitting in the office's corner.

Captain Eagleton asks, "How much will your city pay to be rid of him?"

"Pay? You expect us to pay you for his passage?"

"He's your nuisance. In the tight quarters of a ship, he could become a problem. How long will your sheriff be willing to feed him?"

The agent stares at his desk for several moments.

"I'll consult the sheriff. And I'll inform those looking for passage of your availability."

"Good. Once you know the exact volume of fruit, we'll have our financial negotiation. No loaded rowboat leaves shore until we've got a deal. My ship sails morning after next, loaded or not."

While the partners enjoy after-dinner drinks that night, Sebastian clears his throat.

"Captain Eagleton, I have a question to pose."

"Certainly, Sebastian."

"When we are underway again, I'm not reconvening our deck-side discussions, as there's not a topic we haven't beaten to death."

Lillia and Wellingham nod in agreement as Sebastian continues, "I'm wondering if you, in the course of your many voyages, have ever allowed games of chance to be played on your ship?"

The captain's eyebrows raise as he directs his attention to his drink before saying, "I've been known, when there were no women onboard to offend, to allow friendly card games."

"Bravo! I play a French card game called *poque*. I believe it is similar to the American card game: poker. Always in a friendly way, of course."

"On two conditions, Sebastian: first, you announce your new diversion to the passengers only after we leave Valparaíso. Second, you cannot solicit the crew. Their attention must remain on the ship's operation."

"Of course, Captain. I assure you that time will fly by with this new form of entertainment!"

By the time the partners assemble in the customs agent's office, seven wagons of crated fruit have shown up at the docks, and two of the 'tween decks' berths have been secured by two sisters traveling to California from Vermont.

Lillia takes a deep breath and steps directly toward the seated agent and takes great satisfaction when his eyebrows raise in surprise when she says, "In consideration of the rare opportunity afforded to you by our ice cargo, the risk we take in spoilage, and your brother's unknown willingness to pay us for our freighting service, we expect sixty-five percent of the freight costs to be paid by you, now."

Instantly falling into a red-faced coughing fit, the customs agent gasps, "Sixty-five percent? Only my brother stands to make a profit from the fruit!"

"That is a family matter and none of our concern."

The agent rises from his seat, places his hands on the desktop, and lowers his head in thought. Slowly, his fingers begin to drum, and he raises his face to meet Lillia's gaze.

"Sixty percent and the lunatic."

Lillia maintains his gaze as she does the calculations.

"Sixty percent and one hundred-fifty dollars to relieve your city of the vagrant."

The agent turns his attention to the men standing behind Lillia.

"Why do you make me negotiate with this impossible woman? Women in my country know their place. Or are you all just dull jackasses?"

The men stand grim-faced without yielding to his taunt. Lillia's neck and ears flush with heat knowing what his personal attack means. She has won.

Fuming, the agent directs his statement toward Captain Eagleton.

"We'll begin loading the fruit at first light tomorrow. I will meet you with the money, the fruit, and the lunatic."

Gathered for their last supper on land before California, Sebastian raises a toast, saying, "To our tough negotiator."

Lillia laughs in appreciation, as they all tip their small glasses of claret in her direction. In that moment, over their last plated meal in their delightful inn, she soaks everything in, sure she will revisit the memory when they are, once again, surrounded by the Pacific Ocean and in cramped quarters.

After they all toast and sip, Captain Eagleton nips the celebration short with his directive,

"We sail as soon as the fruit is secured. Our new passengers need to be situated, so coordination is important. Miss Soilleux, can you assist the two young ladies? Wellingham, will you take on the lunatic?"

They both nod in agreement before Wellingham asks, "Do you think we missed something in our interview since the customs agent consistently referred to him as a lunatic?"

Captain Eagleton waves off the question saying, "I think the agent is under pressure to get rid of the man. The deal is done and I, for one, will relish one more night in a comfortable bed."

The thought of her featherbed makes Lillia push back her chair. When Wellingham and Sebastian join her, Lillia hears Captain Eagleton ask, "Miss Soilleux, a word?"

Wellingham and Sebastian continue out but Lillia turns back asking, "Yes, Captain?"

"I didn't want to say anything in front of the others but, I want you to know, Mother would have been very proud of your strength today."

Lillia feels heat build in her cheeks.

"Thank you. I believe Agnes would have handled the situation similarly. Good night, Captain."

At first light, the sound of oars slapping the water's surface and the creaking groan of a block and tackle signal the fruit's loading. Waiting to greet their respective charges, Lillia and Wellingham watch it all from the shoreline.

Over Wellingham's shoulder, Lillia sees the customs agent hand the captain a sack. The captain pulls open the sack strings and reaches inside. After a few moments, he pulls the strings tight and shakes the agent's hand. After the agent marches away, Captain Eagleton turns toward Lillia, a bright grin cracking his bearded face.

Two young women tentatively approach Lillia and introduce themselves as sisters, Hope and Sarah Browning. While timid in their first impression, Lillia sees they both are stoutly built and able-bodied. Eager to know how they became marooned in Valparaíso, she says, "I'm from the Boston area, so we are practically neighbors! How in the world did you come to be in Valparaíso, Chile?"

"We sailed with a group of women looking for our fortunes in California. It turns out the ship's captain blamed some misfortunes during the crossing on the women aboard. When we landed in Valparaíso, he made all the women disembark and then sailed away. We were left to find passage on our own. Hope and I are the last of the group."

Aghast, Lillia fights off the urge to hug the strangers for their bravery.

With the last crate loaded on the ship, the launch returns for passengers and the remaining provisions. The women, Sebastian, and the captain climb into the launch while Wellingham and

Nathanial remain on shore waiting for the jailbird. Clearly agitated at the man's tardiness, the captain wears a grim expression for the duration of their trip to the ship.

Once aboard the *Ornery Agnes*, Lillia shows the women where to stow their bedding and satchels before taking her personal effects to her berth. Returning to the deck, she sees the launch back at the shoreline where the three men are boarding, leaving the sheriff and customs agent at the shoreline.

Returning to her berth, Lillia lays back on her rope cot and feels the hemp stretch under her weight, her memory of the featherbed fading quickly. Before long, she hears the launch being lifted and secured to the boat's deck. The captain barks orders from the helm in anticipation of departure, and Lillia rises to see Wellingham and the jailbird disappear into the hole in the deck leading to the 'tween decks. Moments later, Wellingham emerges alone.

From her position, Lillia happily waits for the sails to be set as Captain Eagleton makes his final walk about the ship's deck. She anticipates the peaceful warmth of the Pacific Ocean without having to face Cape Horn. She also recalls that she must remind Captain Eagleton of his promise to help her climb to the heights.

When their newest passenger emerges from below, clearly searching for the captain, she leaves her position in hopes of eavesdropping. Arriving within earshot just as Captain Eagleton approaches the man, she hears the captain begin, "Sir. . ."

"The name is Nicolas. Nicolas Coopton, Captain."

"Mr. Coopton, have you settled into your berth?"

"With all due respect, Captain, after my last experience, I hope you understand I cannot, in any way, consider a berth below decks."

"There are no available berths above decks. We made that point clear."

"Those dolts were so eager to be rid of me, they failed to convey my conditions for leaving. I simply won't live below decks."

Lillia watches the captain's face twist, his jaw clenching with frustration.

"Well, you can't take up residence on the deck, Coopton."

The captain turns on his heel and walks toward Lillia. Through gritted teeth he says, "We have a complication. Where are Sebastian and Wellingham right now?"

"They are in their berths, I believe."

"Please assemble them and meet me at the helm."

Minutes later, Lillia obediently brings both men to the helm. Oblivious to the situation at hand, Wellingham lightly asks, "Captain, are we ready to heave the anchor?"

The captain brusquely relays his conversation with Coopton. When he finishes, Wellingham contemplates before saying, "Come to think of it, he had no bedding. Only a bag tied to his waist and a haughty attitude."

"I'd wager the officials are hoping his demands will eat up any benefit we hoped to gain."

Sebastian's comment makes the captain flex his fingers on the railing.

"That's it. He's going ashore. I'll return the money. It will slow our departure, but we're better off without him."

Hailing Nathanial, Captain Eagleton flips open his spyglass and trains it toward the shore. Nathanial arrives and the captain hands him the spyglass.

Puzzled, Nathanial takes the spyglass asking, "Captain?"

"Look toward shore. Tell me what you see."

Nathanial lifts the spyglass.

"I see three men facing us. One is the customs agent, and the other two are, based on their uniforms, law officers. All are holding rifles, sir."

As thunderclouds pass over Captain Eagleton's expression, the partners jump into action. Scurrying to solve the problem of Coopton's accommodations, Wellingham and Sebastian flip a coin. Loser gives up their berth for a mate's quarters with the captain; winner has to escort Coopton to his new space. Sebastian loses the toss.

As Sebastian's things are being relocated, Lillia notices Coopton observing, one corner of his mouth slightly askew with smug amusement. Once the transfer is complete, Lillia goes with Wellingham to escort Coopton to the passenger's quarters. Finding him at the bow, Wellingham clears his throat.

"Mr. Coopton, this is Miss Lillia Soilleux. Your berth is ready."

Coopton feigns surprise and gasps, "Am I the cause for the relocation of the portly fellow?"

Lillia fights off a visible cringe while allowing Wellingham to respond.

"Yes, well, let's just say we've adapted to your arrival."

"Ah, well, it's nice to have one's needs met. Miss, is it? Sailing on a ship of men and you've managed to maintain your virtues. Admirable. Perhaps I'll have the pleasure of plucking one or two away over the course of this voyage."

Shocked by this, Lillia turns away and walks ahead of the men toward the passenger's quarters leaving Wellingham to escort Coopton alone. As the men arrive, Lillia opens the door to Sebastian's old berth. Coopton pauses before entering.

"When's the next meal served? I haven't eaten a decent meal in weeks."

"We take our meals at seven, noon, and six."

Coopton enters the space before popping his head out, a sneer spread across his face.

"Better than a Chilean jail but just barely. Where is my bedding?"

"If you didn't bring it when you boarded, you'll have none."

"The sheriff said the woman who owns the ship would see to my every comfort. Are you that woman, Miss Soilleux?"

Wellingham looks to Lillia with surprise. She bristles when considering what the customs agent might have contrived about her following her rigid negotiation. Leveling a no-nonsense stare at Coopton, she leaves no room for misinterpretation.

"To be perfectly clear, I'm only one of three partners in ownership. You've got all of us to contend with for the remainder of this voyage. There's no extra bedding. Be grateful for the cot. As far as your needs, you'll get your bare necessities, nothing more."

"Well, that's unfortunate. Seeing as we're underway, I suppose I must tolerate the conditions."

Lillia leaves Wellingham to answer any more questions, marching toward the midship's railing. When Wellingham arrives moments later, Lillia is still fuming.

"His behavior is appalling. When you interviewed him, did he give any indication of this haughtiness?"

"Oh, no. He was quite contrite, a tragic victim of a shipwreck. An unwitting casualty of an intolerant culture deaf to his humble appeals."

"Don't you find it curious he was the only survivor of the shipwreck? His assertion of being able to release the lifeboat unassisted bothers me. And another thing, he commented on my virtue. Is he devoid of any social propriety?"

Silently, Wellingham looks out across the passing water, deep in thought. Lillia gets impatient.

"It's as if he's lost his civility. Or perhaps his concern for civility. Considering the efforts made by the sheriff and customs agent to get rid of him, I wonder what he did to instill such loathing? Perhaps we should prepare a strategy."

Wellingham pauses before using a low tone, saying, "We could loosen his tongue. Perhaps he is prone to drink. I know the captain has brought some aboard."

"But if he's drunk, aren't you likely to be in the same condition?"

"I'll have to be discrete, no doubt. But I have the only unique reason to insist on a conversation. At a minimum, I must learn what happened to the *Night Call*, in order to explain the tragedy to the overland team."

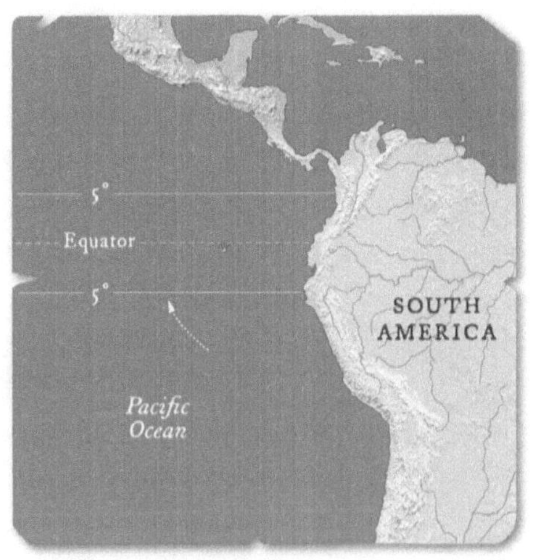

Chapter 8

SEPTEMBER, 1849

PACIFIC OCEAN

The bow deck has become Lillia's favorite place, except for when she is standing at the helm with Captain Eagleton. Extending an invitation to the Browning sisters to join her there, the three young women spend most of their afternoons chatting. One question has burned in her mind since they left Valparaíso, and Lillia decides she is going to ask it today.

"How did you attempt the voyage with no sponsor, no guide, and no idea of what California would hold for you?"

Sarah, the older of the two, answers, "Miss, our pa farms rocky Vermont soil, growing just enough to survive. Hope and I knew our futures would be dim, at best, if we stayed. California might not be any better, but at least we'll have a say."

"What are your skills?"

Hope, whose directness Lillia has come to enjoy, fires back.

"Work. We know how to work hard."

"Well, yes, I suppose you do, but are you literate? Can you do sums?"

After a brief exchange of glances between the sisters, Sarah gives Lillia a sincere stare.

"Imagine everything that happens on a farm. We know how to do every single last chore from birthing animals to killing them. From planting to harvesting, cooking to cleaning, splitting wood to mending. But neither of us reads. Can do sums, though."

Lillia considers the scope of Sarah's response before asking, "What are your hopes for California?"

This time Hope rushes to answer, "Opportunities, mostly. But, I worry about the men. Imagine they are pretty lonely. Do you know anything?"

Lillia takes her time before forming a confident statement. "Sounds like some have lost their civility while prowling for gold. I gathered from accounts I read while still in Boston that women are so scarce in California, when one walks down a street, strangers meet her with marriage proposals on their lips."

The sisters' eyes bulge and fill with tears.

"Just come up to you on the street?" Hope asks, her chin quivering.

Lillia tries to calm them and gently pats Hope's hand while saying, "A woman's got to have her wits about her."

Sarah wipes her eyes with her sleeve before asking, "What are your plans, Miss?"

Lillia explains her business plans with Sebastian.

"Are you staying or returning to Boston when your explorations are over?"

"I don't know yet."

Sebastian's poker games become an anticipated post-supper event since leaving Valparaíso. Tonight, Sebastian asks Lillia to take the dealer's role to afford him the ability to teach the others how to play, a role she eagerly accepts. When the game is over, Lillia decides to get some fresh air before turning in. She goes to the helm and finds the captain changing command with Nathanial for the night.

"Good evening, Captain."

"Up for some fresh air after the card game, Miss Soilleux?"

"It does get stuffy in there. How much longer before the Pacific doldrums, Captain?"

"At our rate, the winds should shift to a whisper in one, maybe two more days. But, if the Pacific doldrums are anything like the Atlantic's, we're destined for a swift arrival in San Francisco."

"As for the doldrums, is it then that you'll help me to the heights?" she asks softly.

Captain Eagleton's genial expression fades and he looks away. Lillia presses him.

"Did you not say . . . ?"

"I think your climbing the heights will be ill-advised, Miss Soilleux. If something should go wrong . . ."

Lillia turns away and looks out at the ocean, desperate to hide her disappointment, but she searches for a way to remind him of his promise. Then it occurs to her.

"Captain, as a child, did you ever ask your mother for something she considered beyond your years?"

The captain thinks for a moment before replying, "Yes, a

knife. I was seven when the idea of carving wood with a blade was interesting.”

“Did your parents grant your request right away?”

“Oh no, they made me earn it. Mother eventually honored her promise once I showed responsibility.”

“And how did that make you feel?”

“At first, I was confused and frustrated, I suppose. She never fully explained when or what was required to realize the reward.”

Lillia lingers for a long moment before saying, “Then you know my feelings.”

Acknowledgment washes over Captain Eagleton’s expression.

“Ah, I see. You’re quite like her, you know. I see it in so many of your mannerisms. Alright then, on my honor, when we are sitting in the doldrums with nothing else to do, I will arrange for you to experience the heights.”

Sebastian’s brass bell summons the night’s players to the card table. Dr. Gibbs, Wellingham, and two of Charles’s boys, who are new to the game, obediently arrive. Wellingham sits across from Lillia, Sebastian two seats to her right. Looking up from her card deck, she sees Coopton staring at the table from his berth’s doorway. Sebastian notices him at the same time and extends an offer.

“Mr. Coopton, care to join us?”

“As you know, sir, I have nothing with which to enter the betting pool.”

Sebastian nods to the statement’s truth and returns to the game. After a few hands, everyone becomes more confident. When Sebastian announces the last hand, Lillia glances in Coopton’s direction. His absence causes a disconcerting chill to run down her spine.

Lillia finds her way to the helm for fresh air, disappointed when Nathanial is at the rudder wheel. Moments later, Sebastian and Wellingham join her where Coopton's unsettling absence forces itself into her mind.

"Did either of you notice Coopton's odd behavior?"

Wellingham shakes his head.

"No, he was too far to my right."

"Uncle?"

"I looked up a few times, but my attention was focused on teaching. What is bothering you?"

"It's probably nothing but he seemed unduly fixated on the table's activities. He never looked away the whole evening, like he was memorizing the flow. And then he disappeared completely at the end."

Wellingham hesitates before staring directly at the Soilleuxs.

"Could he be tracking each player's winnings?"

A realization works through her and Lillia blurts, "Something's not right with him."

Wellingham laughs, "There's the truth!"

Sebastian wishes them a good evening and leaves the helm.

"Miss Soilleux, may I escort you back to your berth?" Wellingham asks.

"Of course," Lillia says, and she joins Wellingham on the short walk toward the passenger's deck.

At her berth's door, Lillia notices him uncharacteristically fidgeting with his vest buttons before saying, "Thank you for the pleasant evening, Miss Soilleux. Gaming is a good release for me. And you are an adept dealer. Another pleasant surprise from you."

"Mr. Wellingham, perhaps you can begin calling me by my given name. It has been several months since we met."

Smiling, Wellingham whispers, "Certainly, Miss . . . Lillia. I'll make the same request."

Lillia nods, saying, "Good night, then, Howard."

Turning to reach for her berth's door latch, Wellingham leans in with a gentle but urgent kiss on her mouth. Lillia stares wide-eyed before Wellingham bobs his head toward her, word-lessly slipping down the hallway and into his berth.

Still reeling with surprise, Lillia enters her dark berth and closes the door. Rather than light the lantern, she plops onto her cot and promptly falls through its bedding-less ropes. Scrambling awkwardly to her feet, she lights her small lantern. Holding it high, the naked ropes shine in the lantern's light. Lillia's mind swims for answers and lands on only one. Coopton.

Defiantly, she fashions bedding from her petticoats and extra skirts. Satisfied, she undresses, extinguishes the lantern, and lays down. In complete darkness, she detects the soft tread of approaching footsteps.

Fear grips her when she realizes, after Wellingham's stolen kiss, she forgot to lock the berth door. Swinging her feet to the deck, she perches on the cot's rigid edge, every muscle tensed.

Through the berth door's slats, she hears Coopton's voice growl lowly, "I know what you're up to."

Terrified, Lillia studies the door, ready to throw herself against it if it cracks open. When she hears the footsteps retreat, she jumps up and locks the door. For good measure, she drags her large trunk against the door. Forcing herself to lie down on her makeshift bed, her mind burns with questions.

At the railing, while Lillia waits for Wellingham to fetch Uncle Sebastian as she had requested, the seawater's spray and morning's fresh air flow over her, and she forces herself to breathe deeply. When the men finally arrive, their urgent steps fore-tell their concern. Panting from the rush, Sebastian grips her shoulder.

"What's this all about?"

Lillia turns to face both men. Her face is drawn with dark

circles looping below her strained eyes. Based on Sebastian's concerned expression, she has his full attention.

"I'm afraid for our ship."

Lillia recounts the discovery of her stolen bedding and Coopton's ominous message at her door last night.

"I can't tell you why exactly, but I believe Coopton's being the *Night Call*'s only survivor isn't an accident. He had to have played a role in its demise. And now he's on our ship."

Wellingham contemplates for a moment.

"But what of his threat to you?"

Lillia's memory of his awkwardly stolen kiss and sudden protectiveness are now overshadowed by Coopton's stunt.

"I don't know if it was a threat or just his effort to unsettle the ship, to force turmoil and create some sort of advantage."

"If Coopton is fixated on you, the captain'll want to know. I believe our captain cares deeply for you," Sebastian says.

At this, Lillia cringes, as her uncle surely knows nothing of Wellingham's attention after the card game last night. Unable to suppress a sideways glance at Wellingham, she sees him staring at his boots, his fingers once again fidgeting with his vest's buttonhole.

"Come, we must go," Sebastian insists, taking Lillia's hand and leaving Wellingham standing at the railing. Expecting Sebastian to haul her to the helm to confess her story to the captain, Lillia is surprised when they make a sharp turn toward the captain's quarters.

At the door, Sebastian calls out, "Hello! Anyone present?"

When no one answers, he opens the door and leads her into the cramped space, only made smaller by his large traveling trunk crammed into a corner. Certain of his discomfort in the strained accommodations, guilt angrily stabs at her for facilitating Coopton's presence.

Taking the edge of his tiny cot, Lillia watches as Sebastian heaves on the trunk. He selects a key from his key ring, kneels in front of the trunk, and inserts the key into the lock.

Lillia jumps when the overstuffed trunk lid pops up dramatically.

"Please indulge me. What I'm looking for is in the bottom."

Lillia's lap fills with men's clothing until he growls triumphantly, "There you are, you little devils."

Lillia peeks around the clothes pile and sees a pair of black scabbards beside him on the floor. Once Sebastian finishes replacing the clothing, he twists the key in the lock and heaves a great sigh. Rather than join her on the cot, he chooses to remain sprawled on the deck, leaning against the trunk.

"Now then, I've not mentioned that I have these to anyone, certainly not the captain."

Sebastian produces a long, narrow item made of ivory and delicately carved mother-of-pearl; its double-lobed pommel surrounded by bands of polished steel. Smiling broadly, he slides the fingers of one hand across the top while using his other fingers to delicately hold the object with a light grip.

Lillia watches as he subtly presses the object's end and then jolts back when a knife blade springs out, doubling the object's full length. Gripping the weapon's handle, Sebastian admires the single-edged blade as it shines from its hilt to its point, even in the dull light of the cramped space.

"This is a gentlemen's folding dagger, a solognot, from Châtellearult where they have been perfecting the art of cutlery since medieval times. They've made everything from swords to epees, but this one, this is my favorite because it can be concealed until needed. For you, I would slide it up my sleeve, like this."

As he talks, Lillia sees him press small pins in the jointed side of the dagger allowing the blade to retract neatly into the body. Once retracted, Sebastian slides the whole apparatus up his sleeve on the inside of his arm.

"See, it fits perfectly between my elbow and my wrist. If I need it, I simply flick my forearm toward the floor allowing the force of this movement to let the dagger slip into my palm."

Demonstrating again, he shows how the smooth dagger slides right out of his sleeve and into his hand, gripping it carefully.

"When you need the blade to emerge, you turn the blade away from your hand and squeeze these pins."

The demonstration of the blade's emergence once again makes Lillia flinch.

"You'll need to practice and become very familiar with how it works. Two points about wielding a blade. First, if fighting facing a person, you will do the greatest damage with a stab and upward thrust, the blade in the vertical orientation. But, from behind, orient the blade horizontally so you are more likely to slice between ribs. In either case, be prepared to use all your strength. The blade is sharp, but human flesh and bone are robust and sinewy. In a fight for your life, don't be afraid to do mortal damage. I assure you, with this under your pillow, you'll sleep soundly."

As he hands the solognot to Lillia, she asks, "How have you come to know these things?"

"A requirement in traveling, I'm afraid. I've not been in an altercation, but I have witnessed many."

She holds it with timid admiration until she finds the courage to press the firing pins. She smiles widely when the blade flashes out brilliantly.

"Try putting it up your sleeve. I believe your forearms are easily as long as mine, but it would be good to understand how it fits in your blouse's tighter sleeves."

Following his suggestion, Lillia retracts the blade and slides the lobed pommel up her sleeve.

"Now, bend at the elbow to make sure it doesn't restrict your movement."

Following his instructions, Lillia finds the solognot fitting snugly without budging.

"Try whipping your hand to the ground and forcing it to slide into your palm."

The motion that had been so easy for Sebastian escapes Lillia, leading Sebastian to suggest a different blouse.

"I will see what I can do. Perhaps I'll have to make some alterations," Lillia says.

"Good. With this, no one will know you are carrying a weapon and yet, you will have something to use, if necessary."

Lillia bobs her head, her mind reeling with the idea of carrying such a weapon, much less using it. After several contemplative moments, she looks up at Sebastian and asks, "What do you think Coopton meant when he said he knew what I was up to?"

Sebastian's brow creases.

"Perhaps he thinks we're rigging the game. Perhaps he's threatened by your role in the ship's business. Whatever it is, we'll be more diligent during tonight's game."

"We are going to play again tonight?"

"Most certainly. A scoundrel can't be allowed to alter our minds with his sinister statements. Before I deal tonight, I'll ask each player to examine the deck so there's no doubt about our honesty."

Lillia's mind whirls with her next question but knows she must ask it.

"When do we tell Captain Eagleton?"

"He should be informed sooner than later. But you need to be the one to tell him."

"I can do that. But, Uncle, what did you mean about the captain having feelings for me?"

"My paternal notion tells me your determination and drive appeal to him. After all, he's a man of similar qualities. It's not surprising you've caught his eye."

Sebastian's comments make Lillia blush, knowing her own developing feelings. Still confused by Wellingham's stolen kiss, she is sure Sebastian's revelation at the railing this morning will sufficiently throttle any further advances.

"Aren't we obligated to warn Dr. Gibbs and the other passengers about Coopton's thievery?"

"Yes and no. His theft of your bedding is in retaliation for what he thinks is a broken obligation. He can't hide anything he might steal. More prudently, the captain will likely inform the crew to be watchful of Coopton's activities below decks."

"But he said he never wants to go below decks."

"His objection was to having his berth below decks. As the equatorial heat builds, the coolness of our cargo will bring temptation . . . for all of us. Now, off to Captain Eagleton."

Helping her uncle to find his feet, Lillia steps into the ship deck's bright light conscious of the solognot's weight and subtle bulge now cradled between her sleeve and forearm. The foreignness of it wears off quickly, and she suddenly feels the confidence of having a reassuring advantage.

Unsuccessful with her search for the captain at the helm and on the deck, Lillia looks below decks before her resolve in the matter starts to slip. Relieved to find him in the ice hold's dim, cool light, she is glad she can have this conversation in some privacy. Nodding politely, she launches to the point.

"Captain, our most troublesome passenger—Mr. Coopton— has stolen my bedding. I don't want it back but think you should have the other passengers and crew be on alert. I would also like a way to secure my berth door when I leave."

Lillia watches a wave of anger cross the captain's face as he says, "Did he steal any personal items?"

"I haven't gone through my trunk. I only know my bedding is gone."

"I can't raise an alarm over a tick mattress."

"Actually, Captain, there's a bit more."

"Out with it, then."

Lillia rubs her forehead while staring at her feet. His lack of reaction suddenly casts doubt on the event's legitimacy. She feels him move closer to her, his fingertips gently lifting her chin to face him. Looking into his eyes, her thoughts sharpen into a verbal deluge.

"After last night's card game, he stood at my door. He muttered something about knowing what I was up to."

Her chin quivers in his cupped hand. Through her welling eyes, she sees his expression soften before he gathers her in his arms and embraces her tightly. Unable to resist his comfort, she raises her arms to his waist and returns the embrace realizing too late that he might be able to detect the solognot in her sleeve. She does not have to wait long to know.

"Miss Soilleux, it's not my habit to ask women what they may have hidden in their garments, but I suspect you've got something sinister lurking in yours."

Lillia pulls away and struggles to extract the solognot from her tight blouse sleeve.

"Uncle Sebastian believes this is my best protection from Coopton."

Captain Eagleton admires the solognot's beauty and ingenuity, tripping the blade's release creating further wonder. His intrigue is so complete, Lillia worries he has lost sight of their conversation's purpose.

"Captain, what do we do about Coopton?"

Continuing to admire the solognot blade's swift action, he does not look at her when he says, "Miss Soilleux, you present me with another first. If the man's unstable, he could become violent if accused falsely. We need to be ready to control him."

"And Wellingham still needs to learn the circumstances of the *Night Call*'s demise."

Captain Eagleton hands the solognot back to her before saying, "Go back to your berth and rest. The doldrums could be upon us as early as tomorrow. I will talk to Sebastian about tonight's game. Do not leave your berth or open the door to anyone but me or your uncle. And for goodness sake, take the time to practice the use of this weapon."

Lillia replaces the solognot in her sleeve and climbs the ladder from the ice hold, the warmth of Captain Eagleton's embrace still present in her limbs.

Secluded in her room all day, Lillia practices with the blade until she can no longer ignore her stomach's urgent protests of hunger. Finally, she hears the sound of the bell, and her door rattles loudly.

"Miss Soilleux, it's the captain. Interested in supper tonight?"

Lillia tucks a few stray strands of hair behind her ear and brushes out the wrinkles from her skirts. Choosing to leave the solognot behind, she tucks it under the many petticoats lining her rope cot. Opening her door, she sees the captain and steps out quickly. He pulls the door shut behind her and locks it with a heavy key. Offering his arm, he whispers, "From now on, you'll be escorted to and from your berth. The door will be locked when you are not within to lock it yourself."

When they pass by the poker game in progress, Lillia spies Coopton studying the table's activities again. She catches Wellingham's eye and receives a subtle nod. Not twenty-four hours since his inelegant kiss, the memory of it makes her strengthen her grip on the captain's arm.

Surprisingly, instead of walking toward the galley, Captain Eagleton guides her toward his quarters. Upon entering, she finds the space nothing like what she had seen earlier with Sebastian. A table for two has been set, complete with crystal glasses and domed plates.

"Why, what's this?"

He pulls out her chair and Lillia takes her seat.

"This way, we can dine in peace and privacy."

He pours sherry into the glasses and removes the plate dome with a small flourish. Lillia smiles at the dinner fare. It's the same as what Barnabas served the day before.

"I hear presentation makes it taste better," the captain says softly.

Eagleton sits, then raises his glass to offer a toast, "To the doldrums. May we root out the nuisances in our lives."

Shortly into their meal, Lillia is relieved when the captain launches into conversation. "Let me start by saying I think you've been harboring this difficulty with Coopton as your own doing. Howard and I share in the pain with equal portions, given that we were justly duped by his interview."

"Does Wellingham plan to use the doldrums to extract the *Night Call*'s information from Coopton?"

"The doldrums will keep us in its grasp for as long as two weeks. Infuriatingly slow but with a threatening passenger aboard, it becomes dangerous. As for Wellingham's plan . . ."

Lillia, her eyes focused on her plate's food, waits for details. When none come, she looks up and sees him gazing at her, to which he offers only a deep sigh.

"As a man who has developed a deep affection for a splendid woman, the doldrums present a glorious opportunity for a plan of my own."

Baffled by his confession, Lillia quickly directs her gaze back to her plate. Cautiously, she raises her head and they silently observe each other until the captain yields, "Have I been too bold?"

"I . . . I . . ."

"Miss Soilleux, after last night's events, I can't treat you like a passenger, or even a business partner anymore. My feelings have leapt far ahead. I fall asleep seeing us together. I see us working, laughing, and having a home together. I can only hope you feel the same."

"Has my uncle said anything to you about my life before this voyage?"

"He has alluded to a painful time, a disappointment in love prior to your departure from Boston. Nothing more."

"While my uncle is quite insightful, he isn't aware of all the circumstances."

Captain Eagleton pushes away from the table and comes to her side. She rises to meet his embrace, melting against him. The power of his hold makes her pulse quicken, but it's the pressure of his lips that makes her knees weak. Donovan had always been brief in his kisses, as if fearing to offend her. This kind of bold kiss let her know the captain didn't fear her offense, but wanted her to understand his sincerity. Rather than pull away, the captain maintains his embrace of her, resting his chin against her forehead and asking, "Tell me, do you still wish to climb to the heights?"

"Absolutely."

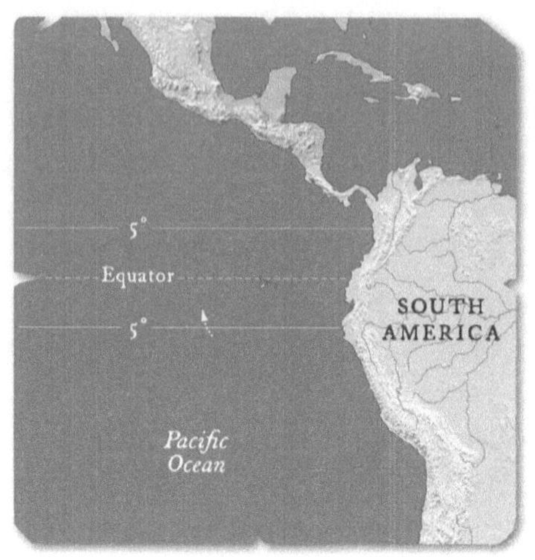

Chapter 9

SEPTEMBER, 1849

PACIFIC DOLDRUMS

True to the captain's prediction, the *Ornery Agnes* stalls her northerly progress days later. Suffocating in the equatorial heat, her camisole drenched in sweat, Lillia impulsively makes an unescorted dash to the ice hold for a bucket of ice chunks. She considers asking the captain for an escort but changes her mind, not wanting to further the image of her being a frightened and helpless female. She ponders taking the solognot, but reasons against it since her trip will be so brief. Just down the ladder and back again. Nothing to fear.

Once there, she pauses to relish the cool darkness. Knowing it is a gamble to linger, she uses the provided ice pick to break off pieces of ice. Turning to leave, she hears a familiar voice and freezes when she sees Coopton emerging from the shadows.

"I'm so disappointed you never came to claim your bedding."

Moving swiftly, he uses his full weight to pin her against the burlap-wrapped ice block, his face only inches from hers.

"I had hoped we could share it. You've got to be so uncomfortable without it."

"Get off me, now!"

Sounding strong against her panic, Lillia re-grips the heavy ice bucket in her right hand while at the same time regretting not having her solognot for self-defense. Then again, she wonders, what if she had the weapon? It would have been impossible to use in her current position. And further, what might he have done had he discovered it?

With her mind swimming in doubt and confusion, she squirms against his body's pressure which prompts him to hiss, "Resist me if you like, Miss Soilleux, but I'm going to teach you to stay in your place. You're a woman who manipulates and pits men against each other without consequences."

"Did you put the crew of the *Night Call* in their place too?"

She feels his muscles stiffen at her accusation before he says, "Those fools underestimated my skills and paid the price. No one knows anything of what happened there and I intend to keep it that way."

"Are you attempting to do the same here?"

"No. My failure with the *Night Call* taught me I'm a lousy sailor. This time I'm counting on you to guarantee my return to California."

"I will never . . ."

"Oh, yes, you will. By the time we arrive in San Francisco, you'll have learned the importance of serving a man's needs. You'll not think so much of yourself."

Spittle drops from his wheezed message collect on his rough beard. When Lillia works her head away from his wretched breath, he grips her left wrist, pulls it up and behind her head, and knots his fingers in her hair. The leverage snaps her face toward his, and she has no choice but to stare into his wild eyes.

"I left California in early spring of '49 half the man I used to be. I had hoped to return to the East, but every ship I boarded set me off at their next port. I was stuck in Buenos Aires when the *Night Call* arrived for provisions. I took passage with them even though they were sailing back to California. I'd have done anything to leave Buenos Aires."

He looks away with the disclosure of his recent history, and Lillia watches him with caution.

"Once again, the captain and crew of the *Night Call* enraged me to where I knew they all had to die. I let us get around the horrid weather of Cape Horn before I went ahead with my plan. My miscalculation was ending everyone's life. I should have left more to do the sailing. They just made me so angry."

He stares at her face again, his expression twisted with madness.

"Here's how I'm doing it differently this time. You're going to help move what's in that dandy's trunk into my coffers. Since you've got both the captain and the dandy ensnared in your web, you'll have to be sly to accomplish all I want from you."

"I most certainly will not!"

"You'll do my bidding. If not, I'll tell the captain about this little tryst of ours. He'll never believe I didn't soil your purity. No doubt I'll be punished, but there's nothing they can do I haven't already endured. You, however, will be shunned."

"He'll never believe your story. Not when I tell him you wrecked the *Night Call*."

"Ah, but your virtue will be in question. He'll always wonder."

Lillia digests his warped logic and its implied consequences before saying, "The doldrums will give you no distractions. Everyone is idle and more likely to detect your activities."

"That is where your skills will shine. Drawing their attention away from my activities is your role in my plan."

Lillia wonders if her best chance at foiling his plan is pretending to go along with it.

"What do you want me to do?"

"Distract the dandy during tonight's card game."

"Tonight? And what will you do? Take all his wealth at once?"

"I've got a plan to neutralize him for the duration."

"And you expect no consequences for your actions from the captain? We're weeks away from California. Why not wait until we get closer?"

Coopton leans in and says, "Unlike my misguided efforts on the *Night Call*, I intend to use restraint this time. I will take command of the ship's crew and demand they continue on to California. No one will stand in my way."

Lillia shivers at the thought that her uncle could come to harm but continues her inquiry into Coopton's plan by asking, "When it's over, you'll leave me alone?"

"It'll be our little secret. Should you breathe a word of it to the captain, however, I'll confess loud and long about what I might have taken from you down here."

Lillia feels his grip soften. She pushes against him with all her rage-enhanced strength, the surprise shove catching him off guard as he stumbles back onto the deck. Rushing to the hold's ladder, Lillia finds the rungs too steep for a quick escape but climbs up to the sound of his sick laughter below her. By the time she reaches the ladder's top rung, Lillia has formed a plan of her own.

Without telling him why, Lillia convinces Sebastian to let her deal in the night's card game. Initially skeptical, Sebastian relents with, "Your presence is most welcome. I believe the men appreciate your style with the cards."

Over the course of the night, Lillia deals the cards expertly. She notices Wellingham is winning more games than he loses. She knows Coopton is lurking and waiting for an opportunity. A chorus of groans from the other players goes up when Wellingham wins the night's final hand. Noting Coopton's usual disappearance, she waits at the table while Wellingham casually counts his winnings.

Eventually, Wellingham leaves the table juggling the coins against his chest. Lillia feels a wave of guilt-ladened dread wash over her. Unaware of Coopton's timing or specific intentions, Lillia condemns her own arrogance for believing she could play both sides. She pushes back from the table and turns for the helm in hopes of finding the captain there. Behind her, she hears sounds of a scuffle and then Wellingham's yelp stops her in her tracks.

"Ah! What are you doing in my . . . ?"

The ring of coins hitting against the hard deck interrupt Wellingham's sentence. A sickening thump of human flesh being beat upon follows. She turns and sees Coopton's fist punching downward into Wellingham's face.

Sebastian calls out, "Captain, Nathanial, someone come quick!"

The brawl blocks all passengers but Sebastian and Lillia inside their berths, who are helpless until the captain bursts in and grabs Coopton's raised fist.

"That'll do, rogue. Nathanial, get a length of rope," the captain calls out.

As he pulls Coopton off Wellingham, Coopton swings his free hand wildly and slashes at the captain's midsection. Lillia sees a red stain develop across the captain's white shirt just as Coopton attempts a second slash. Anticipating the swipe, the captain's fist comes down hard on Coopton's arm and knocks a thin piece of metal from his grip. The weapon skitters across the deck. Before Coopton can inflict more damage, the captain delivers a blow to Coopton's gut that doubles him over.

Satisfied the man's threat has been neutralized, the captain releases Coopton to look at his own wound. Coopton senses his freedom and makes a mad dash for the door, which coincides with Nathanial's hurried arrival. The two collide with full force. Both men crash to the deck, but their collision gives the captain and a few crew members time to pounce on Coopton, quickly binding him tight.

Within moments, a defiant and obscenity-howling Coopton is secured to the enormous timber mast. His cries remind Lillia of a wounded dog, but she finds no pity for him.

"Serves him right. Hope he spends the rest of his days on this ship in that exact spot," Sebastian says.

Lillia doesn't agree. Coopton's position allows him to witness everyone's comings and goings, which makes her very uncomfortable.

She suggests, "Couldn't he be hauled below and forced to remain in a place he despises?"

"I could get my berth back," Sebastian reflects. "Yes, your idea has merit. Share it with the captain later."

The captain! Lillia turns from her uncle and sees Dr. Gibbs tending the captain's slash wound. His blood-soaked shirt has been ripped open exposing his entire chest, and Lillia sucks in her breath at the sight.

Going to his side, she asks the doctor, "Is it deep?"

"No, Miss Soilleux, just deep enough to produce a lot of blood. We're glad the weapon was so slight. Anything more substantial would have had serious consequences."

Lillia's mind races to that afternoon in the ice hold. If Coopton had gotten a hold of her solognot, the captain's wound could have been fatal. She suddenly despairs at the thought of confessing her roll in all this, but she also knows her disclosure has to come before Coopton can vomit out his version.

"Captain, there's something I need to tell you."

"Miss Soilleux," Dr. Gibbs interrupts, "I suggest we give the captain time to recover from tonight's shock before he has any interactions. Can it wait until morning?"

"I suppose it can," Lillia says biting her lip.

Coopton's rants go on all night. The doldrums stillness allows the wails and vulgarities to linger in the stagnate, humid air rather than a breeze blowing them to nothingness. Lillia lies in her berth with the solognot nestled under her pillow. She practices the words she will use to explain everything to the captain. Her fitful dreams have Coopton's angry spewings winding in and out of them, and she wonders where he gets the energy to continue. Finally, at daybreak, he is quiet. She determines it's now time to talk to the captain.

Lillia unlocks her berth and realizes locking it is no longer necessary. The thought brings a touch of levity to her step until she sees Wellingham sitting at the passenger's quarters' table. His face is swollen, one eye completely blackened, and his lip has an enormous crack in it.

"Howard! I had no idea of your condition. Has Dr. Gibbs seen you?"

Wellingham turns to face her, displaying the entirety of his wounds and tries to grin, a movement he immediately regrets.

"Ah! The brute has robbed me of even the ability to smile. Damn him, damn him completely."

"What can I do to help?"

"Doctor Gibbs assures me my injuries are treated only by time. I'm afraid I'll be the ship's monster for a while."

"But surely a cold compress would ease the swelling. Let me get you some ice."

"That would be kind of you. My head aches with such ferocity that I can't bear to stand or move about."

Lillia returns to her berth and grabs her ice pail, determined to be of some comfort to the man in his distress. Leaving the passenger's quarters, she detects no movement and is confident she was not the only one who did not rest overnight. Walking softly toward the hold, Lillia sneaks a peek at the mizzenmast fully expecting to see Coopton tied there. All the blood leaves her face when the binding ropes are empty.

Oh my God! Has he escaped?

Multiple questions pop into her head, their answers turning her to stone. She realizes she left her solognot under her pillow and the door unlocked. Just as she turns to go back to her berth, she hears voices coming from below deck. Tiptoeing toward the hatch area, she leans in low to hear the conversation.

"Go ahead, Hope, give him a tad more."

From her position, Lillia hears a muffled objection before dwindling to silence.

"You'll do as I say, you filthy creature. No one keeps me up all night with their carrying on especially after beating on others and cutting the captain."

Throttled noises come in reply and Lillia gasps as she realizes it's Sarah's voice. Lillia cautiously steps down the ladder, her eyes adjusting to the dim light. Scanning the area, she sees Coopton flanked on each side by Hope and Sarah. Gagged and trussed tightly, like a country ham, his bound wrists and ankles allow for no movement.

"Good morning, Miss Lillia. We had to find a way to make sure he doesn't cause such a disturbance. Gave him a bit of the poppy to make him cooperate and keep him quiet."

Lillia is stunned speechless as she processes the sight before her. Then she finds the words and asks, "Does the captain know what you've done?"

"I don't think so. I'd imagine the entire ship is going to rest given the commotion he made all night. If you'd like to tell him, be our guest."

Lillia slowly nods, her mind rushing to the next, most important question.

"Where did you get opium?"

"Our mum grew a bit, just for medicinal purposes. It came in handy when there was trouble on the farm and something needed to be quieted. Brought some with us, just in case."

Nodding at their practicality, Lillia says, "Alright then. I'll leave you to it. I'm on an errand to get ice for Mr. Wellingham's injuries, but after I'm done, I will notify the captain of the situation. I'm sure he'll want to have a word or two."

Hope says, "We may try to take a nap. Thank you, Miss Lillia."

Lillia turns toward the ice storage and then turns back.

"Actually, Sarah, Hope, thank you. You have no idea."

With that, she picks off some ice chunks, scurries up the ladder, and back to Wellingham with a handkerchief-wrapped ice chunk in hand. After making sure he is situated with the cold compress, she tells him, "I'm going to visit with the captain for a few moments. I can fetch you some tea from Barnabas, if that suits you?"

"A lovely idea, but alas, I don't think my lip will appreciate even the pressure of the cup. I'm satisfied to suck on ice cubes in the meantime, thank you."

"Alright then, I'll return later."

When Lillia taps on the officer's door, Uncle Sebastian greets her.

"Good morning, Lillia. That is, I think it's a good morning. The quiet is welcome, but curious. What has happened? Did he finally go hoarse?"

"It is even better than that, Uncle. I must tell both of you at the same time though."

Sebastian looks over his shoulder before whispering, "The captain's wound made him quite restless last night. Dr. Gibbs's liberal dousing of whisky before bandaging was thought to help, but he's been quite uncomfortable. It might be a few moments before I can convince him to rise."

"It is important news about Coopton. I will meet you at the bow when both of you are able."

Standing still with a tin cup of tea in her hand, Lillia's thoughts wander while she waits for the men. Suddenly grateful for the quiet, she wonders how long they can keep Coopton in his present condition. Having just entered the Pacific doldrums, they wouldn't be going anywhere for a while. And even if they could control him until California, what will they do with him when they get there?

Her thoughts are interrupted by the low growl of the captain's voice approaching from behind.

"Your uncle tells me you have news about our hostage, Miss Lillia."

She turns and sees the captain wearing a fresh but unbuttoned shirt, exposing Dr. Gibbs's bandages along with a generous amount of bare chest. His normal height is bowed, as she imagines that he's protecting the wound or the pain of it. But otherwise, he seems as confident as always. She wants to touch his chest, to stroke away the pain, but she knows how inappropriate that would be.

"Yes, Captain, I can shed some light. It seems our new passengers—the sisters from Vermont—took matters into their own hands. Coopton is below deck, immobilized and quiet. They've done an admirable job of incapacitating him and muzzling him as well."

"However did they do that?" Sebastian asks.

"Opium."

While Lillia smiles smugly, both men gape at her words until Sebastian says, "I must see this with my own eyes. I don't think you should try to scale the ladder, Captain. You are in good hands with Lillia."

Watching him lumber off, Lillia turns to the captain and says quietly, "There is more to this situation, but I'd rather have you hear it from me without my uncle knowing."

"Go ahead. I'm listening," the captain replies tenderly.

Lillia's words don't come easily, at first halting and jumbled. By the time her story gets to Coopton's threat to her and the ship, she has found her confidence.

"I'm ashamed to think I would have betrayed Howard. I thought I could find a way to trick Coopton into making a mistake, and he would be caught. I had no idea he was thinking of acting so quickly."

The captain quietly ponders her words before saying, "Actually, I think Coopton is deranged. Whatever he has said or done should be considered legitimate. The question is, how do we deal with him for the remainder of the voyage? We should be in California in a little over a month. We can't keep him on laudanum for the whole time."

"We can't?"

"Lillia, I've got certain responsibilities to not mistreat even the most vulgar of souls. He will stay restrained, but we've got to feed him, give him water, and manage his needs."

"I don't like the Browning sisters being below decks with him, even if he is tied up. Is there anything we can do for them to come above deck?"

The captain contemplates this until Lillia perks up suddenly and says, "I've got an idea. What if the sisters move into my uncle's old berth, and he remains in his current berth? Considering the circumstances, I'm sure he will agree for another five weeks or so."

"A single rope cot is too small for two people."

"Perhaps we should talk to the sisters about the idea," Lillia says. "They seem to be quite enterprising."

"You're offering us an above-deck berth?"

The Browning sisters look excited at the opportunity as they sit in the galley with Lillia sipping tea. Lillia can hardly keep her glee subdued when she says, "Yes, but you'll have to decide how to make a berth intended for one person capable of accommodating two."

"We'll take a look at the space. Goodness knows we've had to learn to compromise our comfort many times before. I can't imagine passing up an opportunity to breathe fresh air and have sunlight."

"Alright then. You ladies take a look while I find Dr. Gibbs. We need to discuss how to keep Coopton quiet while still treating him humanely."

The sisters exchange a look.

"What?" Lillia asks. "What is it?"

"We wouldn't want the captain to know," Hope begins.

"Because we didn't encourage him," Sarah chimes in.

"Know *what*?" Lillia asks, wishing the answer isn't what she thinks it may be.

The sisters exchange a look before simultaneously staring at their feet until Sarah mumbles, "There's something you should know about Coopton. Something awful but it does explain some of his behavior."

"What is it, Sarah?"

"He would visit us. We never gave him encouragement, but he'd sneak into the 'tween decks and talk loud enough for us to hear."

"Of what?"

"A testimony of sorts, I think."

Hope's statement brings a mutual nod from the sisters before Sarah continues.

"He said he has no . . . uh . . . no, well, he has no man parts."

"Said it had been stolen from him in the southern mining camps in California. He'd gotten drunk on a cold winter night and the next thing he knew, someone was removing . . ."

". . . what he called his jewel sack!" Sarah finishes.

"Why would anyone do such a thing?" Lillia asks, shocked.

Hope is quick to answer. "He said gold dust leaks out of sacks with seams."

Lillia ponders the explanation before saying, "Ridiculous. There are other sources for such things."

Sarah waits for a moment before continuing with the implausible story.

"He said so many needed a way to hold their gold dust, most of the ram sheep in the area had lost theirs. Shepherds had to put a guard over those remaining intact rams. So, when a man died, or those who were assumed to have died, there were men who would harvest the part."

"As he said, 'a dead man no longer has use of it.'"

Hope's statement settles over them like a foul odor. Lillia's mind whirls, trying to understand if what she had experienced with Coopton since his arrival aboard the *Ornery Agnes* had anything to do with this disturbing revelation.

"Back home, if a bull is cut too late, he becomes mean and unpredictable. It was always better to just eat him rather than live with an animal that was unpredictable. Maybe that's what Coopton is dealing with, losing his jewels has made his mind unhinge."

Lillia takes a deep breath before saying, "May I share this with the captain by way of an explanation for his behavior? It may further complicate just how we are going to deal with him until California."

"I suppose, if you have to," Sarah says.

"I think it's best," replies Lillia. "But for now, let's go take a look at the berth and try to figure out how to keep you out of the 'tween decks and Coopton's presence."

After considerable discussion, the Browning sisters decide to alternate between the cot and the deck. Lillia marvels at their strategy and problem-solving skills. After removing Lillia's stolen bedding and taking it to the bow to air out, the sisters begin their move above deck. Forced to walk past Coopton several times, they are met with a barrage of animal noises emanating from his gagged mouth, despite several crew members posted defensively beside him.

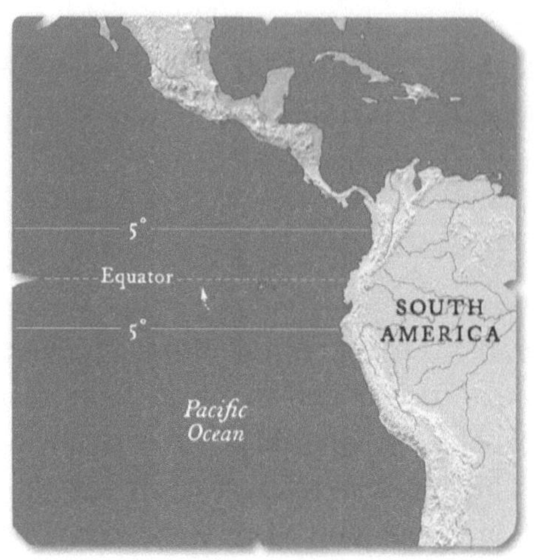

Chapter 10

SEPTEMBER, 1849

PACIFIC DOLDRUMS

"There is no time like the present."

Lillia's heart leaps when, ten nights later, the captain tells her that tonight is the night. Her pulse races with an unfamiliar flutter when he adds, "I will accompany you in case there is the need for assistance, of course."

"But can you climb in your condition?" she asks, doubtful his wound has healed enough in so short a time.

"I have made the ascent enough times to know how to take

care. I will be fine. And anyway, I don't want to send you up there alone."

We will be alone in the heights?

He continues, "I can feel the current starting to tug at our keel. If I'm going to make good on my promise, we must do it before I lose my impetuosity and come to my senses. I will loan you some trousers. You'll need to trim your garments, enough to cover without impeding your progress. Given that your feet don't have the required callouses to climb the rat lines barefoot, you'll also need sturdy socks."

"When do we meet?"

"When the ship goes quiet, meet me at the helm. No one should suspect anything."

"And the trousers?"

"I will get them as we walk back to your berth tonight. But, Lillia, I'm giving you one more chance to change your mind. I won't hold it against you if you do."

"Absolutely not, Captain. My eyes wander to the moon sail atop the mainmast and, after your description, I find myself bursting with curiosity."

The captain lightly kisses Lillia's forehead before saying, "Let it not be said that I don't keep my promises."

Later that night, when the other passengers are sleeping, Lillia pads in sock-covered feet down the deck toward the helm, nervously glancing from side to side on the lookout for anyone who might spoil this opportunity. She wears the impromptu climbing costume she has put together in the privacy of her berth: a chemise tucked into trousers she borrowed from the captain. She has forgone her corset, and instead pulled her short-sleeved chemisette over the chemise, the wide neckline buttoned to its top. Finally, she donned the high-necked, long-sleeved blouse she had been using to hide her solognot, its trim fit sure not to catch or tangle on any rat lines as she climbs. She secured her hair in the tightest of buns, tucked the solognot into her sleeve, and went to meet the captain.

Now, carefully climbing the helm's stairs, she sees him and smiles. Relief washes over her. He takes her by the shoulders to examine her ensemble.

"Good, you've followed my directive to the last detail. Are you ready?"

"Yes, I believe I am."

"Agreed. Here we go."

The captain leads her to the mainmast shroud and lithely steps up to the railing's edge gripping the shroud with his right hand. Gesturing for her to join him, he guides her with his left hand, showing her the proper way to climb the rat lines, and they begin their upward traverse. At the common top, he slips through the small opening, his muscular body wiggling through before extending his hand through the opening to her.

"This is the first of three tops we have to negotiate. You must let go of the rat line and grip the inside of the top before hoisting yourself through it."

Lillia takes a moment to assess the space as well as her hand and foot holds. After a clumsy effort, she stands on the common top about forty feet above the ship's deck. The dark sky is filled with stars, their crispness still dimmed by the dense ocean humidity.

Before she knows it, they are climbing the shroud to the gallant top. Lillia feels her body responding to the rhythm of the climb, and they reach the top quickly. Repeating their ascension through the top's access hole, Lillia stops once again to admire the view seventy feet above the ship's deck. Catching her breath, she feels her pulse racing with excitement for this adventure. Taking the time to look in all directions, she sees that the dim stars are now clearer, and a distant bright flash catches her attention.

"What is that?"

"We are in luck. A distant thunderstorm is brewing for our entertainment. Let's keep going higher."

Following his lead, Lillia eagerly climbs and slips through the top with ease. Now one hundred feet above the deck, she feels her pulse racing and wobbles when she looks down.

"Take my advice and don't look down. It will overwhelm you. Besides, you have more interesting things to observe with the best show to be seen from the sky sail top. How do you feel about going up one more shroud? Remember, we have to come down."

Lillia considers Rupert's question, her eyes searching the distant horizon for the thunderstorm. The occasional burst of lightning rips through the sky and she decides.

"This is a practical stop. I can't imagine being more impressed by another twenty feet."

"Good choice. Shall we get comfortable?"

Lillia's expression betrays her doubts about comfort, and the captain laughs.

"I'm mostly joking, but we could position ourselves to look toward the storm and relax for a few minutes."

"Oh, that would be wonderful."

By leaning against the mast and gripping the attached yard arm, the captain guides Lillia to sit on the top, her foot bracing against the yard arm while one arm holds tight to the mast's diminished girth. Finding his place adjacent to her, he sits. Together, they watch the thunderstorm's lightning crackle high into the atmosphere.

Occasionally a bright blue arc further brightens the sky, and Lillia utters, "Ah!"

After several minutes, she turns to Rupert, her eyes bright with excitement.

"It is so beautiful and peaceful up here."

Rupert takes her hand and looks into her eyes.

"I must tell you something, Lillia. I've spent my life looking for a woman like you. I wanted you to know my feelings before we return to the deck."

His admission makes Lillia tingle, and when his warm hand takes hers, she smiles. A sudden flash of guilt about Donovan fires in her memory, and she quickly turns away to look out toward the thunderstorm. Grasping for words, she decides the truth has to be told.

"Rupert, there are things in my past and my future that may sway your opinion of me. I must accept that fact, but I intend to be truthful with you now."

In the ominous silence of the wide expanse, Lillia feels the throb of both their hearts. When he leans toward her and gently brushes her cheek with his finger, she braces for the worst.

"I don't care what lurks in your past," he tells her.

"Rupert, there's a secret I've borne. I should have been more forthcoming, specifically with my uncle."

"I can't imagine anything that will change my feelings about you, but if it will make you feel better, you can tell me."

Lillia takes a deep breath and starts at the beginning. She tells him about how she first met Donovan, their courtship over learning Morse code together, the plans they hatched to marry in order to free themselves from their respective societal prisons. Then Donovan's mysterious letter and disappearance, and the real reason she set sail for the West.

The captain listens intently without interruption.

She closes with, "My parents and uncle knew nothing of his deeds or my motivations. I lied to them and am ashamed. That is my secret. I guess I just didn't expect to find you along the way."

Rupert quietly absorbs her words before squeezing her hand and giving her a wistful grin.

"I think it's time to make our way to the deck."

"Wait, Rupert. Are you . . . do you take back your sentiments?"

He pulls his hand from hers and puts it against her cheek, drawing in close.

"Not one bit. What a colossal mistake Donovan made. But he's paid you the highest compliment a woman can be given."

Lillia pulls away revealing a confused expression.

"Compliment? I don't understand."

"Think of it. He left you a coded message he knew you'd decode. He knew you would take his challenge. He understands your strength, or he wouldn't have asked you to join him. I'll not judge his actions, because I don't know why he made his decision, but I'm grateful he let you go."

"But I deceived my family!"

"I'm a betting man, and I've got tall odds on their forgiveness."

With that, Rupert lifts her chin with his index finger and gazes into her eyes. The distant lightning reflects in them as he lowers his face to hers. His lips tenderly brush against hers. As they softly kiss, she loses her heart to him.

"Rupert, we should probably start down."

"Yes, of course. I wouldn't want to get carried away up here."

He helps Lillia rise and demonstrates how to descend through the top's hole before going first. Nervous tension ripples through her while her feet dangle, waiting for Rupert to guide them to the shroud's rat lines. Once secure, she feels her way through the opening, her fingers eagerly gripping the rat lines where she holds tightly for a few moments.

"Going down is frightening."

"We'll go slowly through the tops. Just don't look down. Use your toes to find the rat lines. We aren't in a hurry."

Before she knows it, they arrive at the gallant top and Rupert eases her through it. Once again, the idea of not knowing when or where her feet are going to find security has her rigid with fear.

"Lillia, it is important you trust me. I've got you."

Once through the gallant top, she stops long enough to catch a glimpse of the ship's deck. Below them, she sees someone walking, and she freezes when she recognizes his gait. The horror of the realization makes her whisper, "Rupert!"

"What is it?"

"Coopton is walking the deck below us."

Her news makes Rupert's head snap to the deck, his eyes riveted. Lillia stays frozen on the common shroud while Rupert mutters, "How in the . . . ?"

The couple watch the escapee wander about the deck waggling his arms and legs like he is trying to restore circulation. Ever so quietly, they watch him enter the galley. After several minutes, he returns to the deck, one hand holding a bucket and the other a loaf of bread. Casually, he walks around the ship's deck while taking large bites of the bread.

"What is he up to?" Lillia whispers.

"I don't know, but it looks like he's got Barnabas's ash bucket. Oh, my God, no, no. He can't . . ."

At the same instant, Lillia realizes Rupert's terror when it manifests itself in immediate and drenching sweat. Lillia quickly whispers, "Rupert, he doesn't know we are here. If he tries to set the ship on fire, we can hurry to the deck and wake everyone."

"If only I had something or some way of keeping him from even starting it."

Instantly, Lillia remembers her solognot and says, "I have my solognot in my sleeve."

Acknowledging her weapon, Lillia watches him formulate a plan, all the while keeping watch on Coopton's movements.

Rupert whispers, "I don't want to give him any chance with that weapon. Tuck it away unless absolutely necessary. You should have something to protect yourself, if it comes to that. If you can keep him visually occupied, I might be able to sneak across the yard arm and down the opposite shroud without him noticing me. From there, I should be able to surprise him from behind. Do you think you can engage him?"

Lillia contemplates their situation for a moment. She remembers the incident with Coopton in the ice hold, his foul threats about her virtues and says coolly, "Distracting him will not be a problem."

"Good, let me get to the opposite side shroud. Then on my signal, call out to him. He mustn't spread those coals across the deck."

Nodding her understanding, Lillia watches Rupert lithely and silently work his way up to the royal yard, across it and down to the shroud directly across from her. His wave signals the start of their plan.

Taking a deep and calming breath, Lillia's voice breaks the silence with clarity.

"Mr. Coopton, how is it that you are above decks?"

Duly startled, Coopton's head jerks skyward. After a few seconds, he replies, "Miss Soilleux, I must ask the same. How is it you're perched up there like a night owl?"

"I've become enamored with the heights. It's a frequent activity for me these days. But you, how did you free yourself from your bonds?"

"Ah, I can tell you since no one on this ship will live to know of my exceptional escape. Your doctor may have skills, but he's not very observant. He thought I was drugged to oblivion. Actually, I've got quite a tolerance for the stuff. Those farm girls gave me just enough to put me under. Perhaps the good doctor was trying to save some for himself, but his dose never really made me dim. And he wasn't watchful of his equipment. Scalpels are small things and easy to lose. But sharp and in the right hands, they're absolutely freeing."

Lillia looks away from Coopton and sees Rupert working himself down the common shroud. Now is the time to maintain Coopton's attention.

"What is your intent now that you have your freedom?" she asks.

"Actually, Miss Soilleux, your fortuitous location makes you my plan's focal point. See, these coals spread just so around the base of this mast will afford you the honor of being the first to see the ship go up in flames. I'll just spread them and add a little fuel from the lantern. You're going to have a fine view."

"But if I yell for help, someone, all of the crew, will come running, don't you think?"

"I suppose you could do that, but by the time they rise from their slumber, the flames will be well advanced. See, the *Night Call*'s crew thought they could outsmart me as well. They tried to do exactly what your captain did: bind me and toss me in the hold. And yet, I was able to wreck them rather spectacularly."

"What joy do you derive from destroying whole ships of people?"

"I've been irreparably damaged, physically and mentally, and men have to pay. I'll never be compensated for what I've lost. And I've recently decided my future is dim, at best, so I've decided to go down with all of you."

Without further explanation, he begins to shake the ashes and hot coals onto the deck at the mast's base. Lillia sees Rupert advance stealthily from the shroud to the ship's railing, his expression grim and determined.

But Coopton's actions are just as resolute. The glowing coals burst into flame when he pours the lantern's oil on them. In seconds, the deck is alight. Lillia hurries down the shroud and through the common top, her toes frantically reaching for the shroud's next ratline. Just as she wiggles her way through the top's hole, she hears the crew yelling in alarm.

Where are Coopton and Rupert? Why hasn't Rupert sounded his own alarm?

The acrid smoke stings her eyes as she scans the deck on her descent. The two men she had hoped to see are nowhere to be found. When she finally reaches the railing and steps onto the deck, the flames are licking across the deck with discouraging speed. Torn between her fear of the flames and wanting to know where Rupert and Coopton are, she freezes with indecision. Then she hears the grunts of a struggle.

To her right, she sees the two men crouched low and facing each other. Both are completely focused, seemingly oblivious to the fire surrounding them. Rupert advances aggressively and Coopton skillfully avoids the attack. Before Rupert can spin to face him, Coopton is on Rupert's back, his arm cinched tight around Rupert's neck in a choke hold.

Lillia feels the solognot in her sleeve drop to her palm, the blade springing out at her request. Without hesitation, she moves through the smoke and chaos toward the pair. Her arrival is a surprise Coopton could not have anticipated. Coopton's focus on throttling Rupert is so complete that Lillia's swift stab between his fourth and fifth rib barely causes a reaction. Temporarily sickened by the sound of the sharp metal blade piercing and slicing through skin and muscle, Lillia prays he will stop wrenching on Rupert's neck immediately. But he continues without pause.

Desperate to stop him, Lillia uses all her strength to bury the solognot's blade to its hilt into his back. Only then does he turn to look at her, his face a mask of madness. Coopton glares at her as his grip on the captain eases and he slumps to the deck. His lips form words but no sound comes, just a thin line of blood oozing from the corner of his mouth. She stands over him until there is no breath coming from him, her heart beating furiously from the shock of her actions.

Rupert, too, slumps to his knees in the opposite direction, gasping loudly for air. She rushes to his side and hugs him close before pulling back to look into his face. That is when she sees the bruises and lacerations. Theirs had been a silent battle, but one Rupert had been on the losing end of before her arrival.

"Must put out the fire," he rasps through damaged vocal cords.

"The crew is working on it. Let me help you to your quarters before fetching Dr. Gibbs."

"No, I must help save the ship. You need to go back to your berth and stay out of the way. This is no place for a woman."

Just then, Nathanial arrives at Rupert's side with a report of their progress. Stunned by Rupert's last statement, Lillia heads to her berth. Understanding the truth of his words doesn't stop the sting of them, especially when she knows of her role in Coopton's death. That truth will have to wait.

Dodging buckets of seawater being hauled over the railing through hissing clouds of blue-gray smoke, Lillia arrives at her berth and slams the door shut. Eager to strip off her clothes, she is aghast when her fingers detect the moisture of blood splattered on her blouse buttons. Unsure if it is Coopton's from her fatal stab or the captain's injuries when she hugged him, she quickly removes it and tosses it in the corner.

"Lillia, you must come out and see!"

Sebastian's words draw her up and she replies, "In a moment, Uncle, I'm dressing."

Hurrying now, she dresses and presents herself to the passengers amassed in their common room. Wellingham and the Browning sisters watch the crew's efforts to put out the flames at the windows while Sebastian and the Gibbs gather around Lillia, concern etched on their faces.

"How could you sleep through this ruckus?" Sebastian asks.

Lillia glances between him and Dr. Gibbs before saying, "I assure you, I was not asleep. Dr. Gibbs, at the earliest moment possible, the captain needs your immediate attention. There has been an attack."

All eyebrows rise at this information and the doctor leaves to fetch his bag. Sebastian gathers Lillia into a hug.

"Is there something you'd like to tell me, my dear?"

"I'll tell you so many things, Uncle, once the fire is out. For now, I must inform you that the captain, Rupert, and I were . . . he showed me how to climb to the top of the mast. It was during our descent when we noticed Coopton on the deck and had to formulate a plan for keeping him from burning the ship. I did what was necessary to save our lives."

"How did he get free?"

"He bragged that Dr. Gibbs had not been giving him a potent enough dose of laudanum, so he was able to steal a surgical implement from the doctor and use it to cut himself free."

Sebastian considers her words before his expression softens.

"You had to have been terrified. How did you . . . ?"

"You will learn soon enough. I'm more concerned about Rupert. He was beaten by Coopton."

"Where is he?"

Lillia feels her strength wain as she says, "He insisted that he help fight the fire, regardless of his injuries."

Dr. Gibbs arrives, saying, "Where do you think I can find him, Miss Soilleux?"

"He will fight the fire until it is out," Lillia replies, looking toward the windows and the activity outside. "It looks like the crew has it in hand. Perhaps you could seek him out."

"I'll go with you, Doctor," Sebastian says and starts toward the door, stopping when Lillia does not accompany him.

"Are you joining us?"

Lillia smarts at the question before replying, "No, I'll stay here. You can tell me later what you find."

Exhausted, Lillia returns to her berth to calm her mind. So much had happened in such a short time. Time alone with her thoughts would surely help sort it all out. How, in the space of a few hours, could she reconcile the emotions ranging from the high of hearing Rupert's feelings for her, to the panic of Coopton's efforts to sink them, to the overwhelming focus of burying the solognot's blade into Coopton's back? She killed a human, an act she never would have believed herself capable of doing. But he was trying to kill the man . . .

She considers the thoughts going through her mind. The man she loves? Had she truly decided after his admission and her actions that Rupert Eagleton is the man she loves? Admittedly, her feelings for Donovan had diminished to a faint memory, yet she still allowed herself an ever-so-thin tether to honor his promise. But tonight's events changed everything.

By dawn, the smoldering deck is all that is left of the night's near tragedy. When the sun rises, Lillia, dark circles under her eyes signaling a sleepless night, leaves her berth and chooses a chair in the passenger's quarters to linger for her uncle's report. She doesn't have to wait long.

Both Dr. Gibbs and Sebastian arrive at the same time, both wearing dubious expressions. They stop short when they see her sitting at the table. Wordlessly, they pull up facing chairs.

Dr. Gibbs says, "The captain is going to be fine. His facial wounds will heal without scars, but he's going to be sensitive for a while. That rogue must have surprised him to get such an advantage over him."

"I did not see how any of that happened. The smoke obscured my view."

Sebastian quietly places the solognot on the table between them and asks, "Perhaps you can help us understand how your solognot came to be wedged between Coopton's ribs?"

"I took it with me when Rupert and I climbed to the heights. As it turned out, I got to the ship's deck just as Coopton wrapped his arm around Rupert's neck. I stabbed him from behind. My first effort didn't have any effect, so I was forced to drive the blade further. It was then that he released his grip and fell back dead."

Sebastian and Dr. Gibbs exchange glances before Dr. Gibbs says, "Miss Soilleux, did you know ahead of time where to place your blade to have maximum lethal effect?"

Lillia looks at Sebastian before saying, "I suppose I might

have been given some advice on the topic. I have never executed the maneuver before, if that is what you are asking."

Dr. Gibbs raises his hands in mock defense before saying, "No, no, please don't misinterpret my question. It's just that if there was a perfect insertion point for your dagger's blade, that was it; a remarkable placement for a quick death."

"And, you have nothing to fear from anyone on this ship with regard to having killed the man. He was trying to do us all in, and you stopped him, *ma chérie*. You are a heroine," Sebastian adds with pride. "Although, I think I must have a conversation with the captain about his manner of courting my niece."

"Uncle, I asked him to show me the heights months ago. He resisted, telling me I wasn't capable. But, with the doldrums and since our relationship has grown, he offered, and I took him up on it."

"Is that all?"

"I believe you will be very pleased to learn that our conversation was everything you've been hoping for and probably more than you can imagine."

Sebastian looks tenderly at her for a moment before reaching out and clasping her hands in his, satisfied chuckles coming from deep in his throat.

Later that afternoon, Lillia asks Sebastian to inquire about a visit to the captain's quarters to check on him. While worried about his injuries, Dr. Gibbs's reassurances calm her fears, but there were other things they needed to discuss about the previous night's events.

Sebastian leads her into the captain's berth where the stagnant air smells of sweat and rank body odor. She sees him lying in bed, his face bruised and swollen, and his ribs wrapped in bandages.

"Rupert, can I get you anything?" Lillia asks.

"Water. Perhaps with some ice in it?" he responds.

She hurries to act on his request, leaving Sebastian to sit with him while she is gone.

When she returns, Sebastian is chuckling as Rupert says, "Do not make me laugh. It hurts too much."

Arriving at his side with the ice and water, Lillia seats herself on a trunk and quietly observes him until Sebastian says, "I suppose you two need some time to discuss things. I'll leave you to it, then."

"Thank you, Uncle. I will take care of him."

Lillia's assurance brings a faint smile to Rupert's cracked lip, and he winces before saying, "I understand from Sebastian and Dr. Gibbs that I owe you my life. I was just informed you are not one to underestimate. I never could have imagined this outcome."

"Nor I. But when I saw him gain the advantage over you, I had no choice but to use the only two weapons I had. Surprise and my solognot. I had no hesitation."

To this, Rupert reaches his hand to hers and squeezes it, saying, "I meant every word of what I said last night in the heights. I can only hope you do not see me as less of a man for falling victim to Coopton's beating."

"Certainly not. But I am curious. What happened when you engaged him?"

"He was so intent on setting the fires, I thought I had him. But when I tried to restrain him, he surprised me with a quick flurry of punches that knocked me off balance. From there, it was a brawl between us. I was losing. My last effort was when I think you spied us, my lunge was futile, he jumped on my back, and he started strangling me."

"I know the rest."

Quiet settles between them until Rupert rises to take a sip of the ice water and says, "What has become of his body?"

"I have left it all to Dr. Gibbs and Nathanial. If it were me, I would toss his corpse over the railing like filthy trash. But I suppose there will be some kind of minimal service."

"Whatever is to be done, let it be with haste," Rupert says firmly.

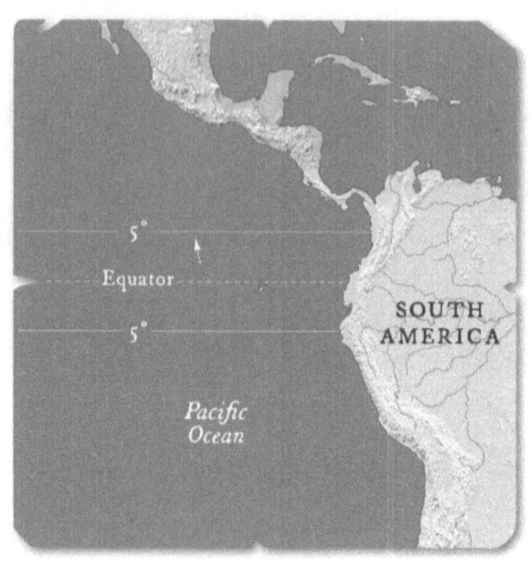

Chapter 11

SEPTEMBER, 1849

PACIFIC DOLDRUMS

Looking across the doldrums' stilled waters, Lillia greets each morning since Coopton's demise at the bow filled with a mixture of relief and melancholy. She wants so badly to remind herself of what Rupert had told her while they shared the heights, but the sight of Coopton's sailcloth-wrapped corpse slipping into the dark waters at dusk a week ago keeps intruding.

She remembers Rupert saying through his swollen lips, "Under normal circumstances, a burial at sea calls for the captain to say words of condolence. I find that quite impossible in this case."

Dr. Gibbs had stepped forward and offered, "This mortal being is better off in the hereafter than he ever was in our realm. May his troubled soul find peace."

She admits to feeling a swell of relief when the knotted line was released and the splash confirmed he was gone forever. Now, though, she wants to find Rupert and have him wrap his arms around her to fight off the images of Coopton that keep haunting her. When she hears footsteps approaching, she turns with an eager expression for Rupert's arrival only to have it be Wellingham.

"Excuse me for interrupting your contemplations," he says.

"Not to worry, Howard. I'm trying to erase the ugly memories of Coopton."

"I've been working on the same and have decided I need a project. Alas, my hands are so mangled from the fistfight that my project is in need of assistance. Would you be available to help me write the condolence letters to the family members of the young men on the *Night Call*?

I've made a feeble attempt at a draft, but I want my words to convey the proper sensitivity given the letter's tragic news. Would you consider the project?"

Lillia smiles compassionately at his humble request and says, "I'd be happy to read your draft and help write the letters. Shall we set up our operation in the passenger's quarters?"

"I'll fetch the list and supplies and meet you there."

At the common table in the passenger's quarters, Wellingham hands Lillia his draft letter while laying out a sheaf of paper, an inkwell, and a quill pen.

"It's such a sensitive matter, a death notice."

Lillia reviews the letter quickly and says, "Your words are perfect, Howard. Not too abrupt but a thoughtful conveyance of the facts. We have seven of these to write, correct?"

"Yes, I've got the list of names from both teams right here."

He reaches into the trunk and pulls out a scroll of paper, pressing it open on the table.

"The Yale team's names, those on the *Night Call*, are on this side and the Boston team's are on the reverse."

Reaching for a piece of paper, Lillia prepares the pen by dipping it in the inkwell.

"Who is our first family?"

"The Shoon family; son's name is Oliver."

The process of writing is tedious, and after the third letter, Wellingham offers to fetch a pot of tea while Lillia rests her hand. Grateful, she sits back in the chair until curiosity gets the best of her. She reaches for the scroll. Observing the remaining names of the Yale team, she casually turns the scroll over and glances through the Bostonians' names. When her gaze falls on the last name listed, she realizes the truth lying before her.

Donovan, alias Dash Truepenny, is on the overland team.

Lillia becomes aware of others entering the passengers' quarters and lifts her head from the tabletop. Wellingham is chattering to Sebastian. Concerned expressions loom large in her vision.

"I found her here, head on the table as if asleep, but when I nudged her, she didn't rouse. That's when I came for you."

"Lillia, what happened here?"

Wellingham offers her a cup of water as both men sit down.

"I . . ."

"Take a moment."

Lillia takes Sebastian's advice and drinks from the cup. When she sets it down, she takes a deep breath and looks directly at both men.

"Actually, Howard, I'd like to speak to my uncle privately. It's kind of you to get me water."

Wellingham bobs his head toward her and leaves. Sebastian watches him go before turning back to Lillia.

"What's all this about?"

"After my question to you last night, I knew I would have to be forthcoming. I just didn't know it would be this soon."

"All right then, take all the time you need."

Lillia takes the scroll from the pile of papers and places it between them. She unrolls it to show the list of names making up the overland team originating in Boston. Her finger points down the list at the last name. Sebastian looks and then turns his face up to hers.

"Who is Dash Truepenny?"

Lillia feels the full weight of her circumstances come to bear.

"It is the nickname I had for Donovan."

Sebastian's gaze lurches from the scroll to Lillia and back. She sees the soft skin of his neck flush, the blotches of red rushing to his graying hairline.

"This is dated April 19, a week before your intended nuptials."

"Yes, Uncle."

"Did you know of this race?"

His question causes the cold sweat of confession to break on her forehead, her head tingling with nervous torture.

"I didn't know of this exact endeavor. He had written me a note—in code—saying he had betrayed his father and had to flee Boston. He begged me to find my way to San Francisco. I was hoping we could start our life together free of his family's treachery."

"And you told no one of this note?"

"No one. I couldn't decide on the right course. If I'd told Donovan's father, he would have hunted him down. And he is not a man I trust to be rational. If I had told my parents, they would have rejected him as a son-in-law. But, more than either of those, I was angry at him for abandoning me to languish in our present society. After our marriage, we were going to leave Somerville and start a new life together, perhaps in Boston, perhaps elsewhere. I was just as desperate to leave that suffocating society as he and yet, he didn't even offer to take me with him. I used your business venture as a way to find him. But then I met Rupert."

Sebastian quietly absorbs her explanation.

"What do you feel for Donovan now?"

"After all that has happened on this trip, I've come to realize my relationship with Donovan was sweet but borne out of a mutual need to free ourselves from restrictions. His was his family, mine was my ill fit into society. My parents did what they could, but I was never going to adapt. Rupert respects and honors my differences. After our time at the heights, I believe he has won my heart."

Sebastian hunches over the table, his head hanging low. After several deep breaths, he tilts his head up, the symmetrical folds of his forehead creases preceding his question.

"I assume Captain Eagleton is ignorant of this as well?"

"When we were at the top of the mainmast, I told him most of it—about my courtship with Donovan and deceiving my parents. And you. But this information about Donovan being in this race is new to all of us."

Sebastian leans back in his chair and folds his arms across his round belly. The soggy air thrums with the silence between them until he says, "You can't live your life without wondering of Donovan's fate."

Lillia sighs before asking, "Have you ever had an intention only to learn it wasn't as important as what you discovered along the way?"

Sebastian answers, "There've been times when I've pursued an interest only to have the original passion change along the way. Most times the change was for the better. But I would be a hypocrite to be upset that you did not tell me of your initial intentions. Lord knows I've not always been forthcoming in my personal pursuits. It's your parents who worry me. You are their sun. They have only the highest regard for you, no matter how difficult it has been for you to conform to society. I'm not sure how they will react when they know of your deceit."

Lillia's eyes well at his use of the word "deceit," but she quickly acknowledges the word's accuracy.

Sebastian asks, "We know of the *Night Call*'s fate, but what if no one survives the overland trip?"

Lillia answers, "I've read the race's rules. Howard has to advertise for two years before he takes control of the assets."

A soft rap on the passenger's quarters' exterior door sounds ahead of Captain Eagleton's baritone voice, "Lillia, are you well? Wellingham just informed me. May I?"

Lillia exchanges looks with Sebastian before he rises and opens the door, saying,

"I'll leave you with the captain. Before I go, you need to know I am here to support and advise you in your decisions. Life is full of twists and turns. Navigation isn't without missteps, *ma chérie*."

When Rupert replaces Sebastian in the small space, he quickly seats himself across the table from her. The bruises and gashes on his face make her want to find a cloth to tend to them but she decides, instead, to keep still.

After a moment, Rupert asks, "Why does Sebastian look so grim?"

"I just told him what I told you in the heights. He has assured me he isn't angry, but he is concerned for my relationship with my parents when they learn my true motivation for sailing to California. I've also just learned Donovan is participating on the overland team in Howard's wagered race."

"Give him time to consider all the information you have just shared with him. He will come around, especially when he knows our feelings for each other. That is, if the feelings I have confessed to you are mutual. Quite a lot has happened since our time at the heights. With this news, I need to know if I should retreat from you since your fiancé is expected in California," Rupert says, his voice dropping to a ragged whisper.

Lillia looks into his blackened eyes and sees them welling with sincerity. For a man of such dignity and stature to be so vulnerable makes her heart melt with pure affection for him.

"I'm overwhelmed with feelings right now. So much has happened. If I could have a little while to consider everything, I would be in your debt."

Rupert smiles gingerly, careful not to stretch his cracked lip, and says, "We have all the time in the world."

Later, Lillia and Wellingham reconvene their letter-writing efforts. Before they can start, Lillia explains to him what all the excitement had been about. He contemplates a while before replying, "I can't believe the overland team has had it any easier that the ill-fated seagoing team."

"Are you saying you think they will all die too?"

"It's just that, well, when I met them in New York City, they seemed rather ill-prepared for the rigors of such an undertaking. Which one was Donovan?"

"He wears an eye patch."

A look of recognition washes across Wellingham's face before he says, "I remember him as one of the less enthusiastic Bostonians. And, if I'm not mistaken, he had two small children in tow. Filthy little mites. When I made a comment about the oddity of their presence, he said he was delivering them to their aunt in Baltimore."

Lillia struggles to hide her shocked expression as her mind runs wild with questions.

Children? What was he doing with children? Whose children?

Before she can say anything more, she hears Nathanial calls out, "Captain! Come quick. The winds have returned!"

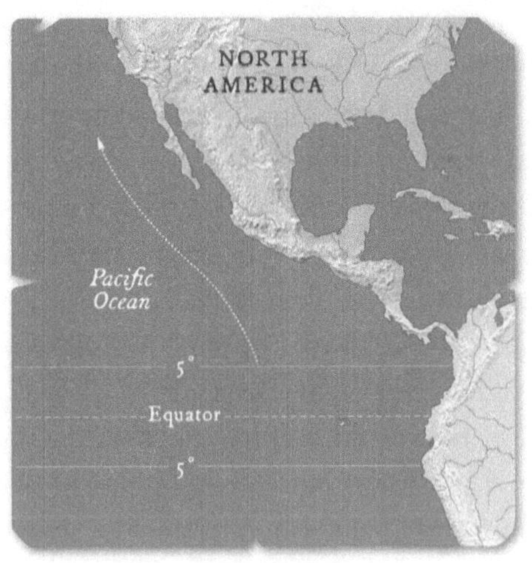

Chapter 12

OCTOBER, 1849

PACIFIC OCEAN

Over the next two weeks, the passengers and crew experience a renewed energy spawned by the ship's progress. With each rise and fall of her bow, the *Ornery Agnes* speeds them toward their respective destinies. Their next stop is California.

From the ship's bow, Lillia stands and lets the cool salt mist remove the anxieties of her past. Every rise and fall of the bow forces her to confront her future with Donovan or Rupert. She owes Rupert an answer, and his occupation with sailing the ship has proven beneficial for her to consider her feelings.

Sebastian has asked for a business meeting, but before she goes, she has decided it is time to give Rupert the news she knows he has been waiting for. Nathanial is at the helm, which means Rupert is still in his quarters. As she approaches, she hears familiar voices in discussion.

"She'll never stand for it, Captain. I implore you to reconsider. Let her participate in the decision."

"But she can't know everything, Sebastian. Where's the fun in that?"

"I'm simply saying I know my niece. She won't take it well, no matter what shine you put on it."

Her curiosity now piqued, she reveals herself with a sharp knock.

"Uncle, our meeting?"

Sounds of scuffling come from inside before Sebastian calls out, "A moment, please. Just straightening up."

The door swings open and Rupert scoops her up in his arms, crushing her against his chest and twirling her away from the open door, "Good morning, Lillia."

She laughs at his gaiety, a welcomed change from the weeks of painful recovery he had endured. The bruising and cuts have all healed, and he is back to his usual self which makes it even easier for her to tease, "Shouldn't we exercise discretion, Captain?"

Her sly smile gives away her true feelings, and he notices with a wink before whispering,

"Once we are ashore, you and I are . . ."

Sebastian interrupts from behind, saying, "Alright, Lillia, come in, come in. Captain, *s'il vous plaît*, unhand my niece."

Rupert drops his arms and steps aside, his full mustache obscuring his affectionate smile as she passes.

Before leaving, he says, "Far be it from me to get in the way of this ship's great business minds. I wish you both a productive session."

After the door closes, she settles herself into a tight corner of Sebastian's berth.

He says, "Given that we're going to be in California soon, we have some business decisions to make. I wonder if we shouldn't approach the Chilean fruit merchant with our canvas. The quicker we sell it, the sooner we can get on with our exploration for new opportunities. I'm eager to know what goods we can make the highest profit from and I'm wondering if getting inland would be better than staying in the city. What do you think?"

Lillia nods in agreement. The morning is spent discussing strategies for selling their canvas, acceptable terms, and whether to compete with established merchants or simply sell out and move on. When Rupert knocks, Lillia is shocked at how quickly time has passed.

"Barnabas has our meal ready. Shall we?"

They rise and join Rupert on the deck, all three enjoying the fresh air.

"Where are we exactly?" Sebastian asks.

"We passed the thirty-sixth parallel today. If the seas stay fair and the winds strong, we will arrive within ten days."

Lillia gasps and claps her hands, saying gleefully, "I dream of a bed that does not bisect my lower half from my upper."

Rupert leans in close and whispers, "Those aren't my dreams."

Lillia covers her mouth at his bold words to which Sebastian interjects, "Have you proper plans for how to achieve those dreams?"

Surprised at his eavesdropping, the pair stare back.

Then Rupert stammers, "I . . . I . . ."

"I didn't think so. As this young woman's guardian, I must insist you proceed in a reputable manner."

"I wouldn't consider any other way, sir."

Just then Nathanial calls out, "Ahead, sir! Whales breaching ahead!"

They had seen other ocean dwellers but had yet to see whales. The passengers rush to the railing and take great delight in the unexpected entertainment. The whales' breeching creates great splashes of Pacific water. Sebastian moves away from the couple for a better view and Lillia senses her opportunity.

"Rupert, since our last conversation, I've taken all things into account and have come to a conclusion."

"About your feelings for me?"

"Yes."

Lillia blushes and looks away. Taking her by the shoulders and with a deep-throated chuckle, he cups her chin and lifts her face to his.

"The suspense is almost unbearable. Please come out with it!"

"You, you make me . . . you have opened up a whole new world to me with new possibilities, and while we don't know exactly how it's going to work, I choose you to walk into the new world with, side by side."

Staring at her with love in his eyes, Rupert smiles widely before hugging her tightly and spinning her around several times.

Laughing by the last twirl, he says, "I want you to be my wife. I will devote myself to making you happy and fulfilled in all respects of our lives together."

As the whales continue to leap and frolic behind them, Lillia meets his lips with her own in a tender kiss, sealing the agreement.

After telling him their news, Sebastian conspires with Barnabas for a special treat for the celebration before retrieving a bottle of champagne from his trunk. He quickly invites Wellingham, the Gibbs, and the Browning sisters to join them in a spontaneous party on the bow deck.

With tin cups held high, he calls out, "*Salut*! To the happy couple, all blessings in your future! Your parents will be so pleased."

From high in the rigging, the crew break out in a series of songs, and a harmonica wails out a lively jig from above, which starts everyone dancing. Barnabas proudly produces small tea cakes with dried fruit topping and is cheered by all for his efforts. The last of the sun's rays disappear behind the vast ocean's horizon before the celebration dies down.

Sebastian takes Lillia's elbow and draws her aside, whispering, "I'm so happy for you. But you must write to your parents straight away when we arrive on shore. About your impending marriage, of course, but also about your transgressions leading up to it. You could probably leave out any reference to Coopton, but you could state your true intentions for undertaking this journey."

"Of course, Uncle. That was my plan too. I can't wait for Mother and Father to meet Rupert. I think they'll love him as much as I do."

"Love who?" Rupert asks, appearing at her side.

"You!" Lillia laughs.

"Exciting, isn't it?" Rupert says, wrapping an arm around her waist.

"Yes, exciting is a good word," agrees Sebastian. "But how is it all going to come together? Rupert, you had promised your mother you would find your brothers before returning home. Will you still go forth with that plan? Will you marry in California or wait until you return to Boston?"

"We should marry as soon as possible," Rupert says.

"In California," Lillia adds.

Their responses evoke a fresh round of laughter.

"Unlike Howard's clear directive to advertise his arrival, I haven't the faintest idea of where to begin looking for my brothers in the vastness of California."

After considering the captain's statement, Sebastian reflects, "It's a big task given winter's arrival in a few months."

"Sebastian, you met my mother. I cannot return home without the repayment for the family loans in my pocket. And I must retrieve the government voucher before the government forgets what they owe me."

"If you are going to spend the winter looking for your brothers, should we plan on finding accommodations on land?"

Rupert rubs his chin before replying to Sebastian's question. "If we can maintain a presence on the ship, that will go a long way to warding off anyone who might conspire to seize her. I'll approach Howard with the idea."

"What of him? He could be waiting for days, months, or even years."

"For the short term, an anchored ship is a better place to guard the wager trunk than on land. We could schedule our respective absences and spread the responsibility around. I don't think we should plan on spending the entire winter in California, Sebastian. We've got too much news to share with the families back home."

Sebastian nods and drips the last bit of champagne into each of their cups.

"Here's to sharing the good news. Now, I'm off to bed. Sleep well, Lillia, Captain."

He busses her cheeks and leaves them. They walk out to the fresh air and starlit night. At the railing, Rupert takes Lillia's hands and pulls her close.

"You know, aboard a ship anchored in a beautiful bay makes for a very romantic setting for a wedding."

Lillia considers his words before saying, "Indeed, it does, but I have my heart set on a comfortable bed that doesn't threaten to tear me limb from limb."

"Trust me, after we are married, you will have a proper resting place, although I'm not sure how much rest you'll get in it."

"I should wonder if you'll not be the one in need of rest."

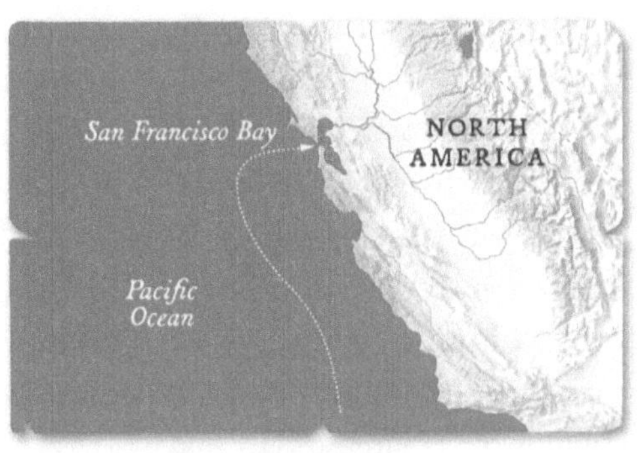

Chapter 13

OCTOBER, 1849

SAN FRANCISCO BAY, CALIFORNIA

Within a week, Captain Eagleton and the crew busy themselves with preparations for their imminent arrival in San Francisco. The California coastline has come into sight off the *Ornery Agnes*'s starboard side.

As has become her habit, Lillia joins Rupert at the helm as the sun sets, shivering against the evening chill. Her shiver gives him a good excuse to pull her close. The two gaze at the distant mountains, the golden twilight reflecting brilliantly.

Rupert comments, "Such mysterious country, even from here. It's easy to understand the world's love affair with California. I'm eager to explore it, but I have to confess, I don't want to make the trip without you. Are you willing?"

"Willing? I'd have it no other way. But what of the crew and Uncle Sebastian? Will they wait for us?"

"Sebastian can entertain himself while we're gone, but I'll need to devise an irresistible incentive for the crew to return."

"Perhaps there will also be individuals who have not had the luck they expected and will be willing to sail back to Boston."

"It may take a little of both ideas to make a crew. You're right. In a year's time, gold fever will have gone bust for some."

The rain begins overnight, and by dawn, low clouds obscured any progress toward San Francisco Bay. Choosing to wait for clearer conditions, Rupert gathers the crew in the galley. The men seat themselves in an arc facing him while Lillia observes from the corner.

"I'll not mince words. Other than Charles's men who are contractually bound to do so, who is intent on scurrying off to the goldfields?"

Lillia joins his scan of the crew's faces. Remarkably, none admit to wanting to leave, which frustrates Rupert.

"Alright, then, I've a proposition for you. I must find my brothers somewhere in those distant hills. I suspect such an enormous task will take six weeks, at the least. If you want to use the same amount of time to try your luck and return in time to sail, I'll offer you solid employment for another go around Cape Horn."

Lillia watches the crew bow their heads averting their eyes from Rupert but giving each other side glances. Their elongated pause thickens the air until one speaks up.

"Captain, do you think six weeks will satisfy our curiosity?"

"It'll give you a chance to test the truth of the easy-wealth stories."

Lillia observes each crew member nodding and speaking as one.

"Aye to your proposition!"

"Alright, then, we'll bring our ship around when this soupy

fog lifts. Until then, stay warm and dry, best you can. When we make our attempt, we'll need to post watches at the railing to keep off the rocks."

After the crew leave the galley, Rupert stays seated for a long moment, and Lillia is puzzled by his mood.

"Rupert, is everything alright? Isn't the crew's response what you had hoped for?"

"I wish I felt more confident. I guess I will feel better two months from now, when I have my brothers by my side, my wife in my arms, and my crew safely aboard my ship sailing for Cape Horn."

Later, Lillia joins Rupert at the helm and finds Dr. Gibbs, Miriam, Wellingham, and Sebastian at the railing, their coats pulled tight against the drizzle, all eager for their first glimpse of San Francisco Bay. Rupert's crew are posted at lookouts above and around the railing, but Lillia can tell he is in a foul mood.

As she approaches, he mutters, "Damn, I'd hoped for better. It'd be a shame to run into the rocks at this point."

Even though there is thick fog, the coastal waters echo with the sound of shanties being sung. Lillia's ears perk at the lyrics, and she listens intently. When a ship flying the Australian flag passes them, their shanty loudly proclaims their anticipation of women ashore. Lillia shoots a look at Rupert who shrugs his shoulders.

He says, "Women, and fantasies about them, are all-consuming to most sailors. That's just the way it is."

"And you?"

"Hardly. I just have better restraint. That's why Coopton's behavior was so appalling. When ashore, you and the sisters must be on guard at all times. Assure me when you aren't aboard this ship, you'll continue to wear Sebastian's gift."

They are interrupted when the crew sights navigational buoys on the ship's starboard. Suddenly, a flurry of distant voices call from the fog, all originating from the north and west.

"This won't do. We'll wait for better conditions to sail into the bay. Ready about!"

Rupert shouts instructions to alter their course while turning the rudder away from the shoreline. Just as the *Ornery Agnes* begins to respond, a ghostly ship's image slices only yards from their bow.

From his watch, Nathanial calls out, "Outta the way, idiot!"

With no way to alter their trajectory, Lillia braces for impact, her eyes squeezed shut. Nothing happens. She looks up in time to see the ship's passing stern missing the *Ornery Agnes* by a hair's breadth. Glancing back at Rupert, she sees he has turned stone-faced.

Shaken by the near miss and chilled to the bone, Lillia returns to the safety of her berth. The clanking of the ship's anchor chain wakes her from a nap, and she dresses quickly. Emerging from her berth, she stares at the sight before her. San Francisco Bay is filled to capacity with ships of all sizes, their masts dancing in the late afternoon sun's glow. The eastern hillsides surrounding the bay are green with trees mingling between massive stone outcroppings. To the west, row and rows of temporary buildings dance with life like an ant's mound.

Walking to the helm, she overhears Rupert talking to Nathanial, his tone oddly grim and very unfamiliar.

"When we go ashore, I want you to find the captain of the *Fleeting Star*. Do not confront him. Just find where he is lodging and report back to me. I'll take it from there."

"Yes, Captain."

After their supper onboard, Rupert addresses the crew and passengers with seasoned authority, "Some advice to those going ashore: first, be cautious of fast talkers. You are easy marks because they can see you coming. Second, in most parts of our world, women are outnumbered ten to one. California is different. White women are outnumbered a thousand to one, perhaps even more since my last visit."

Lillia watches as Hope and Sarah's expressions tighten with trepidation.

"Finally, the *Ornery Agnes* will sail back to Boston in six weeks. Use the time to decide if California is all she's been hailed to be. If she's not, I expect to see you for our return trip. Any questions?"

No one says a word until Dr. Gibbs raises his hand and asks, "When are you and Miss Soilleux going to tie the knot?"

"As soon as we find a church. Who'll be going ashore with me in the morning? I can take six in the launch."

As several rise to discuss the morning's plan, Lillia seeks out Sarah and Hope.

Sarah, sounding despondent, says, "The captain paints a frightening picture. We've no money for return passage."

"Whatever made us believe this was a good idea?" Hope asks.

Lillia takes both of their hands in hers before saying, "This trip was a response to the restrictions we faced at home—yours and mine. When the opportunity for freedom came, we took it. Freedom takes courage. We need to keep that courage as we step off the ship."

"But the captain makes it sound like we're lambs going to slaughter."

"We'll be on our guard. We survived Coopton didn't we?"

"That we did," says Sarah, beginning to smile a bit.

Lillia sees Rupert, Wellingham, and Sebastian approaching. She says, "You're strong and courageous. Just stay aboard until we know more. You needn't join the first boat to shore."

Both young women nod and step away as the men replace themselves in front of her, apparently having important business to discuss. Their heads are down in deep conversation.

Rupert asks Wellingham, "Howard, getting to shore is a priority for you, isn't it?"

"It is, but only to place an ad and then return to the ship. I'm quite certain the trunk is safer here than ashore."

Captain Eagleton nods, turns to Lillia and asks, "How are the Browning sisters?"

"Your speech unnerved them. They are using phrases like 'lambs going to slaughter.'"

"Good."

"Hardly! They are too scared to leave the ship!" Lillia replies, aghast.

"Scared is good. It will make them watchful and diligent, and that makes for sound decisions."

Sebastian adds, "A scared woman is vulnerable to superficial kindness. I've seen such situations go awry, leaving women in servitude and lifelong slavery."

"Slavery! Really now!" Lillia says.

"Just be careful, that's all I'm saying," says Rupert with a twinkle in his eye.

Clearly, he thinks women should feel dependent on men. Lillia, however, wonders if feeling confidence will suit the women better. It will make them less approachable and not so susceptible to false friends.

Sebastian tells his niece, "I'm joining Rupert to find the Chilean merchant, among other small errands. I'd advise you to keep your head low and stay aboard."

Lillia's brows furrow at Sebastian's statement.

"I'll remain with the sisters, for now. They will need to find a plan for their survival here, as they cannot afford the return passage, at the moment. Do me the favor of keeping your eyes open for any opportunities, no matter how menial."

"Certainly, although we already have quite a list of errands to accomplish in a foreign city."

"Of course," Lillia says.

But she sees Rupert and Sebastian exchange conspiratorial looks, and wonders what errands the two men have cooked up, thinking they have plans for going beyond just visiting the Chilean merchant.

As the men board the launch and move away through the morning's thick fog, the Browning sisters come up behind Lillia.

"Did the captain leave already?" Hope asks.

"Yes, but he will return this afternoon with a report and Barnabas's pantry list fulfilled. With our privacy, I'm hoping this fog lifts in time to do some washing, don't you?"

"Perhaps we can combine our labor?"

Lillia smiles, "Agreed. I'll ask Barnabas to heat some water."

Between her quick visit to request heated water and her arrival at her berth, Lillia is surprised to see the sisters' impressive pile of accumulated laundry amassed on the deck. Eagerly, she disassembles her cot of its petticoats and other garments used for bedding since Coopton's theft. She adds some of her daily garments and wonders if she might freshen something from her trunk to wear when Rupert returns. Slowly, she raises her wedding trunk's lid.

She finds Sebastian's lavish wedding gifts and smiles at the memory of Phoebe's reaction to their extravagance. Then her hand brushes against the crinkly paper-wrapped gift her mother had hastily given to her the night before she received Donovan's coded note.

She recalls the soft knock at her bedroom door and opening it to see Phoebe standing there, holding this package in both hands. She had quickly handed it to Lillia without explanation.

"Mother?" Lillia had asked.

"May yours be a joyous union," Phoebe had said before rushing away without another word or look at her daughter.

Without opening it, Lillia had slipped the package into her trunk, choosing to wait until the wedding that hadn't happened to open it. Now, Lillia fumbles with the knotted cord holding the paper around something light and flimsy. When the knot loosens, Lillia feels her curiosity pique.

With delicate care, she unfolds the thin tissue. Her fingers brush against a mass of soft knots and she immediately identifies them as fine silk. She finds thin straps and runs her fingers through them, allowing the bundle to unfurl. In a gravity-induced cloud of gossamer, she recognizes and marvels at Phoebe's handiwork. A wonder with intricate lace patterns, Lillia remembers how Phoebe's minute crochet hook would whirl away in the lantern's dim light until she finished her project.

"Miss Soilleux, Barnabas says the water is hot. Shall we commence with our washing?" Sarah asks from outside the door.

The intimate nightgown had already made Lillia blush, but when Sarah's question interrupts her thoughts, she guiltily gathers up the fine threads and stashes the garment back into to the trunk saying quickly, "Yes, Sarah. I'll be there in a moment."

Working the laundry up and down on a washboard, Lillia begins to tire, but she consoles herself with the thought of how nice it will be to have clean garments again.

Their work is lightened by reminiscences of their past lives—perhaps to distract all three from their shared reality of not knowing what their futures hold in this new land. Hope and Sarah tell innumerable stories from their family farm which, before long, have the women laughing so hard they can barely continue their work.

"And then," Hope laughs loudly, and says, "the rooster chased Sarah right into the house! Ma was beside herself to get it out but it wouldn't go until Sarah let it chase her outside again. I've never heard Ma scream so loud!"

"And he was chicken soup the next day!" Sarah exclaimed.

Lillia, gasping for breath at Hope's tale of chaos, says, "My family didn't have any pets, let alone farm animals. Living in the city doesn't allow for livestock except the horses Father used to pull our wagons. But they were his concern."

"Did you learn how to ride a horse?" Sarah asks.

"No. I had no need to learn. I suppose I'm going to have to learn quickly, since I'm accompanying the captain to look for his brothers after we are wed. I did learn Morse code."

The look of puzzlement on the sisters' faces lets Lillia know they are unfamiliar with the words, and she laughs before saying, "It's a way of communicating over the telegraph wire. Dots and dashes are assigned to each letter of the alphabet. If you string them all together, first words and then sentences can be sent long distances in a matter of minutes instead of days."

As the sisters ponder the meaning of what she has shared, Lillia remembers Donovan's exasperation about how easily the code came to her. She never considered it as being a skill she could use herself, only a way for him to escape his father's control. Now, perhaps, Morse code is something she can use in California.

"I wonder . . ." Hope begins.

"Yes?" asks Lillia.

"Do you think while you and the captain search for his brothers we could use the ship's deck as a laundry? We might take in laundry from other sailing ships, begin to earn some money toward our passage back to Boston."

"We'd be safe enough," Sarah adds. "If only we could catch all of this fog and rainwater. We found a way back home and stored it in barrels. I see plenty of unused barrels on those abandoned ships there."

Sarah points Lillia to several ships sinking in the bay where barrels litter the decks, saying, "We'll just need to convince someone to fetch them for us."

"How will you catch the rain without a roof to shed it?"

"Perhaps we can purchase the captain's used sailcloth. We'll make great funnels to catch the water and drain it into the barrels," answers Sarah.

Hope interrupts her sister, "How can we purchase anything, Sarah? We have no money."

Lillia interjects, "How about if I purchase the sailcloth and we'll be partners until you accumulate enough to pay me back?"

The sisters exchange looks before nodding in unison. With renewed enthusiasm, the women finish their washing. By the time the sun burns through the morning clouds, petticoats and garments hang from the ship's shrouds.

The men return just as the sun drops behind the city's western hills. Rupert pours out rum for everyone to fend against the chilly wind coming off the water. Lillia looks at Sarah and Hope, their combined enthusiasm about to burst.

"So, now tell us about what you found in the city," Lillia says.

Rupert shakes his head as he replies, "I never would have imagined such things as what greeted us today."

Sebastian cuts in, "What an expensive city. It's nearly robbery! A decent bed and a bath for one night is half a year's wages for a working man. But, to our advantage, the whole city—every business and institution—is made of rough wood and canvas. The saloon features two logs cut to height with a plank across where men exchange a pinch of gold dust for a bottle of watered-down whiskey under a sheet of canvas."

He leans toward Lillia, and says, "Henri won't believe the opportunities. There are even more inland."

"What's more," Rupert adds, "the prices for even the most mundane services like hauling freight, sweeping the city board-walks, and even laundry, are all exorbitantly high. Someone willing to do the most menial of jobs could become rich here."

Lillia casts a quick glance toward Hope and Sarah to see them sharing the same astonished expression.

Rupert comes to Lillia's side as Sebastian yawns and says, "I will rest well knowing my accommodations onboard, cramped as they may be, are far better than those on shore."

Lillia turns to Rupert, searching for confirmation through her pending disappointment.

He shrugs apologetically, and says, "It's true. I could no more take you ashore for our wedding night than sail to the moon. The place is filthy with mud and debris. Clearly, the country's civilities have yet to take root."

Before Lillia can brood too long, he grips her by the waist and sweeps her into the air.

"But I did find a preacher who has agreed to come to the ship to perform our wedding service. Honestly, it was his idea. He believes the spectacle of a wedding might incite a riot."

Lillia smiles widely at the idea.

Before she can say anything more, Rupert asks, "How did you pass your time without me today?"

"Funny you should ask. Hope, Sarah, and I took the time we had to ourselves to do our laundry. We were wondering how the men of San Francisco accomplished getting their clothes cleaned, and your observations provided insight. What do you think of a laundry located onboard this ship while we look for your brothers?"

Rupert is quiet for a moment before saying, "The idea has merit."

"They can stay onboard for their safety, do the washing here, and have it rowed to shore. All they need is someone reliable to do the rowing and collect the fees."

Rupert eyes her carefully before asking, "Where will they find fresh water?"

"I've agreed to help them buy your old sailcloth to create a water catch system using old barrels off these ships sinking around us."

Rupert nods his head while considering the idea.

"I believe that can be arranged. But I have a very important question for you."

Lillia stares into his face with concern.

"Yes?"

"Can you be ready to wed in two days?"

Two days later, Lillia and Sebastian lean against the bow railing enjoying the pleasant temperature while they wait for Rupert, Wellingham, and Nathanial to return from the city. Today's trip was the fruit delivery, depositing Dr. and Mrs. Gibbs onto dry land and Wellingham's placement of his first claim notification.

"I tell you, Lillia, reptilian qualities run in the customs agent's family. When we stopped to ask directions, we were warned that the brother doesn't pay his debts. It was very fortuitous to demand payment for the majority of the fruit's value before we left Valparaíso."

Nodding, Lillia says, "Rupert told me he got a similar feeling when the merchant pressed him about delivery. I'm so eager to learn what happened during today's trip."

"Perhaps it would be well worth our time to find another merchant to deal with our canvas."

"What if we left the canvas in the hold while Rupert and I explore the countryside for his brothers? By waiting, the price may go up."

"Lillia, the price is already five times what we paid for it."

Hesitating for a moment, she says, "If you find a suitable individual to sell it to, I trust your judgment."

"When are you and the captain setting out on this expedition of yours?"

"Immediately after the wedding, or so I'm told. He asked me to be ready to wed two days ago, but he has yet to provide further details."

"He's just as eager as you, but he has obligations to satisfy."

At that moment, they see the launch navigating through the bay's thicket of anchored ships, Rupert pulling hard on the launch's oars, Wellingham his only passenger. Lillia rushes to throw down the boarding ladder and hears Rupert shout, "Ahoy, *Ornery Agnes*, your captain returns with good news!"

"I sold half the fruit right out of the containers. When I handed the merchant the proceeds, he made it clear he suspected I'd filched him."

Sebastian leans close to Lillia and whispers, "I told you, a real viper."

Rupert turns to the Browning sisters.

"As for your business idea, name your price. Laundry is being sent as far away as the Sandwich Islands, and they're getting a dollar a shirt. Half the price, and you'll not sleep for the work."

Sarah whispers to Hope, "To think we got paid nothing for doing shirts at home."

"The preacher will be rowed to our ship at sunset tomorrow. Sebastian and Nathanial, it's time for you to find new accommodations. I require the entire officer's quarters for my new bride's comfort."

Lillia blushes at his bold public announcement.

"Barnabas, a modest feast is in order, but I'll warn you that food here is exorbitant. Choose wisely, so as not to bankrupt me. The launch will go ashore in the morning with your list."

Smiling, Barnabas nods his head before turning to wink at Lillia as Rupert continues,

"Finally, Nathanial, I'll need your assistance in my quarters as soon as Sebastian is relocated."

Lillia watches as all nod obediently. Overwhelmed, she excuses herself and returns to her berth. The Browning sisters catch up with her before she gets there.

"May we help with your bridal preparations?"

"Why, that would be wonderful. My best dress has been in my trunk for the whole trip, and it has so many wrinkles."

"We'll take it to our berth and set to work on it, if you're willing to trust us with it."

Lillia accepts their offer, and the three women continue to her berth. Lifting the trunk's lid, she unloads a few things until she finds the burgundy taffeta dress she had planned to wear when she married Donovan. She hands the folded and creased bundle to the sisters. Without unfolding it, they spirit it away leaving Lillia sorting through her trunk's contents.

Suddenly, Lillia hears a trunk scraping across the ship's deck and Sebastian saying, "Nathanial, ease the trunk into the corner if you can. Thank you for your help, young man."

"Sebastian, may I ask your advice?"

When she hears Wellingham ask for Sebastian's time, Lillia has no choice but to listen, the passenger's common room inches from her berth door.

"Certainly, Howard. Let's sit. The rush to vacate my living quarters has left me winded."

"I'm wondering about the creation of posting bills for the race winners' ease in finding me. Perhaps Rupert would take some with him when he searches for his brothers."

Only if you want every rat and cockroach in California knocking at your door.

"Howard, I have thoughts about this. Given the circumstances of the *Night Call*, I'd be cautious of spending money on the chance the overland team befalls the same fate."

Unexpectedly, Sebastian's truthful statement and its reality about Donovan's existence make Lillia sit bolt upright.

"And, correct me if I'm wrong, but isn't it in your best interests to do the bare minimum to fulfill this courier job? Furthermore, posting bills will have every easy-money rogue rushing to say they are the winner. Do you really want to have to wade through a mob?"

Lillia nods quietly at Sebastian's sound advice. But, on the eve of her wedding to Rupert, it's her concern for Donovan's survival that fills her mind. After several attempts to reconcile her feelings, the finality of her decision becomes clear.

Donovan left me behind and took on an uncertain fate. What did he expect me to do? When he disappeared, he gave up his claim to me. Rupert has my heart now. Our love has its foundation in mutual admiration and an exciting future. My life with Donovan would have centered around saving him from a life of soul-crushing tedium and abuse. I choose Rupert.

Chapter 14

OCTOBER, 1849

SAN FRANCISCO BAY, CALIFORNIA

Sarah's nimble fingers wind and tuck at Lillia's dark ring-leted hair using ivory combs to elegantly secure the coiffure up and to one side. She then dabs lavender oil behind Lillia's ears and down her spine to her waist. While she tightens the corset, Hope gently fits Sebastian's Venetian beads around Lillia's neck.

The wedding dress, now impeccably pressed, hangs on its peg behind the closed door, its deep burgundy taffeta glowing in the late afternoon sunlight. Helping Lillia step into it, the sisters fasten the bodice's buttons and secure the skirt before holding a small, round mirror up to Lillia. She gasps at the sight of herself.

Her tanned cheeks have lost their fullness, the high cheekbones now accentuating her dark brown eyes. The dress fits her with a little room to spare given their austere life on the ship.

Lillia smiles and says, "Oh, Sarah, I never imagined . . ."

Sarah returns the smile and says, "I'll fetch your uncle. He will, no doubt, want to see you."

Moments later, Sebastian arrives with a small nosegay of white flowers and green ivy.

"Oh, *ma chérie*, you're a jewel, a rare and precious jewel. You're not the same woman who left home five months ago. No, you're a transformed beauty."

"Thank you, Uncle. I think life at sea suits me. I feel stronger and more myself than I have ever felt in my life."

"I agree. I have seen you blossom during this trip," he replies warmly.

"Have you any advice?" Lillia whispers.

"Be patient. You have his respect. Now give him strength with your heart."

Lillia accepts his hug before taking his arm, stepping out of the passenger's quarters into the early evening light. Her breath catches when she sees many candles arranged on the ship's railing and around the deck. She looks closely at the stranger among them, a kind-faced man positioned in the center of the arc of men—the preacher.

Barnabas and Nathanial, each in his best shirt, flank the preacher behind Rupert. She feels her knees go weak at the sight of Rupert. He has transformed himself with a haircut and mustache trim since she saw him last. A string tie delicately adorns the collar of his white shirt, and he is breathtakingly handsome in a dapper satin vest. Briefly, she worries whether he will be as astonished with her presentation as she is with his, but once she reads his expression, she has her answer.

The preacher's gentle eyes crease into his smile when Lillia and Sebastian enter the gathering's arc. Facing him, Lillia maintains her grip on Sebastian's arm until the preacher clears his throat.

"Who gives this woman into this union?"

"On behalf of her father, I do."

The preacher nods and smiles his acceptance of the statement as Sebastian busses Lillia's cheeks and steps away, offering her arm to Rupert. The preacher speaks of the roles and duties of matrimony before asking if there's a ring to present. Lillia is shocked when Rupert produces a thin band of delicately carved ivory. Blessing it and placing it on her finger, the preacher finishes the ceremony by wishing them happiness and a fruitful life together.

"I now pronounce you husband and wife."

Rupert isn't shy about kissing her, long and hard in front of everyone gathered for this beautiful event. Lillia's emotions spin when she looks about the small arc of the ceremony's attendees and their smiles of approval and clapping.

Barnabas presents a modest but delicious repast while Sebastian unveils one final bottle of champagne from his trunk. Lillia is lighthearted with happiness. Before she knows it, Rupert is arranging for the preacher to be rowed back to shore. Everyone excuses themselves to their berths, leaving the newlyweds alone. She knows their private time has come, but as he takes her hand, she suddenly freezes.

"Oh, no. Oh, my. There is something . . . I must return to my berth, Rupert."

"You're not trying to escape, are you?"

"Rupert, we're on a ship. I'll not be throwing myself overboard."

"Alright then, but don't make me wait too long."

Lillia rushes to her berth and grabs up the gown with its soft knots and threads. Suddenly puzzled with how she's going to transport the item, she tucks it up her dress sleeve. At Rupert's door, she takes a deep breath before rapping softly. Instantly, the door swings open and Rupert scoops her up, twirls her around and steps inside.

Lillia is speechless at its transformation. Billows of white sailcloth have been artfully draped to cover the room's walls. A lantern glows in the room's center, safely away from the sailcloth, providing the only light. Rupert pauses at the lantern to put her down.

"I . . . I need to change," Lillia whispers.

"Indeed."

"No, you don't understand. There is something my mother made for me."

"Let me help you with your dress buttons and then, I promise, I'll turn away."

"Thank you."

Turning to give him access to the bodice's back buttons and hooks, Lillia feels his fingers fumbling with the small hooks. When he peels back the crisp taffeta to reveal her corset, there is a sudden assault of warm and tender kisses on her bare shoulders. Her knees weaken.

"Rupert?"

"I still have the laces to undo."

She feels him tug and loosen the corset laces. The fragrant lavender oil Sarah had placed so strategically wafts intoxicatingly between them. She feels him breathe heavily against the nape of her neck.

"This is a test, isn't it?"

"Rupert, I believe your patience will be rewarded."

"I'm a man of my honor, but hurry. My rogue side is winning the battle."

Rupert steps to the outer room, pulling a section of sailcloth behind him for her privacy. Lillia quickly pulls the gown from her sleeve and slips from the petticoats and corset. Removing her pantaloons and camisole, she shivers, not sure if it's the room's chill or her naked vulnerability.

From the other side of the sailcloth, Rupert whispers, "My dear . . ."

"I'm almost finished."

The idea of being naked in front of a man, any man, makes her tremble. She fumbles with the straps as she pulls the gown over her head, knocking free the combs in her hair. Then the ivory ring, still a foreign presence on her finger, catches and forces her to pause to untangle it.

Finally, the garment's folds fall to the floor in a whispered rush. She presses the thin silk threads against her skin with her fingertips. She blushes, knowing Phoebe's garment has transformed her. Her pulse throbs and her nipples harden as she turns to the side in one last motion toward modesty.

In the lantern's glow, she bows her head and calls out softly, "Rupert."

Rupert gently pulls back the sailcloth and peeks into the room. She lifts her chin, looking over her shoulder to focus on his expression. Instead, her own breath catches at the sight of his naked upper torso. When she looks into his eyes, he is gawking unabashedly.

"Well, I never. . ."

"It is a gift to you from my mother."

"I have never, I mean, I never expected . . . it is . . . you are . . ."

He confirms Phoebe's intention as he steps toward her, his eyes fixated. His hands reach out to touch her. She closes her eyes against their warmth as they run over the soft threads with just enough pressure to sense her body hiding behind the knotted veil. His fingertips follow the swirling contours of the flowing knots, their pattern guiding him to her body's most secret places.

"Rupert, are we to . . . are we to spend our wedding night on the floor?"

As he continues his tactile survey of her body, he murmurs, "Ah, you're not the only one with surprises."

He grins at her as he unbuttons his trousers, the soft folds of wool falling in a pool at his feet. Their vulnerability now equal, he takes her hand and lifts the lantern from the floor. Leading her a few steps forward, he stops to lift the lantern up again.

"I am . . . you must believe . . . I have never known a woman . . . like you."

"And I have never . . ."

Rupert passionately kisses the words back into her mouth. Stopping himself, he continues leading her through a sailcloth-draped hall until they enter a mysterious back chamber. He offers the lantern's light to lead her forward and she cannot contain her gasp.

Voluptuous billows of sailcloth lay mounded in a loose pallet, their crisp linen whiteness lustrous in the lantern's glow while bundles of pink pepper berries adorned the room. Rupert sets the lantern to the side before facing her.

"Yes, you could say we are spending our wedding night on the floor. But I hope you'll never again worry about such a place as long as I'm next to you."

She searches his face until he leans in to gently kiss her forehead, his lips fluttering across her face. With closed eyes, he turns his exploration over to his fingertips, Phoebe's design guiding his caresses. When his fingers come to her breasts, they rest and delicately fondle. She shivers and his eyes flash open.

His control close to exhaustion, he continues to follow the garment's guiding contours to her warm, soft places. His tender touch lights her passion until he cannot contain his desire.

He stops, scoops her up, his arms cradling her close to his chest. Lillia closes her eyes as he steps onto the billows of sailcloth. With the tenderness reserved for the most fragile, he places her in the pallet's center. The fabric gives way under her weight, but it is soft and supportive. As he lies beside her, she feels his body's warmth.

"It feels like a dream."

"It is our sanctuary from the wildness outside. We enter our union together with nothing to keep us from giving everything to each other. I have had my time to explore you. Now, it's your turn."

Lillia hesitates. Unsure of what she should do next, she cautiously brushes her hand across his bare chest and watches his muscles tense at her touch. She can feel his heart pounding. Slowly, she explores the familiarity of his face and neck using the lightest of touches. His breath comes in long, deep sighs.

Suddenly, her restraint passes. Her passion gives neither of them advance notice and she reaches for his lips with her own. He pulls her to him, his hands strong around her waist, rolling her on her side. As they come together, their bodies demand skin contact and instinct takes over.

When the lantern burns through its oil, the profound darkness decreases their inhibitions. Their combined warmth fills the space as they alternate between resting and lovemaking until intimate exhaustion overwhelms their first night together.

Chapter 15

OCTOBER, 1849

SAN FRANCISCO, CALIFORNIA

*I*t takes days to prepare for Lillia and Rupert's inland adventure. Unsure of what to expect when she and Rupert arrive in the shallows of San Francisco's bay, Lillia finds no words. Eyes wide, she soaks in the rush of men of all descriptions. She hears English words, but they are drowned out by many other languages being called out loudly, the din so loud she yearns for the quiet of the open ocean. Men of many heights, widths, and colors move in a continuous flow into which she and Rupert merge carefully.

Sebastian was right. The main thoroughfare is lined with flapping canvas structures, many with hand-painted signs announcing their business. There are a few two-story buildings clad in wood slats, and even a few with glass windows on the ground floor. No matter where she looks, there is little semblance of the organized and stifling life she left behind.

It isn't long before Lillia realizes she is the only woman in the crowd. Suddenly grateful she had compiled a masculine traveling costume before leaving the ship, she feels the camouflage pay off. With her hair knotted up under a hat and the liberal use of a few charcoal smears along her jawline, it provides decent deception, at least from a distance.

She quickly learns to mind her step as the roadway is lined with an endless accumulation of horse manure. Acting on their mutual decision to travel by horseback in their quest to find the Eagleton brothers, Rupert protectively maneuvers her through the throng searching for a livery stable.

Continuing her deception, Lillia rides astride in a man's saddle. She eases her horse behind Rupert's and follows him out of the livery stable. Taking advantage of the autumn's warm, dry weather and Rupert's hunch, they bear toward the southern goldfields. Missing from California's vast rolling hills are the maple trees of her home. In their place, they find oak trees providing shelter in little valleys and crannies along the way. The hills are covered in waves of dry, golden grass, an indication that spring was a wet one. Water flows in meandering streams that are unmolested by the miners' activities. It is easy to find secluded spots for the evening camps where they enjoy their newlywed status.

Working their way up into the hills for two weeks, they query small mining camps tucked away in dark canyons and individual stream bed prospectors, all with disappointing results. After another week, Rupert pulls up his horse at a hand-painted road sign announcing the town of Sonora.

"Can't be too many more camps before we find them," he announces.

They are escorted down the town's center by bawdy music coming from competing dance halls. Women issue full-throated calls of temptation to Rupert from upstairs windows. He looks at Lillia with raised eyebrows.

"I have a good feeling about this place. My brothers would be in the proximity to this kind of activity."

Lillia raises her eyebrows at him.

"How about we board our horses for a few days and see if we can flush those boys out?"

Lillia brightens at his suggestion. Her exhaustion is obvious, which prompts him to affectionately place his hand on her shoulder.

"You're ready for this odyssey to end, aren't you?"

"Not until we find your brothers. But I need a bath."

Rupert eases close to her and gives her a teasing wink.

"An activity for which I'd gladly wish to be invited to join."

Finding the livery stable all the way through town, Rupert arranges for the horses to be boarded. Lillia stays back to listen, once again, to Rupert's routine questioning.

"Where's a good place for supper and a bed?"

Without hesitation, the livery owner says, "There's an inn three blocks yonder. Caters to travelers, not miners. Saloons and gaming houses are the other way."

Rupert nods, handing over his payment, saying, "Not interested in gaming. You wouldn't know the name 'Eagleton' would you?"

Braced for the usual denial, Lillia detects instant tension as the man's tone bristles.

"Don't want no trouble, mister."

"No trouble intended."

"Don't know who I'm talkin' to, that's all. 'Spect they'll be around for the next fandango. Miners'll climb out from their hidey-holes for the dancin' and drinkin'. You stay long 'nough, I 'spect you'll see 'em."

Lillia feels a rush of excitement and steps from the shadows. Rupert looks over his shoulder and says, "Lyle? You coming?"

"Uh-huh."

The livery owner leans in to Rupert as he takes his horse's reins.

"Don't say much, does 'e?"

"Nope, doesn't like strangers. Has a terrible temper. Most think he's a woman because his whiskers are so pitiful. Makes him crazy, so don't stare."

"Gotcha. All us gots our problems."

Lillia leads them away from the corrals, stopping only when Rupert comes to her side. He grins and winks at her, but she waits until they are beyond earshot to speak.

"Seems like you enjoy making up disingenuous stories about your traveling partner."

"The more uncomfortable you can make a curious person, the quicker you squash their questions."

"What do you think of his reaction to the name Eagleton?"

"I say my feeling about this place is spot on. They're close by."

They approach the inn with a sign in the window that advertises, "A bed, a bath, and a hot meal, fifty cents."

Rupert chuckles. "Perfect, as long as we do all three together."

Lillia blushes, ribs him playfully with her elbow and steps toward the inn's door.

Lillia peels off her traveling clothes in their room while she waits for Rupert to return from his inspection of the bathing room's privacy. Even her long underwear sends billowing plumes of dust from her legs. The distant sound of raised voices from within the building make her freeze mid-pull.

Moments later, Rupert returns and quickly closes the door behind him. Lillia looks up to see his face flushed with a giddy expression.

"What was all the whooping I heard coming from the bathing room?"

"Are you ready for your bath?"

"Yes."

"I believe it is ready for us. Let's go."

Lillia wraps herself in a blanket and stumbles out the door ahead of Rupert. He guides her toward the bathing room door where he reaches around her to push open the door. Inside the dimly lit room, the air is ripe with the smell of wet wood and soap. A tin bathtub sits in the room's center, steam rising intoxicatingly from the tub's water. A few thin blankets lay folded on the table next to it, and a lantern gives off a warm glow. She steps toward it, tracing her fingers across its warm surface.

"Do we have the place to ourselves?"

"Not entirely."

Rupert's tone is unusual. When Lillia turns to see why, another man steps from the shadows. Standing side by side to face her, their expressions are identical.

"Lillia, my new bride, meet my brother, Paulo."

Lillia gapes while reflexively tightening the blanket around herself.

"I'm so glad to meet you."

"And I, you, my new sister."

"How . . . ?"

"We'll sort it out over supper. For now, Paulo's going to assure our privacy."

"Lock the door behind me. Supper'll be late. I don't eat until the dining room closes. I've got plenty of news to share."

Rupert follows Paulo and throws the heavy metal latch into its cradle when Paulo closes the door. Lillia is still stunned when Rupert turns to face her.

"What's wrong?"

"It's just you found him, or rather, he found you. Here,

in an inn, not in a canvas tent or a stream bed. It's not what I expected."

"Our water is chilling. Shall we slip in? I'll answer all your questions while I wash you. And then, you can wash me."

Lillia smiles and lets the blanket fall to the floor. She slides down the tub's smooth sides, the water's steamy warmth welcoming her as Rupert strips off his dirty clothes. He joins her and they squirm into a tangle of arms and legs until only their heads are above the waterline.

"Where did Paulo get his interesting name?"

"Let's see, I believe he was named after Paolo Veronese, an Italian Renaissance painter. Mother loves all things Renaissance, so my siblings were named after famous painters, sculptors, mathematicians, and in my sisters' case, models. All except me."

"Why not you?"

"Father insisted I be given my grandfather's name. Just so you know, my brothers may spew a disastrous nickname that continues to haunt me, even after all these years."

"And what is that?"

"Perty."

Lillia breaks out into a fit of laughter, her eyes watering at the image. Rupert wraps his arms around her shoulders and pulls her against him.

"Go ahead, have a giggle at my expense. I delight in your laughter."

But then he leans in, and her giggles are suppressed by his urgent kisses as the water laps against the tub's sides.

By the time Paulo knocks on their room's door, Lillia and Rupert are ravenous. He escorts them to the back of the dining room where a table is set with three plates of food. They devour their meal in silence.

Then Paulo asks, "When did you marry my brother, Mrs. Eagleton?"

"Please, Paulo, call me Lillia."

"We met on our ship. She and her uncle are partners with me until we can pay back Mother. Charles Forsythe owns part of it too. All the result of you boys' sudden departure in San Francisco."

Paulo looks up at Rupert as he chews, swallowing before he speaks.

"So much to explain, Perty."

Lillia gulps at the ease with which he uses the nickname. She covers her mirth by asking Rupert a question.

"How many years are between you and Paulo?"

"Paulo is eight years younger. Then Mona Lisa and Seraphina."

"Why didn't I see evidence of Agnes's interest in art when we visited?"

Paulo chokes on his food and asks, "You've met our mother?"

"Yes, they met before we . . . well, brother, that is another story. Yes, Lillia and Agnes have met. And they actually liked each other."

"Immensely," Lillia says earnestly.

"Interesting."

Finished, Paulo takes the large cloth napkin from his lap and wipes his mouth before shoving the empty plate far enough away to spread his elbows wide in front of him.

"Where would you like me to start?"

"From the time you hooligans left me on the ship and rowed away under the cover of night, my personal bag switched with Donatello's."

Paulo starts their story, telling of his travels with the other brothers, their successes and trials. After half an hour of talking, he finishes with, "That's when I came to work here, the need for a steady place for our brothers to come once in a while. And my salary helps to fund their diggings."

"How long since you've seen them?"

"It's been around three weeks. They'll be here for tomorrow's fandango, but the weather's about to put a damper on traveling. They'll have to decide whether to stay in town or winter at the compound. No matter, it's my job to work here and keep up our place in town."

"Where is the compound?"

"It's in the hills southeast of town. Each has built their own cabin. All but Rafael's are small, meant for one or two people. His is where they eat and have their meetings."

"Why do I get the feeling the Eagleton name makes some wary?"

"Anglos aren't the majority here. Mostly Mexicans, Europeans, and Indians. Last summer was hot and tempers were running high. The boys came to town and got a little tight at a Mexican fandango house."

Lillia glances sideways at Rupert in time to see his expression harden.

"Giorgio and Rafael were dancing with a couple of señoritas, buying them drinks, pretty harmless stuff. A fella wanted to dance with Giorgio's girl. He let the guy dance with her once, but when the dance was over, Giorgio wanted her back. The guy refused, held her too tight, and she started to squawk. Rafael stepped between them to let the woman choose. The guy thought Rafael was bustin' him and moved to draw his knife."

"Uh-oh."

Rupert leans over to Lillia and whispers, "Rafael has always been lightning fast with throwing knives."

"The guy didn't stand a chance, fell still reaching. Some thought Rafael should stand trial, but others saw the dead guy go for his knife first. Rafael made it out of town, but ever since, we've kept a low profile."

Rupert is quiet for a few long seconds before broaching his key subject.

"What are the chances of me getting any of you boys to sail the *Ornery Agnes* back to Boston and settle up with Mother?"

Paulo rubs his chin in contemplation.

"There's a chance a few will go if they know you'll come back west again. I'm not leaving, though. This job is too good. Rafael might go to let the air clear around here. They're bringing in pay dirt at the claim, so someone has to stay to keep it from getting jumped. If squatters move in, there'll be a fight for sure."

Rupert stares at the table, drumming his fingers.

"Well, I guess Mother isn't going to get her wish. But I do have to find the government claim voucher."

"Oh, I have it. It wasn't half a day before Donatello knew he had the wrong bag. We knew you'd be back for the voucher. He gave it to me so nothing would happen to it at the compound."

"Do you think we'll meet them tomorrow?" Lillia asks.

"I'd bet on it. They'll go to town first to drop their things off at our cabin before coming here for a bath and a meal. Aren't they in for a surprise this time?"

Rupert winks at Lillia as a broad grin stretches across his face.

"We best turn in. Tomorrow's going to be an eventful day. When do you expect them?"

"May get here tonight, depends on the weather. They'll try to beat the downpours if they can."

As they leave the dining room, Rupert pulls Lillia close and whispers with a tease, "I can't wait to see my brothers' expressions when they see you."

Lillia falls asleep to the rumble of thunder and flashes of lightning. Several hours later, they are jolted awake by a sharp rap at their door.

"Perty, there's trouble."

The urgent tone of Paulo's voice jerks Rupert into instant action. As he pulls on his trousers, he turns back to Lillia.

"Stay here until I get back. Not sure what this means, but you need to be safe."

Lillia nods, wincing against the door's abrupt slam as he rushes out.

In the dim morning light, Lillia paces impatiently, occasionally pulling back the window's thin cotton covering to survey the street below. When footfalls pound in the hallway, she rushes to the bed and sits expectantly. At first, Rupert carefully opens the door and peers around the edge. As soon as he sees her, he rushes in and closes the door carefully behind him.

Like a gleeful child with a surprise to share he blurts, "Lillia, you won't believe what happened!"

"I'm eager to know what has kept you away for so long."

"Luca was plenty surprised when I rumbled down the stairs behind Paulo last night. Turns out, the rain made their trip treacherous. Then they were ambushed outside of town. Apparently it's a common occurrence around here. Giorgio has a knife slash and Donatello has a broken nose."

"Oh, my goodness!"

"The good news is they'll survive and the robbery was unsuccessful."

"Where did you find them?"

"Luca and Paulo took me to their town cabin. When Luca opened the door, they were so tired they didn't even move. But, when I entered the room unexpectedly, they found all kinds of energy."

"I wish I could have seen the reunion."

"They were a mess. We got the wounds bandaged before I shared why I'm here. But I kept my news of you close to my vest."

His voice trails off unexpectedly and Lillia suspects something is wrong.

"Rupert, what is it?"

"They've changed, all except Rafael. I left them as kind-hearted, honest, good young men. Rafael's hot head has had its influence. Of all of them, he and I have the most difficult relationship."

"Why is that?"

"When Father didn't return from his last trip, Rafael and I took on new roles. I assumed the role of father figure, and I think Rafael resented it. I'm certain he persuaded them to abandon me in San Francisco."

Lillia lets the statement rest for a moment before leaning in to hug him.

"Had he not, we would never have met. You'll know who they respect when you ask them to return to Boston."

Rupert contemplates quietly before saying, "I guess I don't really need them. I just need their money."

Following the departure of the inn's guests, Paulo rearranges the dining room in anticipation of the Eagleton brothers' arrival. Rupert and Lillia pitch in to help, the activity helping ease Lillia's anticipation. As a group, the brothers arrive, fresh from bathing and hungry for their meal. When they see Lillia, they turn quiet, almost suspicious of her presence. Without wasting time, Lillia greets them.

"It's so nice to meet my husband's brothers. I've heard so much about you!"

The already quiet room crackles with tension before a rowdy cheer rises from their lips. Several pat Rupert on the back while others reach for Lillia's hand and plant polite busses on it. Even Donatello, with broken nose and blackened eyes, welcomes her.

They spend the next two hours retelling events that have happened in their mutual absence until Rupert takes the floor and makes his pitch.

He finishes with, "Who'll join us? Mother is eager to see her boys."

"I'll stay at the compound, watch over the claim," Rafael quickly responds.

At this, Lillia shoots a side glance at Rupert, whose expression flashes from jovial to stern. Discussions between the young men are vigorous and Lillia recognizes that Paulo had been correct about the need for some to stay.

"Lillia and I are eager to leave. Make your decision tomorrow so we can leave for the ship early the next morning. Rain or shine. Regardless of your decision, I need your portion of the family loan money to satisfy Mother."

Dark, moisture-heavy clouds drape themselves threateningly around the Sonoran hills when the Eagleton brothers are due to gather and depart. At breakfast, Lillia asked Paulo about the heavy weather and his answer made her heart sink.

"Since we've been here, autumn brings bouts of rain followed by the winter snows. I don't know what to tell you, except you don't want to be here when the snow starts. Last year, it forced the boys to come to town and even here, the snow piled up our town cabin roof's eaves. I imagine you all will be riding into the rains the whole way back to San Francisco."

Lillia regrets not considering a weather change and wishes they had brought the Cape Horn slickers from the *Ornery Agnes*. But when Luca, Donatello, and Giorgio emerge from the murk, she is relieved and sighs contentedly knowing Rupert will be pleased.

As the group pack their saddlebags and prepare their horses, Lillia is impressed by how they distribute their wealth. Some gold dust goes in the saddlebags, but there is also some tucked into coat pockets, boots, and hat linings. Luca approaches with two leather sacks tied tightly.

"Would you mind stashing these in your satchel?"

"Happy to, Luca."

Hardly fifteen minutes on horseback, the heavens open. Lillia pulls down her hat's brim, determined to not start her relationship with her new family by being fainthearted. The rain comes in great sheets, but they continue to ride all day. She witnesses an unfamiliar side of Rupert that is unrelenting and singularly focused on getting back to the ship.

They approach the outskirts of San Francisco after sleeping in canvas shelters with no means to build fires for two days and nights. Grateful to have had Rupert to curl up next to, Lillia marvels at the fortitude of the Eagleton men.

But, on the morning of the third rainy day, fatigue and fever begin their fiendish crawl across her skin. Lillia sways rhythmically in the saddle, her motion more exaggerated with each stride until she slowly slides out of the saddle, landing in a heap on the muddy roadside.

"Perty! She's fallen!"

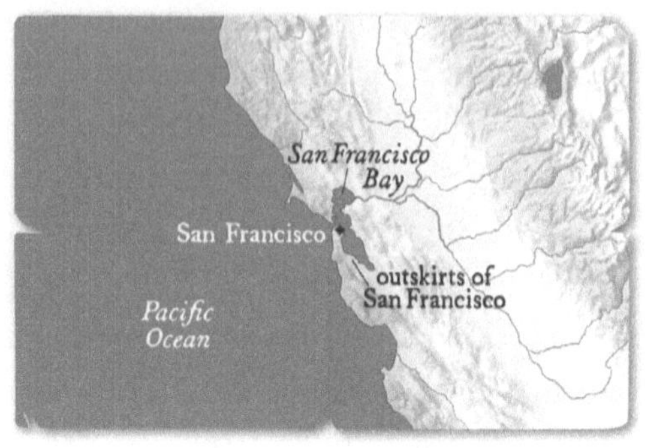

Chapter 16

DECEMBER, 1849

SAN FRANCISCO, CALIFORNIA

A bright ray of sun pierces into the small room, its beam waking Lillia from a deep sleep. Without moving her head, she looks around and sees she is tucked tightly into a bed. When she detects no sound, she brings her hand to her ear and discovers her head is wrapped in bandages. Vibrations tell her of approaching footsteps just before the door cracks open cautiously.

"Well, well, Miss Soilleux. I mean, Mrs. Eagleton. So nice to see your eyes open!"

"Dr. Gibbs?" she whispers hoarsely.

"Yes, my dear. Serendipity, that's my only explanation. When Captain Eagleton brought you to this boardinghouse, the owner called me. Miriam and I had only introduced ourselves to him the day before. It has taken us all these weeks since we left the ship to find proper lodging on the outskirts of the city's filth."

Dr. Gibbs barely finishes his sentence when another set of footsteps shakes the floorboards. The door swings open and Rupert steps in, his hopeful expression shifting to a broad smile when he sees she's awake.

"Hallelujah! It's so good to see you awake, Lillia!"

"Miriam will be here soon with some broth. She's been at your side the entire time you've been fighting the fever."

Rupert comes to her side and takes her hand gently, his voice low, "It hasn't stopped raining since I brought you here. I've never seen anything like it."

"And how long ago was that?" Lillia asks. "How long have I been here?"

"It's been almost two weeks. You've been quite sick with fever. We are coming up on the six-week mark and I'm glad to say, most of the crew has returned. They are standing by for your recovery. I'm awfully glad we gave them the time to explore so they are happy to make the trip home with no regrets."

While Rupert stays at her side, Dr. Gibbs runs a quick examination and concludes, "I imagine the two of you would like to catch up. I'll tell Miriam to wait on your meal for an hour, if you think that's sufficient. Continued rest will be important for your recovery."

Dr. Gibbs leaves the room and Rupert takes the armless chair next to Lillia's bed, spins it around, and sits astride it. He rests his chin on his crossed arms to stare unabashedly with an admiring expression on his face.

"I never considered I would miss anyone like I've missed you. The boys are good fun to be around but not like you."

"And what have you learned from your brothers?"

"They've changed. Matured. I think they've seen and done

some disturbing things they wish they hadn't. They talk of all manner of killings, mutilations, and robberies."

"Oh, my."

"Yes. I'm glad they had each other. They said they got to their claim just before the hills began to crawl with gold seekers. I think they got a good share of the gold when it was easy to find. But that's not what they want to talk about."

"Really? What could be more interesting?"

"You."

"Me? Whatever for?"

"They can't believe I finally found the right girl. They say the scarcity of women here is a big part of why they want to go home—to bring wives back!"

"But don't men come here to escape Eastern society women?"

"Maybe some do. And I don't think the boys are looking for the preach-and-screech types."

"Hmm. I wonder if Sarah and Hope would be of interest to them?"

"I tried that idea. I think they've got certain someones in mind."

Lillia nods her head, the slight movement initiating a dull pound. She rubs her temples absentmindedly and Rupert is quick to tighten the covers.

"I'll leave you to rest and wait for Miriam. Sebastian will be beside himself when he hears you are on the mend."

A week later, Lillia is strong enough to get out of bed and walk slowly around the room. She is dressed and ready for Rupert's visit, eagerly anticipating the sound of his boots coming down the hall. At their familiar thud, she opens the door to greet him.

"Hello, my beautiful wife. So good to see your eyes sparkling again. May I?"

He leans in and places a tender kiss on her lips.

"Oh, Rupert, I'm ready to return to the ship. What is happening in our world?"

He gestures to his soiled boots.

"Mud, my dear. The Browning sisters are doing a fine lot of business. Wellingham hasn't had a claim on his trunk's contents and this called out to me today."

Rupert reaches for something in his breast pocket, removes it, and hides it in the palm of his hand. Holding it out to her, Lillia cups her hands together and he plops the heavy object into her palms. She draws her breath when she sees a broach of silver feathers swirling around a dark red, faceted stone.

"Where did you find such a thing?"

"I passed a vendor this morning and it practically jumped out at me. May I pin it over your heart?"

Dr. Gibbs arrives just as Rupert is admiring his handiwork and says, "Well, well, I'd say my patient has made a solid recovery. How are you feeling? Any headache?"

"None. I think I'm ready to get back to the ship."

"I agree. But, Captain, I must impress on you to be cautious with her. No rough weather heroics, no unsavory characters, and no stress. Just take it easy. Perhaps you could wait for another month before leaving for Cape Horn?"

Lillia watches Rupert's expression droop.

Later that afternoon, Rupert, with Lillia perched in front of him and her satchel secured behind the saddle swell, directs his laboring horse through the street's mud ponds and potholes. At the launch, Nathanial rows them to the *Ornery Agnes* where Sebastian greets her with one of his enveloping hugs. Lillia learns of the Browning sisters' successful laundry business, that Wellingham still hasn't found a place to live, and Sebastian has dragged his feet in regard to the sale of their canvas.

"I'm holding out. You were right, the longer we wait, the more valuable it becomes. The city is a sea of canvas and each day more souls arrive, all requiring cover."

"Aren't you worried another merchant will take our market?"

"The need is too great. It will take ten ships with their holds as full as ours to meet the demand. Our canvas will be the last item to leave this ship before we sail back to Boston."

A staccato splash of oars signals the arrival of Nathanial, Donatello, Luca, and Giorgio, along with two strangers. As each man crawls over the railing, Rupert greets them. Lillia quietly observes that one man is scarred in the most unnatural way and tries not to stare.

"Captain, remember the *Fleeting Star*? The one that almost hit us as we came into the bay?"

Recognition washes across Rupert's face and he replies, "Yes, I do, Nathanial."

Giorgio steps forward and gestures toward the strangers, saying, "May we introduce two of her crew? Hum and Dingle. Men, Captain Rupert Eagleton, his wife, Lillia, and her uncle, Sebastian Soilleux."

The two men doff their caps toward Lillia. Donatello eagerly continues, "Nathanial told us of your interest in the *Fleeting Star*. We met these fellows ashore, and when we learned their story, we thought they should be the ones to tell you. We promised them a meal if they would come out."

Barnabas takes the clue, and while chairs are added to the table and the men seat themselves, he returns with several plates of food. Clearly ravenous, everyone quietly waits until they finish and push back their plates. As promised, the scarred one, Hum, takes up the story.

"Like I tol' these'uns, we sailed in from them Sandwiches over two months ago. Been whalin' for a year by then. Gold fever hit the ship while we was in Lahaina. Once word got out that the *Fleeting Star* was California bound, all abandoned the whaler. Me and Dingle have been tryin' to get out to them hills but cain't come up wi' the coin for the tools."

Luca urges him, "Tell him about your whaling."

Dingle clears his throat and stares earnestly at Rupert.

"Honest, Cap'n, I never could get used ta seein' only the blue plane o' water, nothin' else ta look at but waves an' water. I like my solid ground. Won't miss the stink, that's for sure. Them try pots used for cookin' the blubber to oil were the worst for stink. I'd give a hard nickel to have been the lucky cuss cuttin' an' heavin' blubber strips over the railing and up to the deck from the cuttin' stage. At least th' air was clear down close to the water. They did have sharks circlin' below 'cause o' the blood. Wouldn't want to lose yer balance! Bein' as we was the last to join on, our job was the lowest—keepin' them try pots hot and stirred good 'til the oil was ready to be poured into the casks. Tricky business gettin' oil poured without spillin' or burnin' yerself."

Hum nods after hearing Dingle's statement, saying, "I learnt that . . ."

Dingle pulls Hum's collar open to show a mosaic of burn scars running from his left temple down below the shirt's opening. Horrified at the sight, Lillia looks away as Dingle continues.

"Left our captain, the whole crew did. Rowed the launch as fast as we could to the *Fleeting Star*. Left the ol' man standing' on the ship's deck, wavin' his fists and hollerin' to beat all. Don't think he was a' wishin' us well."

"He was a tyrant. A year at sea with 'im and we all knew he wouldn't make good on our pay. Stingy, 'e was. Food was rotten, forbid our goin' ashore. 'Ope he sits there, the 'old full ta the brim and no one to unload it."

Caught up in their story, Lillia interrupts, "How much is 'full to the brim'?"

"Probably a hundred-ton worth, I'd guess. Got bones and baleen too."

"Of what whale?" Rupert asks.

"Mostly rights but there's a sperm whale too. Captain was mighty proud o'gettin' that big bloke. Said the oil from 'im would make good money. With no men to serve 'im, Captain will get what's comin' to 'im, I'd say."

Lillia looks from one man to the next, her gaze finally settling on Rupert. She is astonished to see her husband wearing a rather silly expression before he stands and offers his hand.

"Hum, Dingle, it's been a pleasure to make your acquaintance. Our best to your success in the goldfields. If it were me, I'd head north rather than south."

Donatello adds, "Less likely to get stabbed in a bar fight."

"Luca, Giorgio, will you row these men back to shore?"

The brothers nod as Hum offers, "Thank ye, Cap'n, fer the meal. Been a while since we've had a square one."

Rupert keeps his silence until he hears the sound of oars splashing away from the ship. Then he pulls Sebastian and Lillia aside.

"I have a plan. It involves a visit to the Sandwich Islands to find that whaler."

"When do you want to leave? I still have to sell our canvas."

"There are things to do before we leave. The crew has to be rounded up after our prolonged delay. I have to find ballast until we fill our hold with whale oil in Lahaina."

Lillia asks, "How long will it take for us to get to Lahaina?"

"I'll do the calculations, but I believe we should arrive in about a month's time. We have to get the sisters settled on shore, Wellingham has to find lodging, and time is of the essence. There's a fortune waiting there!"

Ten days pass until the crew of the *Ornery Agnes* has finished their preparations for sailing. The last item is the canvas, and

Sebastian resigns himself to selling it after the Christmas Day celebrations. As they prepare for bed, Rupert comes up behind Lillia and tenderly kisses her neck.

"So, my lovely wife, it is Christmas Eve, and I have something for you."

Lillia turns and sees him holding a wrapped present.

"That's not fair. I've not been allowed off this ship to find a gift for you."

"It isn't a grand item. I had only a few minutes at the mercantile before we returned to the launch."

"You didn't need to get me something."

Scuffling boots interrupt her statement before Nathanial's voice calls out, "Captain, come quick!"

Rupert tosses the present to Lillia and pulls on his trousers, the gift-giving mood dissolving. Lillia rushes to dress as many pairs of boots stomp on the ship's deck. When she gets to the door, she smells it before she sees it . . . smoke.

On deck, she stares wide-eyed toward the shoreline. The city's surreal display reflects in the bay's mirror-like surface. The entire San Francisco waterfront is burning. Aggressive flames are licking from one canvas-topped structure to another. Winds blow the flames from the waterfront up the populated hills. The smokey air is punctuated by shrieks and frantic calls for help from the city's residents, audible even at the *Ornery Agnes*'s distance.

Sebastian joins her from behind, the ship's occupants watching in silence, helpless to do anything. After several minutes of distressed quiet, Sebastian's low voice rumbles, "At the risk of being callus, I believe the market for our canvas just brightened. Our last trip to shore will be our most profitable."

By mid-morning, the flames had subsided, but blue-gray smoke obscures Lillia's ability to see the city. Nothing deafens the wails and calls for help. Rupert organizes a group to survey the situation on the shore.

Wellingham approaches and says, "Now that you know when you are sailing, I best go along to determine where I'm going to live and how I will store the wager's trunk."

"Howard, I'll bet people are ready to leave this place, and you'll find somewhere to live."

Rupert calls for the launch to be lowered and Lillia watches the group descend the Jacob's ladder. At the splash of oars against the water, Sarah and Hope join her at the railing.

"We've decided to stay. When they return, we need to talk to the captain for suggestions about where to begin," Sarah states.

"We have the money to pay you back and find a place to live. Maybe in the same neighborhood as Mr. Wellingham, so we know someone."

Lillia smiles at Hope, who after her brave announcement, has tears in her eyes.

"A conversation with the captain is in order but as to paying me back . . ." Lillia pauses, "I'd like to leave my investment with you. Use it to build your business and keep me as a partner. When we return next year, I'll take great pride in seeing how well you've done."

The women exchange hugs before Sarah says, with a serious tone, "We best write our arrangement down so your participation is recognized. You never know what can happen in a year."

When the launch returns, the women greet them with tin cups of water as they pull themselves over the railing. Exhausted, the men lay on the deck hardly able to hold the cups to their lips. Lillia is shocked by their blackened faces and the ash on their clothes. She also notices Wellingham's absence.

"What happened to you? And where is Howard?"

Rupert fumbles in his vest pocket and produces a fistful of paper slips, charred and wrinkled.

"I've sold all of your canvas to those who'll pay whatever you ask. Based on the conversations I heard, the city will be rebuilt within a week like nothing ever happened. Howard found a desperate soul who watched his livelihood go up in flames. His despair was so complete that when he saw us approaching, he rushed up and offered his lot for sale. Howard agreed. He's waiting for his percentage from your canvas proceeds to pay the man."

Luca adds, "The canvas structures are so close together that when the wooden structures light up, the fire spreads in one great fire chain. The only way to have stopped the fire was to pull down the buildings ahead of it."

Donatello continues, "Their water brigade was useless. A bucketful equaled a thimble in the fury's wake. Blame seemed to be everywhere, but the facts are, the water pumper ordered from the East Coast just didn't arrive in time to be helpful."

Rupert chimes in with, "There are also a fair number of men who have had enough. Much like the whaling sailors we entertained, equipment is so expensive they can't get to the goldfields on the odd jobs they've picked up. Rumor is that prices for everything double once outside the city. A poorly financed fellow doesn't stand a chance. We'll benefit by their disappointment when they become our paying passengers tomorrow."

Later that same afternoon, the first large bundle of canvas is wrestled from the hold. There is only room in the launch for one bundle of canvas along with Sebastian and two oarsmen. Rupert made arrangements for two wagons to meet them—one empty for delivering the canvas and one loaded with ballast stones. As the canvas leaves, the ballast stones arrive. The men put in an exhausting afternoon. By the time the sun goes down, the exchange is complete.

Wellingham returns with the last load of stones to gather his personal items and the wager trunk. Eager to know what he accomplished with his time on shore, Lillia and Sebastian invite him to eat one more meal with them and leave in the morning.

"What are your living arrangements going to be?"

Sebastian's question makes Wellingham pause before answering, "Not ideal but there's a sinking ship near the wharf I've agreed to purchase. I'll salvage what I can of its respective parts, most notably, the lumber from the helm and captain's quarters. I'll stay in a hotel until it is done. It will allow me to forgo the expense of haggling with others over freshly sawn lumber."

"Howard, do you have any insights for Sarah and Hope as to where they should relocate?"

Turning his attention to the Browning sisters, Howard offers, "I'll help you locate a safe structure until something can be constructed. As the fire has taught me, there are many who've had enough of chasing the elephant and are giving up. Each one leaving California allows hearty souls an opportunity."

Sarah smiles and says, "Thank you, Mr. Wellingham. We will be ready to leave with you on the morning's launch. We appreciate your help and guidance in finding our place in this new city."

As they lay in their bed that night, Rupert whispers softly to Lillia, "A ship full of passengers and a complete crew, all ready and willing to return via the Sandwich Islands. I never would have guessed we'd have this kind of good fortune. You know, there's a chance the whaler is long gone and a trip to the Sandwiches is foolhardy."

"But didn't you say we needed a valuable cargo to add to the ballast?"

"Yes, but what if . . . ?"

"There will be something, Rupert. Your information is too good not to follow up. Besides, I'd like to see the Sandwich Islands."

At first light, Lillia helps get the Browning sisters with their accumulated bundles and laundry equipment to the railing where the men lower it into the launch. At the railing, they share hugs and a wide-eyed moment with Lillia.

As the Browning sisters disappear over the railing and scale down the ladder, Lillia fights the urge to yell out encouraging words. She watches the launch's progress toward the shore and then, through Rupert's telescope, as the young women join Wellingham and disappear into the crowds.

Fighting back tears, she lowers the telescope, vowing to see them again.

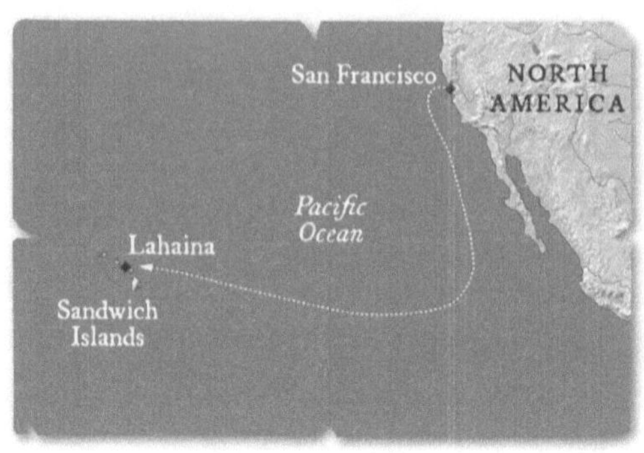

Chapter 17

JANUARY, 1850

SANDWICH ISLANDS

Rupert's eagerness to act on their exclusive information and get to Lahaina had prickled through the entire ship's crew. He had rushed to board paying passengers and to round up any straggling crew. They had left San Francisco without adequate provisions and were forced to stop at several coastal California towns. Rupert's odd behavior had made Lillia fret at this new facet of her husband's character until she had realized he had fallen prey to a variety of gold fever.

After confiding her concerns to Sebastian, he had said, "Your husband is a very accomplished captain and would never put us or his crew in danger. I'll admit we've not witnessed this passion for treasure hunting from him before, but I advise you to trust his instincts."

Taking his words to heart, Lillia had let them echo in her thoughts all the way to Lahaina. With the Sandwich Islands now in view, she is in awe of their rise from the ocean's horizon. Without knowing how long they will be staying, she has a hard time fighting off her curiosity about the islands and the relief of stepping foot on dry land again. And yet, her chest tightens with apprehension for what is—or is not—waiting to ease Rupert's obsession. Uncharacteristically, she feels ill and is haunted by the memory of Miriam Gibbs's seasickness on their way to California.

Sailing into Lahaina Bay, Rupert stands at the helm, unconsciously twisting at the ends of his full mustache while scanning the water from horizon to horizon. Lillia, too, searches the water's plane but finds it void of a whaling ship. She considers what will happen when he learns the ship is gone, sunken, or looted already. While Rupert and his three brothers lower the launch to row to the quaint village lining the beach, she fights off her skepticism. Silent dread fills her for what they are going to learn until she rationalizes he might come to his senses and sail away from this wild goose chase.

Content to sit at the railing and observe the lush green, Lillia spends the day contemplating what life might be like on a tropical island for a foreigner. So far removed from her understanding of civilization, she wonders if this kind of place would test her desire for freedom beyond anything she could ever imagine. How would she know if she never got the chance?

Crawling over the railing from his visit that evening, Rupert's rogue expression tells her he is far from sailing away. Rather, he has turned into a possessed warrior on the hunt for a rare bounty.

"She just disappeared, they say. No one bothered to find her. Just glad she and her foul-mouthed captain were gone."

Giorgio leans in close to his older brother's shoulder and grins broadly.

"But we're going to find 'er."

That night, lying beside Rupert, Lillia makes her feelings known as tactfully as she can.

"I wonder if this is what 'gold fever' feels like? Following a hunch about a treasure that may or may not exist?"

Rupert looks at her for a long moment, saying, "You could be right. I thought I was immune but really, I'm just the last to catch it."

"How many of the crew know why we're in Lahaina?"

"Only my brothers, Sebastian, Barnabas, Nathanial, and you heard the whaler crew's story. I didn't tell the crew or passengers the true reason for sailing here. I just said we were taking an exploratory detour."

"If you are determined to continue with your hunt, you must tell the crew and passengers the truth."

The next morning, Rupert takes Lillia's advice and calls a crew meeting.

"The passengers will be set ashore to partake of this paradise's gifts for the day. We'll sail around the island looking for the whaler. We should easily negotiate the island in a day and if we find nothing, we'll be back by sunset."

Following his crew meeting, Rupert tells all the passengers, including Lillia and Sebastian, that they get to enjoy the island for a day, maybe overnight.

"Captain," one of the new passengers calls out, "a day in paradise is one thing. What guarantee do we have you'll not just strand us here?"

"There are no guarantees in life. California should have taught you that. But I'm leaving my newlywed wife and her uncle with you on the island. They are the best promise I can offer you. If nothing fatal happens to us, we will return to pick you up and continue to Boston."

Rupert's words of assurance should have had a confidence-building effect for Lillia, but his use of the word "fatal" sent a pang of trepidation through her. Rather than fill her head with fears and what-ifs, she leaves the gathering and collects a few items into her satchel for their visit to a tropical island.

After a lengthy embrace, Lillia joins Sebastian and the other passengers in the launch going ashore. Setting her bare feet into the warm water and vast sandy beach of Lahaina, Lillia pauses and looks back at her ship. She knows Rupert is busy preparing for their departure while he waits for the launch to return. She fights off feelings of rejection at being told to spend time away from him and replaces them with determination to make the best of the time she has in such a unique place.

Determined to walk off their sea legs, Sebastian and Lillia eventually pass the island's Christian mission just as a white woman leaves the building with her flock of children. She looks up and smiles genuinely saying, "Good day, my name is Charlotte Baldwin, the wife of Reverend Dwight Baldwin."

"Hello, Mrs. Baldwin," Sebastian replies. "I'm Sebastian Soilleux and this is my niece, Lillia Eagleton. We are here for the day to explore this lovely island. What brings you here and for how long have you been in Lahaina?"

"We are Presbyterian missionaries originally from Connecticut and New York. We've been here since June 1831. I'm happy to help you in any way."

"Thank you," Lillia says, "we don't want to bother you. We are just here while my husband sails the islands looking for a lost whaling ship."

"Oh, my, does he know of the whaling ship's circumstances?"

"He does. But having traveled all the way from San Francisco, he isn't willing to give up until he has satisfied his quest."

Charlotte's face draws tightly as she replies, "I wish he would have come to us before venturing out."

"What is it, Mrs. Baldwin?"

Sebastian's sober tone tugs Charlotte into further explanation.

"We've had many sicknesses here in the last year. First, whooping cough and then measles, followed by dysentery and influenza. Ships coming from California bring the sickness for which the natives have no defense. By the time the whaler you speak of arrived, suspicions of any ship in Lahaina Bay were quite high. When the whaler's crew rowed to another ship and did not come ashore, everyone was relieved. After a few days with no activity on the ship, we suspected foul play. Some brave souls rowed to the whaler only to find the captain aboard, alone. Offers of help were rebuffed in a shower of obscenities. Days later, we awoke to see the ship was gone. Some guess she had been boarded, the captain overpowered, and sailed away under the cover of night. Others theorized the captain had raised anchor determined to sail it out to sea alone and died aboard his ship."

Lillia feels her earlier dread return.

"Won't you come to midday meal with me and my children? It has been so long since I've had news of the world and adult conversation."

Glad for the invitation, Lillia and Sebastian accept. Over a simple lunch of fish and potatoes, Sebastian turns on his story-telling charms, and it isn't long before they feel like they have been friends with Charlotte for years. Following their meal, Lillia feels a wave of nausea wash over her and abruptly leaves for the washroom. After retching into a basin, she feels the warmth of Charlotte's hand patting her on the back.

"Since you're newly married, I must ask, when was your last bleeding?"

Initially shocked at the woman's personal question of her, Lillia considers it before finally answering, "I guess, I think, oh, my, it's been . . ."

"Having had five children, my dear, I know the signs. Congratulations!"

"But, what if?"

"He will return. Given your uncle's stories, it sounds like your relationship is a special match."

Taking the damp cloth offered by Charlotte, Lillia dabs the sweat from her face as her thoughts ricochet with the consequences of raising a fatherless child.

Charlotte and the children accompany Sebastian and Lillia to the harbor before supper. Lillia turns her face into the breeze, looking to the western horizon for any sign of the ship. The rhythmic crash of the waves on the distant reef are so different from the other beaches and shore fronts she has experienced that she's temporarily enthralled at the sound. As the tendrils of waves and their light foam tickle at her bare toes, she smiles at the sensation. The breeze is warm and gentle, and the loose strands of her hair softly brush against her cheek.

While enjoying the moment, she hears Charlotte say, "Ah, the zephyr wind. It is one of the best parts of living in this remote place. It is always stirring but never fierce. I enjoy it myself when I come to the beach."

"It will be the zephyr wind that blows my husband back to me, won't it?"

Charlotte smiles at Lillia and answers, "Indeed. He will be back, one way or the other, for you and for your new baby."

The sun sets with no sign of the *Ornery Agnes*. The Baldwins graciously take Lillia and Sebastian into their home with the reassurance that Rupert had warned them they might have to spend a night on the island.

But it is more than one night. For two weeks, Lillia scrutinizes the western horizon, the zephyr wind constantly reminding her of Charlotte's kind words. But she realizes the tropical pleasantness is no match for her ill ease.

Even her casual strolls on Lahaina's beach and its warm water swirling around her ankles can't soothe her. Under normal circumstances, she knows she would be entranced by the opportunity to walk barefooted in the shallow waters and search for interesting shells and oddities. She feels none of that. Her walks are an evening ritual meant to will Rupert and the *Ornery Agnes* back to her.

Eating has become especially difficult, the fault of pregnancy or anxiety, she isn't sure. Sebastian, having learned her news, has become a doting uncle, helping her to and from her vigil site on the beach every day. But her expectations for seeing Rupert and the *Ornery Agnes* wane with each passing day.

As the sun sinks into the western horizon, Lillia contemplates the very real possibility of a future without Rupert. Tears spill from her eyes, their cool tracks skid down her cheeks, and she doesn't try to stop them. She knows Sebastian will arrive soon to escort her back to the mission for their supper, but the thought of enduring another encouragement-ladened conversation from the Baldwins makes her melancholy.

Unable to keep from sobbing, she turns for one last survey of the western horizon. Temporarily blinded by the green flash of the sun's last light, she strains her eyes when they catch a shape silhouetted there. Unsure if the shape is an illusion brought on by the bright light, she wipes her eyes and looks again. While distant, she sees an unusual shape that wasn't there earlier. Hoping against hope, she squeezes her eyes tight, pressing any moisture away with her fingers. Then, once again, she studies the growing shape.

At the sound of soft steps behind her, she turns excitedly to face Sebastian.

"Look, Uncle. He has returned!"

Sebastian squints into the bright sunset.

"Are you sure, Lillia? It could just be another ship sailing into port. Please don't set yourself up for disappointment."

Staring at him defiantly, her gaze falls on the rising moon, its brightness signaling it to be almost full as she says, "I'm willing to stand here all night to prove it to you."

"All right then, *ma chérie*, I'll stay with you as well."

Willing herself to stand in the growing dusk tempered by the moon's light, she sees the ship getting closer, the bright white of its fully stretched sails sending her the signal.

Only Rupert would have his sails full at this time of night. It has to be him.

Sebastian's warm embrace encircles her as they continue their vigil. Afraid she might be dreaming, she presses her face into his chest until she hears him whisper, "*Mon Dieu*, you're right, Lillia! Rupert has returned."

"How can you be certain?"

"He is on the bow with his spyglass searching the waterfront for you."

Lillia faces the ship and waves with all her strength. In a visual reply, she sees a white shirt enthusiastically whirling and knows it is Rupert.

"We must go to him, Uncle!"

"No, no, we'll wait until morning. Come now, we must get you to bed so you can be refreshed for your reunion. He's going to tell quite a tale."

For the first time since Rupert's departure, Lillia sleeps soundly, waking only at Charlotte's gentle shake. She notices the usual wave of morning nausea is absent. Gathering her things, she thanks the Baldwins, then joins Sebastian and rushes to the waterfront. She watches the *Ornery Agnes* for any movement, but there is nothing. Forced to hire a launch, she impatiently waits for she and Sebastian to be rowed to her ship.

With each oar pull, Lillia feels her pulse quicken. When the ship's Jacob's ladder invitingly tumbles over the railing, she scales its awkwardness with newfound strength. Falling into Rupert's outstretched arms, she clings to him, breathing in his scent, gripping his arms, shoulders, and neck, all to convince herself he is real.

Once they are aboard and the cheers are quieted, demands to tell their story force Rupert and the crew into it.

"When we left, we only planned to explore around the island. We sailed until midday and came upon a native fishing boat. We hailed them, bought some fish, and asked if there had been any sighting of the whaling ship."

Giorgio interjects, "Those natives thought we were soft in the head for attempting to track down the ship. They told us the captain had become daft and the ship had disappeared in the night. We asked them which way it would've drifted without an anchor. They pointed to the southwest, out to sea, saying the current would have driven her all the way to India."

Rupert reappropriates the telling.

"I pulled out my maps and found some islands and shoals northwest of the Sandwiches. A Frenchman had charted them about a decade ago. I showed the natives the maps, and they said they'd never gone there. I pressed them about the possibilities of the lost whaler being able to drift in that direction. They doubted it saying the current didn't flow that way."

"Clearly you didn't take their advice," Sebastian says, his voice edged with sarcasm.

Luca replies with a solidly honest expression, "When Perty—I mean—when the captain makes up his mind about somethin', there's hardly anyone who can change it."

Rupert surveys his crew wagging his finger into their faces saying, "It was less of that and more for an adventure. You have to admit boys, it was quite an adventure, no?

In unison they reply, "Aye, Captain!"

Luca takes up the telling,

"Everyone agreed to figure out the lost whaler's mystery. To do that, we had to think like a deranged ol' captain with no crew and a hold full of valuable cargo. He would want to sell it, especially since he didn't have to share the profits with his crew. We decided the old boy didn't trust anyone, so he tried to sail his ship to another port, waiting until night to pull up anchor.

We figured he would have sailed toward Molokai to get to Oahu except, being alone, he got caught up in the channel current. It pushed him out further than he could navigate. We're guessing there must have been a great storm or some other event; a storm so strong, it blew him against the ocean's currents, beyond Kauai, and he found himself headed to the northwest with no land in sight. After a few days, the ship wrecked onto the shoals of the coral surrounding a narrow chain of semi-islands inhabited only by seals and birds."

"And you know this because?" Sebastian queries.

From behind the crowd, Donatello cries out, "Because we found the ship!"

The whole crew burst into excited chatter until Rupert holds up his hand.

"Boys, boys. One at a time."

One after another, the crew tells of how they had sighted the whaler, her hull embedded in and supported by the coral reef above the ocean's surface during low tide. Once examined from the spyglass, the men had decided they would have to swim to the wreck to better understand the situation. Luca and another had volunteered, wrapping their hands and feet in cloth and swimming the distance to the whaler.

"Once on the reef, we gained access to the ship through a mighty hole in its hull. Inside, we tiptoed through the exposed barrels and bundles and called out to the whaling captain. The only sound came from the surf and seabirds. In the 'tween decks and the forecastle, all looked like the crew had just left. Berths were still filled with mattresses and blankets, and the ship's equipment was stowed in its proper place.

Silence met our calls, so we cautiously climbed to the main deck. We didn't have to look far. The poor old geezer lay face down on the ship's deck. We used a blubber hook to flip him over, and the smell of him turned me green! We wrapped the bloated corpse in sailcloth and pushed it against the stern railing, away from our activities. We waited until the salvage work was done before we gave the old boy a proper sailor's burial."

"Any sign of how he died?" Sebastian asks.

"We didn't see any wounds, but the corpse was so grotesque, none of us was too interested in a thorough examination," Rupert replies.

"The hold was full of oil barrels. The whale bones and baleen were all bundled neatly at the bow," Donatello adds.

Now Giorgio speaks up. "We built a raft to transport it all to the *Ornery Agnes* and its construction took us the rest of that day. The next morning, we started with the whaler's tools and equipment including the huge blubber try pots, valuable to us for their weight. For every load of equipment or oil, we tossed ballast stones! We spent a week moving two hundred oil barrels, some of 'em sperm oil that'll bring a bloody fortune. All we had to do was load it into our hold."

"After we gutted the ship, we gathered on the stern deck and said a few prayers for the ol' captain. Then we slid him into the drink and rushed back to our ship. We didn't want the sharks getting confused about who was dead and who wasn't," Donatello guffaws loudly.

"That was two days ago and here we are, safe and sound and

with a cargo in our hold that is perfect for our return voyage to the states," Giorgio said.

Lillia and Sebastian quietly absorb the brothers' story until Luca clears his throat.

"Ah, Perty, er Captain, about that shore leave?"

"Right, right, all who want to go ashore are free to go but behave yourselves. I'll have no part of any mischief or lawbreaking. I'll give you today and tomorrow ashore. Be on this ship at sundown tomorrow night. We'll leave at dawn. If I have to come after you, there'll be hell to pay, understand me?"

Rupert, Lillia, and Sebastian, now tucked into their berths, are all who remain onboard as the eager crew rows to shore. Even Barnabas went; the opportunity for more fruit and pantry items is more than he can pass up.

"You were lucky, you know, Captain," Sebastian says.

"Yes, I know, but we were brilliant too, wouldn't you say?" he says, smiling broadly.

"Of course, but, can we all agree taking risks like that . . ." Sebastian starts.

"Are no longer done without giving some sort of notice?" Lillia finishes for him.

Sebastian snorts at Lillia's response.

"Well, yes, in so many words. Have you . . . ?"

Lillia interrupts him, saying, "I'm only now getting the opportunity."

"Opportunity for what?"

Lillia turns to face Rupert, her eyes welling at her news.

"I learned, while ashore, you're going to be a father."

"I am?" Rupert whispers excitedly before gathering her in his arms and holding her in a long embrace.

"Rupert, we've been guests of Pastor Baldwin and his wife

Charlotte since you left. Is there anything we can give them to thank them for their hospitality? Perhaps a memento from your adventure?"

Seizing the opportunity presented by Lillia's question, Sebastian chimes in, "How about showing us the hold? I've never seen whale bones before they have become scrimshaw."

"In due time, sir. The bones aren't going anywhere. You should get resettled. I'd like to get reacquainted with my wife."

Agreeing, the trio part ways. Lillia accepts Rupert's guiding hand to their quarters. Once inside the door, he gathers her in his arms.

"I've never been so lonely and yet so determined to succeed in my life. I slept with your silk scarf on my pillow. I missed the tease of your smile and your comfort next to me. And now, to find out you carry our child. How do I deserve all of this?"

"We are both blessed. I, too, have learned something. I can't abide being away from you. When you travel, no matter the adventure, the unknowns, I will travel with you."

"I love that about you. For now, tell me of the baby."

"What do I say? I was ill from the moment you left until the moment I saw the ship approaching last night. Every morning but this one. I don't know why but Charlotte Baldwin tells me illness can be just a short time or months. I'll be happy when it's over."

"I can't wait to be a father. You might have the baby at sea. Maybe we'll make it back to Boston, but it'll be close. Your family is going to be in for several surprises."

Lillia hears him but her thoughts fill with the joyful picture of her parents learning of both her husband and a baby.

Lillia knows Rupert is eager to get underway, but as the sun rises following their promised two days of shore leave, they wait for a few remaining crew. Hoping Barnabas's coffee will soothe his grumbling mood, she hands Rupert a cup and learns it has no effect.

"Damn them. We'll have to make another trip to the shore. We might even be required to search the entire island for them."

"Who's missing?"

"That's the worst of it! It's Donatello, Luca, and his new pal, Ned. They did this even after my warning."

"Permission to come aboard?"

The distant call comes from the starboard and they rush to the railing. Peering over, Lillia sees a native vessel, rowed by four powerful-muscled men. In the bow sit Luca and Ned along with Donatello, each staring up with eager expressions. Rupert tosses the ladder over and the men scurry up its rope rungs.

"It's a good thing," Rupert growls as Luca climbs over the railing.

"We've got a good excuse, Perty."

As Donatello follows Ned over the railing, Luca waves at the native men who strike their oars and move away from the ship. The three young men stand in front of Rupert like penitent children until he can't wait anymore.

"Out with it. What kept you from being here last night with the others?"

After casting glances in both directions, Donatello speaks up.

"We got wind of a plot to rob the *Ornery Agnes* of all her wealth. We stayed to deny the buggers the opportunity. Don't worry, no one's hurt. But if you'd take my suggestion, we might want to hurry on our way before they realize what has happened."

Rupert stares at the young men and Lillia watches his mustache twitch until he barks his command, "Raise the anchor, Nathanial! Time to set sail."

Turning back to the trio, he hisses, "How did anyone discover our wealth? Wait. Don't say anything to anyone. Take your positions. We will talk later. We're underway!"

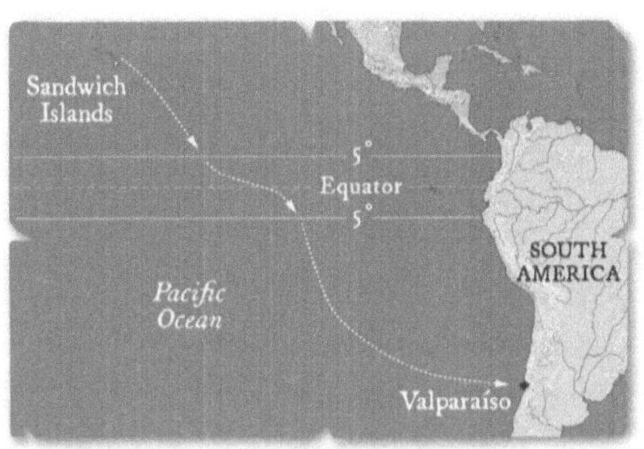

Chapter 18

FEBRUARY, 1850

PACIFIC DOLDRUMS

Pushed by the combined strength of the strong Pacific current and the blustery westerly winds, the *Ornery Agnes* is in the Pacific doldrums ten days after leaving Lahaina Bay. Lillia is relieved for the calm. Her morning sickness has abated but the constant motion had been far from comfortable, vacillating between dizziness and nausea with every rolling swell.

Rupert's frequent, and uncharacteristic, backward glances make Lillia suspect he has learned what transpired in Lahaina from his brothers.

Impatient for him to share the details with her while they relax on the ship's bow at sunset, she asks, "Rupert, is there something you'd like to share with me?"

He looks at her quizzically before a penitent expression crosses his face. He takes her hand, saying, "There is so much. Where am I to begin?"

Astonished at his peculiar answer, Lillia blurts, "I suppose at the beginning!"

When he speaks again, Rupert's tone is conspiratorial.

"I owe you an explanation. There's more to the whaler's story. I swore the crew to secrecy that Luca and the others were trying to protect with their tardiness, but I'm afraid someone couldn't hold their tongue."

Lillia feels a chill flow down her spine as she says, "I have a feeling there are facts either more significant or more sinister than I had previously understood."

"Yes, well, when the boys told you of our adventure, they left out what the whaling captain's logbook hinted to as 'additional cargo.' When he began to fail, his writing became more oblique."

"Such as?"

"Such as his going adrift was intentional. He said his cargo was too precious for anyone to have, and if he couldn't realize the benefit of it, the sea would reclaim its own."

"Whale oil? Too precious? What makes his whale oil any more precious than the next whaler's?"

"That was my question. So, I took it upon myself to slip down to the hold and remove a barrel's lid. It was pure whale oil. I examined the next barrel. Again, whale oil. After I popped the lids on twenty barrels, I realized only whale oil would be evident. If he had hidden anything in the whale oil, it would have settled to the barrel's bottom. So, I flipped the next barrel and removed the bottom."

"What did you find?"

"Remarkably, pearls."

Lillia gasps, "Pearls? Where would a whaling captain come into contact with pearls?"

"I was just as puzzled. I went back to the logbook and searched it again for any clue as to where a whaling ship would come into contact with pearl oysters."

"And?"

"Indeed, the whaling captain had a particular affinity for sailing in and around shoals and atolls that stretch even farther to the northwest than where we found the wrecked ship. He referenced one area in particular as being ripe with pearl oysters and, between whale kills, the ol' whaling captain sent his men to gather the oysters after they had finished rendering.

"It seems his men were pleased to have a break from their shipboard duties. They brought back thousands upon thousands of pearl oysters. But the captain made notes insisting he be the one to shuck them. Shucking oysters is not a captain-worthy chore, unless greater treasure would be found within the shell. My guess is he'd pull out any pearls before handing the half shell over to the crew.

"On their way to the Sandwich Islands, they enjoyed their last raw oyster binge until it had an effect on the captain. He wrote in his journal about suspicious behavior within his crew and seeing things that didn't exist. I suspect there might have been some bad oysters in the bunch."

"Bad? Like what kind of bad?"

"I've sailed through algae blooms that created a toxin which would contaminate algae-eating shellfish. Perhaps there had been a bloom, and the toxin had concentrated into the oysters. Why the captain would have been more susceptible to the toxin than the others, we'll never know. Perhaps he hoarded them and got a greater dose."

Lillia considers the idea before saying, "That would explain why the men were so eager to leave their percentage behind. The captain had gone so mad, they left him to die. And now our whole crew knows of the pearls?"

"Yes. It was impossible for me to keep it a secret, but I swore them to secrecy on their mothers' graves. Apparently, someone doesn't have a mother."

"Between the whale oil, these pearls, our brothers' gold, and Sebastian and my proceeds from the cloth, my goodness, Rupert. When you count it all, we're a floating treasure chest!"

"I've made sure the other caches are well stowed. No one will find them easily."

Lillia's conviction strengthens when she says, "We don't want to lose any of it. You risked your life and our future to salvage it. But, sooner or later, someone is going to come for the pearls. How many barrels have pearls in them?"

"It's hard to know if pearls are in every barrel and just how to go about extracting them."

"Are there any empty barrels?"

"We retrieved fifty deconstructed barrel kits, which have to be fitted together and sealed."

"Could the whale oil be strained to separate out the pearls?"

Rupert grips Lillia's hand enthusiastically and says, "Good idea! Until then, we must plan for the sale. The whale oil could be a valuable trading commodity during the return voyage, especially the sperm whale's case oil. I've not examined all two hundred barrels, but the greater percentage will be clear: either #1 or #2 grade and refined to its purest. A smaller percentage will likely be graded #3 and #4, refined with meat and bones in the blubber, so the oil is dark brown."

"Our whaling captain certainly had high expectations."

"Indeed. He must have been a devil to deal with for his crew to leave their share of the profits. Which returns me to who spoke of our treasure."

"Did Luca offer any insights about the culprit?"

"He only heard the plotters discussing their attack—a plan he and Donatello thwarted with a few good nicks in their launch's oar handles. They were tipped off by someone on our salvage crew."

"Are you familiar with the backgrounds of the crew members who are new to us since San Francisco?"

"Only that they had sailed before."

Just then, Nathanial's voice rises to a high-pitched alarm, "Ship ahoy, coming in from the north!"

"Damn, they are on to us! I'm sure of it," Rupert mutters.

"How do you know?" Lillia asks, continuing. "Aren't all sailing vessels at the whim of the doldrums?"

"Yes, but, it's an enormous ocean. Their proximity is suspicious. Until we work our way out of these damned slack winds, I'm keeping an eye on them."

Day after long day, Lillia watches Rupert stalk the deck, spyglass in hand, his whole attention focused on the adjacent cutter a mile or so off their port side. As if delighted in Rupert and the crew's mental torture, the winds are anemic for a week longer than expected. Everyone is visibly relieved when the winds finally do arrive and push them south of the stillness. The cutter moves off without further incident and is nowhere to be seen as they progress to Chile. Sailing into Valparaíso's bay two weeks later, Rupert identifies the same cutter at anchor. His hackles go up again and he is blunt in his address to the crew before they go ashore.

"Open water piracy takes courage and planning. Lacking the courage, they've been in Valparaíso long enough to create a plan, and I'll not make us easy to be preyed upon. Only three crew go ashore at a time. The remaining crew will be on guard at all times, as well as undercover in case we are being surveilled. Every day not on the open sea is a day we risk being boarded."

Following his lecture, the crew hardly speak as suspicion clouds the air. His address to the passengers is less ominous, telling them to enjoy the comforts of Valparaíso but only for brief visits ashore. It is clear to Lillia that the threat of piracy has not escaped the passengers' ears when she hears some of them grumbling about their personal safety.

"It is hard not to blame them."

"She killed him."

Rupert's potent words and the Valparaíso customs agent's reaction to them give Lillia some satisfaction. Knowing his deceptive role in Coopton's arrival on the *Ornery Agnes* eight months ago still makes her blood boil.

"Did you expect another outcome? Surely you had your suspicions," Rupert continues.

"No, no, I didn't know what to expect from that lunatic. I wouldn't have thought he would have become . . ." the agent hesitates, searching for the right word.

"Deranged?" Sebastian inserts.

"Yes," he says with an acknowledging wave of his hand, adding, "and to try to burn your ship. I'm sorry."

His weak apology is brushed aside with little acknowledgment. Leaving with their documents, Lillia between Rupert and Sebastian, Rupert swiftly hugs her to his side and says, "You make such a great story. Especially now that you are so . . . different."

"You took a little too much joy in sharing the Coopton incident," she tells her husband.

"He asked! He'll walk with more care around you. I like that. Especially since I have to stay aboard the ship for the entire time we're here. I hope Barnabas can get his restocking done quickly. I really don't want to stay a minute longer than we have to."

The trio separate, Sebastian and Lillia turning inland toward accommodations as Rupert strides in the direction of Nathanial and the ship's waiting launch. Over her shoulder, Lillia casts a longing glance toward her husband and realizes this is the first time since Lahaina they've been apart. For reassurance, she lightly pats her growing belly knowing that even though they are not together, they are not too far away either.

March brings autumn to the Southern Hemisphere. The vibrant spring flowers Lillia remembers lining the streets last September are now fading into the lush green foliage. She and Sebastian walk along on the city's upper streets, hoping to find an inn with a view of the bay and the *Ornery Agnes*. Around each turn in the ascending street another hotel appears, each one newer than the last—another product of the California gold rush. They pass the American Hotel, the Tremont Hotel, and the Eagle Hotel. Lillia stops and stares. Startled by her sudden halt, Sebastian follows her gaze toward the elegantly carved figurehead mounted under the hotel's name. The figurehead has remarkable similarity to the *Ornery Agnes*'s.

"*Mon Dieu*, could they be the same?"

"Uncle, we must know. It is too similar to be a fluke."

Walking through the front door, Lillia feels a wave of familiarity wash over her. She looks at Sebastian and knows he feels the European flare. Even the scent of ground coffee and pastries coming from the dining room press against her memory.

"Good morning, *mes amies*."

A woman's melodic voice lilts toward them from behind. When they turn, Lillia notices Sebastian's unusual reaction to the woman and hers to him. Her accent is clearly French, not uncommon in the culturally diverse city, but it is the warmth of her stunning smile that transfixes Sebastian and Lillia. The woman is the first to gather her composure.

"I am Madam Deschamps, owner and manager of the hotel."

"*Bonjour*, Madam Deschamps, I am Sebastian Soilleux and this is my niece, Lillia Eagleton."

"Eagleton?"

"Yes, my husband is Rupert Eagleton, the captain of the *Ornery Agnes*."

Madam Deschamps nods slowly, her silence nudging against awkwardness until she asks, "How long will you be staying in Valparaíso?"

Sebastian's answer rushes out as his bold gaze continues, "We're here only long enough to gather provisions before crossing the Horn back to Boston."

"Can I interest you two in joining me in the dining room for coffee? I always appreciate a cup before the midday meal."

Nodding their acceptance, Lillia and Sebastian follow Madam Deschamps through a comfortable dining room to a table with a slim view over rooftops toward the bay, including a full view of the *Ornery Agnes*. While Madam Deschamps fetches their coffee, Lillia wants to get to the bottom of Sebastian's odd behavior.

"Uncle, please explain your infatuation with Madam Deschamps."

"To be honest, I don't know. There is just something about her."

"I wonder why she reacted like she did to the Eagleton name."

Returning with a tray laden with coffee, cups, and sweet-crusted rolls, Madam Deschamps interrupts their conversation. Skillfully, she pours a cup for Lillia and offers a small pitcher of milk as she says, "I have so little opportunity to talk with people who do not have gold dust dancing in their eyes. I would love to know more of your adventures, if you don't mind sharing them."

"Where does one begin?" Sebastian asks as he takes her offered cup.

Lillia sips and listens to Sebastian talk of their import business and their success in California but also their eagerness to return to Boston.

"It is your turn, Madam Deschamps. I'm hoping your story will answer Lillia's greatest question."

"Oh? What is that, *ma petite*?"

"How is it you have the same figurehead as our ship's?" Lillia asks.

"Ahh, you saw my talisman hanging above the door, *n'est-ce pas*?"

"It is what drew us in, most certainly," Sebastian adds.

"Several years ago, I found myself alone with nothing but my wits. I won it and a captain's logbook in a card game. The sailor who lost them said he had salvaged them from a wrecked ship. The captain's log was written by a man named 'Eagleton.' The figurehead and the logbook have brought me good luck ever since."

Sebastian and Lillia exchange curious expressions with Madam Deschamps, their eyes begging for more of her story.

She continues, "The old boy was so distressed at losing the eagle masthead and the logbook to a woman, he was almost speechless. It took a few more drinks for him to loosen his tongue."

"Had the sailor actually read Captain Eagleton's logbook?" Sebastian asks.

"I doubt he had, didn't seem like the type to have an education."

Turning to Lillia, Sebastian says, "Rupert is going to want to read it, I can guarantee you that."

The Frenchwoman smiles and tips her head to one side before asking, "Who is Rupert?"

"My husband, Captain Rupert Eagleton," Lillia replies.

"Ah, that is where your keen interest rests! Could they be from the same family?"

"My husband's father was lost at sea when he was just a teenager. This might solve a long-awaited mystery for him," Lillia says.

The woman smiles warmly and says, "I can offer you accommodations. Two separate rooms with their own tubs for the hot baths that I'm sure you'll enjoy. This way I will get to meet your Captain Eagleton. And to make our conversation more comfortable, please call me Esmé."

Lillia notices her uncle's rapt attention and marvels inwardly at why she has never seen him behave like this before.

She considers their conversation and decides she trusts Esmé enough to ask, "There is a clipper ship anchored in the bay. Do you know anything about it?"

"What does it look like?"

Lillia turns to Sebastian who says, "I'd describe it as a light craft of moderate dimension. I don't recall any distinguishing features."

Esmé takes a long pause before saying softly, "I know of only one clipper ship that is in our bay regularly. It is owned by the Defois brothers."

"What do they do with it?" Lillia asks.

"One is the local customs agent, Paco Defois, and the other is a successful merchant in California named Stephano. He sails back and forth quite frequently. Paco uses his maritime position to acquire goods for Stephano to sell."

"All according to the law, correct?"

"I suppose a certain amount of it is legally obtained, but they have a reputation for, shall we say, heavy-handed persuasion?"

Lillia's mind twists with the realization that, not only are they once again matching wits with the conniving Paco Defois— at least she has learned his given name—but, unfortunately, Stephano likely knows of the treasure aboard the *Ornery Agnes*. Paco may have gotten the best of her with Coopton but this time things will be different. What is important now is that Rupert understands their connection.

Despite her inner agitation, Lillia feigns fatigue and says, "Thank you for extending accommodations to us. I'm ready to lay in a real bed for the afternoon. Shall we, Uncle?"

Agreeing, they leave the dining room and Esmé fetches them their room keys. At her room, Sebastian sets her satchel down and spins around quickly, saying, "It is conceivable that Stephano learned about Rupert's salvage plans while in San Francisco. He could have planted someone in our crew to report to him about the salvage's success in Lahaina. Stephano's cutter followed us just close enough to ensure we were going to Valparaíso, speeding ahead when they satisfied their assumption. My concern is whether it is to Rupert's advantage to know who he is dealing with, or if it matters at all. After our last encounter with Paco Defois . . ."

Sebastian paces for several minutes without finishing his sentence.

Lillia breaks the silence with, "Rupert has forbidden our involvement. If Paco Defois uses his authority and some fabricated legal claim to board the ship, perhaps with the sheriff's involvement, Rupert would certainly be at a disadvantage. We need to reach him right away to warn him! He needs to know not to let either the sheriff or Paco board the ship, no matter the charge."

"Perhaps, after your rest, we should take a walk to the waterfront. We can deliver the message ourselves under the guise of checking the status of pantry provisions."

Lillia acknowledges the wisdom in resting but knows that while her body may be relaxing, her mind will be fully engaged.

An hour later, Lillia knocks on Sebastian's door. Before they could leave the hotel, Esmé stops them and asks, "Going out? Do you mind if I accompany?"

Lillia and Sebastian exchange glances before Lillia offers, "We would love your company, Esmé. We're going to the waterfront to check on our ship cook's progress with provisions."

Esmé reaches for a light wrap, gracefully draping it around her shoulders as she says, "Wonderful. If he is having any trouble, I'm only too happy to assist with a good word to any merchants I know. The stores are getting quite low on the necessities with all the California traffic. I might be the grease needed to turn some wheels to your benefit."

Lillia tries not to betray her urgency as they walk down the cobbled road, but her heart jumps when they arrive at the waterfront. She immediately recognizes Luca rowing the launch toward them with Barnabas and Rupert inside. Waiting for the men to get to shore, Lillia can hardly contain her excitement. Sebastian takes the lead and introduces Madam Deschamps to Barnabas, allowing Lillia to pull Rupert away for a private conversation.

After a long embrace, she shares her news of their accommodations, Madam Deschamp's connection to the Eagleton family, and the cutter belonging to Paco and Stephano Defois, as well as her theory about their intentions.

"Well now, isn't that interesting? I would wonder, same as you, if Stephano had planted someone onboard with the intention of making his play here in familiar territory. I've been watching the crew like a hawk and have seen nothing peculiar other than my own brothers' itch to visit the local saloons. I swear they didn't have that habit when I left them a year ago."

Lillia asks, "Have you seen Paco or the sheriff? What if they devise some fraudulent legal ruse to force their way onto the ship?"

A deep furrow forms on Rupert's brow as he says slowly, "They can, certainly, fabricate a reason to come aboard and it would be hard, short of violence, to keep them from it. Barnabas is off to find the quantity of fruits and vegetables we'll need to get to the Caribbean. If there is any hint of those scoundrels thinking they're going to mount an ambush, I want you and Sebastian to get to the ship as fast as possible."

"Our dining room has a view of the *Ornery Agnes* anchored in the bay."

"Perfect, I'll signal you when it's time to return, even if we are not truly ready."

"What kind of signal?"

Rupert thinks for a moment before he says, "I'll light a barrel of whale oil on the bow. Be watching and take turns with Sebastian. The signal could come in the middle of the night. If in the day, the smoke will be black; at night, it will glow. I'll have no other reason to light it."

With that, they turned to see Sebastian and Esmé deep in conversation. When the Eagletons approach, the pair share a sly smile. Rupert extends his hand toward Esmé's and busses it saying, "Thank you for taking such good care of my wife and her uncle. If my attentions were not focused on gathering provisions for our trip around Cape Horn, I'd love to know more of your ownership of an identical masthead as my ship's."

"Captain, I was just proposing to Monsieur Soilleux that we have supper together. Perhaps we could all retire to the hotel tonight?"

While flattered by Esmé's offer, Lillia knows Rupert is struggling between his duty and his heart and she counters with, "Esmé, would you consider a night on our ship? We can make accommodations for you. It may not be as comfortable as your hotel, but not too awful either, and we would so enjoy the pleasure of your company."

"A compromise. I like it. I'll make the arrangements at the hotel. I haven't been away in quite a while. It would do my staff good to operate on their own for a night. Oh, and I will bring our evening meal from my kitchen. Tell your cook he can have the night off."

Smiles of satisfaction are erased when the sound of several boot scuffs come from behind them. Lillia turns with the rest to see the sheriff and Paco Defois.

"We meet again, Captain Eagleton," the sheriff says officiously.

"Sheriff, Customs Agent Defois. What is your business on this fine day?"

"We understand you are sailing back to Boston. Agent Defois says you have declared a hold full of salvaged whale oil. Would you have any interest in selling a quantity of it? There aren't as many whalers trading with us since the gold rush started."

Rupert stares at the officials. Lillia wonders what is taking him so long to reply until he says, "I believe I can part with some second-grade oil."

"Perhaps we should take a look before we agree to take it. No good to have it smoking up our homes."

"I'm afraid you'll have to wait until tomorrow for that inspection. My crew is loading provisions at this time. We'll bring a barrel or two up from the hold, first thing in the morning. How does that sound?"

"When are you leaving for the Horn?" Defois asks.

"We're having some trouble finding a few dry provisions so, perhaps in a few days."

Lillia knows now that Rupert is spinning a tale. He had just told her they had all the flour they needed onboard and were waiting for more fruits and vegetables. She watches the officials' expressions and gleans nothing. If they aren't buying Rupert's story, they aren't giving away any clues.

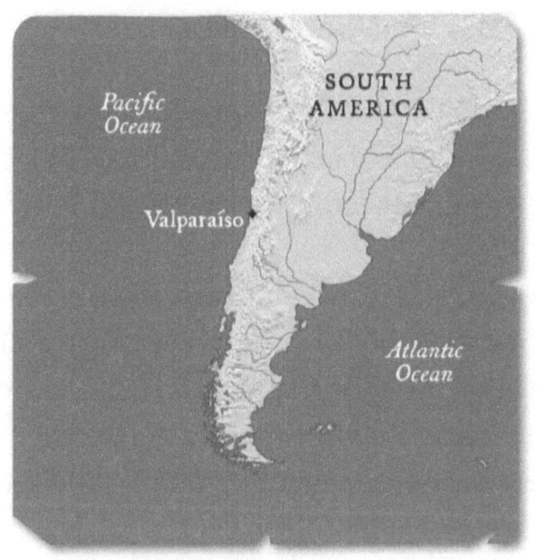

Chapter 19

APRIL, 1850

VALPARAÍSO, CHILE

Their evening meal aboard the *Ornery Agnes* is better than Lillia could have imagined. Madam Deschamps's preparations were delightful. Her beef bourguignon brought tears to Sebastian's eyes. Accompanying the stew were all the familiar staples of a French meal, including crusty bread, pickled cornichons, cheese, and a Nicoise salad, with a perfect pear tartine in its gooey caramel for dessert. The conversation is even more captivating. It is like they have been friends for years. And yet, Lillia finds the most intriguing part of the evening to be watching her uncle devolve into a lovestruck schoolboy around Esmé.

Meanwhile, when Esmé answers Rupert's question on the subject of the missing logbook, he exclaims, "In a card game? It goes without saying, Madam Deschamps, I'd be very interested in that logbook."

"Alas, I was in Nassau when I won them. I left the logbook there, in secure hands, not knowing where my travels would take me. The masthead, my good luck charm, and I ultimately landed here where I've become a rather successful hotelier. In truth, I've always wondered about the captain's family. You should have the logbook, Captain."

"That is very generous of you, but how do you propose we retrieve it?"

"I've been thinking about that very question. I could give you names and directions but I'm not sure if those watching over it will allow you to have it without me."

"Which means you'll need to accompany us to Nassau," Sebastian says, his voice pitched with enthusiasm.

Esmé smiles mischievously at him. She says, "I'm considering the idea. Tonight's experiment will tell me if I've found reliable management for my hotel."

Then to the rest of them she says, "Sebastian tells me you plan to return to California in less than a year."

Lillia speaks up, "If all goes according to plan, we do. Would you be willing to join us?"

"Indeed, *ma chérie*. Not only will you need my help with procuring the logbook, you'll need my help with the baby."

Before Lillia can answer, Rupert reaches for Esmé's hand saying, "I'd be pleased to have another woman aboard. I'm prepared to do the midwifing, but I'll gladly play the understudy. You should know our departure may be quite spontaneous, depending on the sheriff and customs agent's behavior tomorrow morning."

They all shoot startled glances at him, and he expounds, "During our conversation with the officials today, the sheriff let it slip that we had 'salvaged' whale oil onboard. I intentionally did not mention anything 'salvaged' to the customs agent in my documents. Someone has been talking."

"Do you have a plan?" Lillia asks.

"If they arrive in the light of day and our launch rows them to the ship, that will tell me they are not up to anything. But, if anyone else accompanies them, I've a mind to raise the flag of quarantine. It'll be an effective means of discouragement for the short term, allowing us to leave the port, but all who want to leave had better be aboard."

"But what about the passengers expecting to depart in daylight?" asks Sebastian. "Our belongings are still back in *The Eagle Hotel*. What about Madam Deschamps's need to make arrangements with her staff?"

Rupert replies, "Our ally is the cover of darkness. Rather than our original plans of staying aboard the ship tonight, I suggest we make a show of you all returning to the hotel, just in case someone is keeping an eye on us. Your return in the wee hours of the morning should go unnoticed. As for the other passengers, I have a way to inform them."

Dim lights shine from only a few houses when Luca rows Esmé, Sebastian, and Lillia to shore. Lillia's heart races at Rupert's suggestion that their movements are being monitored. She knows he's probably right, since the Chilean officials have proven themselves as dirty scoundrels.

Lillia sighs with relief when she is safe in her hotel room. She rushes to pack her bags while her mind busily rehearses Rupert's parting instructions: return to the launch separately, in one-hour intervals, using different routes. Luca will meet them at the launch to row them to the *Ornery Agnes*, starting with Lillia.

Lillia folds and rolls her clothes into tight bundles, putting them in her traveling bag. She places her solognot strategically on top. Before leaving the ship that night, Rupert had insisted she have immediate access to it. She tests the bag for its weight. While not overly heavy, she frets about carrying it the entire distance to the launch.

Two hours fly by and before she knows it, Sebastian knocks lightly on her door whispering, "It is time, *ma chérie*. Watch your step."

Stepping out into the moist night, Lillia takes a deep breath and lets her eyes adjust to the darkness. A mist tickles her face and hangs on her eyelashes. No lights are visible in the city's windows to aid her hesitant steps on the cobbled street. When, finally, the launch comes into view, she fights the urge to rush.

Tiptoeing into the shallow water, she feels raindrops and hears their gentle splatter on the surrounding water. At the launch, she finds Luca snoring in its bottom, a thin blanket pulled up to his chin.

"Luca, I'm here," she whispers as she raps on the launch's railing with her knuckle. Her words bring him bolt upright. Startled by his reaction, Lillia gasps as well. When he looks at her, or rather, over her shoulder, his sleepy expression shifts to one of alarm. Rising slowly, he extends his hand toward her traveling bag as a familiar voice drones from behind her.

"Well now, Mrs. Eagleton, why is a lady in your circumstances out traipsing about in this rainy autumn night?"

Lillia recognizes Paco Defois's sneering voice immediately and freezes. Thinking quickly, she turns and sees the sheriff and another brute with Defois.

"I missed my husband. I intend on surprising him in our bed."

The sheriff coughs before saying, "How convenient to have someone waiting in the launch for you."

"Luca is a kind collaborator. Why are you sneaking about meddling in people's private business at this time of night?"

"It's our duty to surveil the waterfront, especially when there is a ship carrying enormous wealth anchored in it."

"Enormous wealth?" Lillia asks.

Defois grins like a wolf cornering a lamb, "Madam, it is hard to keep sailors from talking after they have enjoyed Chilean rum. Several mentioned your husband's good fortune in the Sandwich Islands. I applaud his boldness. His risk paid off. But I'm afraid he's guilty of falsifying his records when he stated he has just whale oil aboard. Since I can no longer trust his word or his ethics, I am legally bound to come aboard, do a true valuation, and charge accordingly."

"So you're demanding a true valuation fee? I don't believe we paid such a fee when we came through with ice and canvas in our hold."

"Ah well, ships sailing to California don't usually carry the riches those sailing from California do."

"And why do you think my husband will allow you to board at this hour?"

"If he wants our protection from those who'll steal, and kill, for their own benefit, he'll let us board. Your romantic surprise won't be the only one he gets tonight."

Lillia glances at Luca, his expression clouded with anger. She steps into the boat and settles at the bow's plank seat where Luca had placed her traveling bag. While the three officials find their seats, her mind whirls to find a way to foil their plan. In every scenario, she holds no advantage. Somehow, she has to throw them off balance.

Luca rows obediently, the rhythmic clap of the oars on the calm water eventually signaling their arrival at the ship's side.

The Jacob's ladder is already down so hailing it is not necessary. Lillia waits in uncomfortable silence as Luca gently stirs the water with the oars to position the launch close enough to tie the bow line to the Jacob's ladder.

"Now what, Defois?" Lillia hisses.

"Your sailor is going to go up and fetch the captain while we wait. Tell him the longer he waits to let us board, the longer his wife will be exposed to the impending rain, potentially compromising her health. His deliberate action will be best for all of us."

Watching Luca scale the ladder, Lillia considers Defois's truth about the weather. She remembers the onslaught of rain in California. At the same time, she is determined not to let these fiends get their hands on Rupert's hard-earned treasure.

Rupert's head pops over the railing and he growls, "What's this about, Defois?"

"I only want what my city is due in an accurate tariff for your cargo. The word is out about the treasure aboard. Who knows what evil element is waiting to relieve you of it as easily as you lifted it from the whaler. If you need further incentive . . ." he whistles shrilly and three boats ease through the thickening fog toward them, ". . . these men are under instruction to assist with anything I might need with regard to your entire cargo. It would be best for all if you let us board."

Lillia feels her breath catch at his audacity. Simultaneously, she wonders how Sebastian and Esmé will learn of the trouble aboard the *Ornery Agnes*?

To complicate things further, the heavens open into a bona fide downpour. Lillia's mind races with the implications of Rupert's submission, or not.

"Alright Defois," Rupert shouts down to them, "I'll cooperate and let you board."

Positive Rupert's plan doesn't include true cooperation, Lillia knows Nathanial and Barnabas stayed aboard after supper, along with the six crew members keeping a strategically low profile for just such an occasion. She also knows her presence on the ship will be a liability.

I need to row myself back to shore. None of them will expect it, just like Coopton didn't expect anything.

"Since you have clearly ruined my surprise for my husband, now I'm left in this terrible rain and at risk of falling ill. Why I should have to suffer for your greed?"

"I sincerely hope you won't consider any kind of escape. I have men at the ready on both sea and land."

"You've little to worry about on that account. Just don't plod through your assessment. The rain seems to be coming down even harder."

"Have it your way," Defois says and gestures for the sheriff and his deputy to begin the climb.

As soon as they are halfway up the ladder, Defois hooks his boot into the ladder's rope and turns back.

"Madam Eagleton, I sincerely hope your husband plans to make this a simple process, for your sake."

Lillia doesn't respond. Instead, she unties the bow line and reaches for an oar.

At the movement, Defois stops. He glares at her and taunts, "Do you actually know how to row a boat, Mrs. Eagleton?"

In answer, she grabs the oar handles, swivels them in their oar locks, and pushes the launch away from the ship's side. The oars are long and awkward, and their handles are substantially large for her small hands. She flails for the first few strokes. Then she produces only a wobbly arc after her port oar's blade misses the water completely.

Desperate for progress, she squares her shoulders and focuses on making the oars' blades hit the water's surface in unison. After a dozen successful strokes, she sees the sheriff's launches break through the clouds and start in her direction. At the same time, the fiery arcs of firebombs fly from the *Ornery Agnes*'s deck.

"*Mon Dieu*, Lillia! What has happened?"

Sebastian's question hits her ears at the same time that the sand grabs the launch's bottom and brings it to an abrupt halt. She releases the oars and leans forward, gasping for air after her sprint to the shore. From under her mop of wet hair, she lifts her gaze enough to observe the scene in front of her. Men bob in the water, their launches floating in flames. Judging by the way the fire is spreading within the small boats, she muses that Barnabas has found another use for Chilean rum.

By now, Sebastian is shaking her, his eyes wild with alarm as rain drips from his face.

"Tell me, what happened?"

"Defois, the sheriff, and one of his beasts ambushed Luca and I as we left the shore. They want to assess our cargo's value and for us to pay them protection money."

"I suppose someone couldn't help but talk," he mutters.

Lillia continues, "Once Defois boarded the ship, I decided to row to shore and draw some of Defois's boats away from the *Ornery Agnes*. I was about twenty yards away from the ship when someone threw firebombs at the sheriff's launches. Without that distraction, I would have been intercepted."

"And Rupert?"

"I don't know. He had Nathanial, Barnabas, and Luca with him plus the six crew he had hidden from observers. I wonder if the firebombs weren't Barnabas's doing. No one considers the actions of a cook or a woman."

Lillia watches the sheriff's boats burn in the harbor. Despite the drizzle and early morning hour, a crowd gathers along the shoreline. Through the rain and commotion, Lillia hears Esmé's voice join Sebastian's as he fills her in.

From behind, she hears Donatello and Giorgio's shared exclamation, "What the . . . ?"

Lillia sees both brothers and another crew member gaping at the sight.

"We've got to get to her," Giorgio says as they splash into the shallow water toward Lillia and the launch. Stepping out of the launch and into the shallows, Lillia takes her traveling bag from Giorgio. She watches the quiet ship's deck for any movement until Sebastian tugs at her sleeve and says, "Let's return to the hotel. Rupert will send someone," he says.

Gathering up her soaked skirts and lifting her traveling bag above the water's surface, Lillia takes Sebastian's hand and wades through the tepid seawater. Further down the beach, the sheriff's men slog out of the shallows as well, their burning launches now useless. None make any effort to go to their boss's aid.

In the hotel, Lillia's fingers twitch with the cold as she struggles to undo her dress hooks. Leaving her soaked clothes in a sodden pile, Lillia pulls her nightgown from her traveling bag and lifts it over her naked body. Believing she needs to stay vigilant, she decides against sleep and lies in bed long enough to warm herself. The baby's kicking along with her own chattering teeth force her into a tight curl. It is not long before the slow flow of warmth takes hold and the dark curtain of fatigue unfurls around her.

The thud of abrupt door knocks brings her back from the depths of sleep. Groggy, she rises and opens the door to Esmé and Sebastian. Esmé is quick to assess the situation and briskly directs him, "You must find a coach and driver. Meet us at the front door in ten minutes. I will have Lillia there. Go, hurry!"

Sebastian closes the door quickly and Esmé turns to Lillia.

"Dear, you must dress, in something. What have you got that isn't soaked through?"

Silently, Lillia pulls garments from her traveling bag, the solognot working its way to the bottom and out of sight.

Frustrated by what she sees, Esmé says, "None of this is going to work in these circumstances. I have an idea. Remove your nightgown. I'll be right back."

With uncharacteristic lethargy, Lillia removes the nightgown. Esmé returns with her arms full of fabric and finds Lillia sitting on the bed's edge modestly holding her nightgown over her front and bulging belly.

"I had this habit made for the winter, but I've never worn it. It has just the right amount of shapelessness to suit our needs in this moment. Hurry, pull it on, and I'll wrap this sash around your waist."

Lillia obediently pulls the habit's tunic over her head, the warmth and softness of it caressing her skin. Her head is enveloped by a generous hood as Esmé wraps the sash around her pregnant belly. The light in her quarters is enough to tell it is the most beautiful indigo blue, almost purple in color. Fashioned like a monk's habit, it is simple but functional in its ability to cover the wearer completely. The fabric is the softest she has ever felt in her life.

Esmé grabs the traveling bag, Lillia's wet clothes and boots, and opens the room's door.

She whispers, "No time for footwear. This way. Your uncle is waiting with our transportation."

Thoroughly cocooned by the lush garment, Lillia eases out the door and down the hall toward the front door, her bare feet hidden in the cascading fabric. As she approaches, the door swings open and Sebastian gasps when he sees her.

"What a fantastic disguise! Hurry, we're going to be late."

The faintest dawn light cracks the night's pitch black. The rain has been replaced by a coastal fog heavy with the odor of burned wood. Lillia climbs into the coach's interior followed quickly by Esmé and Sebastian. As the coach rumbles down the steep road toward the waterfront, the jolting cobbles make any conversation impossible. Once the carriage comes to a stop, the three hastily pile out.

The launch bobs in the shallows, the other *Ornery Agnes* passengers crowded together on the plank seats and Giorgio ready at the oars. Lillia leans low and gathers her garment in her arms, hoisting it just above the water's level. Once in the launch, Sebastian and Esmé exchange looks of satisfaction as they are rowed to the waiting ship.

"Why are we sneaking away?" Lillia asks.

"We learned from my hotel manager that the sheriff, his deputy, and the customs agent never returned from your ship. It is quite likely that Stephano Defois is planning some sort of retaliatory kidnapping. We can't risk getting caught. By moving quickly and disguising you, we could only pray to outrun them. It looks like we were right."

Lillia looks over her shoulder at the shoreline. A contingent of men are gathering, forced to mill about when they discover the burned remnants of their boats washing up onto the sand. Fully awake as the launch nears the ship, Lillia eagerly watches the Jacob's ladder clatter to the water's surface to welcome them. Quickly pulling the garment's back hem between her legs and tucking it into her sash to form pantaloons, Lillia grips the rope ladder and begins to climb. By the time she pulls herself over the railing, she is completely winded.

Shocked to see the disarray before her and with no sign of Rupert, she wonders what exactly went on during the struggle with the three officials. Before she knows it, Esmé, Sebastian, and the other passengers arrive at her side and the launch is being hoisted to the deck.

Rupert's familiar voice calls out, "Raise the anchor and prepare to set sail."

The earsplitting clatter of the anchor's chain winding through the capstan obediently answers his call. Through the brightening morning light, Rupert appears standing confidently at the helm. The Eagleton men join the crew as they race up the mast's shrouds and scurry out onto the yard arms in anticipation of further commands. Lillia heaves a great sigh of relief to leave Valparaíso without further incident.

Chapter 20

APRIL, 1850

PACIFIC OCEAN

The familiar pitch and roll of the ship rocks Lillia in their bed, the smell of fresh salt air tingling in her nose. Still wearing Esmé's disguise, its hood is draped around her face and shoulders such that she isn't quite sure what time it is for the darkness. Struggling to rise, she feels the weight of the fabric fall in limpid folds as she stands.

Determined to wear her own clothes, Lillia parts with the garment and searches her trunk for a comfortable dress. When properly clothed in a simple tunic with a loose-fitting skirt tied around her expanding waistline, she reaches for the door. She sees Sebastian and Esmé seated at the passenger's deck table sharing a pot of tea. She sits and joins them while hearing another conversation coming from the helm.

"Now what do we do, Perty? They're raging like bulls down there. No telling what kind of trouble they'll raise against us."

"Not if they can't tell anyone," she hears Rupert reply.

Lillia smiles, positive Rupert had turned the tables on Defois and the two lawmen.

Outside the officer's quarters, she sees sailors moving confidently from shroud to yard arm, their familiar shanties breaking through the crisp air, the Chilean mountains in the far distance. The familiar faces of the ship's passengers set her mind to rest that everyone was able to make it aboard before their swift exit from Valparaíso.

Turning to climb the stairs to the helm, she meets Luca and asks, "What's happened?"

Luca smiles widely, replying, "Perty'll be pleased you're out of bed. With all the goings-on, I think he was most relieved when he learned you were safely on the ship. The plan he had concocted worked perfectly except when you rowed away. Even he didn't see that coming. We've got the dogs in the hold. None too happy about it. I'd best let Perty explain it all to you."

Eager to know more, Lillia rushes to Rupert's side and hugs him firmly around the waist.

"Well, there you are! Did you rest well?"

"I did, but tell me what has happened."

"Those belligerent fools. Thinking they could coerce more fees out of me. I knew they were trying to line their pockets. After Defois and the sheriff's sneaky prank with Coopton I decided this would make us even. I'll put them ashore before we head around the Horn. They'll find their way home."

"Did anyone get hurt after they boarded?"

"No, we nabbed them as they came over the railing. Pretty arrogant to think they could board us without consequences. They probably thought they'd get help from their buddies. No one expected the chaos after Barnabas opened fire with his rum bombs or that you would row away! We probably won't stop in Valparaíso on our way back to California. We've pretty much burned our bridges there."

"Esmé gave me the most amazing disguise."

"I saw it. You were stone asleep when I got to our quarters, but you looked perfectly angelic in that outfit. We owe her so much for her quick thinking. I didn't know who we could trust. When she found out what Defois had threatened to do to us, I could barely keep her from going down to the hold and lashing both of them. And now, she's got Sebastian twisted around her little finger. By the way, Barnabas told me he'll fix your heart's desire now that his pantry is full again."

Hugging him tightly again, Lillia smiles to herself acknowledging her exceptional fortune.

When Defois and the others learn they are being put ashore in Talcahuano, Chile to find their way back to Valparaíso, their combative behavior calms, but their curses do not. In Talcahuano's port, Donatello and Giorgio row the bound and irate men to shore, unceremoniously forcing them out of the launch into the knee-high surf. The Eagleton brothers leave them screaming vulgarities at the top of their lungs.

Now southbound, the fresh ocean winds flip wisps of Lillia's hair into her eyes while sitting at breakfast with Esmé.

Lillia, looking ahead of the ship, wistfully says, "I wonder what this crossing of Cape Horn holds for us. The last time I had no idea what it meant, but now I'll admit I have my trepidations."

"This will be my third crossing. I have faith in your captain, Lillia. He is skilled at his work and his crew respects him. After his clever dealing with the Valparaíso officials, I trust him implicitly."

"So Esmé, tell me about the magnificent habit you lent me. I've never seen something so beautiful."

"Yes, well, I had it made for me out of alpaca wool. I didn't want to be misunderstood as a monk, so I had them dye it the lovely indigo. There have been times when I've felt the need to move about the city without anyone detecting my identity. But, as I said, I've not had the occasion to wear it. Ultimately, it was used just as intended."

Sebastian approaches Lillia and Esmé from the opposite deck, his face unusually clouded.

"Good morning, Uncle. What's the matter?"

"I find myself without purpose."

"On a sailing ship in the vast ocean, all passengers find themselves without purpose. But what to do about it?"

"There are games and such, but I surmise there might be a rather profitable exercise for the three of us, if you are willing."

"Oh?"

"A pregnant woman, her old uncle, and a new friend could certainly go fishing . . . for pearls."

He looks at the women, and Lillia says enthusiastically, "Why yes, Uncle, let's do that! Rupert won't mind, I'm sure of it. What a wonderful idea."

"What's this about pearls?" Esmé asks.

Very quickly, Sebastian explains Rupert's salvage bonus and the need to release the true treasure from its packaging. Lillia senses Esmé's excitement when she rubs her hands together and gives a little squeal.

At their midday meal, Lillia pitches Sebastian's idea to Rupert. Impressed by the trio's willingness to get started on the project, Rupert gives them full permission to start immediately with a few caveats.

"You've got about a week before we hit rough water. And I hope you're prepared to wear the same clothes for the duration of this exercise. Whale oil is messy stuff."

Rupert sends Sebastian to fetch three bailing buckets while he escorts the ladies to the hold. In the dim light, Lillia sees the whale oil barrels arranged in neat rows. When Sebastian returns, Rupert flips over a barrel and pries off the lid. Peering into the barrel's oozy contents, Lillia doesn't see anything but gelatinous goo that reminds her of Phoebe's soup bone gelatin.

"Now, you've got to hustle to scoop the pearls out before they sink."

Rupert grabs Lillia's hand and thrusts it into the thick whale oil with his fingers spread wide and grabbing into the void. She gropes into the mass for something, anything solid. And then she feels it: a perfect sphere between her fingers. Squealing, she brings out her hand and admires the pearl she holds between her forefinger and thumb. Seeing her success, Sebastian and Esmé follow her lead, beaming when they produce a few goopy orbs.

"See? I told you they were there!"

The three grin at Rupert as he flips two more barrels and then expertly pries off their lids.

"You can start with these. Once you have a system, we'll take the lids off more barrels. I'll check on you after a while."

Agreeing, they plunge their hands back into the whale oil and the treasure hunt is on. They labor for the rest of the day finding about two handfuls of various sizes and colors of pearls per barrel. Each morning, the trio is energized to get to work. After the fourth day, they've cleaned all but twenty of the barrels of their precious cargo.

As the afternoon light wanes on this day, Lillia decides to do one more barrel before calling it quits. She calls out for Rupert's assistance. When he arrives, he flashes a quick smile before reaching for the next barrel.

His face washes with a surprised expression as he strains, saying, "Either my arms are getting weak, or this barrel is heavier than the others."

Lillia feels a flash of anticipation when the lid pops up. Even in the dim light, she knows why the barrel weighs more. The surface of the gelatinous material is dimpled with orbs of various sizes. Everyone gasps in unison.

"*Mon Dieu*, would you look at that!" Sebastian exclaims.

"Fetch them out, quick," Rupert says, offering up the bucket.

Three pairs of greasy hands thrust into the oil and start the salvage. Each hand holds more pearls than any of the other barrels combined. Even though her shoulder muscles protest, Lillia doesn't stop until all she feels is whale oil.

"That's all I can reach, but I know there are more."

Lillia hears Esmé give a suppressed giggle. Pearls of all sizes and colors reflect the light. Lillia looks up into the other's faces and meets their grins.

"How much longer before rough seas, Rupert?" she asks.

"You've got one, maybe two days. The swells are kicking up, and I'll have to start giving all my attention to navigation. These few barrels can wait until we are on the other side. I suggest you use your time around the Horn to sort your harvest."

The next three weeks prove to be less challenging than Lillia's first crossing. The winds, while ever present and fearsome, are at least blowing them through the great waves of Cape Horn. The eastbound current sucks at the ship's beam and secures it in the current's flow.

The pearl divers spend their confinement sorting the pearls, cataloging them by size and color. Lillia begs for a few flour sacks from Barnabas to create small pouches to store them in after they are inventoried.

Finished with the day's pearl sorting, she is eager to compare her harvest with Sebastian's and Esmé's when Rupert arrives at their quarters. He hugs her and unexpectedly, she groans with discomfort.

While rubbing her bulging belly, she moans, "Ugh, our little one is tired of my sitting all day, I think."

"We are almost out of the tempest. Nassau will be a very welcome stopover, won't it?"

"Have you been there before?"

"I have. I knew my father's route and went there to learn anything of his disappearance—always disappointed. Esmé's revelation has given me more hope than she could ever know."

"I wonder if our baby will be born there."

Taking her in his arms, Rupert nuzzles her neck, whispering, "You're in good hands with Esmé and me onboard. You have nothing to worry about."

The smooth seas of the Atlantic are a glorious change to Cape Horn's tempest. Eager to return to the last few oil barrels, Esmé and Sebastian do the plunging. Now in her final months of pregnancy, Lillia's bulk keeps her from bending low. Satisfied to hold the bucket, she watches as more pearls appear, almost equaling their entire previous haul. Finally, after the last barrel has been thoroughly seined and the lid replaced, everyone lets out a cheer.

Lillia catches the shared expression when Sebastian winks at Esmé and says, "How fortunate we are to have you aboard to help us. Kismet has embraced us completely."

She sees Esmé blush slightly as she softly laughs and says, "It is my pleasure to participate in this adventure. I, too, believe our time together is most serendipitous."

Esmé throws her head back and laughs joyfully, her gaiety catching up Sebastian and Lillia until their mirth overwhelms them. The ease with which her uncle and their new friend interact and tease each other makes Lillia wonder if pearl sorting has been the only activity happening in the passenger's quarters during the crossing.

The paradise of the Bahamas greets the *Ornery Agnes* with bright blue water lapping gently on the island's white sand beaches. In the two months it has taken them to reach Nassau after rounding Cape Horn, Lillia has endured high seas and the doldrums. Being in her last weeks of pregnancy and decidedly uncomfortable already, the tropical heat of late July is unwelcome.

Resigned to watching Esmé and Rupert depart on their quest for the Eagleton logbook, she watches the fully occupied launch go ashore. At the bow deck sitting with Sebastian, Lillia lets the zephyr breeze blow the wisps of hair away from her face. She thinks of Charlotte Baldwin's definition of the wind, and her mind wanders to her time in the Sandwich Islands. Four months and so many events have transpired since she walked on the sandy beaches of Lahaina.

Barnabas's announcement of their supper wakes her from a nap. Startled, she looks at Sebastian, her alarmed expression communicating her worry that Esmé has not yet returned.

"Don't fret, Lillia. It may not have been as simple a task as she had hoped. She has Rupert with her. No doubt he'll be a great help. And he always comes back to you."

"Indeed, as did his father to Agnes—until he didn't."

Offering nothing to her curt truth, Sebastian helps her to her feet and they walk to the galley. While eating, Lillia hears, "Ahoy, *Ornery Agnes*, your captain has returned!"

The first to arrive over the railing is Esmé, the agile woman heaving herself over the railing with admirable skill. The men hand up basket after basket of fruits and vegetables, bottles of what Lillia assumes are island liquors, and Barnabas's requested pantry items. The last to arrive onboard is Rupert. Giving Lillia a reassuring embrace, he stands back and looks her square in the face and says, "The mystery continues."

"I suggest we pour out some of the local's best before delving too deeply into our efforts," Esmé offers.

Lillia sets out their tin cups while Sebastian works on a spirit concoction, taking a quick sip before smiling with satisfaction.

"Ah, rum. If one adds a squeeze of this orange and lemon, and a bit of sweetening, then rum punch is the product. It's one of my specialties."

Sebastian distributes the rum punch among the tin cups and hands one to Esmé, both of them giggling like schoolchildren.

Lillia and Rupert take theirs, and Sebastian offers a toast, "To a gallant effort to retrieve the elder Eagleton's logbook and our renewed efforts for a swift voyage to our families in Boston and Newburyport!"

Taking a quick sip of the concoction, Lillia asks Esmé, "I take it your efforts were unrewarded?"

Esmé smiles wistfully before replying, "There is no trace of the logbook."

Quickly, Rupert raises his tin cup and toasts, "And here's to releasing the past in anticipation of the future."

Just as Lillia raises her cup the baby shifts its weight. Gasping, she grips her belly with her free hand and exclaims, "Oh, my! Our little one has a strong opinion about your rum punch, Uncle Sebastian."

Esmé comes to Lillia's side saying, "I think it's time to consider making some preparations. Shall we retire to your quarters?"

Nodding her agreement, Lillia takes her offered arm and the two women leave the men to their punch.

At dawn, Rupert calls for the anchor to be raised for Boston at the precise moment Lillia feels a gush of water saturate her petticoats. Lillia's labor is quick, and after only a few hours, Esmé makes her way to the helm.

"Captain, may I have a word?"

"Excuse me, Miss Esmé, but we are about to tack out into the northbound current. Perhaps in an hour?"

"Yes, well, I understand. Perhaps before we speak again, you can contemplate your son's name."

Rupert turns to her abruptly, immediately understanding her question as he whispers hoarsely, "She did it? Without me?"

"The baby came as you were guiding the ship out to sea. The boy is healthy and has a powerful resolve. He wasted no time coming into the world. Lillia is resting, but she wants me to tell you she can wait to see you until you are confident in turning command over to Nathanial."

Esmé watches as Rupert commands a sail adjustment before responding, "Tell her I'm proud of her, and we should consider my father's name."

She smiles like a proud grandparent and whispers, "A perfect choice."

Justus Henri Eagleton carries the Eagleton physical traits, and Lillia is grateful to acknowledge he is an even-tempered baby.

"How fortunate, Lillia. I've known children to fuss and fit for weeks on end!" Esmé says.

While eager to meet the new baby, his uncles allow Lillia a week of confinement. She is touched by their tenderness as they stroke his soft skin with their calloused hands. When Barnabas's turn comes, he grins like a proud father.

"He'll be a sailor for sure."

"How do you know?" Lillia asks.

"Born on a ship, the motion will be his comfort. Other children will get seasick. He'll be at ease."

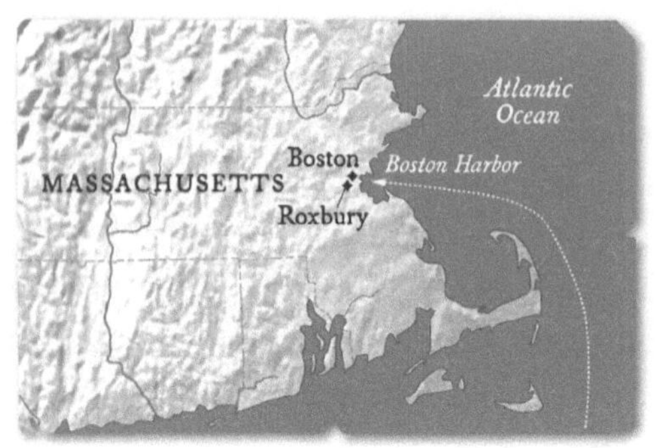

Chapter 21

SEPTEMBER, 1850

BOSTON, MASSACHUSETTS

Two months from the tropics of the Bahamas, the *Ornery Agnes* slips uneventfully alongside the dock in Boston Harbor's wharf, the thick September heat welcoming them. Even though Lillia longs to see her parents, she knows her surprise will be better received in the morning. Her decision does not stop Sebastian and Esmé from suggesting a celebratory meal on shore.

Waves of nostalgia wash through Lillia's mind as she steps down the boarding plank carrying Justus in a blanket-wrapped bundle. Familiar sights make it hard to believe she has traveled to the continent's opposite shore and was gone for over a year. She stifles the emotion that wells up when she thinks of the woman she used to be when she last set foot on the planks of

244

Boston Harbor's wharf. Wounded and defiant after Donovan's departure, she had been determined to prove she could accomplish what he had asked of her in his note.

I wonder where he is now?

But then thoughts of sailing around Cape Horn, Coopton, the sight of San Francisco, marrying Rupert, riding a horse through the California foothills, and having a baby all fill her memory. She knows she is a much different woman with her arrival in Boston.

That night, sleep is elusive. Her mind dances with anticipation of introducing her parents to Justus, and for that matter, Rupert, since she has no idea if they had received her letter announcing her marriage. She can only hope they are strong enough to handle all the news she and Sebastian have to share.

Dawn brings the rowdy calls of dockworkers, stevedores, and ship crews preparing for departure along with Justus's announcement of his hunger. Lillia rises from bed, weary but tingling with excitement. Rupert is absent from their bed, and she wonders if he forgot to tell her about his early morning business. She urges Justus to finish his morning feeding in hopes of a quick conversation with Sebastian.

Catching him as he starts down the boarding plank, she can tell he, too, is anticipating the reunion.

Knowing what is on her mind, Sebastian says, "I'm going to inquire of the Soilleux ship docked at the India Wharf. I will fetch you and your men when I understand the situation from our ship's captain, Captain DuBois. It is all so very exciting, isn't it? Henri isn't going to believe everything we've brought him!"

Smiling and nodding her agreement, Lillia decides to search for Rupert. She finds him at the helm talking to his brothers and hears the last of his directive to them.

"We'll leave for Newburyport in a few days. That should be enough time for you to finish this list, and I can finish my business with the Charleston Navel Yard."

Satisfied, Lillia returns to her quarters where Justus is fast asleep. She fights the urge to hum as she bustles around the room, filling her satchel with gifts and baby items.

Suddenly, Sebastian's frantic voice cuts through the placid atmosphere, "Lillia, come quick!"

Startled and confused, she steps from her quarters to the railing. She sees Sebastian, his face pale and drawn, calling to her from the dock.

"What is it, Uncle?"

"I just talked with Captain DuBois. It seems there has been an accident. Your mother is incapacitated and your father comes infrequently to the docks now. Please fetch Rupert and Esmé while I hire a coach. We must go to them now!"

Lillia feels her knees soften but she rushes to Esmé and asks her to join them. Then she returns to Justus and quickly wraps him, the baby squirming against her tight grip. Outside her quarters, she holds the baby in one arm and her full satchel gripped in her other hand. She heads straight to the galley. Dropping the satchel in order to grab the galley door handle, she swings it open with such force that everyone inside vaults to their feet, Rupert among them.

"Lillia, what is it?"

"We must go to my parents. My mother . . . my mother has . . . Sebastian is arranging for a carriage," Lillia sputters before handing the baby to him and returning for her satchel.

Without asking questions, Rupert takes the baby and meets Lillia and Esmé at the galley doorway. Sebastian has the coach waiting when the group walk down the boarding plank. Rushing toward it, Lillia feels tears welling in her eyes. Rupert sees her distress and turns to Esmé.

"Could you please hold Justus?" he asks her.

Esmé nods and swoops the child from his arms. Rupert turns to Lillia and gathers her in a tight hug.

He whispers to her, "Lillia, we'll see her. You must pull yourself together and be strong for her and for your father. This isn't how we imagined it, but all will be managed."

"We'll take care of our girl, Perty," Giorgio's voice calls out from over Rupert's shoulder. "You have your hands full. Good luck."

Thanking him, Rupert escorts Lillia to the carriage where Sebastian helps the women in before he and Rupert find their seats.

"Driver, you know the way. Make haste."

Lillia snuffs into Sebastian's offered handkerchief and he leans in close, saying, "Be strong. Your arrival is going to do wonders for Phoebe. We will, no doubt, bring joy to her heart, the kind of joy that heals."

Lillia tries to drive the fear and panic from her heart. She wonders how Henri has fared having to take over the household. She focuses on their return, pushing everything else to the back of her mind.

They pass the trip in tense silence. Rupert looks out the window at the passing countryside and small communities while resting his arm around Lillia's shoulders. The carriage's gentle roll has lulled Justus back to sleep, and Lillia focuses on his peaceful face. Sebastian and Esmé sit facing them, his stylish cane impatiently stabbing the floor while his gloved hands rest on its top. Nearing the Soilleux's home, he breaks the tense silence.

"It may be tempting, you two, to change all your plans because of this situation. You are young and have wonderful opportunities in front of you. My only request is for you to keep those plans in sight, even as your hearts tell you your parents' lives would be easier with you here to help."

Lillia hears his words but tingles with anticipation when the coach turns into the Soilleux's yard. Her back to the house, she watches the sunlight dance through the familiar trees' leaves. After the carriage pulls to a stop, Sebastian unlatches the carriage's door.

"Let me assess the situation before we release the carriage."

Lillia listens for Sebastian's rap on the kitchen door and waits for what seems like an eternity for the door's familiar creak to break the silence. The joyful sounds of brothers greeting each other brings a smile to her face. She hears Sebastian talking and Henri replying while their voices get closer.

The carriage door opens and Sebastian beckons Esmé to step out. Sebastian introduces her, and Henri graciously greets her. When Rupert exits, Sebastian makes a quick introduction.

"Henri, Captain Rupert Eagleton, the man on whose ship we sailed from Newburyport to California and back."

The two men shake hands. Then Rupert reaches for Justus, hands the baby to Esmé and returns for Lillia's hand. As their eyes meet, Lillia sees her father is overwhelmed and speechless. Silently, he takes her in his arms with a smothering embrace.

He whispers, "You are back. We haven't heard anything since your letter before leaving Chile for California. Thank you, Heavenly Father. Our prayers have been answered."

Through her tears, Lillia squeaks as she gestures to Rupert, "Father, I did write you. I wrote to tell you I've brought you a son-in-law."

"Captain Eagleton? Oh, Lillia. Welcome to the family, sir."

Taking the baby from Esmé, Lillia pulls back the blankets to reveal the child's face while offering Henri a look.

"And our son, Justus Henri, now just over a month and a half old."

"A grandson? All of this? Your mother will be thrilled."

"We know Mother is not well. Captain DuBois told us when we met him this morning. Will she see us?"

"Oh, most certainly. But she has lost her ability to speak. The doctors believe it is a case of apoplexy. Her left side is useless, although we've seen some progress in recent months. She can hold her teacup without spilling it. She just can't say what she is thinking. She has a slate and is getting better at using it.

"Come in, come in. Wait, no, stay here. I've left her in bed. She has a hard time getting up. It seems she has to reconnect every day. I'll signal when we're ready. Please forgive the wait, but if I introduce all of you without preparing her, she'll be quite upset with me."

With that, Henri returns to the house. Sebastian and Rupert fetch everyone's satchels and release the carriage. Lillia and Esmé casually walk Justus around the Soilleux's humble grounds. It seems like forever before Henri rushes into the yard.

"Phoebe is at the kitchen table. I propose Lillia go first. I worry Phoebe might be too overwhelmed if all of you arrive at once. This is more good news than we have received in a very long time."

"Mother, I'm home!"

Lillia lets her words precede her arrival into the kitchen. She scans the space and finds it exactly as she had left it, except for the woman seated at the table. Somehow, her mother has diminished in her scale. Perhaps it is the limpness of her left side. Henri made an attempt at fixing her hair but the bun is looser than Lillia remembers her mother arranging it on her own. Her typical ruddy complexion is absent, and Lillia reminds herself that Phoebe probably hasn't been outside in quite a while. But nothing has changed the spark in Phoebe's eyes when she sees her daughter. When she starts to cry, Lillia knows her mother understands.

Sobbing, Phoebe lifts her right hand and beckons toward Lillia. Rushing to her side, Lillia falls to her knees and wraps her arms around Phoebe's shoulders. The two weep with mutual joy.

Hearing them, Henri calls out, "Are you two alright in there?"

Lillia pulls away and looks into Phoebe's face. She asks, "I have others for you to meet. Are you ready?"

Phoebe's eyebrows arch as if wondering what to say. Lillia reaches up and tenderly wipes Phoebe's tear trails with a napkin, brushing back the gray wisps of hair from around her mother's face. Going to the door, Lillia motions for Rupert to come to her. Taking his hand, Lillia brings him through the doorway. When his large frame blocks out the kitchen's light, Phoebe's right hand flies to her mouth.

"This is my husband, Captain Rupert Eagleton. His was the ship Uncle Sebastian and I sailed on to California. We married a year ago when we arrived in San Francisco Bay. Rupert, my mother, Phoebe Soilleux."

Phoebe babbles nonsensically. Lillia had not noticed Henri's presence until he pushes to Phoebe's side, trying to calm her. Phoebe forcefully pushes her chair away from the table and Henri helps her stand. Reaching as high as she can, Rupert accepts her one arm embrace.

"Mother Soilleux, I'm delighted to meet you. I'm proud Lillia agreed to be my wife."

Phoebe cranes her neck to look into Rupert's face, a genuine smile on hers. Her eyes speak the words of love she cannot utter. Losing strength, she stumbles backward, but Henri catches her and she lands heavily in her chair. Lillia waits until she is settled before speaking.

"There's more, Mother."

Again, Phoebe's eyebrows arch. Lillia walks to the doorway and takes Justus from Esmé's arms. This time, when Phoebe sees the blanketed bundle, she hums. Tears cascade down her cheeks as she excitedly taps the tabletop with her right hand. When Lillia approaches with Justus, Henri slides his arm around Phoebe's shoulders.

He whispers in her ear, "My sweet girl, you must be still, or you'll wake him."

Lillia bends low and places Justus on Phoebe's lap. Henri reaches out and holds the baby's side while Lillia pulls the blankets away from Justus's face. Phoebe goes still until her lips form an "O" as she watches the baby take deep sleeping breaths.

"He was born on June 29 when we were sailing home. Due to his being born while aboard a sailing ship, he will always be comfortable at sea," Lillia says. She smiles at her mother before adding, "One last guest I want you to meet is a new friend of Uncle Sebastian's. She is Madam Esmé Deschamps. We found her in Valparaíso, Chile."

Esmé steps forward and smiles warmly at Phoebe and Henri as Lillia continues, "It is quite a story, Mother. But there is time for that. We have many, many stories."

Phoebe nods and reaches for Lillia's face, her wrinkled and fragile hand cradling it tenderly. It feels better to Lillia than anything she can imagine.

Henri heats water for tea and Esmé joins him, arranging sweet buns on a platter. Lillia sits between Phoebe and Rupert with Justus on her lap, the sleeping child having cast a spell over Phoebe. The group chats over their drinks and the plate of buns disappear as they talk. The California trip is the main topic. But after a while, it appears that Phoebe is becoming agitated. She taps Henri's arm to get his attention.

"Yes?"

Phoebe holds one hand flat and pretends to write, a perplexing expression on her face.

"Do you think you can?"

Phoebe nods to Henri's question.

"Alright, I will fetch your slate," he says as he pushes back his chair and leaves the room.

While they wait, Phoebe glances at Rupert. When she reaches for Lillia's hand and squeezes with unexpected force, Lillia knows Phoebe is eager to communicate something. Henri returns to the room and hands Phoebe a slate with a chalk piece. Bracing the slate between her left forearm and her stomach, Phoebe letters her message.

"LILLIA. ME. ALONE."

"I believe we've been asked to leave," Henri announces.

"Very well," says Sebastian. "We've got business to discuss. Brother, I think you'll find our new family member has quite a bit to offer beyond being Lillia's perfect fit."

Rupert winks at Lillia, saying, "And I must arrange a meeting with a certain naval agent."

Lillia knows the importance of this meeting, and she wants to go with him, but Phoebe's emphatic request is more important.

"Is a trip to the waterfront enough time for you two to be alone?"

Henri's question is met by Phoebe's nod. Lillia assures him they will get along just fine. With her confidence, the group files out the door, but not before Rupert steals one last kiss before he leaves. Phoebe smiles at their affection and Lillia blushes.

"Mother, can I get you anything before I feed Justus?"

Phoebe shakes her head and then motions for Lillia to sit close to her.

"I'll have to feed him while we talk. Is that alright?"

Phoebe answers with an emphatic nod but her quivering chin and welling eyes betray something more. To Lillia's alarm, more tears pour down Phoebe's cheeks. Lillia wonders what her mother is feeling.

Moving closer to Phoebe, Lillia embraces her with one arm while holding Justus in the other. After several moments, Lillia pushes back and looks Phoebe in the face.

"You've nothing to fear, I'm here. Nothing can come between us now."

Retrieving a handkerchief, Lillia hands it to Phoebe before preparing to nurse Justus.

Phoebe focuses on the slate in her lap and starts writing. When she finishes, she holds the slate up.

"I KNOW."

"You know what, Mother?"

Phoebe uses the handkerchief to wipe the slate clear and starts anew.

"WHERE DONOVAN IS."

Lillia's face goes pale at the name.

"How do you know?"

"YOUNG MAN. RETURNED INJURED. KNEW DONOVAN."

"How was he injured?"

"STEAMER EXPLOSION. LOST ARM. DONOVAN THERE."

"When did you find out?"

"IN DECEMBER. WOMAN'S MEETING. UNABLE TO SPEAK AFTER."

"You haven't spoken since you found out?"

"YES. YOUR FATHER DOESN'T KNOW. O'CREIGH EITHER."

"I suppose that's for the best. Neither of them would be able to handle the information well."

"WHY NOT SURPRISED?"

"I know too."

"HOW?"

Lillia tells the story of the race to California, and about Wellingham and his role as the wager courier. She tells of the *Night Call*'s loss but having no knowledge of the overland team. When Lillia tells her of finding the contestant's names on the ledger in Wellingham's trunk, Phoebe gasps and scribbles.

"WHAT DID YOU DO?"

"I was shocked, at first. Then I . . ." Lillia stops.

Her mind blurs knowing it is time to share the truth about decoding Donovan's note, but she hesitates when she considers all that Phoebe has endured these past months.

"WHAT IS IT? TELL ME."

Lillia lifts Justus to her shoulder to burp him.

"Oh, Mother, I'm so ashamed."

Lillia hardly gets the words out before she feels penitent tears escape. Justus lies heavily on her shoulder while Phoebe waits, helpless and confused, for Lillia to find her composure. After what seems like a long time, Lillia feels her resolve build. She wipes her face with her sleeve while balancing the sleeping Justus, determined not to keep this ugly secret any longer.

"I didn't tell you the whole truth when Uncle Sebastian and I left. You have suffered because of my selfishness."

"WHAT?"

"Donovan told me of his plans to go to California in his note in Morse code. He asked me to meet him in California."

Phoebe listens and begins to slowly nod her head.

"YOU SO EAGER."

"I thought he was the only man who'd love me."

"BUT CAPTAIN CHANGED YOUR MIND?"

"Yes. Rupert is kind and strong. He listens and admires my opinions. He encourages me to be myself and not to be ashamed of having a strong voice."

"GOOD. WHAT OF DONOVAN?"

"I don't know yet."

"HIS FAMILY NEEDS TO KNOW."

"Oh?"

"THEY BEGGED FOR NEWS."

"But I don't really know anything of him."

"SAY NOTHING?"

"He did something to betray his father. Donovan's as good as dead to him."

"HIS MOTHER WON'T CARE."

Silence develops between them for a moment. Then Lillia breaks it.

"Please forgive me, Mother."

"NOTHING TO FORGIVE."

"But I deceived you and Father. I should have told you."

"YOU WERE CONFUSED. A LOT FOR A YOUNG WOMAN."

"I wish I could make you better."

"YOU HAVE. RETURNED WITH THE CAPTAIN AND GRANDSON."

"But, I mean, physically. You and Father have so much more time to live together. Your not speaking is difficult for both of you."

"NOW I STOP WORRYING."

Lillia sighs with relief knowing Phoebe's truth and that her need to keep her secret has evaporated. By the time Rupert and Henri return to the Soilleux home, Phoebe has relaxed and only Lillia knows why.

Rupert announces, "We are sailing to Newburyport in the morning to share our news with my mother, but don't worry, we'll return soon."

A flash of sadness crosses Phoebe's expression as Lillia bundles Justus up and gathers her things. When Lillia leans down to give her mother a warm embrace, she is surprised when Phoebe whispers a soft, halting message, "You are my best work."

Tears spring to Lillia's surprised eyes and she quickly looks to Henri and his own surprised expression.

"Eagletons, return soon! Your mother may just be back to her old self before we know it!"

Following Rupert out the door, Lillia quickly looks over her shoulder to see Phoebe's face aglow with maternal love and knows all is well.

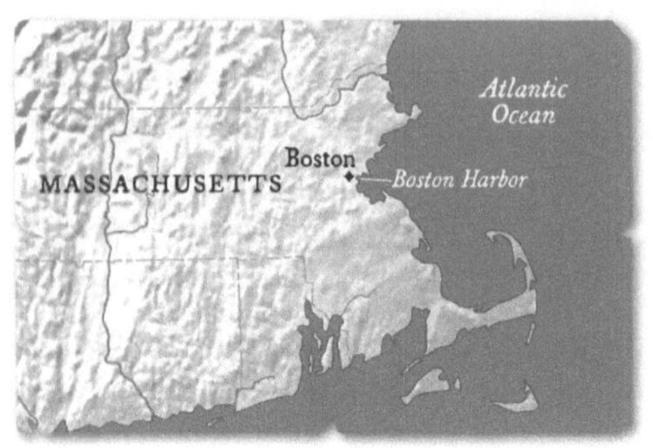

Chapter 22

SEPTEMBER, 1850

BOSTON, MASSACHUSETTS

Lillia feels the sweet release of dread's grip on their way back to the ship. She nuzzles Justus and lets the autumn breeze, rich with late summer's scent, wash across them in the open-topped carriage. Her back to their forward progress, she looks into Rupert's face and finds it suddenly anxious.

He stands abruptly and growls, "Where is she? What have they done?"

Lillia strains to look over her shoulder in the ship's direction and immediately understands his distress.

"The ship is gone! Why would they disobey my orders? There better be a damn good reason for leaving."

"Could someone have taken control of the ship?"

Rupert stares at her. She realizes, too late, the impact of her question. As the couple reach the height of their panic, the carriage pulls up to the docks and Sebastian hails them from the Soilleux ship, *Mon Coeur*, Esmé at his side.

"Rupert, Lillia, good to see you. I have news. Come aboard!"

Rupert silently maintains his inner fume while he fetches their baggage, pays the carriage driver, and assists Lillia out of the carriage.

At the ship, Sebastian welcomes them up the boarding plank where they find Captain DuBois and Esmé sitting on deck in no state of anxiety whatsoever. Confused by their lack of alarm, Lillia waits for Sebastian's explanation, but Rupert is not as patient.

"What of the *Ornery Agnes?*"

"No need for alarm. She's on a quick errand. Rupert, the crew were quite confident they would be back before nightfall."

"Under whose orders? I explicitly told them to wait for my return."

"When your brothers got back from having their gold assayed, they were jubilant with their good fortune. They asked Captain DuBois and I if we thought they could sail to Newburyport and be back by tonight without causing you distress. I believe they simply wanted to see their mother."

Reluctantly, Rupert responds, "You're sure they are returning tonight?"

At this point, Captain DuBois stands and offers Rupert a champagne flute and says, "While we wait for your ship to return, I'd like to propose a toast to your success, both financially and personally."

Sebastian takes up a flute as Captain DuBois makes a flamboyant exercise of opening the champagne. Sebastian tries to ease Rupert's ruffled feathers as the frothing liquid is poured out between them.

"It will do me no good to tell you not to worry, but perhaps my own observation is in order. I believe your brothers are very capable sailors."

Rupert is silently biting the ends of his mustache while pacing the ship's deck when the *Mon Coeur's* cook arrives with their supper. Uninterested in eating, he moves to the ship's bow and its view of the harbor. Sebastian, Esmé, and Lillia are discussing their evening accommodations when they hear Rupert's voice boom, "There she is!"

Moving to his side, Lillia sees the *Ornery Agnes* tacking in from the north, her trimmed sails reducing her speed into the close harbor. Through the darkening shadows, Lillia also sees Agnes proudly standing at the bow, searching the Boston waterfront for the familiar face of her oldest son. Lillia smiles to herself and wonders whose idea it really was to have this reunion.

Expertly approaching the dock, the ship glides in smoothly until close enough for the crew members to vault off the railing. They gracefully land on the wooden deck and secure the ship's lines to the dock ties.

"Hello, *Mon Coeur!*" Giorgio salutes the Soilleux ship from the *Ornery Agnes's* helm.

Rupert barrels off the *Mon Coeur* and lopes to his ship without a word to anyone.

Thanking Captain DuBois for his hospitality, Lillia juggles Justus into her arms and follows him. Sebastian and Esmé come to her side, and she takes Sebastian's arm.

Lillia asks, "Just whose idea was this sojourn to Newburyport?"

"You may not believe me, but it was the boys' idea. It was as I said. They had finished their business and were bored waiting for Rupert to return. We agreed it would give them something to do and make a wonderful surprise. Now the Soilleuxs can meet Mrs. Eagleton, and we can celebrate your marriage all together."

"Seems like a plan sprinkled with a little of your seasoning, Uncle."

"Well, perhaps the boys needed a little prod. To their credit, they were very uncomfortable leaving without their captain's approval. I assured them their mother would be thrilled with the idea. It looks like I was right."

Lillia observes Agnes surrounded by her sons, along with Charles. At the *Ornery Agnes*'s boarding plank, Lillia, Esmé, and Sebastian stop to absorb the scene in front of them. When Agnes sees Lillia, she rushes toward them, tears streaming down her cheeks.

"Oh, my heart is so full. I knew the moment I met you that you were the one for my son. And now this little one."

Handing Justus to his eager grandmother, Lillia asks, "You and Charles? After all that time?"

"Yes, dear, you left us and the next thing I knew, he had captured my heart. I learned why he had never returned to me. It was all so unfair. I had no knowledge of his accident. But now, well, I'll tell you before my own children. We are betrothed. It's never too late to love."

Lillia's hand flies to her mouth before reaching for a warm embrace. Charles, his hearing ever acute, comes to Agnes's side and whispers, "I hear you can't keep a secret."

"Charles, can you blame me? There is so much happiness around us, we should be able to share ours."

"Not without proper permission from the family."

Charles raises his voice and calls out, "Attention! Attention!"

Everyone turns and looks at the older couple who cut a striking figure of ageless beauty between them.

"Eagleton family, I, Charles Forsythe, do hereby request the permission of you, most all of whom are her children, to marry your mother."

Without a second's hesitation, a loud cheer goes up from the male voices onboard, and Agnes embraces Charles.

"I think we have their permission."

From behind them, Sebastian clears his throat, and

announces, "Now then, it seems Esmé and I have a similar announcement."

The entire group turns away from Agnes and Charles and faces Sebastian. He has his arm around Esmé's waist. Lillia feels her mouth drop open.

From behind her, she hears Rupert say, "Why Sebastian, you old fox."

"Uncle, really? You have waited all these years."

Sebastian hugs Esmé and laughs. Then he says, "The gold bug isn't all that's catching these days."

Sebastian suggests Charles and Agnes join him and Esmé and return to the Soilleux's family home for the evening. Grateful for the privacy of their own quarters on the *Ornery Agnes* after all the excitement, Lillia and Rupert lay quietly in their bed.

Rupert whispers, "I learned that Luca, Giorgio, and Donatello have repaid their shares of the family trust with some left for themselves. I need to explore the sale of the whale oil and attend my appointment to present my voucher at the Charlestown Naval Shipyard. Would you like to join me for either of those activities?"

The thought of all their fortunes coming to bear so quickly after so long makes Lillia ponder the situation for a few moments.

"I'll let you tromp the docks with the whale oil merchants, but I would like to accompany you when you present your voucher. Perhaps a woman's presence will help in the agent's willingness to settle it."

"Perhaps. I've tried to quell my doubts about the government making good on their promise. It has been a long time since my bid was authorized."

Lillia understands his concern. Two administrations had come and gone since President Polk's Secretary of War had granted Rupert the bid to transport Army goods to the Pacific Coast at the end of the Mexican War. It has only been a month since President Taylor died in office and that fact alone puts Rupert's arrival and request on tenuous footing.

"I'll stay here with Justus and count the pearls while you're at the wharf. I'd like to lay them out to see exactly what we have before we decide what to do with them. We'll be ready to go to the shipyard right after midday. How does that sound?"

"Like a true partner. Thank you," Rupert replies and snuffs out the candle.

Rupert leaves at first light, and while Lillia knows the whale oil will sell, the demand will dictate the price. The pearls are not items dealt on the regulated market. She places Justus on the bed to kick and play before pouring out each bag into the sunlight to begin the count.

Predominately white, Lillia is excited to see some have subtle color differences: pink, rose, champagne, gold, blue-gray, and some almost black. She finds a cloth sack from her trunk and removes some of her favorite colored ones, including one that is rosy gold. After an hour at her task, Justus begins to fuss. Reluctantly, Lillia sets her work aside to nurse him. When he drowsily falls asleep at her breast, she quickly places him in his crib and continues her sorting.

When she hears thumps on the ship's deck, she thinks Rupert has returned too soon. But when a voice calls out, "*Bonjour, Madam Eagleton! Ca va?*" she recognizes Captain DuBois of the *Mon Coeur* and is baffled why he is calling to her.

Leaving her pearls, she greets Captain DuBois on the ship's deck, and Sebastian lumbers up the boarding plank behind him.

Panting with his effort, Sebastian greets her, "Lillia, we need to talk. Captain DuBois has some remarkable news I think you will find quite interesting."

Lillia turns a curious expression toward the captain and he begins, "Your uncle has told me of the whale oil salvage Captain Eagleton and his crew made. Truly fantastic. But my interest is piqued at what your uncle tells me was hiding in the oil barrels."

"The pearls."

"Yes, yes, Lillia. Have you considered their value?"

Sebastian's question is ironic given how she has spent her morning.

"Actually, I do not understand how to value pearls. Is it by weight like gold?"

"No! That's what the captain has spent the morning explaining to me. But I'll let him tell you," Sebastian says as he waves the captain closer.

Captain DuBois explains, "The 'chow' of grading pearls measures their diameter, their weight, and their luster. Taking all three into account is how a jeweler values an individual pearl."

Impressed, Lillia asks, "How have you come to have this knowledge?"

"My brother is one of the leading jewelers in Paris, and Paris is the center of pearl jewelry design in Europe. Bombay has been a center for pearl jewelry for centuries because the Gulf of Persia is where most of the world's pearls are found. But because of the West's recent infatuation with pearls, Paris is where the royalty and those who can afford such things go for the most beautiful creations."

"I had no idea. And your brother is involved? How fortuitous. So, Uncle, why are you so excited?"

"I'm thinking Esmé and I will escort the pearls to Paris when Captain DuBois leaves. Once we arrive, he can introduce us to his brother and hopefully learn their value. If the price is right, we will sell them for as much as possible. What do you think? And, just as importantly, what do you think Rupert will say?"

Before Lillia responds, she hears loud boot steps coming up the boarding plank. As Rupert strides toward the trio, Lillia detects a sly grin on his face, which wanes under the scrutiny of their combined gazes.

"Why am I under such observation?"

"A most interesting turn of events, Rupert. Captain DuBois has a connection in the European pearl world, and I have a proposition for you. Do you have time to hear it?" Sebastian asks.

"Honestly, no. I have an appointment to see the Charlestown Naval Yard's agent to try to convince him to make good on my voucher. Lillia, Justus, and I must leave immediately if we want to be on time. Perhaps over tonight's supper?"

"Very well, tonight it is. I'll inform Barnabas there will be five for supper. Esmé should be present as well."

Agreeing, the Eagletons return to their quarters to gather Justus from his nap.

When Rupert shuts the door behind them, Lillia reacts to his most ridiculous expression and asks, "What has gotten into you?"

"I don't know what Sebastian and the captain are up to, but nothing is better than the news I have about the whale oil."

Lillia's attention now rapt, Rupert continues, "The going price for spermaceti oil is more than I could have dreamed. Eighty dollars a barrel! And the common oil is going for sixty. If I do my math right, the salvage crew is going to be thrilled. I'll know more tomorrow morning, when the merchant and his clerk arrive to do their valuation and count."

"Is there a reason for the increased value of the oil?"

"It turns out there are fewer and fewer sperm whales being taken these days, which means their oil is becoming more valuable. Who knew? I can't believe our good fortune."

On their way to the carriage, Lillia gets lost in quiet contemplation of Sebastian's kismet and hopes for its continued influence on the naval agent's benevolence.

Their arrival at the Charlestown Naval Shipyard is welcomed by the ringing sound of men busily attacking their work on ships in all stages of construction. Inside the office building, Rupert fidgets with his freshly trimmed mustache to the point of distraction.

"Why are you fretting?" Lillia asks.

"It has been a long time. It'll be easy for him to reject."

"A claim is a claim, isn't it?"

"Not if the government doesn't have the money to pay it."

"Why wouldn't there be enough money to pay it?"

Before Rupert answers her question, the naval agent's office door opens, and a young man motions for them to enter. Lillia stands and takes a deep breath. Entering the office, a man no older than Rupert steps forward and extends his hand.

"Agent Ben Knobbs, pleased to meet you. What is your business?"

"Captain Rupert Eagleton and my wife, Lillia. We're here to surrender a certified government voucher for payment."

Rupert hands the folded document to Knobbs and steps back as the man unfolds the paper to examine the wording.

"Good God man, this is four years old!"

"Yes, well, it has been quite an experience. But, as you see by the signature at the bottom, the terms of the contract were fulfilled, so I'd like to be paid."

"Captain," Knobbs begins, "your claim is quite valid, no doubt. But you are aware of the government's circumstances, correct?"

"Sir?"

His slight hint of default makes Lillia's stomach drop.

Agent Knobbs continues, "With the untimely death of President Taylor, our government has been shaken to its economic foundation. When Vice President Fillmore assumed his duties, the majority of President Taylor's cabinet resigned. President Fillmore has had to fill positions, such as mine, as quickly as possible. In my case, I've only been here for two days.

If you hoped to arrive today with this claim stub and leave with a satchel of government gold, I assure you, that isn't going to happen. Even if this claim is approved for payment, it could take weeks before you'll have anything to put in the bank."

The weight of his words is dizzying. Lillia feels potential failure sucking the oxygen out of the room and yet, the government's reputation is at stake.

Standing, she faces Agent Knobbs and asks, "Sir, may I speak?"

"Certainly ma'am."

"We appreciate the difficulty of your position. At the same time, I'm sure you can appreciate my husband's unique circumstances. It is imperative the government, through you, show no sign of being incapable of honoring its contractual promises to its citizens. Consider the impact to the greater community of states, not to mention the international realm, knowing that the United States can't pay its debts to one of their own, let alone foreign countries."

Agent Knobbs stares at Lillia, his mouth slightly agape until he clamps it shut, his jaw ticking with the effort. He turns his gaze to the voucher, intently studying it. After a few moments, he turns to his assistant.

"David, will you please escort the Eagletons to the waiting room and fetch me whomever it is I need to confer with on this matter?"

David shows them to a waiting area and scoots down the building's hall. When the assistant is out of earshot, Rupert turns to Lillia.

"My dear, where do you come up with those words?"

"What do you mean?"

"I mean, you told Agent Knobbs that while he was an honorable gentleman, the government of the United States would lose face if we aren't paid."

"Yes, I suppose I did," Lillia admits.

"Well then," Rupert whispers close to her ear, "We can only hope your diplomatic challenge works."

Just then, quick footfalls crack against the wooden hallway floor, and David returns with another gentleman, both rushing past the Eagletons to enter Agent Knobbs's office. After several moments, the office door opens.

"Captain and Mrs. Eagleton, Agent Knobbs would like to speak to you."

Rupert jumps to attention while Lillia stands slowly, adjusting Justus in her arms. Once in the office, Agent Knobbs silently offers them each a chair.

"Let me begin by saying you make an interesting argument, Mrs. Eagleton. Captain Eagleton, I am sure we can resolve your claim. My advisors tell me the issue is not that our government lacks the means to pay you, but rather that it lacks the currency to do so. All of that said, I think we may have gotten off on the wrong footing today. Perhaps, over a cup of tea, you could explain what has happened since this voucher was issued?"

Rupert clears his throat quietly and says, "Certainly, sir. Glad to fill in the time gaps. But my tale may take more than a cup."

With that, the Eagletons spend the rest of the afternoon sharing their story with Agent Knobbs, including the first trip to bring provisions to the military during the Mexican War. Then he tells of the trip loaded with ice, and finally, the most recent salvage of whale oil and pearls.

"What has me intrigued, Captain Eagleton, is the ice. Do you think you could do it again? I mean, specifically, the speed and the lack of spoilage?" Agent Knobbs asks, coyly swirling the liquid in his teacup.

"Well, Agent Knobbs, anything can happen when sailing around Cape Horn, especially westbound. But this will be my third trip. I'd like to think I've learned a few things about making the passage. As far as the ice goes, it's ballast—like wheat or whale oil. It just needs to be enough to get all the way to California."

"Hmmm, good to know. Captain Eagleton, give me time to figure out how to make the payment owed to you. I'll send a note to you when I have a resolution."

Lillia can't help herself and demands, "Can we expect to hear within the week or the month?"

"Given the state of the government, ma'am, notice anytime within a month might set a speed record."

On their way home from the shipyard, Lillia explains the premise behind Sebastian and Captain DuBois's idea. Genuinely surprised at the captain's unique connection, Rupert practically glows with enthusiasm.

"To have the pearls in Sebastian's capable negotiating hands, second only to yours, of course, is ideal."

"I counted all the pearls this morning, and removed a few for myself," Lillia says. "I hope you don't mind."

Rupert grins and wraps his arm around her.

"I'd call that a fair trade."

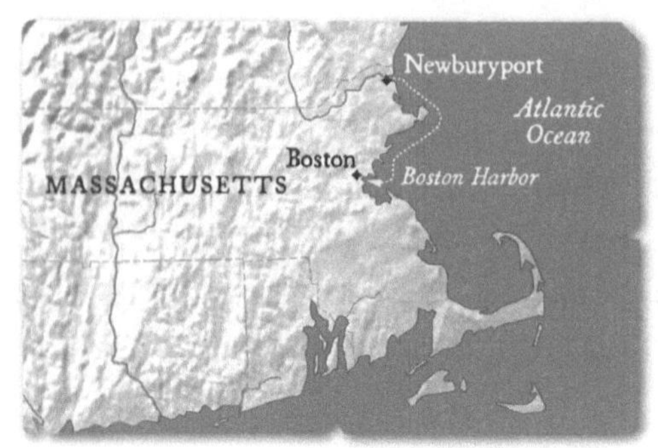

Chapter 23

SEPTEMBER, 1850

BOSTON, MASSACHUSETTS

It is hard for Lillia to tell who is more giddy between Sebastian and Rupert. But two weeks later, Lillia stands with her parents at the stern of the *Ornery Agnes*. They watch and wave as the *Mon Coeur* sails away with Sebastian and Esmé onboard. A hit of melancholy fills her when she acknowledges their last eighteen months together and Sebastian's steady hand during the tumultuous and happy times.

Rupert is absent because of meeting the oil merchant at the bank to take receipt of the proceeds from the oil's sale. She recalls when Rupert had finished his negotiations with the oil merchant weeks ago and had come back to the *Ornery Agnes* with a beaming grin. He had lifted Justus from her arms, gently tossed the child above his head, and said, "Justus, your daddy and uncles are going to be wealthy."

Now, it's her turn to feel the tingle of excitement when she hears, "A message for Captain Eagleton from Agent Knobbs of Charlestown Naval Shipyard."

Lillia takes the note. She anxiously rips it open to read:

```
Captain Eagleton, I have news on your
claim. Please report to my office tomorrow
so we can discuss the details. Yours,
Agent Ben Knobbs.
```

When Agent Knobbs's assistant, David, escorts the Eagletons through the building's hallways, Rupert is quick to strike up a conversation.

"David, do you know what news Agent Knobbs has for us?"

"I know he has been diligently working on your claim. I suspect he's found a solution."

Lillia glances at Rupert, her eyebrows peaked with questions. They find Agent Knobbs at his desk, his quill working furiously across a page.

Without looking up he says, "Please seat yourselves while I finish this last thought."

When his scrawling ceases, Knobbs blows on the ink and gestures to David to take the document away.

"Now then, Captain and Mrs. Eagleton, so good to see you again."

"Indeed, Agent Knobbs, we're surprised to be back so soon."

Agent Knobbs's long fingers press the worn claim voucher across the hard desktop as he starts, "I've been discussing your claim with the Treasury Chairman and the Secretary of the Interior, Mr. Alexander Stuart. We find ourselves stuck in a predicament. Congress's inability to find a compromise over the free versus slave state issue is throttling us. While Mr. Stuart is in full agreement to settle your claim, he is powerless to enforce it until that debate is decided.

As I have said, there is only so much I can do. We must wait, but in the meantime, I have a proposition. Care for a cup of tea while we discuss?"

Rupert and Lillia, their expressions solemn, both nod to Agent Knobbs's offer. He continues speaking while pouring from a tea set conveniently placed on a sideboard.

"Congress has allowed California to be granted her statehood without going through territorial status. And, as a free state. With statehood comes the need for a military presence.

The Second Infantry Regiment and the Third Artillery Regiment have been residing on a parcel of land adjoining a city called Benicia on its east. Benicia is located up the Sacramento River just beyond the chaos of San Francisco Bay. The talk is that it will become an ordnance supply depot.

I have to admit, I'm enamored with your ingenuity. One of the Army's challenges is shipping perishable goods to our distant outposts. California, as you know, is a godforsaken wilderness. Anything we've shipped to the Pacific Command has arrived green with mold and spoilt beyond salvage. We need a more consistent method of moving provisions to forts being established along the coast of the Pacific Northwest.

Your experience with ice storage could go a long way toward solving those problems. I think that will take some arm bending, but regardless, by the time you arrive, we'll know if Benicia will get the Army's nod. I'm wondering, would you consider an official position?"

Lillia regards Rupert, who asks, "Where would I be located? Could I remain a civilian or would I have to join the military?"

"You'd be a civilian under contract, paid monthly. You could find a home in the Benicia area for your family."

"Clearly, Agent Knobbs, we'll need some time to consider your proposal. Even if we agree to it, we'll have to wait until after the first of the year before the ice has frozen thick enough to harvest. At the earliest, we'd arrive in San Francisco by late April or, early May 1851."

"Certainly Captain, I understand. And we have to wait for Congress to hammer out their differences. I expect you'll have plenty of time to consider my proposal while we wait to hear about your original claim's status. Until then," Agent Knobbs says as he lifts his teacup, "here's to your health."

Lillia can't believe their good fortune. The whale oil sale was incredibly lucrative, and now they have another reason to return to California, other than to see if there's been a claim on Wellingham's race wager. Initially, she hesitates to share Agent Knobbs's proposition with her family. Why make them fret about their departure having only just arrived? But then, she counters, she has vowed to never keep a secret from her parents.

"If we accept the agent's proposition, Rupert will transport Army goods from San Francisco Bay to Fort Vancouver in Oregon Territory. Isn't that a wonderful opportunity?" Lillia asks enthusiastically.

"Fort Van . . . ?" Phoebe asks, struggling to form the word.

"Fort Vancouver. It's along the Pacific Coast in the northerly direction," Rupert replies. "I have to retrieve my maps to have a better understanding myself."

"It's an interesting development," Henri replies.

Lillia detects a note of sadness in his statement and fights the temptation to let it cool her enthusiasm.

Eagerly, she says, "The Pacific Coast's doors are open wide for our future business expansion."

"Yes, but it means you'll be away from us, maybe even for

good. These last few weeks have meant more to your mother and I than you can ever imagine, *ma chérie*."

Rupert breaks Henri's somber sentimentality with more imminent news when he says, "Once we've settled the details with the naval agent, we'll return to Newburyport to contract with a New Hampshire ice cutter. Keep in mind, we'll likely be in the neighborhood until at least January. We will be here to share the holidays with you and my mother."

Lillia watches the effect Rupert's words have on her parents. Despite the nodding smiles and their departure being three months away, she knows they are already reconciling themselves to it.

Upon their arrival in Newburyport, Agnes sweeps Lillia into the kitchen to prepare tea while Charles and Rupert discuss the agent's proposition in the front room.

Arriving with tea and cakes on a tray, Lillia hears Charles ask Rupert, "And what has become of my investment in Wellingham and my gold seekers?"

"Wellingham arrived in San Francisco in decent condition given he was physically attacked by an odd nut we picked up in Valparaíso. We left your gold seekers in the hills. I hope you hear from them, but honestly, Charles, it is a frightful country fraught with danger."

"By the time you left, had Howard found a claimant for the race's wager?"

"He had not. The race's agreement gives Howard the money if no one claims it by May 1851. It's my opinion he hopes to become the sole beneficiary."

Charles ticks his head to one side and asks, "Is that so? What would make him think no one was coming for the money?"

Rupert explains the *Night Call*'s loss of life and the assumption that the overland group may have experienced similar difficulties.

"It is hard to imagine there wouldn't be one survivor . . ." Charles says as his voice trails off.

Agnes pipes up, "Lillia told me your plans, Perty."

Lillia watches Rupert reactively wince to his nickname as Agnes continues, "Do you think your brothers will want to return to California with you?"

"They can if they want to. It will be interesting to see if Rafael and Paulo are still in one piece."

"What do you mean by that?"

Lillia pats Agnes's hand protectively and explains, "The southern goldfields are dangerous. And there is quite a bit of tension among the ethnic groups. There was talk of a Foreign Miner's Tax when we were preparing to leave. If it's implemented, there will be increased hostilities between the Americans and the foreigners."

"So, once you arrive in San Francisco, you're going to race to Paulo and Rafael and entice them to leave that dreadful place?"

"We'll do our best, Mother. But Paulo and Rafael are two hundred miles inland. I'm sure the boys are well enough and surviving just fine. Rafael may even be married by now."

"What?"

"Oh, yes. He found a lovely little French girl. From what Luca said, they had been spending a fair amount of time together."

"Where did he find a French girl in California?"

"There are quite a few French in the southern goldfields. Most of them were fleeing the unrest in their country, but all of them are on the take for cheap and easy earnings."

Agnes looks up at Rupert, her lips pierced tightly.

"I believe I understand the nature of the relationship."

Based on Luca and Giorgio's mischievous grins, it becomes clear to Lillia that the Eagleton brothers had returned home for more reasons than to pay their debt to their mother. Arriving at Agnes's house at noon the next day, they join the family on the back porch, where Agnes is quick to ask, "Where's Donatello?"

"He'll be along shortly. He's bringing a surprise."

Luca's statement causes a ripple of curiosity that quickly dissipates when Rupert shares his news of the government's pending offer.

"We'll be here until the ice is harvested, so we won't leave until after the first of the year. Being at home will be good for the families and will give Justus's grandparents time with him."

Luca and Giorgio trade glances before Luca mutters, "We should know by then."

"Know what by then?" Agnes asks.

Before he can answer, Donatello rounds the porch corner, holding the hand of a young woman. With low-key bravado, Donatello announces, "Mother, Charles, all, I'd like to introduce you to Marisse, my wife."

Stunned, the group rises while Agnes joyfully throws up her hands and chortles, "Welcome, dear! It seems my sons are in the recent habit of surprising me with brides. I love new daughters! Can't have too many daughters."

Luca and Giorgio look at Donatello, who gestures encouragement with his free hand until Giorgio says, "That's good to hear."

Luca takes over, "Because we hope to be introducing you to our wives in short order. Two more daughters, Mother. Wonderful, isn't it?"

Agnes's mouth gapes wide and retreats to Charles's shoulder for feigned support. With his offered handkerchief, she dabs at her eyes and stammers about daughters and sons who like to create scenes. Charles wags a knowing finger.

"I understand your motivation. There aren't many women in California, so you're taking some with you."

October passes with no word from Agent Knobbs. Back in Boston Harbor, Rupert tries to pretend the lack of news is not bothering him, but Lillia knows better. Her husband becomes so crotchety that, when he decides to preemptively arrange contracts with New Hampshire ice harvesters alone, she is relieved to spend the day and night with her parents.

In the carriage ride back to the ship, Lillia busies herself with Justus hoping to avoid any topic that might darken Rupert's sullen mood. At the *Ornery Agnes*, they find Barnabas seated at a galley table playing solitaire. When they enter, he grins broadly and offers an envelope.

"There you are, Captain. Had this message delivered this mornin' and was beginnin' to think I might have to figure out where to find you. Guessin' it's from the government, fancy seal and all."

Lillia feels her heart lurch as Rupert tears open the offered envelope. She watches him scan the letter. When he looks up, his expression is intense.

"We have a meeting with Knobbs tomorrow. Says there is much to discuss. Damn if he doesn't say anything else! How am I supposed to sleep tonight?"

"But it's news! And a meeting tomorrow. I'm so glad there is some kind of progress."

"I'd be honored to keep the little one if you'd like to make this meetin' without him."

"Thank you, Barnabas," Lillia says. "Let's see how he is in the morning. If he has a solid sleep, I'll take you up on your offer. It would be good to discuss important business without interruption."

Outside, she inhales the brisk November air deeply and offers a silent prayer of thanks, grateful to be close to having one more question resolved.

Leaving Justus bouncing in Barnabas's arms the next morning, Lillia and Rupert hold hands on the way to the shipyard. Unlike their previous visits, Rupert does not wait for an escort to Agent Knobbs's office. Lillia puts a gentle hand on his forearm just before he turns the knob of the office door.

"Whatever happens in there, you are my champion. I will always be by your side, no matter where life takes us."

Rupert looks at her earnest face and bends to kiss her quickly. Then he opens the door.

Agent Knobbs's radiant expression greets them as he says, "Captain and Mrs. Eagleton, so good to see you again."

The men's hearty handshakes fill Lillia with encouragement before Agent Knobbs asks,

"Shall I pour out?"

Teacups are accepted as the trio sit down across from each other. Rupert holds his cup and saucer low in his lap where Lillia notices a slight tremor.

"Captain Eagleton, Mrs. Eagleton, I've got good news. I've been able to negotiate a compromise on the voucher from 1847–48. They didn't want to pay it, but I helped them understand that you're going to become a real asset to the Army. I'm assuming you're willing to accept my proposition for transporting perishable goods along the Pacific Coast?"

Lillia goes deaf after hearing "negotiate a compromise" and she sits in stunned silence as Rupert starts, "I have tentatively contracted with several ice harvesters."

"What do you mean 'negotiate a compromise'?" Lillia cuts in.

Both men turn to stare at her until Agent Knobbs finds his voice and says, "Well . . . uh . . . Mrs. Eagleton, I'm sure you can appreciate the difficulty of getting one administration to recognize the commitments of a past administration."

"Certainly, Agent Knobbs, but I'm sure you can appreciate the importance of the successful fulfillment of a contract to the government's credibility. There are signatures and dates, all made by men who had the proper authority to do so. How can there be room for negotiation when there is an executed contract?"

A tense crackle fills the air between Lillia and Agent Knobbs. She waits for a reply and when none comes, she turns toward Rupert. When he offers nothing, she realizes she has overstepped.

"Please excuse me, I believe my ill-mannered statement has compromised your discussion. I apologize and will leave you to walk back to the ship, Rupert."

Lillia stands, places her teacup on the agent's desk and turns to leave. Rupert does not stop her. By the time she reaches the door, unsure if it is embarrassment or indignation causing the throb in her ears, Agent Knobbs clears his throat.

"Mrs. Eagleton, please stay. Your point is well taken. An explanation is due."

"Yes, Lillia, we should hear Agent Knobbs's explanation and proposal together. We've come too far for a misunderstanding now."

As she returns to her chair, Rupert leans in close and whispers, "Perfectly played."

Once they are settled again, Agent Knobbs leads with his strategic government proposal.

"As I see it, we have a three-pronged requirement: payment for the 1847–48 shipping contract, a new contract for goods to be shipped in early 1851, and a long-term contract for hauling perishable goods to and from San Francisco to Fort Vancouver. To get two of the three, I had to compromise and only get half the amount of the 1847–48 contract. But I insisted the Army pay you the entire amount for the new shipping contract before you leave as well as providing a written, unchallengeable document of your hire, your salary, and your job responsibilities to present personally upon your arrival in California. I guess, Mrs. Eagleton,

I tried to provide assurance for your future with two of the three, since our government disappointed you both on the first count. It is the best I can do."

Lillia quietly absorbs the offer. Ultimately, she knows the decision lies with Rupert. His expression tells her he is torn, but what he says next makes her remember why she loves him.

"My wife made a good point earlier. I trusted my government to make good on a mutually agreed-upon contract. You, Agent Knobbs, have done more than I could have ever expected. I am grateful for your dedication to my cause. It is disappointing not to receive the full value of my original contract, but I concede that too much time passed. In a new administration's shoes, I, too, might hesitate to settle a claim from three years and two presidents ago. It's clear you have given this considerable personal effort, and I accept your proposal, including relinquishing half of the original contract's value."

Agent Knobbs leaps from his chair, his hand outstretched in Rupert's direction, while beaming from ear to ear.

"You're perfect for this position, Captain Eagleton. I'm so glad you're onboard. I'll have the employment papers drawn up and the payment checks authorized and signed for both shipping ventures for you to pick up here in a week."

Satisfied, Rupert and Lillia leave Agent Knobbs's office and silently walk out the building. Lillia casts a quick glance at Rupert as they walk but his expression gives away nothing. It is not until they are a few miles down the road that Rupert stops in his tracks.

Confused, Lillia looks into his eyes and asks, "What's wrong?"

"I don't know how I've gotten so lucky."

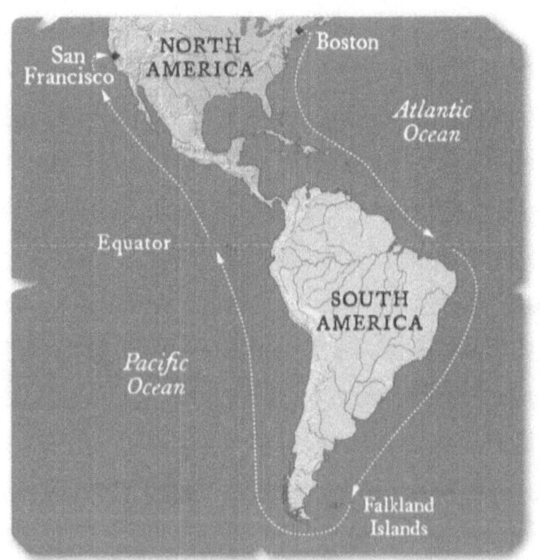

Chapter 24

DECEMBER, 1850

ROXBURY, MASSACHUSETTS

Before Lillia knows it, Christmas is upon them. Rupert has been working tirelessly to prepare the *Ornery Agnes* for another ice-packed voyage. He learns they will be hauling barreled pork, smoked meats, rind cheeses, as well as apples, potatoes, and other root crops to further test the ice's effectiveness.

When Agnes and Charles arrive, the families celebrate the holiday in warm camaraderie. But their impending separation hangs over them. Justus is adorable and brings joy to the

279

gathering, and yet Lillia's heart is torn at the idea of separating the grandparents from their new grandson. It feels like there hasn't been enough time since their surprise arrival.

The Eagleton brothers and their wives, Marisse, Theresa, and Sally, also arrive for the celebration. They will be along for the voyage back to California as well, and Lillia looks forward to the companionship of her new sisters-in-law. While younger than her, the three brides have an easy way about them. Sally, in particular, has a riotous sense of humor and an infectious laugh. Marissa and Theresa are less outgoing, but Lillia finds them interesting, and she's eager to have the long conversations she knows will be coming aboard the ship.

Two days later, it's time for their departure. Stepping outside their berth into the frigid air, Justus wrapped in warm blankets in her arms, Lillia takes one last look at her home city. She is startled to see Henri's wagon, mounded high with crates, parked on the dock next to the *Ornery Agnes*. She welcomes her parents aboard with a puzzled expression but before she can ask, Phoebe takes Justus.

Henri says, "We've accepted that we aren't likely to see you again, Lillia dear."

"Don't say that! We'll come back for visits once we get established."

Henri takes her hand and holds it gently, saying, "Then we will celebrate. But you have nothing with which to start your household in California. We want you to have some things that will remind you of us. These crates are filled with items for you and your children as they grow. There are household items, personal things, and many treasures that will spark memories of us when you use them."

"Of course . . . Sebastian contributed," Phoebe adds.

Lillia hugs Henri and Phoebe before saying, "Thank you. I will cherish them. I am going to miss you both so much. Take care of each other."

"I can . . . enter my life's final chapters . . . knowing you've a loving husband . . . and my only grandchild—so far," Phoebe says slowly but earnestly, a twinkle in her eye.

"Don't worry about us," Henri says. "We have plenty to do to prepare for Sebastian and Esmé's return. Please write us about your adventures. Hopefully a letter or two will actually reach us this time."

Her eyes suddenly welling with tears, Lillia replies, "I will. When you have news of the pearls, send it to us. I'm so eager to know what Sebastian and Esmé end up doing with them."

The *Ornery Agnes*'s westbound passage is uneventful when compared to Lillia's first time around the Horn. Different from the usual trip's challenges, this voyage centers around building new family relationships as the Eagleton brides become new sisters. They choose to stay together and talk, knit, or do piecework while being tossed about by the waves. Gratitude fills her heart as Lillia enjoys their hardiness and overall sense of adventure.

The men are all good-natured, and Rupert announces on several occasions he has never had such a fine group of sailors. Having four married couples aboard makes the time pass quickly as they play competitive games and have their own nighttime companionship. Lillia can't be positive, but given the dark and cold time of the Cape Horn crossing, she ponders the idea of all the Eagleton women presenting babies within days of each other.

Justus entertains the crew with his good-natured antics. Once they sail into the calm seas of the Pacific, everyone watches carefully as he crawls around the ship's deck. He quickly learns that Barnabas always has a treat for him, and the ship's cook takes on the role of surrogate grandfather. Eager to teach him to say something, Barnabas finally succeeds when the child blurts out, "Keeee," when Barnabas hands him a cookie.

Knowing they dare not stop in Valparaíso, no one is bothered when they sail past the city, their load of ice performing all the necessary requirements. Lillia looks toward the east and the mountain range she used when navigating into Valparaíso for the first time. So many ugly things came from their stops there, with Esmé coming into their lives as the only positive.

On May 4, 1851, only eighteen weeks since leaving Newburyport, everyone stands at the railing and watches San Francisco pass by on their way to Benicia, located more inland. Most are stunned at their record pace, but Lillia chalks it up to their combined energy for getting back to a place of promise. She knows the Eagleton brothers are eager to get back to their Sonoran home to introduce their wives to Paulo and Rafael. Lillia is determined to help Rupert adapt to his new role as a civilian employee of the Army of the West.

Holding Justus on her hip, she stands at Rupert's side as he navigates the ship eastward through the narrow bay.

She asks her husband, "Do you know what you are looking for?"

"I don't think there'll be a sign. Our first clue will be the only army barracks anywhere else in this area. This map is barely useful, but it says we'll come upon the barracks beyond the city."

Several minutes pass before the ship rounds a river bend and Lillia sees the organized streets of a tranquil village present itself on a hillside running right down to the water. She guesses there are close to one hundred structures of varying sizes dotting the gridded hillside along with a new wharf attached to a large warehouse.

There is clearly a city center, several large structures suggesting government buildings, a hotel, and a building with a steeple suggesting a church. As they sail past, she studies the buildings for anything familiar, seeing only a few wooden structures. Most are made of what looks like mud and are single storied with just a few windows for light. But there are many open lots still waiting for construction to happen and the thought of the little town's potential makes Lillia's pulse race.

Rupert sails the ship around another bend where a large encampment comes into view. There are long, low buildings clearly meant to house many men. Further in the distance are several barns and corrals for horses and equipment. But dust billows from the area where several more buildings are in different phases of construction. Men and their horses strain to pull wagons with great square stones rumbling in the beds.

Rupert expertly brings the *Ornery Agnes* to the wharf's dock. Giorgio and Luca spring from the railing with lines to lash to the dock's cleats. A cheer rises from the deck as the crew scrambles to secure the ship, reef the sails, and prepare the boarding plank.

After a reasonable amount of time, a group from the base arrives at the dock. Rupert welcomes the commanding officer, extending his hand.

"Rupert Eagleton, sir. I and my ship, the *Ornery Agnes*, are carrying foodstuffs from New England on orders from the Charlestown Naval Base. Here are my papers for your review."

As the officer takes the offered folded papers, he straightens and stares directly at Rupert, a dubious scowl clouding his expression.

He snorts, "Brevet Captain Charles P. Stone. Foodstuffs? From New England? Can't imagine any of it is useful. Who in God's name thinks anything will be edible after such a long trip?"

"We left 126 days ago, sir. I checked it this morning and save for a little mold at the edges, most of the cargo is first rate. Ice has a way of keeping decay at bay."

"Ice?"

"Yes, sir, the majority of my cargo is New Hampshire ice, which surrounds the edible portion of the cargo. Agent Ben

Knobbs wanted to see if I could sail here with minimal loss, and I believe I have proven the technique to be quite effective. Again."

"I should like to see for myself. May I?"

"Certainly. Happy to show you around."

With that, Rupert leads Captain Stone up the boarding ramp and to the hold. Lillia watches them from her quarters. Eager to walk on solid ground, she prepares to leave the ship with Justus, when she hears Rupert's voice rise from the hold.

"You'll want to take possession of the goods right away, am I correct?"

"Remarkable, Eagleton, I never would have imagined something like this, but yes, I'll have my men here first thing in the morning to begin unloading. How about a stroll around the barracks to regain your land legs?"

Just then, the men step onto the ship's deck directly in front of Lillia and Justus.

"Oh my, who have we here?"

"Captain Stone, this is my wife, Lillia, and my son, Justus."

"Good to meet you, ma'am. This little fellow is a stout boy, isn't he?"

Lillia smiles and says, "Yes, Captain Stone, he's quite active. We're just going for a walk."

"How about sharing supper with me tonight in my quarters? I would love some company, and my cook is pretty decent. Nothing fancy. It is the Army, after all."

Lillia and Rupert exchange glances before Lillia smiles widely, replying, "Supper at your quarters would be lovely. Thank you for the invitation."

"I must coordinate with my crew, but that shouldn't take long," Rupert says. "We will be along, say, around six o'clock?"

"Very well. Bring the little one too. A youthful voice will be a nice change."

Lillia knows Rupert's brothers are eager to show their wives their world in Sonora. Before they leave for dinner at Captain Stone's, Rupert has a conversation with them.

"I know you're in a hurry to get to Sonora, Paulo and Rafael. I urge you to be patient. We have quite a bit of unloading to do for the army and it might take a while. Because of where we are docked, think about how you are going to get to the other side of the strait. I know you have the funds to take a ship to Stockton, which is what I have learned you did the first time you arrived, so perhaps giving yourselves a few days to finish up this business won't feel like all that long."

"We've been thinking about it, Perty," Giorgio starts. "What if just one couple goes ahead now and leaves the others to help with unloading and preparing for the trip to Sonora?"

Rupert thinks for a few moments before replying, "I suppose I can ask Captain Stone to lend me a few soldiers if we need them."

"Right, then," Luca says, "let's flip a coin for who gets to take their new wife to Sonora and tell Rafael and Paulo about our new family members."

Agreeing, the three go through a series of coin flips until it is determined that Luca and Sally will find their way to Sonora with all the good news.

After their meal, the evening's pitch-black sky engulfs the barracks and Captain Stone offers to escort the Eagletons from his quarters to their ship. Stepping carefully along the unfamiliar trail, a brisk and chilled north wind blows in, causing Lillia to hug her sleeping child close.

"Glad to not have to fight a gale like this at sea," Rupert remarks.

"Odd to have such a wind at this time of year. May is usually quite . . ."

Captain Stone gasps as he stares wide-eyed toward San Francisco. Both Rupert and Lillia follow his gaze and see a slight glow blossom into an intense orange and red glare.

"Damn, damn it all, another fire!"

Lillia watches in horror as the intensity of the color rises enough to reflect off the low-hanging clouds. The wind rips tendrils of hair across her eyes and she feels panic well inside her knowing that Wellingham, Hope, and Sarah are somewhere in the city.

"This makes five fires the city has experienced since its establishment. When are they ever going to learn that canvas isn't a desirable building material?"

Lillia looks at Rupert, knowing a large part of her wealth was derived from selling canvas to the people of San Francisco.

"We were here for the Christmas fire, Captain. There have been three others since then?"

"Yes, and we're powerless to help from here. There's so much money there that, rather than using other materials, they rush to rebuild with the cheapest materials which, unfortunately, are also the most flammable."

Lillia asks, "But don't they lose everything? How do they start over?"

"Gold keeps coming out of the hills and goods keep arriving from the sea. They might be set back for a few weeks until new goods arrive, but as long as they don't die in the fire, most recover and plow ahead."

The group continues their walk to the ship, and the captain gives them a brief history of Benicia along the way. At the boarding plank, he offers his last comment of the evening.

"If you intend to get established here, I suggest you get in touch with Dr. Semple. He is generally considered the founder of Benicia. He's a land speculator and has the overall vision of the place. You'll find his land office in town. He's a lanky one, so you can see him coming from quite a distance. And, if you can afford it, please build your home with quarried stone like we are using for the arsenal."

As Lillia takes her first step up the boarding plank, a question pops from her lips.

"Captain Stone, if we need to visit San Francisco, what is the best way to get there from here?"

"Actually, your ship is the most direct. You'll need a carriage to take you around the city. Wouldn't bother going too soon, though. The cleanup will take some days."

Taking Captain Stone's assessment under advisement, Lillia watches the fire and concludes her friends have been, or are currently, in grave danger.

Rupert leans in and says, "Don't fret. We'll go as soon as we're unloaded. Focus on preparing Justus for the trip."

Despite Rupert's consoling words, Lillia's rest is fitful. She rises early to feed Justus, and sets him next to his father before leaving to fetch their morning coffee. Tendrils of blue acrid smoke taint the clear sky of dawn. Striving for calm, she only finds dread.

Two days pass before the ship is empty and they can sail to San Francisco Bay. Lillia is shocked at the swath of blackened and charred buildings when she steps into the bay's shallows from the launch. Wagons, loaded to overflowing with debris and ashes, leave the destruction as quickly as empty wagons enter the scene. In his effort to hire a carriage, Rupert is directed to a stable north of the waterfront with the explanation that the fire had been blown by north winds so everything to the south was destroyed.

As they walk to the stables, Lillia sputters, "I wonder where Hope, Sarah, and Wellingham settled."

Rupert gives her a hug and says, "We'll find them. It might take a bit of searching, but we will find them."

Making their way through the ruined streets, Rupert stops to ask about any laundry houses in the area. Most say those they know of were burned to the ground. Lillia aches at the idea of their friends' loss.

When they finally reach the untouched dwellings on the opposite street, they ask again for stables and are directed to one several blocks away. Seeing a small tailor's shop, Lillia enters.

"We're looking for a laundry run by two sisters. Do you know of such a place?"

The small man peers at her through bifocals, his eyes magnified by the extreme lens, his expression one of deep concern.

"I know of one such laundry. It is located to the south. I'm afraid to say that it would have been in the path of this last fire. The women were very good at their work. Never had a complaint when I took my garments to them. Meticulous, they are. I hope you find them."

Lillia feels her mouth go dry, but she isn't sure if it's from dread or excitement with his news.

"Can you tell me how to get there?"

"Because of the mess, I doubt you could make the journey the way I know to go. You'll need to venture around to the ocean side of the city, drop over to the Mission Dolores area, and then enter the city from the south. Your best information will come from those in that area. Good luck."

After securing a buggy, Rupert heads toward the ocean. Lillia sits next to him on the right, holding Justus on her lap. The afternoon sun shines brightly, the crisp ocean breeze belying the devastation and stink behind them. Picking their way along the narrow road, they frequently stop for directions to Mission Dolores.

After several miles, a woman holding a little girl's hand walks toward them and Rupert slows the buggy to a stop.

"Excuse me, ma'am. We're trying to locate friends in the city who may have been in the fire. Do you have any idea of where those who may have lost their homes and businesses would go?"

"Some poor souls used the plank road to escape to Mission Dolores. If you keep goin' yonder," she pointed back from where she had come, "down the road 'bout ten miles or so. If your friends had any luck, they lived on the west side. Nothin' happened on that side. Winds blew in from the north and pushed the flames to the south and east."

Thanking the woman, Rupert slaps the carriage lines on the horse's rump and the buggy lurches ahead. It is sunset when they find Mission Dolores and its grounds. Lillia leaves Justus with Rupert and enters the mission, hurrying back quickly.

Surprised at her haste, Rupert asks, "Not there?"

"No. We should find a place for the night."

In a few miles, a lone boardinghouse comes into view. Rupert secures the buggy and goes inside to inquire about a room. Returning, he takes Justus from Lillia and says, "We got the last room. But there's a surprise for you inside."

Lillia stares at him, a mischievous, crooked grin on his face.

"Are they . . . ?"

"Go inside. Supper's on the table."

Lillia vaults from the buggy, gathers her skirts, and rushes to the front door. Entering the dining room, Lillia scans those sitting at the table until her gaze stops on a familiar face. Hope.

As Lillia gasps in recognition, a small head of red, tangled hair wiggles in the chair next to her friend. Hope is so focused on placing food in front of the child, it is only when Lillia says her name does she look up.

"Captain Eagleton! Lillia, is that you?"

"Yes! Yes, but how? Where? Who is this? Are you alright? Where's Sarah?" Lillia gasps with surprise.

Before more can be said, Rupert pulls back a chair and offers it to Lillia saying, "Come, let's take our seats for supper. And we'll tell you everything,"

Rupert takes Justus and balances him in his lap as he sits. Two full dinner plates are set in front of the Eagletons when Lillia asks again, "Where is Sarah?"

"She stayed behind. She sent me away with our important papers and the child. I didn't know where to go but to the west. Flames were chasing us in all the other directions."

"Why didn't she go with you?"

"She's determined to save our establishment. We've built it into a fine business, Lillia. I wish you could've seen it. We have been doing so well . . . until now."

"Was the fire close?"

Hope flinches at Rupert's question before replying, "I left when it was still a ways off. It sounded like an endless roll of thunder. The wind was blowing so hard and choked with smoke. We breathed through wet rags as we left. Sarah was throwing water on the porch from our wash basins. When I looked back, the fire was jumping from rooftop to rooftop. I don't know."

Cups of water arrive, and Lillia drains hers with one tip. She looks at the child.

"Who is this?"

"The daughter of a friend of ours. Her name is Amalee. She's precious, but hefty. I made poor progress since I had to stop and rest so often."

Once they settle in their room, Rupert barely rests his head on the pillow when Lillia asks, "What do you make of Hope's story?"

"It sounds like Sarah. She was always the one to protect her little sister. But how could she think she could save the place alone? And how did this Amalee child come into their possession?"

Lillia's mind whirls with the same questions, but her husband's snores tell her she will have to wait until morning for answers.

White fog mingles with the blue smoke haze, shrouding the bay's low hills and waterfront when the Eagletons, Hope, and Amalee drive their buggy through the destruction. Hammer shots cut through the murk with a staccato frequency. Hope speaks over the noise.

"They're fast to rebuild. I'm sad you won't see our laundry in all its glory. It was a thriving establishment."

Trying for a confident tone to belie her own disappointment, Lillia replies, "Don't worry, it's just a building. As long as you and Sarah are safe, the entire thing can be rebuilt, maybe even better than before."

Hope produces an envelope from a worn satchel and hands it to Lillia.

"I almost forgot. One of the important things Sarah had me take was this letter to you from Mr. Wellingham."

Confused, Lillia takes the ash-smudged envelope and asks, "A letter? Why not just tell me himself?"

Hope looks at her chapped, cracked hands and sighs, "So much has happened. Mr. Wellingham died last October during a cholera outbreak in the city. Once his body was taken away, we decided we were his only family. We helped ourselves to his desk drawers and some of his other personal effects before the authorities arrived to confiscate things for themselves. This letter was on his desktop. He must have written it in his final days."

"Did you find the trunk he was protecting?"

"Sarah knew it was important. We turned his place upside down and found nothing."

"But it was buried," Rupert interjected.

"Where?"

"He told me he intended to bury it under his office floorboards until he found a bank he trusted."

"He had become so possessive. He told us he wanted to invest in our business with part of the proceeds, and he wanted to buy land."

Lillia contemplates Hope's words as she looks at the envelope. Wellingham's penmanship graces the front of the stained envelope, the heading of "Captain and Mrs. Eagleton" neatly penned across its length. Lillia opens the flap and removes the piece of paper.

28 October, 1850

Dear Rupert and Lillia,

I regret the necessity of this notice, but it seems my time on earth is done. Hopefully the sisters will have the presence of mind to find my personal documents before the place is looted. It's the cholera, brought by a ship from Panama. Bad luck has struck again. I hope to find more peace in the afterlife, with my beloved Lenora, than I have known these last few years.

With regard to my obligation to the wager, I have advertised since our arrival a year ago. It is my opinion that no one survived the overland trip. As you know, the ocean goers failed to make the turn at Cape Horn, and all hands were lost. I began advertising every other week beginning in April 1850. You'll find the trunk beneath the office floorboards directly under my desk. No matter when you receive this note, you are under no obligation to advertise for a claimant.

Tell Charles California was a most glorious experience, even though it did not end as either of us had planned.

Warmest wishes for a successful life together,
Howard Wellingham, Esq.

Lillia's hand flies to her mouth when she finishes the letter, and Rupert looks away from his driving with concern, asking, "What is it?"

"He's bequeathed the trunk to me. What a disappointing end to his troubled life."

Rupert keeps his thoughts to himself, but Lillia can see by the clenching of his jaw that he is privately working over Wellingham's loss.

Following Hope's direction into the city, they pass innumerable wagons hauling burned timbers and debris in the opposite direction, the drivers skillfully maneuvering their teams and mounded loads, all dwarfing Rupert's buggy.

He slows the buggy when Hope announces, "Around the next corner, we'll know of Sarah's efforts."

Lillia covers her eyes, only peeking through when she hears Hope scream, "There she is! There she is! It didn't burn!"

Still smoldering remains of buildings surround the small laundry shop on three sides. Sarah is at a washtub on the covered front porch and is busy rubbing clothing against the ribbed metal when they approach. Getting closer, Lillia sees blistered paint and smoke damage to the building's outer walls.

Hope nearly topples the buggy as she struggles to extricate herself, her screams and their embrace a heartwarming example of what two siblings can mean to each other. Rupert and Lillia watch the reunion with a child in each of their laps, tears in both of their eyes.

After several moments, Hope pulls away and points to the buggy. Squinting into the morning light, Sarah races in Lillia's direction. Lillia lifts Amalee and steps from the buggy before wrapping Sarah in a strong embrace, which produces a flinch from Sarah. It is then that Lillia notices the bandages on Sarah's arms.

"What happened to you?"

"The fire was so close. If it hadn't been for Horatio, I . . ."

Rupert arrives with Justus in his arms and interrupts, "How did you save it?"

"I just decided it wasn't going to burn. I used our washing barrel water and splashed the walls and porch and such. I got up on the neighbor's staircase there," she points, "to get the roof wet. I ran and ran and ran until Horatio and others came my way and started helping. Everyone was impressed at my water supply, but when I showed them all the water barrels we use, they understood."

The child, Amalee, reaches for Sarah and asks, "Where Pa?"

Sarah squeezes the child and kisses her forehead.

"He's helping clean up the fire's mess, Amalee. He'll be back when it gets dark. He's going to be mighty glad to see you!"

"Let us help with whatever you need here. Perhaps we can start the hunt for Howard's trunk tomorrow?"

Lillia's question pulls Rupert up short before he replies, "If we are going to be here for a few days, we should find a place to stay as well."

"You'll stay with us. It is not fancy, but we've got the space and we'll do our best to make you and your little one comfortable."

Agreeing to Sarah's offer of accommodations, they settle in. Unfortunately, Lillia is so filled with anticipation she struggles to sleep deeply so when she hears activity in the kitchen the next morning, she eagerly joins Sarah.

"Do you think you could take us to Wellingham's place and Hope would consider staying here with the children so our trip will take less time?"

"As long as we leave now, before the laundry starts arriving. It's a sure thing, there'll be loads of it."

Lillia rushes to wake Rupert and joins Hope feeding Amalee in the kitchen with Justus. The sky is barely lit when the trio set out in the buggy. Remarkably, some buildings are already repaired enough to be functional.

Seeing this, Rupert announces, "Seems fires are more of a nuisance than a coffin nail around here."

Sarah gasps as they approach Wellingham's home, or what is left of it. Not only had the structure burned to ashes, but debris from the buildings on either side are heaped on top of it. Lillia stares at the refuse.

"I suppose since no one was there to advocate for it to not become a dumping ground, it has indeed become one. As I see it, we can either walk away or we can pay the required amount to have the mess removed."

Rupert thoughtfully twists his mustache ends, saying, "Once we get settled in Benicia, we can begin clearing everything and start the exploration. The trunk is safe enough in its present state."

True to Sarah's word, they are greeted by mounds of laundry on the sisters' front porch. Now underfoot, the Eagletons return to Benicia. Driving away, Lillia's only regret is not having learned more about how Amalee and her father, as well as someone named Horatio, have become part of the sisters' lives.

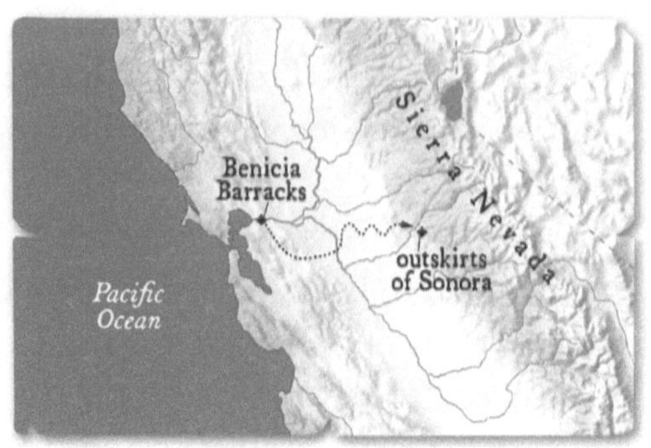

Chapter 25

MAY, 1851

BENICIA, CALIFORNIA

While waiting for an assignment, Captain Stone offers Rupert a semi-permanent dock for the *Ornery Agnes* at the Benicia Barracks. Since their return from seeing the Browning sisters, Lillia and Rupert explore Benicia's dirt roads, planning their future and enjoying the promising May weather. The inland hills from Benicia are rolling oceans of thick grasses, the westerly winds tossing the grasses in hypnotizing waves. Otherwise, the land is bereft of any trees, and Lillia chalks that up to all of the construction in the area.

On this day, as they approach the boarding plank from their walk, they see a man disembark from a San Francisco bound steamer at the barrack's wharf and run toward them. Curious, they both stop and stare at the man's direct route toward them until Rupert realizes who it is.

"Paulo, what are you doing here?"

"There's trouble in Sonora," Paulo gasps. "Luca told me where to find you and the others and I took the steamer from Stockton to get here fast."

The three quickly walk up the boarding plank and Rupert calls out, "Giorgio, Donatello, meet at the helm!"

Rupert hands Justus to Lillia, who decides to put him down for a nap before joining the discussion.

Keenly interested in Paulo's news, she arrives just in time to hear him say, "Rafael is flirting with big trouble. The kind he could get killed over."

"How's that?" Rupert asks.

"Since you boys left, the California legislature put on a Foreign Miner's Tax of twenty dollars per month on miners who don't speak English. This drained Sonora of most of the Chilean, Mexican, and French speakers. Those who stayed agreed to pay it, begrudgingly. Over the next few months, they got tired of gettin' hit for twenty dollars every month. That's when Rafael was deputized to ride with the sheriff for additional protection.

As the summer went along, murders started happening between collection days, usually a foreigner taking his anger out on an American miner. If the killer was caught, someone would run for the sheriff, who would calm the lynch mob. Rafael was usually in the sheriff's group."

"Rafael, a deputy of the law. That's a hard image," Giorgio mumbles.

"After a year of the tax, the foreigner's got the tax stopped, and the tensions lifted for those who knew enough English to read the papers. But some collecting kept happening in the isolated mountain valleys and creeks. It's been two months since the tax repeal, which brings me to the trouble.

Rafael says he's going to rob the imposter tax collector and return the miners' taxes. But it's just a matter of time before he's caught. They'll fabricate some charge, get rid of him, and then go back to taking the taxes for themselves."

Lillia sees the skeptical expression cross Rupert's face when he asks, "You're sure Rafael is giving the gold back to the foreigners?"

"I'm sure. He told me he wasn't keeping any for himself, and I believe him. Said he's tired of the constant tension and trouble in the hills. No one trusts anyone anymore, especially if they don't speak English."

"And no one has been hurt during his retrievals?"

Paulo hesitates at Giorgio's question.

"Not that I've heard. He goes to camps where he can't be connected to Sonora. But it's only a matter of time. Rafael is taking a huge chance by acting on his own."

"What can be done?" Lillia asks.

Rupert clears his throat and answers, "Ultimately, the illegal tax collecting has to stop. Either someone has to tell the miners not to pay it, or someone has to end the collecting."

"Or both."

Lillia feels the weight of everyone's gaze realizing the words had come from her lips.

"We could use your bargaining skills," Rupert says to her. "The miners are more likely to trust a woman. We just have to figure out how to keep you from an encounter with anyone dangerous."

Rupert's request shocks Lillia until she realizes the unique opportunity to help the family. She knows timing is critical to their mission. Just as important, she considers the consequences of leaving Justus. Agreeing to stay on the ship while their new husbands participate in the heroics, Marissa offers to take care of Justus, with Barnabas's help.

Lillia hastily packs an extra dress along with her solognot, and dons her man's costume. At the last minute, she stuffs the sack of her favorite pearls into a corner of her bag, for insurance. Against what, she does not know, but she follows her intuition. Then she presents herself to Rupert.

"I'm ready."

A broad smile flashes across his face as he leans down and whispers, "I'd forgotten how fetching you are in that costume."

Lillia gives Justus one last kiss and tight hug before leaving him in Marissa's arms with the determined promise, "We'll be back when we've convinced Rafael to stop his dangerous plan or dealt with the threat, somehow."

With that and an official copy of the Foreign Miner's Tax abolishment notice in hand, the Eagleton men and Lillia ride their rented horses off into the night.

They ride for three days. Paulo estimates Rafael's location, and they head into the hills. As they get closer to the miners' camps, the group discusses the next day's strategy.

Rupert asks Paulo, "Do you feel confident enough in your Spanish to get our point across?"

"I think so. I've had a hard time with the nuances of Chilean, but once they understand we don't want their money, we should be alright."

"When are the taxes normally collected?" Lillia asks.

"The first of the month. They should be collected by now, so we have a few weeks to get the word out. Everything hinges on whether they believe us," Paulo says.

"What will make them suspect us?" Lillia asks.

"Our English," Paulo explains. "It only brings trouble. We have the tax's abolishment notice but it, too, is in English. We have to do something to make them trust our word."

"If we need credibility, I better not disguise myself."

Paulo says, "I agree. You will draw their attention in a dress. Few will doubt a woman's sincerity."

"Besides, we'll protect you," Rupert adds, wrapping his arms around her, his words lingering in her mind with a mix of comfort and dread.

When the six Eagletons approach the camp the next morning, the miners are seated on stumps around a campfire drinking their morning coffee. Paulo's hail brings the tattered group to their feet, each free hand flashing for either a belt scabbard or firearm.

After a quick exchange, the miners relax, and one man hoists the coffee pot in welcome. The Eagletons dismount and fetch their tin cups from their saddlebags. In the miners' midst, Paulo starts in Spanish as Lillia displays the tax abolition notice. The miners' low-cast, sidelong glances foretell that convincing them will be challenging.

Paulo keeps at it. After several questions and their answers, he turns to Lillia and Rupert.

"They paid their tax a week ago. We're in the right place to spread the word, but no one has any idea of Rafael. No gold has been returned. And they're very suspicious. Do we have anything to prove our sincerity?"

The group exchanges puzzled looks before Lillia gets an idea.

"What if I use a pearl to demonstrate our good faith? If we don't come back for the pearl, they can keep it. It would be worth all my pearls to save Rafael."

The men nod in agreement. Paulo approaches the miners and explains the pearl's promise to them. Lillia then removes a pearl from her sack and hands it to the miner who had asked the most questions of Paulo. His only reply to her is a hard stare. A quick burst of Spanish causes Lillia to turn to Paulo for interpretation.

"He wants to know why an English-speaking woman cares?"

"Tell him it's because we're trying to save a brother's life. Enough killing has happened."

The miner maintains his intent look, his face an illegible canvas of suspicion. She returns his stare's intensity until he mutters something, and all his compatriots stand to face her. Following the man's lead in unison, they sweep their tattered, crumpled hats from their heads with a wide arc in her direction.

Riding away from the camp, Rupert comments, "I'd say your idea worked."

"How many pearls do you have in your sack?" Luca asks.

"There are now thirty-five."

"Thirty-five camps. We have a lot of riding ahead of us."

Over the next three days, they stop in all the foreigner camps they come upon. Lillia takes the lead at the French-speaking camps and has similar results to what happened in the first. With each camp, Lillia leaves a pearl. Unsettlingly, each camp has one thing in common: no one has heard of Rafael Eagleton. Paulo is stymied.

"Why would he tell me his plan only to not do it?"

His question makes Rupert flinch slightly. Lillia knows of his skepticism toward Rafael.

They run out of camps and pearls with twelve days before taxes are due. Eager for a rest, they ride toward Sonora following a narrow trail for several hours. Interrupting the serenading hum of late afternoon insects, Giorgio whistles a quick lick. A corresponding whistle mysteriously replies. Lillia looks at the oak trees on the surrounding hillsides trying to spy who whistled until she realizes they must be approaching the Eagleton compound.

A narrowing path protects its entrance for several yards until it crosses a sweetly flowing stream. Beyond the sound of tinkling water, the path widens into a lush green meadow with several small cabins tucked into the hillside. Its seclusion is a marvel to her.

Unlike the ramshackle camps they had ridden through, the Eagleton compound is neatly organized. A larger cabin and adjacent kitchen space denote the family dining and meeting location, while the other cabins are smaller and likely only slept in. This is a place where one could tell the family intended to stay, rather than the other camps where it was clear the inhabitants were transitory.

Riding up to the hitching posts in front of the cabins, they are dismounting when a woman emerges and rushes toward them saying frantically, "Luca, Giorgio, Don, *vous etes ici!* Hurry! Rafael has been shot!"

Rushing inside behind her, the brothers see Rafael laying on his bed.

"I'm a lousy bandit."

"You were ambushed. You're lucky they thought you were dead."

"No, you're lucky you fell off the cliff and they left you for dead. Otherwise, they would have come in for a closer shot to finish you off."

Lillia listens to the brothers' banter and tries not to stare at Rafael's chest wrapped in bloodstained bandages

Rupert interjects, "But the threat continues. If someone is suspicious enough to shoot Rafael even before he acted, that person is still among these hills, and no one is safe."

After nine days at the compound, it is time to implement their plan. Through Paulo's clever efforts at the Sonoran Inn, they learn the tax collector's route. For added assurance, they send Luca and Giorgio to Stockton to learn the whereabouts of the traveling judge and fetch him to the camps. The remaining members, Donatello, Rupert, and Lillia plot their itinerary, intending to put themselves just ahead of the tax collector at the first camp they had visited.

Their arrival at the camp is met with the same suspicion. The miners gather around them before they can dismount and focus their broken English toward Lillia.

"Dona Perla, we didn't think you would return," the grim Mexican miner says.

Lillia feels her cheeks warm at the moniker he uses before replying, "I said we'd be back. I keep my promises."

"You're the only English who does," he says, flinging the words and turning to walk away.

"And I want my pearl back."

He stops still at her statement. A flash of fear replaces the warmth in Lillia's cheeks, and she regrets her words and their potential offense. She sees him probing his small vest pocket, his dirt-stained fingers fishing in it until, with a flourish, he holds the pearl between his thumb and forefinger.

"I want to return it. But only if you keep us from paying the tax."

To set their trap, the Eagletons make camp behind the miners' camp to prevent the tax collector from shying off. Laying in their bedrolls, Lillia's thoughts flash to Justus. For the first time since leaving him, a raw maternal ache threatens her resolve to bring justice to the miners. Quietly, she whispers her melancholy to Rupert.

"Don't fret, we'll be done with this in a few days. Then we'll race back to the ship and reunite you with his pudgy highness. He won't even know you've been gone. I admit I've been missing him myself."

"What if, " Lillia chokes, "something happens to us?"

"The only thing that is going to happen is the righting of a wrong, especially when the judge arrives and puts an end to the fraudulent collections."

The call goes through the camp before they finish their morning coffee. Lillia feels her knees go weak and she wonders if she can actually accomplish the task. Then she hears English being barked above the camp's din.

"'Tis time, you Mexican dogs. I hope you've had a rich month. Gather 'round and pay up. No excuses. Move along. I have ten camps to get to today."

The tax collector sets up a makeshift desk of a plank across two tall stumps that two accomplices pull from a buckboard wagon. Lillia is mystified that only three men have commanded such obedience by the miners. When no one lines up, the tax collector slams the plank with a thick wooden baton, and his sidekicks make a show of cocking their rifles loudly.

The baton's reverberations prod Lillia into action. Gripping the worn tax notice, she starts her march. Rupert and Donatello flank her as the crowd of miners part for their passage. She stares straight toward the repeated rapping sound. Courage fills her veins when she reminds herself of the document she carries. The tax collector barks with contempt when he sees her coming toward him.

"What's this? You've recruited a woman into your flea-bitten ranks?"

"You can pack up your scales and ledger. There won't be any taxes collected here today. These men are fully informed as to your theft in the past two months."

The tax collector's eyes narrow at her approach. He growls under his breath while leaning on his plank countertop, his fingers drumming ominously. When both of his sidemen threateningly lift their weapons, Lillia stops in her tracks. Behind her the symphonic sound of unified gun hammers being cocked sweeps through the camp.

The outnumbered officials survey the situation through wary eyes. When the tax collector gives an almost imperceptible motion with his hand, both hired guns lower their weapons. His voice drips with condescension as he grimaces at Lillia.

"Perhaps we need a clarification, ma'am. The state has repealed the Foreign Miner's Tax, but the respective counties still have the authority to collect what they believe is a just tax for the activity in their county."

Lillia unrolls the notice and reads the bulletin out loud. It clearly mandates the abolishment of the tax over the entire state. When she finishes, she raises a challenging eyebrow at the tax collector.

"Sir, you've no grounds for collection. I suggest you return to your office, close it, and go back to wherever you're from. We've notified all the Mexican- and French-speaking mining camps throughout these hills of your illicit activities. You'll be met with the same resistance throughout."

The tax collector's face flushes in anger. He drops his chin to his chest, his fingers flexing along the plank's edge with frustration. Clearly vexed, he launches the plank into the crowd of miners. With equal passion, he hurls a colorful stream of profanity in Lillia's direction.

She feels Rupert and Donatello hug in close while the miners' ranks enclose around them, their sweat and grime-encrusted bodies acting as a shield until all that remains of the tax collector and his cronies is the dust from their wagon's wheels.

"Viva Dona Perla! Viva Dona Perla!"

The miners' shouts echo against the hills. Lillia feels Rupert's grip on her release as he joins them.

"You did it! I'm so proud of you."

She smiles and, in response, triumphantly lifts the rolled paper notice above her head before asking Rupert, "Do you think he'll try to go to another camp before we can get there?"

"Maybe. But the word is going to travel fast."

Lillia's pearl guardian works his way through the crowd until he faces her. He fetches the pearl out of the same small vest pocket and holds it out to her.

"Dona Perla, you have kept your word. But those banditos are very angry. We're sending two men ahead with the news of your success and two more with you as escorts. *Muchas gracias.*"

Accepting his offer of additional support, Lillia, Rupert, and Donatello walk through the crowd toward their campsite. As they pass, miners press small nuggets into Lillia's palm. Initially, she tries to resist their gifts, but when the men insist, she relents and accepts their tokens.

On their way out of camp, Donatello laughs out loud, and says, "Lillia's going to find more gold in these hills than any of the Eagleton brothers!"

They visit five more camps without a sign of the tax collector. In each camp, they are serenaded with cheers as the miners proclaim her their heroine. They return her pearl while pressing a small communal sack into her hand without her even dismounting.

On their way to the next camp, they rest by a stream in the afternoon heat, the two Mexican escorts insisting on keeping watch. In the shade of several live oaks, the Eagletons relax, and Lillia feels the tension in her neck and shoulders ease. Lying in the tall grass, Lillia lets the warm air waft over her, and it isn't long before she hears Rupert's familiar snores.

Maybe this will all work out. Peace will come to the hills of the southern goldfields, and we can return to the Ornery Agnes *and our son sooner than expected.*

A man's scream jolts Lillia from her reverie and spurs everyone into action. Rupert and Donatello reach for their weapons and lurch to a crouch while Lillia lays low, the solognot sitting useless in her saddlebag.

"Don't bother. I've got a clear shot at the woman's head. If you move, it'll be over for her before she can suck in her next breath."

Lillia recognizes the tax collector's voice before he comes into view, urging his horse through the brush with his gun trained directly at her. While the gun barrel demands her full attention, she can tell he has gathered more men to his cause.

"Do you feel like a heroine now, pretty lady? You think you're mighty smart, wrecking my little charade, don't you?"

"Just trying to bring peace to these hills," says Rupert.

The tax collector whirls in his saddle, faces him, and snarls, "Peace? Who cares about peace when everyone wants gold?"

"People do terrible things when they lose their humanity," Lillia says.

The tax collector snorts and says, "Listen woman, we were gettin' along just fine without civility and morals. Those things need to stay back east."

"Your actions aren't going to go unnoticed," Lillia tells him. "We've got a judge coming. The miners know what you're up to now, which makes you an easy mark."

"Do you think the law matters here?" the man says, chuckling and lowering his gun. "Just so's you know, I've taken care of the traveling judge. You can search high and low, but there ain't no help comin'. And, while I'm madder than a badger, them Mexicans need to know there ain't a friendly face what's gonna save 'em. They need to see what happens to someone, anyone, who tries to help 'em. Am I right, boys?"

A few affirmative grunts come from his posse.

"So, are you a legitimate civil servant or just a regular thief?" she asks.

At that, the man turns rigid. His next words crackle through the tension-filled air.

"Boys, I'm goin' to need three ropes."

Bound and gagged, Lillia, Rupert, and Donatello sit inside the wagon which travels along a trail through the tree-covered rolling hills of the southern goldfields. All three are choking on the dust from the tax collector's buckboard. A posse of ten armed men ride behind them. With no idea of their destination, Lillia watches for any kind of marker, in case they can escape. Despair sets in when the landscape is painfully nondescript.

The afternoon sun unrelentingly beats in on them, and she notices more cliff edges etching into the horizon beyond rolling, grass-covered hills. When the tax collector holds up his hand, she sits up to see where he is directing his men.

"Box canyon. One way in, same way out. There's a spring and a couple of strong-limbed trees for the hangin'. Goin' to leave 'em to hang and no one'll look for 'em in here for a long while."

Leading the way, the tax collector brushes aside some scruffy bushes that hide the entrance. The opening is so narrow that the buckboard scrapes its sides on the rocks. As they pass through the thicket, the bushes' prickly branches unexpectedly slap and drag across the wagon's bed, lacerating the faces and shoulders of its unsuspecting occupants and raising welts on any exposed skin.

Once through, the area opens up into what would be, on any other occasion, a lovely oasis. A small spring bubbles out of the canyon's furthest wall which then falls into a tree-lined pool. The spring grasses form a thick meadow dotted with wildflowers in the sheltered space. One could live here fairly protected, its vertical rock walls posing some difficulty if one might want to scale them. The buckboard pulls to a stop and the tax collector stumbles off the wagon's seat to stretch before turning to the bound Eagletons in the wagon bed.

"I been thinkin', we ain't had some entertainment for some time now."

A sickening cheer of affirmation goes up. Lillia feels her body being yanked from the wagon bed, a rough man's hands running across her breasts and down to her hips before he sets her feet on the ground with a thump.

"Boss, it's been so long since I touched a woman. Don' ya think we could have a little fun with 'er?"

Rupert bristles from the wagon bed, "Keep your hands off my wife!"

"Wife? Oh, really?"

The tax collector joins the rough man standing in front of Lillia.

"Come to think of it, Oscar, it's been quite a spell since I had the pleasure of fondlin' something soft."

Lillia cringes, but there's nowhere to go, the wagon providing a backstop to his advances. She feels his fingers grab at her right breast; the coarse manner of his touch painful since her weaning of Justus. His gross manipulations stimulate the still full milk glands and suddenly, his hand is wet with warm milk.

"Ugh, what's this?"

"It's what happens when a mother is nursing a child. Milk."

"You're . . . you've got a baby?"

"I do. You're considering hanging a woman who is nursing a nine-month-old child. A boy. What would your mother think of you?"

The tax collector pulls his hand away and wipes it on his pants, an indecipherable expression spread across his face. Not sure if it is the presence of breast milk or the image of his mother's disapproval, but Lillia lets out her breath in relief when he retreats.

"No one touches the woman, or I'll beat you myself," the tax collector tells the others.

Rupert and Donatello are yanked from the wagon bed and join Lillia before they are marched toward the great oak tree. At its trunk, they are pushed to the ground. Lillia looks between Rupert and Donatello, her mind whirling. Armed with the baton from earlier, the tax collector begins his charade.

"It's clear to me, woman, you are the ringleader of this gang of three."

"At least I'm not a scoundrel passing myself off as a credible law officer. Your time is coming. You see just three of us, but there are many more aware of your misdeeds. It's only a matter of time before you are brought to justice."

"I've heard enough out of you."

Lillia watches with despair as the buckboard is backed up under one of the oak tree's sweeping branches. Three ropes with crudely fashioned nooses hanging from one end are flung over the branch's girth. A zephyr breeze whispers through the dark green leaves ironically contrasting with the ominous sway of the three dangling nooses.

With a remarkable calm settling into her mind, Lillia fondly remembers the other occasions when a zephyr had visited her.

"Boys, string 'em up," says the tax collector, with a jerk of his head.

Her calm switches to dull disbelief as she, Rupert, and Donatello are roughly herded toward their makeshift gallows. Muted by her horrific reality, Lillia prays to herself:

It's going to happen. I'm going to die by hanging. Our son is going to be an orphan. Oh, my dear God, help us.

After some formidable resistance, the bound trio are roughly hauled into the wagon bed and the nooses jammed over their heads. The noose's coarse rope scrapes open the clotted brush wounds on Lillia's face and ears as it slides down to her neck. She detects the low murmur of Rupert and Donatello mumbling to each other, but the deafening throb in her ears keeps her from understanding their exchange.

Time slows to a crawl. Wisps of her dark hair brush against her cheek and she fidgets against the binding rope. Sweat streams down her temples, and when she looks over at Rupert, then at Donatello, she sees sweat beading and running off the scruff of their unshaven faces.

"Lillia, you've made me so happy," Rupert whispers softly.

Tears well in her eyes such that when she turns to look at him, he is a blur.

"Oh, Rupert, our love can't end this way. We have so much more to live for."

A shrill whistle interrupts her, and she squeezes her eyes tight before bracing for the wagon bed to move out from under them.

Suddenly, two rifle shots crack the air. When the anticipated movement of the wagon does not happen, Lillia's eyes spring wide open. The horses make a deflated sound, their whinnies of pain issued only with an agonizing sigh. When she twists her neck around to look in the horse's direction she sees instead, the canyon walls swarming with multitudes of men racing toward them. Moments later, she hears Giorgio's familiar voice replace the pounding in her ears.

"Lillia, I'm going to cut you down."

The upward pressure on her neck releases, and she gasps for air as her feet find the floor of the wagon's solid bed. Looking around, she sees Giorgio release Rupert and Donatello from their nooses.

Once their hands and feet bindings are severed, they loosen and rip the nooses from their necks before jumping from the wagon. Rupert embraces Lillia, the strength of his grip resuscitating her from her shock.

"Dear God, that was close," he softly says into her ear.

Content to bury her face in his chest, she hears Giorgio and Donatello join the hunt for the men that, only minutes before, had been their captors. Her breathing returning to normal, Lillia's attention is drawn to the canyon wall and she sees Luca in conversation with a bearded stranger.

In the same line of sight, she sees the horses lying in their death pose, blood pulsing from the holes in their respective chests. When Luca and the stranger turn away, their movement catches her attention again, and she watches them disappear beyond the rim of the canyon wall.

The area churns with Mexican miners bent on revenge as they single out the tax collector and his cronies. There is the occasional pistol pop and taunting shouts as the men are forced to beg for mercy. Her fingertips absentmindedly exploring the noose's raw mark under her jawbone, Lillia, still in Rupert's protective arms, turns away from the violence. That is when she sees Luca striding through the crowd toward his oldest brother, a broad grin spread across his dirt-smudged face.

"Bet you never thought you'd come that close to hanging, did you, Perty?"

Rupert grabs his younger brother by the shoulder and pulls him in for a hug saying, "You've got a lot of explaining to do, but I've never been happier knowing how good of a marksman you've become."

"I can't take all the credit."

Turning to Donatello, Luca says, "Giorgio and I found him, just like Rafael said. Clear over in San Fran. Found him doing road work. Sheer, unadulterated luck, I'd say. We rode as fast as we could and not a moment too late!"

"Found who?"

Luca turns to Lillia to address her question directly.

"Rafael said if we couldn't find the judge, we were supposed to hunt down a sharpshooter by the name of Dash Truepenny. He's the one who took the other shot so's we killed both of them horses simultaneously."

Lillia's mouth falls open in shock. Her mind explodes with only one detail from Luca's statement.

My Dash Truepenny?

Lillia and Rupert exchange exasperated expressions—the name clearly recalled by Rupert as well.

"When do I get to meet this marksman?" Rupert finally says. "We owe him a debt of gratitude."

"He'll be around soon enough," Luca said. "Rafael says he's a reserved fellow, had some kind of accident on his way across the country, so he's got a little different appearance. He doesn't talk much but he sure can shoot like the dickens."

Just then, a man emerges through the bushes, a thunderous cheer greeting him. Leading a dark horse, a long-barreled rifle thrown over his opposite shoulder, Lillia studies his confident stride.

Rupert steps forward and says, "I'm Captain Rupert Eagleton, oldest brother of the Eagleton clan, and damn glad to make your acquaintance. To say my wife, brother, and I owe you our lives is no exaggeration."

Rupert wraps a bear-like arm around the man's shoulder and turns him to face Lillia. She stares at him, her eyes searching for anything familiar through the facial hair and the egregiously scarred left side of his face. His low-slung hat casts just enough of a shadow that she isn't quite sure.

Then the man says, "Hello, Lillia. It's so good to see you again."

Quizzical looks pass among all the Eagleton brothers, except Rupert, as Lillia rushes toward him and throws her arms around him, embracing him fully. When she turns her head and whispers in the man's ear, Luca asks Rupert, "How do they know each other?"

"Oh, they go way back. But its up to Lillia how much explaining she wants to do. Come on, we have to clean up this mess."

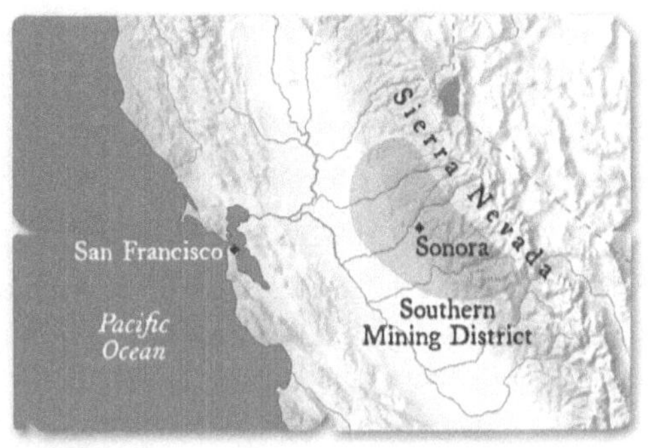

Chapter 26

Lillia waits, mounted back on her own horse, for the men to haul the tax collector's corpse onto the wagon, gather his accomplices, and prepare for their return to Sonora. She watches the skill and swiftness of the Mexican miners as they extract the dead horses from their harnesses, then carve the animals into quarters. Destined to be food, the meat is strapped to the men's backs and then stuffed into saddlebags. Lillia is so focused on their efficiency that she does not hear Dash's horse approach.

Dash looks at her and says, "Nothing goes to waste here. Every bit of the animal has a use."

"Don . . . Dash, I can't believe it. How long has it been?"

"First thing, Lillia, I'm Dash to everyone here. Second, I've counted the months since I left Boston. It's been just over two years since I left you."

Lillia bows her head and forces her eyes to stay focused on the saddle horn at his acknowledgement of that painful time. After several moments, she realizes that that pain no longer exists and raises her head, her expression showing him her confident admiration.

"I kept your secret from your father as you asked, even kept it from my parents so they wouldn't have to face him dishonestly."

"I put you in a terrible situation. I have so much to explain."

"You do," she agrees. "But I do as well."

"You're married," Dash says.

Lillia sees his eyes move away from her face and follows his gaze to see Rupert riding toward them, a warm feeling for the man flooding her as she says, "I am. That's just part of the story."

Rupert arrives and says, "We're ready to head back to Sonora. How about you two bring up the rear?"

Lillia nods and sees Dash give an unfamiliar gesture with the upper fingers of his hands casually stacked on the saddle horn to acknowledge Rupert's directive. Her husband turns his horse, gives a shrill whistle, and waves to Giorgio who slaps the newly harnessed horses with the lines. They give a startled heave and the wagon, full of bound accomplices, lurches forward awkwardly. They wait until the remaining Eagleton brothers fall into line before taking their position on the trail.

After a few moments, Lillia starts with her truth by saying, "I spent many days and nights being confused and angry at you for leaving me. But honestly, your departure forced me to do what my intuition had been telling me to do all along. Your disappearance steeled my nerve to leave Boston and its suffocating culture. I've found who I truly am. Now that time and events have passed, I can say I'm grateful to you."

Dash lets her statement wash over him before replying, "I, too, have found a new life here. I can't imagine returning to the life my father expected of me."

"Along the way, I found Rupert. I hope you have found someone too?"

"I've . . . well, I've been hesitant to commit because I . . . I did so poorly by you. My note contained an unrealistic request, and I didn't want to betray you twice."

"Is she here in California?"

"She is. She and her sister run a laundry in San Francisco."

Unable to hide her astonishment, Lillia's mind leaps ahead and she blurts, "Which one, Hope or Sarah?"

Dumbfounded at her precision, Dash stammers, "H. . . Hope. But how do you know?"

"We sailed together from Valparaíso on Rupert's ship. Wait, are you the friend with the little girl? I can't remember her name."

"Amalee. Yes, she's mine. I mean, she's not mine by fathering," he is quick to add. "I adopted her from a woman whom I met on the overland trip. Oh, Lillia, we need more time to tell this right."

"I agree. But perhaps if you start with how you came to have two children by your side when you first met Howard Wellingham?"

"You know Wellingham too?"

"He sailed on Rupert's ship as well—on our first passage from Newburyport. I was with Uncle Sebastian. Howard said he needed to beat the race's teams with the wager, and Rupert's ship was his best option. About the children?"

"Yes, well, on the night I wrote you the coded note, I learned my father and brothers were involved in the white slavery market. My father asked me to buy two children from an Irish woman living in his tenement building at Fort Hill. When I got there, the woman, their mother, had just died, and they had no one but an aunt in Baltimore. I had all the money Father had given me to purchase them. Hugh let me join his race since they were sailing to Baltimore to catch the Cumberland train west. When we got to Baltimore, the aunt had already left to go west, so I left them in a church orphanage."

"I knew you had taken money from your father. He came to our home and pleaded to know where you were. After how he treated you in my presence, I knew you had hit him in his soft spot, his treasury."

"I was in a panic, Lillia. I feared he would hunt me down, and well, it's hard to know with him. I couldn't take the children where he asked me to, so I ran away. For the longest time, I believed I should have asked you to come with me. But, after surviving what I have, I'm relieved I didn't. You might have died like all the others."

His genuine words wash over her and her only response is, "What's done is done, Dash. So, who is Amalee's mother?"

"That is the remarkable thing. Nora was the children's aunt who left Baltimore! Her husband, Ace, and I became immediate friends. It's hard to explain our connection. We met on the road to Brownsville before my team split off and went to Wheeling. He died of cholera before they got to St. Louis, which left Nora as a pregnant widow. Instead of turning around, she chose to go on. Before he succumbed, Ace asked me to help her any way I could. By the time we got to St. Louis, four of our team members had either died or been wounded."

Lillia holds up her hand to interrupt him, "At a women's meeting last spring, my mother heard a young man telling of his experience being injured by a passing steamboat explosion. He told of the race to the goldfields and mentioned your name. My mother was so distraught that she got apoplexy. It paralyzed her left side, but once she learned that I already knew, she started an immediate recovery."

Dash stares at her with an incredulous expression before saying, "How did you know I was in the race?"

"We sailed past the *Night Call,* or her remains, when we came around Cape Horn. Wellingham needed help writing condolence letters to the families and asked for my help. I used the race ledger and discovered your name on it, rather, my nickname for you."

Quietly, Dash folds his hands across the saddle's horn in contemplation.

"I used the nickname because I was afraid my father would track me down. I took it as my own when I became the last living member of the overland team. No one knew any different, and it was my chance to start a new life. By the way, I learned you had left Boston with your uncle. I just didn't know where you had sailed."

"How?"

"My partner and I were driving a freight wagon eastbound across the Great Basin returning to Fort Bridger last July, and a fellow from Quincy recounted the story after it had been printed in a Boston newspaper and the advertisement my father had placed. He mentioned the woman had left the city."

Lillia says, "Uncle Sebastian caught his own kind of gold fever, and we set out to California with a load of canvas to sell. That is when I met Rupert, Wellingham, and the Browning sisters. But I still have to ask, are you truly the only one left from your overland team?"

"Yes. Wellingham died and without him, no one can verify my true identity. Besides, he hid the trunk somewhere and we could not find it."

It is Lillia's turn to be silent. She struggles with whether to tell him of Wellingham's letter revealing the trunk's location, but she ultimately decides he needs to know.

"I know where the trunk is. Wellingham bequeathed it to me after he died, since no one from the overland team had shown up."

"I arrived at his doorstep minutes after he died."

"Really?"

"That's when my partner, Horatio, and I first met Hope and Sarah."

"Sarah mentioned someone named Horatio helped her save the laundry in the last big fire."

"I was there too. Hope took Amalee away to keep her safe."

"We met Hope and Amalee in an inn by Mission Dolores just last month."

The two stop their horses and stare into each other's eyes, marveling at how closely their lives had entwined, despite everything. It is then when Lillia gets a good look at the scars running along the left side of Dash's face.

"What happened to you?" she asks.

The question causes Dash's expression to harden, conveying how painful the memory still is for him. Clicking their horses back to walking, Lillia waits patiently for him to respond. Several moments later, he coughs softly and begins, his eyes staring ahead as the words tumble out.

"We joined Nora and Ace's Baltimore company in St. Louis. Risks were taken because it was mid-May before we started out from St. Joseph. The guide we hired, let's just say he was not what he professed to be. The gist is, he led us on what he called a shortcut to Fort Bridger from Fort Laramie. And then he abandoned us."

Dash hesitates again trying to keep his composure and Lillia lets him have the time.

"There was a mutiny among the company men. Nora, Nora's baby, another woman, and I were the only ones who survived. My two remaining Bostonian friends died on that day too. I was the only one left trying to save the women and the baby. When I attempted to catch an outlaw horse, it reared up and pawed out, striking a crushing blow to the left side of my head. Nora bandaged me and we set out to Fort Bridger with two wagons and six horses.

"A cold front moved through and the temperature plummeted before the snow moved in. Because of my injury, I couldn't drive, so I was holding the baby to keep her warm next to Nora. At the Green River, we became enshrouded in thick fog, and we got lost in it. Nora was following the other woman's wagon. By the time Nora heard the woman's screams after driving her wagon over a cliff, she was barely able to stop our wagon. I got out to untie Grunt, my horse, from the wagon and Nora insisted I take the baby in her basket, just to be safe. Moments later, the horse drug Nora and the wagon over the edge. I was helpless to go after her."

"Oh, my God, Dash! How are you still here?"

"I wish I knew, Lillia. So much of my survival and recovery is improbable. I owe my life to so many strangers. Especially at Fort Bridger, their kindness was overwhelming. The day after the accident, we rode through the fog and storm until we arrived at Fort Bridger. Louis and Narcissa Vasquez took us in and tended my wounds. Narcissa nursed Amalee next to her own newborn. Jim Bridger helped repair and strengthen my eye such that I have better sight from it than before. He taught me to shoot the long shot. I can now hunt with the best of them."

It takes some time for Lillia to absorb his story. She has so many more questions, but she does not want to overwhelm him.

"Do you mind if I ask you a question?" Dash asks.

"Not at all, go ahead," Lillia replies.

"Luca told me his brother's wife killed a man with a unique weapon. Did you really kill someone?"

Lillia nods slowly, the memory of the event aboard the *Ornery Agnes* less than a year ago filling her mind. As she tells the story, she is shocked at just how unbelievable it now sounds. When she finishes, Dash says with astonishment, "Wouldn't Coopton be committing suicide by setting a ship afire in the middle of the ocean?"

"He lost some of his sensibilities due to the loss, as Hope and Sarah put it, of his 'family jewels.' Seems like there was some kind of event in the winter of '48 when he was accidentally castrated."

Dash pulls Grunt up abruptly and stares at her before saying, "Horatio believes the Eagleton brothers might have been involved in an event like that. Could they be the same?"

"They've never breathed a word of it to me," Lillia replies.

"My advice? Don't bring it up. If it is the same situation, you took care of the problem. One last question, why did the miners refer to you as Dona Perla?" Dash asks.

Lillia tells Dash of Rupert's adventure of recovering the whaling ship full of oil as well as a secret stash of pearls. Dash slowly nods his head at her good fortune before Lillia, with a slight smile asks, "How is it that you know Rafael Eagleton well enough to have him ask his brothers to find you in case they couldn't find the traveling judge?"

"Horatio did me that favor. Turns out there was some bad blood between the Eagleton brothers and Horatio. The Eagletons ran him off his claim. When we arrived in San Francisco last fall, Horatio tried to win back his claim from Rafael in a card game. Of course, Rafael won and the only way he would let Horatio out of what he owed was to have a shooting contest with me. I won, and Horatio was released from his debt. I guess my shooting impressed Rafael."

Lillia sees Dash shaking his head and asks, "What is it, Dash?"

"I just can't believe what we've experienced in the last two years," he replies.

"It is all so remarkable, isn't it?" she admits. "I owe you my life, the life of my husband, and his brother. I am so grateful to you, Dash. And I am glad to know you again. You should know, Rupert and I have a son, Justus, named after Rupert's father. It sounds like he is a year younger than Amalee. Maybe we could introduce them at some point?"

Dash smiles and says, "I know Amalee would like that. She is a very happy little girl, despite all the difficulties she experienced in her early days. And Hope is going to be shocked to learn our history."

Lillia smiles at the thought before turning serious and saying, "You were my best friend for a time—nearly my only friend back in Boston."

When she sees an alarmed look pass across Dash's face, she hurries to continue.

"But I am so happy we both have met our true loves. The love you and I shared was something real and true—no disrespect to that—but we were younger. It was love between two hopeful and desperate dreamers. We've both seen the world now and learned who we really are, and who we're meant to be."

Dash quietly contemplates her words before saying, "Lillia, while I need to apologize for what happened in Boston, I want you to know I am grateful for your friendship during those difficult years with my father. You made me believe in myself, and I was better than he let me think I was. We could have made it, a marriage, I mean. Now we know neither of us would have been satisfied living there. That said, I'm not as confident as you are that I have learned who I am. But I have somehow survived through so many close calls that I must be meant to accomplish something."

"Perhaps use your Morse code?" Lillia asks.

"It could be useful here. Right now, though, I've got to think about my immediate future and my life with Hope and Amalee. I'm pretty sure Horatio and Sarah are smitten with each other, so if I were to suggest a double wedding, I can't imagine I would get an objection from either of them."

"I couldn't agree more," Lillia says, flashing Dash an enthusiastic grin.

Chapter 27

JUNE, 1851

BENICIA, CALIFORNIA

After all the excitement of Sonora, Lillia and Rupert's return is joyous. They wrap Justus in kisses and hugs, surprised by his changes in their absence. Only two months away from his first birthday, Justus pulls himself up to stand at every opportunity, smiling boldly at his accomplishment.

"He's so close, Lillia!" Marisse laughs. "And he's starting to say words. At least, I understand what he wants."

With Justus settled into her lap, Lillia marvels at the sweet smell of his hair when she kisses his head. He turns quickly to look into her eyes and giggles, a joyful sound that no one knows how close she and Rupert came to never hearing.

Aboard the *Ornery Agnes* docked at the Benicia Barracks, they enjoy the mild weather of June in relative peace before the

Eagleton brothers announce their return to Sonora. Lillia feels the sting of their parting having become good friends with each of the young women. At their last supper together, Luca stands and offers a toast.

"Here's to our reunion. And, well, a quick announcement to you all: Sally and I are expecting!"

A round of cheers meets his news before Donatello stands and says, "Congratulations to you. It seems our time around Cape Horn was quite beneficial to growing the family as Marisse and I are also expecting."

Lillia turns to Rupert and whispers, "I had a feeling."

Before he can respond, Giorgio stands, raises his glass and says, "Add another!" winking at a blushing Theresa.

The cheers of astonished celebration rise from the ship's deck and drift across the bay as Lillia squeezes Rupert's hand, saying, "I'm going to miss them all."

Rupert, ever eager to get on to the next thing, begins working with Captain Stone on the next plan for transporting supplies up the coast to military bases as far as Astoria in Oregon Territory.

A week before their agreed-upon rendezvous with Dash at the Browning sisters' laundry to dig up Wellingham's trunk, Lillia uses her spare time and takes Justus on afternoon strolls through Benicia's rolling hillsides and winding dirt roads. Inside the municipal boundaries, the strict street organization makes it clear someone intends to grow this little town in importance. Besides the putrid smell of the tanneries along one side of its coastline, new industry has begun building along its opposite edge, and the air is thick with the staccato ring of construction. San Francisco's May fire has displaced several families who have all taken up residence at Benicia's California Hotel while waiting for their new homes to be built.

During today's walk, Lillia gets caught in an afternoon deluge and takes refuge under a generous awning extending over the main road's plank sidewalk.

"'Tis quite a pour, isn't it? Won't you and the child come in and wait it out indoors?"

The deep-voiced question catches Lillia by surprise. She whirls around and sees a kind-faced man grinning from his open door. The aroma leaking from inside is more than Justus can resist, and he starts wriggling in her arms.

"It seems my son is going to take you up on your offer," Lillia says, struggling to keep Justus under control.

"I just pulled a few loaves out of the oven, so I imagine that's what's got him hooked. Care for a slice with butter? Happy to share with a newcomer."

Upon entering, Lillia stops to admire the room. Shelved canned goods neatly line the adobe walls and the wooden floor is an organized labyrinth of lidded bins and barrels. Clearly a provisions store, Lillia sighs as the fond memories of her favorite store in Boston Harbor wash over her.

The proprietor bustles past her toward the store's rear leaving Lillia to restrain Justus from all of the store's temptations. It is not long before the man returns with two large slabs of steaming bread wrapped in a napkin and offers them to her.

"This'll take the edge off a rainstorm."

Finding a seat in the store's front, Lillia tears small bites for Justus as the man seats himself across from her.

"I'm Edgar Klibben. Came to Benicia after the first proprietor, E. H. von Pfister took off to the goldfields in '48. Did you know that news of gold was broken right here on the front porch of this establishment in April '48? I'm just as happy to make my money off those who've caught gold fever than to wreck myself in the streams."

"It's a pleasure, Mr. Klibben. I'm Lillia Eagleton and this is my son, Justus. We arrived for the second time just a month ago."

"You've been to California twice? That makes you a rare breed."

"Well, my husband and I first arrived in September 1849. We returned to Boston in 1850, and then he was hired by the Army's Pacific Division to haul provisions to their outposts along the Pacific Coast. Now we will be making Benicia our home."

"Well, your arrival is going to make Semple happy."

"Semple?" Lillia asks.

"Ah, yes, well, our Lieutenant Robert Semple is the young, energetic fellow who's invested his life into making Benicia San Francisco's main rival. He has courted industry, the military, and higher education in the effort. While he has stumbled along the way and his partner, Larkin, hasn't matched Semple's same passion, it seems the recent fire in San Francisco has allowed the phoenix to rise again. With your family's new blood and willingness to speculate in the future, perhaps Semple's dream will find stronger footing."

This tidbit of a revelation makes Lillia disguise her personal delight by taking the last bite of her bread.

"What is the industrial building I see from H Street between 6th and 7th Streets which extends down to the water and has its own wharf?"

"Oh, that is the Pacific Mail and Steamship Company. It was established here last summer and has been doing great business hauling their freight and mail from here to Panama. They are the biggest employer in town."

"They certainly have a nice location for such matters."

"Indeed, they do. You should also know that Benicia is the county seat for Solano County. Good things are coming to our humble little town, Mrs. Eagleton."

Noticing the rain's abatement, Lillia wipes Justus's face and rises to leave, saying, "Thank you for your hospitality, Mr. Klibben, I look forward to bringing my husband by for an introduction."

Using restraint as she opens the door to leave, Lillia is fairly bursting with her new knowledge. Her mind races ahead with the potential gains to be made in Benicia. Eagerly, she heads back to the *Ornery Agnes* hoping all the opportunities to invest have not passed.

That night, after Justus has fallen asleep between them, Lillia tells Rupert what she learned that day. When she finishes, Rupert chuckles before whispering, "I'm not sure California is ready for a woman of your talents. Before we know it, you will be running for public office."

"I don't have any ambitions of the kind. I'm just eager to take advantage of opportunities," she whispers back.

"Speaking of opportunities, the time is coming for us to dig up Wellingham's trunk with Dash. Have you thought about what you are going to do since Wellingham bequeathed it to you in his last letter?"

"Honestly, I haven't really thought about it," Lillia replies. "Since our surprise meeting in Sonora, I've only thought about how serendipitous it was that Dash was the man who saved our lives."

After a few moments of silence, Rupert asks, "Do you still have feelings for him?"

Lillia considers his question before saying, "I have different feelings for him. Nothing romantic, if that's what you mean. He's like an old friend, but at the same time a new friend. He isn't the same man I knew in Boston, for many reasons. And I'm not the same woman I was."

"His journey to California sounds incredible. It is remarkable he survived. I just hope when it comes to Wellingham's trunk, you will consider all the options you have."

Rupert's words linger for several minutes as Lillia mulls the idea of what to do with the contents of the trunk and what all that money could mean to both Dash and her.

A week later and per their agreement, Lillia sees Dash and a stranger waiting on the porch of the Browning sisters' laundry as Lillia, Justus, and Rupert arrive in their rented buggy. Dash introduces his business partner, Horatio Fontainebleau, to Lillia and Rupert.

Politely, Lillia says, "It's very nice to meet Dash's business partner. He has told me about your skills and adventures getting to California from Fort Bridger."

"And you, ma'am. To think you are our girls' business partner! With all the miles between us, we got that tie to bind us," Horatio replies.

Rupert's expression shifts and he asks, "Did I hear you say, 'our girls'? Does that mean what I think it does?"

Dash bows his head slightly and says, "Yes, you heard right. We both proposed to Sarah and Hope last weekend when I got home from Sonora. And, remarkably, they accepted!"

"What do you mean, 'remarkably,' Dash? We're fine catches. Goin' to do right by those ladies, we are," Horatio states with sincerity.

The sound of the front door slamming and Hope's gleeful screech causes Dash and Horatio to step back, allowing her to rush past, while handing Amalee to Dash on her way. Lillia embraces Hope fully while taking note of Amalee's buoyant crimson curls shining bright from under her bonnet in the morning light. While her face is mostly obscured by the bonnet's brim, Amalee peers out from under it, her large brown eyes surveying for who they are joining. It is clear to Lillia that Hope is smitten with the child, her clothes pressed and coordinated in a way only a mother would do.

When Amalee glances at the street and spies the Eagleton's buggy, she wiggles and calls out, "Buggy! Ride, ride!"

Sarah hands Horatio a basket saying, "We thought we'd take a picnic with us today. Who knows what kind of time the digging is going to take."

Horatio groans at the basket's weight before saying, "Good idea, Miss Sarah. Might be downright starved after all the treasure huntin' we're goin' to do."

Dash sets Amalee down and says to Rupert, "Horatio and I have spent some time clearing the debris from Mr. Wellingham's lot. That'll make today's work a little easier on our backs and might give us a quicker resolution."

"Thank you!" Rupert replies. "After what we saw the last time we were here, I was concerned about finishing in one day."

The men load the buggy with the picnic basket, a large blanket, and shovels. Dash notices the women whispering among themselves.

Lillia says, "Why don't you all take Amalee and go ahead? Sarah, Hope, and I will walk with Justus so we can talk along the way."

Nodding in agreement, Rupert flicks the buggy horses' lines, and they set out. Amalee, her curls escaping from under the bonnet, sits between Rupert and Dash while Horatio bounces along in the back seat with the picnic basket. When the buggy disappears around the corner, Lillia picks up Justus and they begin their walk.

"Well, my friends, have you any news to share with me?"

"Do you mean the part about Dash being the man who ran out on you in Boston?" Hope asks.

Lillia laughs at her friend's frankness. How she has missed these sisters.

"Indeed. He is the same. But, after we had a chance to talk about the circumstances, I believe his departure, however painful and confusing at the time, was the best for both of us. His family put him in a precarious position. Had we married, I'm certain, our lives would not have been altogether happy. And I would have never left to learn my true love is a ship's captain."

"So, you won't have a problem with me accepting his marriage proposal?"

Lillia stops in her tracks and squawks, "He asked you? Did you accept?"

"Yes, yes I did."

Lillia stops walking and looks Hope in the eyes before saying, "I can honestly say he is not the same person he was when we were betrothed. He was so beaten down by his father, but he had the ambition to try to break free of his family's business and start something new. His ordeal across the country has allowed the best version of him to emerge. I believe he's a much better man and will make you a fine husband."

Hope turns to her sister, and they share a long hug. When they break free, both have tears in their eyes.

"We're having a double wedding!"

"Oh, my. You'll marry Horatio?" Lillia asks Sarah.

"Yes. He proposed alongside Dash. The two of them planned a picnic in San Jose last weekend and asked for our hands as we overlooked the Pacific Ocean."

With that, the women continue their walk toward the ruins of Wellingham's home, their conversation lively with wedding ideas.

"I expect to be allowed to reciprocate your kindness and help with making the wedding plans. Especially after what you did for Rupert and me at our wedding given our limited means," Lillia says.

"I know we would like to be married on the *Ornery Agnes*, just like you. I wouldn't be surprised if the boys are asking Captain Eagleton right now," Sarah replies.

Arriving at Wellingham's lot, they see Amalee happily playing with her dolls in the buggy and the men, their shirts soaked with sweat and grime, shoveling in the general area of where Wellingham's office would have been. She sees Rupert look up at her approach, turn to the others as he stabs his shovel into the ground and make a suggestion to which Dash and Horatio follow suit before picking their way through the debris toward the buggy.

Once together, they put Justus and Amalee together on one corner of the blanket while Sarah and Lillia lay out the lunchtime offerings on the other side.

Lillia watches as Amalee offers a pickle to Justus and hears Dash ask, "Are you hungry, Amalee?"

"Oh, Da, Missope has pic . . . pic . . . piclies. One for you?"

"Sure Amalee, I'll have a pickle."

Observing his easy way with the child, Lillia wonders about their shared trials along the way and how well he has adjusted to fatherhood. She catches herself thinking about what other things she would never know about him now that their lives are going in different directions.

It does not take long to devour the picnic lunch. While the women fold the blanket and pack the basket into the buggy, the men return to their excavation. Lillia casually looks around and is relieved when the passersby pay them no mind.

She jumps when Horatio yelps, "I hit something!"

Working together, the men clear away the sandy soil. The women gather around to block any onlookers' view of the proceedings. Running their hands along the trunk's ends, they locate the handles and with a great heave, yank the trunk from its earthen hiding place, the padlock still in place.

Rupert recalls as he strains on his end of the trunk, "I remember Wellingham had it padlocked. It's a good sign no one has tampered with the contents."

Lillia quickly adds, "Rather than break the lock off for all eyes to see, let's take it back to the laundry and open it in private."

Energetically, all six adults and the children pile into the buggy and rumble through the streets toward the laundry. Once inside, Horatio uses a hammer and chisel to break the trunk's lock, ceremoniously sweeping his hand toward Lillia to do the honors. She takes a deep breath and makes an announcement.

"Before we open it, I've been thinking we should split the contents between the three couples here. The funds will benefit all of us in our different life avenues. Considering all the lives lost, the wager will honor them by being used in diverse and positive manners."

Each adult casts glances, but no one objects to her proposal. Lillia lays her hands on the encrusted trunk lid, her mind returning to the last time she saw its contents, the participant ledger and fourteen bags each holding three hundred dollars inside.

Lifting the lid, Lillia feels the others press against her. Their curiosity is too much for manners. She reaches into the trunk and extracts its entire contents: the name ledger, an envelope, and sand.

"What the. . . ?" Rupert growls.

Sarah and Hope gasp in unison, "How could he?"

"What's in the envelope?" Dash asks stoically.

With shaking hands, Lillia removes the folded letter from the envelope. She recognizes it as Wellingham's penmanship but realizes it is much more legible than his bequeathment letter Hope had handed her after the fire. Then it hits her.

He wrote this letter long before he became deathly ill.

Holding back her suspicions, she unfolds the letter and reads the script, her mouth sounding the words with no emotion.

Lillia,

If you are reading this, I have succumbed to something terminal—either natural or human. You know as much as anyone; I have a fatal flaw. You and your Uncle fanned its flames to life on the ship. I tried to overcome it, but the demon of gambling owns me. Please try to remember my better points.
        Admiringly,
        Howard Wellingham, Esq.

Lillia looks at the others. No one speaks. First, she looks at Dash, who has walked to the laundry window and is silently staring into the distance.

Rupert comes to Lillia's side and wraps his arm around her shoulders saying, "I have no words. Howard had his weaknesses, but I didn't realize excessive gambling was one of them."

"Perhaps he was lonely."

Sarah looks up as she says the words, her eyes full of tears. "He approached me on several occasions. I just didn't have a good feeling about him. I should have been more sensitive."

"No, Sarah, you trusted your instincts. I, too, can attest to Howard's peculiar streak."

Hope joins Dash at the window, takes his hand, and leans in to whisper something Lillia can't hear. Dash's reaction, a warm and committed embrace, reconfirms to Lillia that her friends have the makings of a fine partnership.

Horatio whips around to Sarah and cracks a wide grin before saying, "Well, now, out of disappointment, the future rises!"

With that, he picks up Sarah and swings her around while Dash and Hope hug quietly at the window. Rupert turns to Lillia and squeezes her hand before bending down and kissing her firmly on the mouth.

"Seems we have some planning to do," she tells her husband when they break their embrace. "I'd like to have the weddings on the *Ornery Agnes.*"

"It did well by us," her husband says, kissing her again.

"At sunset, just like yours, Lillia," Sarah says, eagerly.

"Sounds like we best be gettin' down to business," Horatio says.

A month later, Lillia helps both Browning sisters into their wedding dresses just as they had done for her. The sisters wanted to replicate the candles lining the ship's railing as in Lillia's wedding, but because they were all more familiar with California and its abundant offerings, Lillia made arrangements for garlands of flowers, eucalyptus, and pepper berries to grace the staircases on either side of the helm.

Just as the sun drops below the western horizon, Amalee emerges from the passenger's quarters dressed in green with a head wreath of white flowers and pink pepper berries holding Lillia's hand. Initially, the child walks slowly but ends up trotting to Dash before jumping into his arms. Barnabas quickly sneaks around and lures Amalee away from her father with a treat and brings the child to stand next to him. Lillia takes her place next to Barnabas and Amalee, smiling when she sees Dash and Horatio exchanging a quick comment.

They suddenly stop when Rupert emerges. Hope is on his right side, and Sarah is on his left. Lillia watches as both men become emotional at the sight of their brides. Each woman smiles warmly as they approach and Rupert gives them away. Rupert comes to stand alongside Lillia, taking her hand as they listen to the preacher state their respective roles before announcing the couples married. After exchanging a kiss and long hugs, they turn to face Lillia and Rupert. Lillia can see their joy and squeezes Rupert's hand.

"Congratulations! Barnabas, let the festivities begin!" Rupert calls out.

Mouthwatering dishes of all kinds line the dining table. Barnabas, ever the proud uncle, brings Amalee and Justus to their parents once all the food is served. The children add their excitement to the party sampling all the food on their parents' plates.

The preacher tells tales of his life, and Horatio tells his own stories. Before long, Rupert stands and holds out his wineglass for a toast.

"To the new couples. May they have years of joy and prosperity. May they have peace in troubled times, and may they bring children into the world."

Horatio whispers to Sarah loud enough for Lillia to hear, "I like the idea of having a passel of little ones, don't you?"

Lillia watches Sarah blush before giving him a peck on the cheek.

Dash stands to begin his toast, "To the Eagletons who have blessed us with this lovely place to celebrate and the promise of future friendship."

As everyone raises their glasses, Lillia sees Dash look her way and raise his glass specifically to her and Rupert before taking a sip.

Before Dash can sit, Horatio blurts out, "While you're standing, you goin' to tell them our good news?"

Lillia sees Dash bow his head and watches curiously as he quietly looks around the table.

"On a recent trip to explore San Jose as our new home, Horatio and I met a man leading the effort to get a telegraph line established between San Francisco and Marysville via San Jose and Stockton."

Horatio interrupts, "And when he learned Dash knows Morse code, he jumped at the chance to get us involved."

"Yes, but it is a project in its infancy," Dash continues. "They need funding and state support, which could be a year out. We would be part of the construction process initially, but we could work ourselves into other, less-taxing roles once it's established."

Unable to contain her enthusiasm, Lillia exclaims, "That's wonderful news, Dash and Horatio!"

Sarah quickly adds, "We will keep the laundry going until we get established into homes of our own. In the meantime, the boys will continue to do freighting work."

"All very exciting news," Rupert says as he smiles at the young couples.

Horatio asks, "What about you, Captain? What plans do you and Lillia have coming up?"

Rupert pats Lillia gently on the back before saying, "You

know I sail with the Army on August 1. But, Lillia, would you like to share your news?"

Surprised to be put on the spot, Lillia can't help but blush when she admits, "As it happens, Rupert and I will welcome our second child in November!"

"Hooray!" Sarah and Hope exclaim in unison.

"Which means I will oversee the construction of a proper stone home in Benicia while Rupert is away. Also, we are speculating on several land lots. We are anticipating that Benicia will become a major California city."

Lillia sees Dash stiffen when Horatio blurts out, "Gosh, Lillia, you can do all that without Rupert around to help you?"

Rupert is quick to respond on Lillia's behalf saying, "Once you get to know her, Horatio, you'll learn there is very little Lillia can't do on her own."

Rupert's comment lightens Dash's discomfort and Lillia smiles at him knowingly.

"That said, I have one more toast to make," Rupert says, standing once again.

Lillia looks up at her husband, curious about what exactly he is up to.

"I must offer a toast, with my most sincere feelings, to Dash and his ability with the long shot. Without you, my new friend, Lillia and I would not be here now. I am so very grateful to you, knowing your trials and losses along the journey west, that you willingly came to our rescue, just in the nick of time, and your shot was true."

Lillia feels her chin suddenly quivering at her husband's moving words. Lifting her glass to Dash, her eyes uncontrollably fill with tears that spill down her cheeks unchecked. When she looks at Hope and Sarah, she sees that they, too, are weeping.

Dash nods his head humbly toward both her and Rupert, his emotion held more in check.

"I have no words of explanation except to say that it feels

good to be able to contribute to making a difference in this world. My life wasn't always this rewarding."

Leaving it there, the group cheers, "Here, here!"

Settling into more quiet conversations, the party begins to break up. Both Horatio and Dash had made reservations at the American Hotel in Benicia for the night. Lillia had graciously offered to have Amalee stay on the ship with them until tomorrow afternoon to allow the new couples time away from the responsibilities of life.

She watches as Amalee takes Justus' hand, and the two little ones make their way toward Lillia and Rupert's quarters where Amalee has spent the day building a pillow fort.

As the couples walk down the ship's boarding plank, there is laughter between them. She feels Rupert come up behind her and slip his hands around to her slightly swollen belly and nuzzle her neck. The warmth of a zephyr breeze whispers through the ship's rigging and she knows kismet is present. Everything is exactly as it should be.

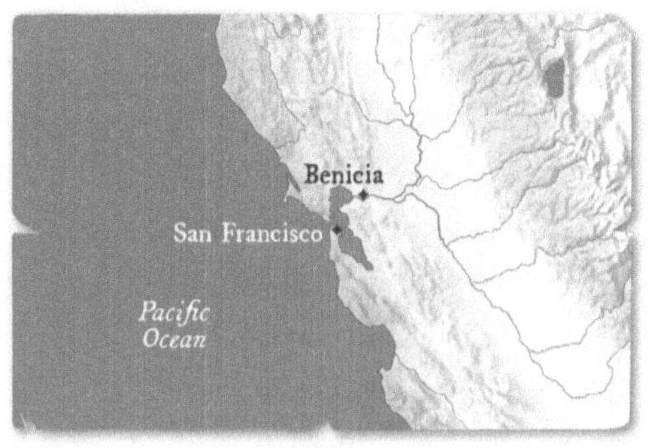

Chapter 28

JULY, 1851

BENICIA, CALIFORNIA

"If you'll take lots 12, 13, and 14 at East Fifth Street and M Street, I will reduce the price. I also want to encourage you to set a construction date as soon as possible. Our little town needs to continue to expedite its population if we want to impress the lawmakers into making her California's capital city."

Lillia and Rupert exchange surprised looks in Robert Semple's land office.

"We didn't know you had ambitions for Benicia to become the state capital, Mr. Semple. Is there really a chance of that given Monterrey's and Vallejo's similar ambitions?"

"We are in the perfect position to make an outstanding capital. Think of it. We are inland enough to be safe from coastal weather. We are surrounded on three sides by water, so we have endless opportunities for trade and industry. Additionally, we have immediate access to the inland of Sonoma and Napa, both vast expanses for agriculture from which we will easily feed our little oasis. And who knows, with the proper investment, we could be the western-most station to the first eastbound railroad linking the coasts of this great nation."

After signing the documents and handing Semple his money, Lillia and Rupert step out into the July afternoon, their arms around each other's waist and their respective minds whirling with what the future holds for them both. Rupert is the first to share his thoughts.

"I have to say, Wellingham put a kink in our plans with his thieving. But, it's nothing compared to the pain Dash must feel. I admire his doggedness. And Hope is his perfect partner."

Lillia quietly considers his statement, her feelings pinching a bit.

"Yes, he is nothing like the young man I knew, and Hope brings him further strength. I can't get over his willingness to take on another woman's baby. He had never shown me that side of himself. I suppose he discovered all kinds of new traits after uncovering his father's ugly secret."

Rupert, not wanting to dwell on Dash's past, says, "What do you make of our good fortune in Benicia?"

"We stand to be a part of a grand idea. I'm grateful we were not relying on the wager money for our future. We risked our lives and fortunes for our money, and now we have the opportunity to continue its growth."

"I learned this afternoon at the barracks that Captain Stone is gathering materials and products for me to sail up the coast. Will you join me or will you stay here to begin the plans for our home's construction?"

Lillia stops and turns toward him, her face etched with worry.

"I told you I'd never let you sail without me again after what happened in the Sandwich Islands. But the timing is rather difficult, isn't it? How long will you be gone?"

"I have no idea. This will be the first time I have sailed north of San Francisco. It may be the right idea for you to stay behind with Justus while I explore. You can accompany me on my next run."

Lillia turns back to walking, her head low in thought. She is silent long enough to make Rupert uncomfortable and he asks, "What have you learned of Sarah and Hope's plans now that they are married to two freighting men?"

"They will continue with their laundry while Dash and Horatio help with the construction of the first telegraph line set for use in the spring between San Jose and Marysville. I'm happy they are confident enough to carry on without their men. They haven't had time yet to feel the fear of potentially losing their loved ones."

"Now then, Lillia, we all take chances. You are most capable in whatever task you set your mind to. How about we make arrangements for you and Justus to board in the American Hotel? You can begin coordinating the selection of materials for the house as well as designing the rooms just the way you like them. Make sure we have the best view of the bay coming through our living room windows. When I return, we will sign contracts to begin construction. I know you'll find ventures to occupy your time beyond mothering Justus."

Lillia quietly absorbs his words before looking up at him with a sly grin saying, "You'll be returning within six months, correct?"

Rupert stops in his tracks, grasps her shoulders, and spins her to face him.

"Absolutely! I'm looking forward to welcoming another Eagleton into the world. We'll need to make sure there is plenty of space in the new house for children, won't we?"

Laughing and sharing a long hug, they continue down the dirt road toward the barracks in happy silence. The warm June afternoon breeze whispers through Lillia's hair blowing loose strands mischievously. Her mind floats back to Sebastian, his concept of kismet and how so many things had turned out so well for her since leaving Boston following Dash's disappearance.

Finally, she says, "I think I'd like to make room for a proper office in our house. One where I can have my ledgers and notes. Perhaps look at starting an import company with Father. Or help Semple make something big out of this little town. There seems to be endless opportunities at hand."

"I have no doubt you have the skills to do whatever you wish, Lillia. And you can count on my unconditional support for whatever you set your mind to doing."

She turns her face and lovingly looks at him, admiring the twinkle in his happy eyes.

Ah, yes, kismet is among us.

Author Notes for Kismet

This is a work of fiction. While most names, characters, businesses, places, events, and incidents are either the product of my imagination or used in a fictitious manner, my stories weave around actual events and places. I do have some historical figures represented, but all of their interactions with my characters, including dialogue and activities, are the product of my imagination. Otherwise, any resemblance to actual persons, living or dead, or actual incidents or events is purely coincidental.

During my efforts toward accurate research, I was continuously taken aback by how similar the mid-nineteenth century's social, global, immigration, financial, technological, and political issues parallel the first quarter of the twenty-first century. I have created a blog on my website to delve more deeply into the different areas of what life was like in 1849–51 so I wouldn't add hundreds of pages of historical notes to my books. You can read the blogs at www.jjameswheeling.com if you would like to explore the time frame and how they run eerily tandem to our current times.

I have read multiple diaries and accounts of the emigrants sailing around Cape Horn, their preparedness and their trials. I did not use one particular journal or diary to make up the sailing part of the story, I think it would be better to describe the travelers in my story as an amalgam of many individuals and their accounts.

I have tried to travel to many of the settings in the story, but I have not been able to sail on a three-masted sailing ship, cross Cape Horn, or visit Valparaíso, Chile. Many of the places that existed in 1849–51 have either been torn down, built over, or repurposed, so experiencing them is a real challenge.

Below please find the lists of places, events, historical figures, and common practices used in my story.

- Places that existed in 1849–51:

  › India Wharf was an international import/export warehouse that was a major entity in the Boston Waterfront.

  › The area known as the Northwest Territory in 1849 was comprised of Ohio, Indiana, Illinois, Michigan, and Wisconsin, along with what would become Minnesota.

  › Lowell Mills was the great textile experiment responsible for many societal shifts, including women working outside the home and living in dormitories, as well as making the first effort to unionize in the United States.

  › Roxbury, Massachusetts was a thriving trade community in the mid-nineteenth century, its population further bolstered by the flood of Irish immigrants in the 1840s and establishing the first predominantly Irish Catholic Church in 1846.

  › Newburyport, Massachusetts was a busy shipping and whaling town in the mid-nineteenth century that has continued to keep its maritime history alive.

› Valparaíso, Chile is a South American city that was an integral stopping point for sailing ships as the first major city along the Pacific Coast for ships traveling northbound and the last for those traveling south and east. It has a diverse blend of European ethnicities and cultures that make up its colorful history.

› California cities mentioned in the story that exist today: San Francisco, Sonora, Mission Dolores, San Jose, and Benicia

› The Sonora Mining District was a hotbed of mining activity in the Southern Mining District of California, where Mexican, Chilean, and other Central Americans were the predominant cultures mining there. While not considered being part of the "Mother Lode," this area was still worked and mined heavily.

› The Sandwich Islands, known as modern-day Hawaii, were named by Captain James Cook after the Earl of Sandwich, a major donor to his exploration. By the mid-nineteenth century, Europeans of all kinds had brought "civilization" to this amazing culture, as well as diseases which diminished the Hawaiian culture dramatically.

› Lahaina, Maui, in the mid-nineteenth century, was a key whaling port for ships plying the trade in the Pacific Ocean.

› Talcahuano is another Chilean city with a port well known to nineteenth century American whaling ships.

› The Bahamas were another island nation in the Caribbean that played a role in the sailing routes as a stop for water and food.

> The Benicia Barracks was established in the 1850s on 345 acres deeded to the government by Semple and Larkin, with its first buildings being brought from the East Coast as wooden kits. It became the headquarters for the Army of the Pacific in 1849. In 1855, the United States Government purchased a herd of camels for military use in the American Southwest. When their military usefulness became inconclusive, thirty-five of the animals were driven from Southern California to Benicia and were stabled there until they could be auctioned off in February of 1864. The Benicia Barracks and Arsenal played a military role through WWII.

- Historical events I use in my story:

  > On February 2, 1848, the Treaty of Guadalupe Hidalgo ended the Mexican-American War and gave the United States much of today's American West, including California, western Colorado, the southwestern corner of Wyoming, Utah, Nevada, western New Mexico, and almost all of Arizona for $15 million dollars and the assumption of $3.25 million of Mexico's debts. Mexico also gave up all claims to Texas.

  > After research done at the National Archive, I learned that the US Navy did call on private contractors to ship goods to the American forces involved in the Mexican-American War.

  > Gold was discovered at Sutter's Mill in the spring of 1848, but President Polk did not announce it to the American people until his address on December 2, 1848, giving many gold seekers along the entire Pacific Coast a distinct head start.

> The Christmas Eve Fire in San Francisco happened on December 24, 1849.

> At this time in history, the world relied on whale oil for lighting lamps. When the California gold rush happened, every sailing ship, including whalers, were susceptible to mass sailor exodus when they got even close to California. There are some who hypothesize that the interruption in Pacific whale hunting caused by the California gold rush combined with the discovery of crude oil in Pennsylvania ten years later saved many species of whales from extinction.

> President Zachary Taylor died in office, cholera is suspected but not confirmed, on July 9, 1850, and Millard Fillmore became president.

> California became a state on September 9, 1850, the only western state to have skipped territory status and gone right to statehood.

> The European Pearl Trade blossomed when pearls became fashionable in the European royalties in the 1840s and established a craze of demand and inventive jewelry designs.

> The Foreign Miners Tax was established in 1950 to tamp down the amount of gold profits leaving California by those from Mexico, Chile, and other Central American countries as well as Europeans, Chinese, and Australians. Repealed in 1851, it reared its ugly head again later but was much less aggressive in its taxation.

> The San Francisco Fire of May 5, 1851, was one of five fires to take place after the 1849 Christmas Fire. This particular fire was driven by a rare and extraordinary northern gale that drove the fire into the heart of San Francisco's

business district until, unexpectedly, the winds turned back on themselves. Many thought the wind's change was a miracle.

- Actual people and entities I weave into my story:

  › Eliza Farnham was a novelist, feminist, abolitionist, and, most famously, appointed as a matron for the women's ward at Sing Sing Prison, New York, in 1844. After the death of her husband, Thomas Farnham, in San Francisco in 1848, she resigned from Sing Sing and organized the California Association of Women as her effort to accomplish some greater good by her required journey to California. It was her belief that the presence of women would be one of the best ways to keep the evils she saw in California in check before she had left her husband there. She tried to persuade single, virtuous, intelligent, and efficient women to pay for passage on the same ship, the *Angelique*, with the intent of gaining employment. To qualify they must be at least twenty-five years old, have written testimonials of their character from a clergy, education, and work capacity, as well as the sum of two hundred fifty dollars and enough to live on in San Francisco until they could get established. As it happened, only a few women qualified and had the money. Farnham sailed with her two young boys to settle her husband's accounts but became so difficult during the voyage that she, her boys, and the other women sailing with her were put off the ship in Valparaíso, Chile. They eventually made it to California to settle her husband's affairs before she returned to New York in 1856.

  › The administrations of Presidents Polk, Taylor, and Fillmore were all in power during this time.

> Isaac Webb opened his shipyard, Isaac Webb & Co., in New York City around 1818, where he built many ships from small sailing ships to ferries, sloops, and schooners. His son, William H. Webb, took over the business in 1843 after his father's death and subsequent insolvency. William Webb became one of the most renown shipbuilders in American history.

> Fredrick Tudor was known as "The King of Ice" and was the first to successfully sail a ship of New Hampshire ice to Calcutta, India. Ice, and its preservation qualities, was the sole way of keeping food fresh in the mid-nineteenth century. Tudor started his business by shipping ice to the Caribbean and, after many failures and stints in debtor's prison, finally succeeded enough to earn his moniker.

> Chatellerault and Laguiole were French knife making cultures in the mid-nineteenth century and were on the leading edge of developing personal weapons like switch blades.

> Dr. Dwight Baldwin and his wife, Charlotte Baldwin, were American Christian missionaries on the island of Maui, one of the islands in the Kingdom of Hawaii, known to the western world as the Sandwich Islands.

> There was a corrupt sheriff in California in 1851 who did collect taxes from the English-illiterate miners even though the Foreign Miners Tax had been repealed in 1850. I decided to dispatch him, but I do not know if that is how he met his demise.

> Lieutenant Robert Semple (a dentist from Kentucky) and Thomas O. Larkin (a wealthy businessman and former American consul in Monterey) were integral in the creation of Benicia, California. Semple dreamed

up the idea and then enlisted the influence of Larkin to persuade General Vallejo to sell off some of his Mexican-granted land (Rancho Suscol). In trade for one hundred dollars, one hundred lots, and naming the city after his wife, Francisca Benicia Carrillo de Vallejo, General Vallejo blessed the creation of the city (named Benicia to avoid confusion with San Francisco) by Semple and Larkin in 1847.

› Captain E. H. von Pfister arrived in Benicia in 1847 and used one of the early adobe houses as a store and a community gathering place. Local legend has it that an employee of Sutter was sent to ask Governor Mason for a grant to a large tract of land, which included Sutter's mill, and let the heavily guarded secret news of a gold strike slip while visiting von Pfister's store. Von Pfister left immediately along with all the able-bodied men of Benicia.

› The Pacific Mail and Steamship Company set up shop in Benicia in 1850. It carried mail and freight between California and Panama and employed one hundred men in Benicia. It was the first large industrial works in California.

› The American Hotel was one of several hotels in Benicia by 1851.

› Benicia was surveyed for the army's Pacific Division soon after statehood in 1850, and Semple and Larkin were persuaded to turn over 345 acres to the army. This led to more than a century of army involvement in Benicia.

• Practices and beliefs at that time:

› Upon marriage, most women fell under the legal doctrine called "coverture," where her legal identity was merged with her husband's. She lost control of the ability to own property, earn a salary, get an education without her husband's permission, and could not sue anyone, including her husband for control.

› "Chasing the elephant" or "Seeing the elephant" were common phrases used to describe people who had fallen under the gold rush's spell and were going to California and leaving everything, and everyone, behind in their quest for riches.

› No one understood germs, contagion, or the importance of cleanliness, so diseases like cholera ran rampant.

› Opium, also known as laudanum, was used as a sedative without any regulation, which made it common in all kinds of practical applications in everyday life. Its addictive properties were generally known and fundamentally accepted.

› I found stories of the harvesting of dead men's scrotums for use as gold sacks in the Yukon Gold Rush specifically but believe the practice could be plausible wherever the pressure of gold fever, scarcity, and survival exist.

Acknowledgments

Since these are my first publications, I'd like to acknowledge a few important lights who, over the many years of learning to write and get my story out, have encouraged and supported me.

First, Will Grey, who taught the courses on writing fiction and non-fiction for Fort Lewis College's Continuing Ed program. His last words to me were, "We are going to see your name in lights one day." Those few encouraging words have kept me going.

Louise Powers-Ackley, my seventh-grade French teacher and a really good friend. Louise was the very first person I shared my story with thirteen years ago. She is a trooper. I know now that manuscript was a mess. But she waded through it and gave me enough positive feedback to keep the fire burning.

My North Carolina Lake Logan Writer's Group who changed my life by helping me find my voice. Jenn Browning continues to encourage me and be my "English teacher lady" when I don't know what to do with grammar.

Liz Trupin-Pulli came into my life with a bang at a Women Writing the West conference in 2016 and gave my ignorant self a break by agreeing to read my manuscript. After a few pages, she stopped and provided me with a list of editors. For the next eight years she coached me, represented me, and furthered my knowledge of the writing profession.

To my first editor Bill Greenleaf, my New York editor Andra Miller, my copy editor Candace Sinclair, and my proofreader Sean Strain, thank you for your insights, perspectives, and encouragement. Bill told me that learning to write is like learning to play an instrument. After all these years, I now understand.

To the team at Mayfly Book Design, Julie, Ryan, and Jess, I am so grateful that Fate brought us together on the day I decided to self-publish my stories. It was the good omen that proved I needed to take that next step. Your insights and professionalism brought Matt Kania of Map Hero into my life, and his work blesses each of these stories.

So important in these last few years is the sanctuary and friendship I have found with Suzanne Zerbe-Erickson. She gave me a quiet place to be away from my ranch life to write. She reads my manuscripts and offers valuable feedback. She mothers me after I lost my own mother and has given so much kindness and encouragement. I have a hard time putting my gratitude into words.

To Bill Brown who taught me how to shoot a rifle and handgun just to experience the sensation in order to put it into words for my characters, thank you for your time and enthusiasm.

My husband, Joe. We've been married for thirty-nine years and these books represent a new adventure for both of us. We have gone through the early married chapter, the corporate chapter, the children chapter, the homeschool chapter, the farm and cattle chapter, and we are now onto the publishing chapter. There were tough times along the way, but we knew and trusted each other so we made it. I am grateful for his love and support. Our daughters, too, for their patience on family trips when I had to stop at one more museum or historical marker. Just one more.

And then there's my greater James family whom I live next to, work with and for, and are partners with in our family agricultural land. I can credit them for teaching me to trust my instinct and believe in myself. Ours is a dynamic, competitive, and complicated family structure held together with a firm commitment to being stewards of our land and our family legacy.

There are so many others who have been my cheerleaders, never forgetting to ask about how the book is coming along, what can they do to help and eagerly awaiting the release. I can't mention all of you but I hope you know how much you mean to me.

Without you all, it would have been easy to get frustrated and give up on this project. These books represent well over a decade of perseverance and prayer. Thank you.

About the Author

J. James Wheeling lives on the James Ranch in Durango, Colorado. The mountains surrounding her home are rich with stories of the miners, railroads, and ranchers who settled in the Animas Valley after the Brunot Agreement was signed with the Ute Indians in the 1870s.

Raised on the ranch, she graduated from Colorado State University where she met and married her husband before living in five major American cities. They returned to the ranch to raise their children where she taught herself to be a chemical-free produce farmer. She homeschooled her daughters, ran the produce farm, was a 4-H leader, dance and swim mom and helped escort the local livestock judging team across Colorado. She works beside her husband and extended family to steward their land using regenerative practices as well as marketing grass-fed beef directly to the consumer.

Her curiosity about American history has her dragging her husband to museums across the West in the off-season. Her best writing ideas come when she is working in her vast flower beds. She has two new son-in-laws and two corgis.

*You won't know the whole story until you read both books!
Available now wherever you like to buy your books including
the James Ranch Market in Durango, Colorado*

Sneak Peak

HERE'S WHAT I'M COOKING UP

NEXT FOR LILLIA

It's October, 1853. Lillia Eagleton has a strong incentive for Benicia to become California's state capital. When things don't work out the way she wants them to, she digs in to figure out why. Rupert has decided this run to Fort Vancouver will be his last before leaving the his civilian employment with the Army to help Lillia further their mutual business interests. He leaves her behind partially because she is busy with business and politics but also because their second child, a son, has recently passed while the family sailed home from Portland.

Expecting Rupert to return by Christmas and disappointed when he doesn't arrive, Lillia is shocked when Nathanial and Barnabas, the Ornery Agnes's first mate and cook arrive with astonishing news. Their beloved ship sank, wounding Rupert and that he has been shanghaied in Astoria, Oregon Territory. Lillia doesn't hesitate to push her affairs to the back, gather her things and get to Astoria.

The Siskiyou Trail to Portland is fraught with dangers for anyone, especially a woman. Lillia hopes to surround herself and Justus, now three year old, with the right people for the arduous journey. Once in Astoria, it becomes clear that the only way to figure out what has happened to Rupert is to become a crimper herself. Her only concern is whether or not the ship captain who shanghaied Rupert will return to Astoria and if it does, will Rupert remember who she is?